Epitaph

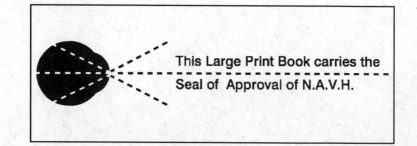

EPITAPH

A NOVEL OF THE O.K. CORRAL

MARY DORIA RUSSELL

THORNDIKE PRESS
A part of Gale, Cengage Learning

GALE
CENGAGE Learning®

Farmington Hills, Mich • San Francisco • New York • Waterville, Maine
Meriden, Conn • Mason, Ohio • Chicago

GALE
CENGAGE Learning·

Copyright © 2015 by Mary Doria Russell.
Thorndike Press, a part of Gale, Cengage Learning.

ALL RIGHTS RESERVED
Thorndike Press® Large Print Historical Fiction.
The text of this Large Print edition is unabridged.
Other aspects of the book may vary from the original edition.
Set in 16 pt. Plantin.

LIBRARY OF CONGRESS CATALOGING-IN-PUBLICATION DATA

Russell, Mary Doria, 1950–
    Epitaph / Mary Doria Russell. — Large print edition.
        pages cm — (Thorndike Press large print historical fiction.)
    ISBN 978-1-4104-7820-7 (hardback) — ISBN 1-4104-7820-3 (hardcover)
    1. Earp, Wyatt, 1848–1929—Fiction. 2. Gunfights—Fiction. 3. Peace
officers—Fiction. 4. Outlaws—Fiction. 5. Tombstone (Ariz.)—Fiction.
6. Large type books. I. Title.
PS3568.U76678E65 2015
813'.54—dc23   2015004131

Published in 2015 by arrangement with Ecco, an imprint of
HarperCollins Publishers

Printed in the United States of America
1 2 3 4 5 6 7 19 18 17 16 15

For Richard Doria:
a story about brothers for my own.

For Louise Hope Dewing Doria:
better late than never.

With thanks to Jeff Jacobson:
welcome to the team.

Beneath history, memory and forgetting.
Beneath memory and forgetting, life.
— PAUL RICOEUR

AUTHOR'S NOTE

The poles of American politics have been stable since the presidential election of 1800. A federalist party proclaiming, "We are a nation of laws" has always been opposed by a "Don't tread on me" party that resists regulation in the name of personal liberty. Since the passage of the 1964 Civil Rights Act, they've been called the Democratic and Republican Parties, respectively. Please note that in the 1880s, those labels were reversed.

All characters and the main elements of this story are based on real people and events.

Sing, Goddess, of Ruinous Wrath!

— THE ILIAD OF HOMER

To understand the gunfight in Tombstone, stop — now — and watch a clock for thirty seconds. Listen to it tick while you try to imagine one half of a single minute so terrible it will pursue you all your life and far beyond the grave.

Begin your half minute with righteous confidence though you stand six paces from armed and angry men. They have abused you. They have threatened your life. Your rage and fear are justified. They are in the wrong. You are within the law. About all this, have no doubt.

Two quiet clicks. A breathless instant. The gunfire becomes deafening. When a sudden silence falls, just thirty seconds later, the life you thought was yours will be over.

Imagine. Your name is Earp or Holliday. Your name is Clanton or McLaury. Your name is Behan. Your name is Marcus or Sullivan, Houston or Harony. You were in the middle of the gunfight. You watched it, stunned. You heard the fusillade and thought,

11

Dear God, not my man. Please, God. Not mine.

Whatever your name, it will be blackened.

Every flaw, every mistake held up for scrutiny, condemnation, ridicule. Your secrets made public. Your reputation twisted and sere as a blighted leaf. Every accomplishment, every act of kindness or courage forgotten. Everything you were, everything you hoped for, everything you planned . . . gone.

Whether you live another five minutes or another fifty years, those awful thirty seconds will become a private eclipse of the sun, darkening every moment left to you. You will be cursed with a kind of immortality. Year after year, everything that did and did not happen during those thirty seconds of confusion and noise, smoke and pain will be analyzed and described, distorted and disputed.

A century will pass, and decades more. Still, the living will haunt the dead as that half minute becomes entertainment for hundreds of millions around the world. Long after you die, you will be judged by those who cannot *imagine* standing six paces from armed and angry men.

Not even for thirty seconds.

■ ■ ■ ■

For the Sake
of Helen:
Princess, Prize

■ ■ ■ ■

SINCE I WENT AWAY AND LEFT MY NATIVE LAND

"You're Russian."

She looked over her shoulder.

He was thin-faced and bent a little to his left, but tall enough to spy on her over the swing doors that separated the Cosmopolitan Hotel's busy lobby from its rarely used music room.

She swiveled on the piano stool and fixed him with a bleary, red-rimmed, adolescent glare. "I'm as American as you are!"

A slow smile. Leaning on a silver-topped walking stick, he stepped inside. "Not 'Russian,' " he said, enunciating more clearly. "You're *rushing*."

Everything about the man seemed slightly askew. His smile, his posture, his demeanor. With an unhurried stateliness he came closer and handed her a handkerchief.

"Blow your nose, sugar."

Resentfully, she did as she was told. Annoyed to be treated like a child. Aware that wiping snot on her sleeve was not a sophisticated alternative.

Without introducing himself, he placed his hat and walking stick on a small walnut table and sat in the wingback chair beside the piano, casually crossing one knobby knee over the other. "Right hand only. And slow down."

"Are you a piano teacher?"

"Never mind what I am." He took a slim dark cigar from a flat silver case and lit it with a few short, shallow puffs. "First eight measures," he said through a cough. "Right hand. Slowly."

"It's useless! I could play this last year, but I've forgotten everything. The music just looks like dots again!"

Cigar at a jaunty angle, he leaned on his left elbow and settled into the upholstery. "Just play," he said, lifting his chin toward the piano.

She got a note wrong in the second measure and banged on the keys. "You see? I told you!"

"Start over," he said patiently. *Staht ovah,* it sounded like. "Give your hands a chance to remember."

Six more attempts. Finally she got through eight measures with just a single muttered "Drat," in the middle. Eyes bright, expecting praise, she turned toward him with juvenile elation.

"Better," he acknowledged neutrally. "Now the left hand. *Slowly.*"

16

She applied herself to the bass clef. He let her try three times, then placed his little cigar in a heavy crystal ashtray on the inlaid table. Sliding forward on the silk upholstery to the edge of his chair, he paused before getting to his feet. Despite his care, the movement set off an ugly coughing fit and he pulled a stack of clean cotton handkerchiefs from a pocket, selecting one to hold over his mouth. The others were returned from whence they came. When the episode passed, he put the used cloth in a different pocket. Each motion was practiced and nonchalant.

"Let me show you something."

She got out of his way. He sat at the piano and played six notes, right hand only. "That's the refrain. You'll hear those six notes again and again, but Mr. Schumann has varied what follows."

He demonstrated, playing plainly. Quarter notes, without pedal or dynamics. She tried to listen, but she was distracted by his hands. They were elegant but seemed too big for the rest of him. The prominent wrist bones were circled by fraying shirt cuffs so loose, she wondered if he was wearing a slightly larger and more prosperous man's castoffs. The clothing was quietly tasteful but certainly not new.

"Y'see?" he asked. "No need to rush . . . And there are those six notes again . . ."

He played it all the way through explaining

the structure and the harmonies. His voice was soft and his diction blurred, but his language was precise. The music had her attention now, becoming clearer with his comments. Then he paused and gathered himself, so self-contained she dared not speak for fear of breaking his concentration.

"And this," he said gently, "is the way my mamma taught me to play it. As though a child were sleepin' in the very next room."

Silent, face still, he cut the tempo in half. His fingers did not so much strike the keys as caress them. Releasing the sound, not demanding it. If she had taken so long between each phrase, it would have been a sign that she simply hadn't practiced. When he played, it was as though he knew just how long each note should linger in the ear and in the heart.

She had been weepy since the argument with Johnny. The music was so beautiful, and so beautifully performed. She sank back into the chair and began to cry again, though not as noiselessly as she hoped, for the gentleman heard the shuddering sniffle that escaped her.

"Yes, it is more tender when you take your time," he said, as though it were the music alone and not her own self-pity that had brought her to tears. "Mamma loved that piece," he said softly. "My earliest memories of her are at the piano." Then, without warning, he rolled through a dazzling five-octave arpeggio. "I have read about the Chickering grand, but this is the first one I have played. There is a little banjo in the tone," he observed, "but it has a lovely touch. Now, here is something that ought to be done at full gallop!"

He ripped into a sprightly sonata, his fingers dancing, the notes crisp and slyly joyous, as though he were sharing some private joke with the composer. She blew her nose again and began to cheer up. His hair was more ash than blond, but he was not as old as she'd first thought. Maybe only forty, she decided. Not *very* much older than Johnny Behan.

Johnny was almost thirty-eight, but still youthful and handsome. And, God! Those Irish eyes, those thick dark lashes! Still, the pianist had a good face. It was intelligent and refined, though lined, she thought — schooled in melodrama — by tragedy or suffering.

Having been caught blubbering like a baby, she suddenly felt it imperative to make this man see her as a woman. When he finished the piece, she cleared her throat and pitched her voice low to say with as much authority as an eighteen-year-old could muster, "You're a professional, aren't you!"

He smiled, but his hands never paused. He was playing a waltz now, the melody simple but pretty. "Guilty as charged."

"I knew it! Are you in Tombstone to give a concert?"

"Cards, sugar. I play cards for a livin', not piano."

"Then you're wasting your talent, and that's a crime. Honestly! You could be a concert pianist."

Another small smile. Amused, not flattered. "I am good, but not *that* good."

"Well, you could play for the theater, at least. I know. I used to dance professionally, and let me tell you — you're better than just good. Of course, my judgment is suspect." She lowered her voice and her eyes. "I can be a fool for a musician."

His hands came off the keyboard, mid-measure, and he turned to look at her, his arched brows lifted high. "Why, Mrs. Behan. Are you flirtin' with me?"

He knew who she was. And from the way he said "Mrs. Behan," he knew what she was as well. Refusing to be ashamed, she manufactured a saucy grin, but the cut in her lip abbreviated the performance. She made her eyes sparkle instead, tilting her head in a way she knew to be provocative and alluring. She had seen it used to good effect by several actresses.

"And what if I am?" she asked, bold as brass.

Several hotel guests had tarried near the door to the lobby, listening to the music. Now that the gentleman had stopped playing, they went on about their business. A few blocks away, a steam whistle shrieked the shift change in Tombstone's silver mines. For a moment, she was freshly aware of the ceaseless industrial noise out beyond Toughnut Street.

With slow care, the pianist rose and moved toward her, his slate-blue eyes resting steadily on her own. She blinked, uncertain about what she had just set in motion, for he was close now. Reaching toward her chin. Lifting it, studying her face with an unnerving, unwavering gaze. He smelled of soap and of tobacco. There was liquor on his breath, and the faint, sweet odor of decay. She thought that he might bend to kiss her on the lips. She decided that she would let him. Why not? she thought, lowering her lids, letting him come to her. It would serve Johnny right.

Her eyes snapped open and she pulled away when she realized that he was tracing with one finger — lightly, lightly — the bruise developing on her cheek. "I — It was my fault," she stammered. "I shouldn't have — Johnny doesn't usually . . ."

The man stared, his face unmoving.

"Honestly! It was my fault!" she insisted. And she meant it. She knew that she'd embarrassed Johnny. She just wanted the house clean when Wyatt Earp came for lunch, but then somehow it turned into another fight about Albert, and she'd made a mess of everything. "I'm unreasonable. I argue, and I always want my own way, and . . ." She fell silent under the wordless scrutiny, the heat of shame rising in her face.

"You have terrible taste in men," he told her. "I am no prize, and I have friends who treat their livestock better than Mr. Behan treats you." He retrieved his hat and cane from the table. "Raise your sights, sugar," he advised as he walked toward the door. "Aim low? All you'll hit are rats, snakes, and rock bottom."

She stood, furious, and considered throwing that crystal ashtray at his bony old spine, but he stopped, leaning on his cane, head down.

"If you had the money," he asked, "could you go home?"

There was something about his voice. An unexpected kindness.

"They think — I told them Johnny and I were married."

He snorted softly. "My people think I am still a dentist." He straightened then, as much as he could. "There will be fifty dollars deposited in your name at the front desk of this hotel. If you ever decide to leave that presumptuous, third-rate, overdressed Irish bigot, ask for the envelope, y'hear?"

Mouth open, she watched him leave the music room. The swing doors creaked on their hinges. He stopped at the front desk for a brief conversation with Mr. Bilicke, the hotel owner, who glanced at her and nodded.

When the man was gone, Mr. Bilicke left the desk and pushed the swing doors to the music room aside. "Do you know who that was?" he asked.

She shook her head.

"Doc Holliday," he told her.

She looked sharply toward the street, hoping to catch another glimpse of the notorious gambler Johnny had argued with yesterday, during the stagecoach journey the two men had shared. Johnny was fetching his eight-year-old son back to Tombstone to live. Holliday was, presumably, coming in from Tucson to play cards. He had a fearsome reputation, but Johnny Behan was convinced he could make friends with anyone. Things seemed to be going well until a short, sharp dispute erupted over the Non-Partisan Anti-Chinese League. "All I did was invite him to join when he got to town," Johnny cried. "I never heard a white man take on so about Chinks. He just tore into me, and with a little kid sitting right there! No consideration at all for Albert."

Johnny had been tedious on the subject, and he turned the conversation toward it whenever *she* tried to find out why on earth he expected her to raise his ex-wife's child, just because Victoria was getting married again.

Mr. Bilicke spoke again: "Word is, Holliday hates your . . . husband."

Always. That little hesitation. That tiny pause. Angry again, she was tempted to snap, "Well, that makes two of us!" but it would have sounded childish. *"Kwand meem!"* she said breezily in what she believed to be French. "It's all the same to me!"

Mr. Bilicke shrugged and went back to the front desk. Soon he was busy with a guest's query about telephone service to the silver mines. "Just between the pits and the stamping mills, sir, but more wires are going up, and the Cosmopolitan is on the schedule for early '81. Shall I arrange for a messenger in the meantime?"

Their voices faded. Alone, homesick, overwhelmed by the shambles she'd made of her life, she began to cry again.

"Oh, thank God!" she heard Johnny cry. "There you are!"

He was standing in the doorway, his beautiful brown eyes moist with freshly relieved anxiety, that handsome open face a complex mixture of concern, dismay, and irritation. Coming close, he gripped her by the shoulders, lifting her to her feet, taking her in his arms.

"Josie, honey, you can't just wander around a town like this on your own. I've been wor-

24

ried sick."

"I'm s-sorry," she wept, her head against his chest. "Really, I am. It was all my fault —"

"Come home," he murmured into her hair. "I'm sorry, too, Josie. Come home."

The streets of Tombstone were crowded, day and night. A thousand people must have seen them as he walked her back to the house. Soon the story would be all over town — Behan's little filly got away from him again! — but he tried not to care. With an arm around her shoulders, John Harris Behan made his voice soft and urgent as they approached the door.

"Just give Albert a chance, all right? Arguments scare him, honey. He's been hard of hearing since he had the measles, so he can't always make out the nice things people say to each other. He just hears what they say when they're angry and upset." Which meant that Al had heard most of what Johnny Behan and Josie Marcus had said to each other since the boy arrived last night. "Honest, Josie. Al's a good kid. And none of this is his fault. He's just a little boy."

Finally, she shrugged and looked away. It was assent if not enthusiasm. He was willing to settle for that.

"I have to get back to town," he told her. "There's a meeting at the marshal's office.

But we'll go someplace special tonight. Would you like that? How about a show? Or dancing, maybe. What d'you say? Let's go dancing tonight!"

She smiled, just a little, but when he kissed her, she kissed him back.

Albert was waiting inside, his little face pinched and pale. He must take after his mother, Josie thought, for she saw none of Johnny's vigor in the child.

She had hardly closed the door when the boy asked, "Are you going to be my stepmother?" Before she said anything, he told her, "I'll ruin it."

It was more like a prediction than a threat. The boy sounded sad, not belligerent.

"My real mother doesn't like me anymore," Albert confided with the blaring voice that partly deaf people had. "She got fat when she had me, so Dad stopped liking her. She's getting a new husband, and she says I'd just ruin things again. She sent me to live with Dad so I'll ruin things for him instead."

She stared at him, her mouth open. What kind of mother would say things like that to her own child? No wonder Johnny divorced her! Who'd stay with a woman like that?

Distracted by a sudden craving for something sweet, she opened a cupboard to see what she had on hand. "Do you like cake, Albert?" She looked over her shoulder. "Of

26

course, you do! Everybody likes cake."

He nodded but warily, not sure why she was asking.

"Let's bake a cake," she suggested. "Which do you like better: chocolate or vanilla? Or molasses, maybe, with currants? I know a good recipe for that."

They settled on a marble cake and had a good time together. Assembling the ingredients, tasting the batter, managing the woodstove. Later they took turns with the whisk, beating the buttercream frosting until their arms ached.

They'd each had two big slices when Albert asked, "Can I call you Mamma?" Eyes on hers, waiting for her answer, the little boy licked a finger and pressed it onto the crumbs to carry every last morsel from his plate to his mouth.

She wanted fame. She wanted to travel the world. She wanted adventure and excitement, not a boring, ordinary life — that's why she'd run away from home! Then she met Johnny Behan. He was dashing and handsome, important and prosperous. A man who might be governor or even president one day. For a while she was sure she wanted to be his wife, but now . . .

Albert was still waiting.

"You have a mother," she reminded him.

"I knew you wouldn't like me," he said. Stoic. Resigned.

"Of course I will! I like you already."

She didn't quite mean it. Albert could see that, and his lonely skepticism made her warm to him.

"All right, listen. You shouldn't call me Mamma, but . . ." She put her mouth close to his ear so he could hear her speak quietly. "I have a secret name."

She reared back to see his reaction, which was wide-eyed.

"You have to promise not to tell anybody," she said sternly. "You can only use it when we're alone together. Promise?" He nodded. Once more she leaned in close to say a single word, then sat back with a conspiratorial smile.

"Sadie," he whispered. "I get to call you Sadie."

They were children, the two of them, without a tiresome adult to say, "No more sweets! It'll spoil your supper." So they celebrated with more cake.

An hour later, she was emotional again and frighteningly queasy. She'd begun wondering if the butter had gone off and was making her sick when a much worse possibility occurred to her. Unbidden, a dismal future rose up. A squalling baby. A sad little stepson. A thick waist. A husband who liked slender girls. Exactly the kind of dreary, domesticated life she'd fled.

Face in her hands, she began to cry again.

■ ■ ■ ■

A lifetime later, when she was a stout old woman, all by herself for the first time in nearly fifty years, she would bury her face in one of Wyatt's shirts and weep hour after hour. For Wyatt. For herself. For their blighted lives.

It was all gossip and slander and libel — newspapers calling Wyatt a killer, a cheat, a bunco man. And now he was gone, and she was the only one left to defend his good name. If only she could get Mr. Hart to make a movie about Wyatt! William S. Hart was a big star, and he admired Wyatt so. He could set the record straight.

"My husband was a hero," she told the nice man who always visited on Sundays. "None of it was his fault." Or mine either, she thought. "All I did was love him. Never be sorry for loving someone, Albert."

"I'm John Flood," the man reminded her, "not Albert Behan."

Wiping her eyes, she snapped, "Of course you're not Albert. Albert's only eight. I know that."

"I'm sure you do, Mrs. Earp."

"Mrs. Earp!" she muttered, staring resentfully at ringless fingers. Then she shrugged. "All the world's a stage. That's what dear Mr. Hart would say. You just have to learn your lines. I helped Wyatt learn his after the gun-fight."

She giggled then — a naughty little girl remembering sailors — and put a flirtatious hand on the nice man's arm.

"It's not lying," she told Albert, or John, or whoever he was. "It's just pretending. That's what Papa said."

"Now, what you gonna tell your *Mutti*?"

"I was helping you at the bakery."

She was rewarded with fond eyes.

"That's my girl!" her father declared. "I can always count on my Sadie."

She wasn't quite seven when they started sneaking off to the Brooklyn docks together. Her father never explained why Mutti shouldn't know, except to say, "She got enough worries. Why give her *tsuris*?"

For a while, they stood with their backs against a warehouse wall, trying not to get in the way of swearing sailors and sweating stevedores. The docks were scary and exciting. There were rats and stray dogs. Hopeful new immigrants and hopeless old women with painted faces. Casks of stinking whale oil. Huge coils of rope almost as thick as her father's arms, which were heavy with muscle that came from kneading big batches of dough.

"Why not?" her father decided. "We go take

a look. No harm in that." He scooped her into his arms, grunting, "Oy, you getting big," and carried her out to the end of the central pier. There he turned slowly on his heel, Sadie clinging to him like an organ grinder's monkey.

They were surrounded by ships tied up at the dock or anchored out in the harbor. More ships than she could count, though she'd recently counted all the way to fifty-three before she got bored and quit.

"Look at all them masts!" her father cried. "Like a forest, eh, Sadie?"

"What's a forest, Papa?" She was a city child, after all.

"You seen trees, right? Well, you gotta imagine places big as Brooklyn — bigger, even — with nothing but trees and trees and trees."

After her father explained it, she could sort of imagine a forest. Except rigging didn't look a bit like leaves. Rigging looked like scribbles.

"You want a good heavy ship for passage around the Horn," he told her as they started back along the pier. "Maybe you don't want so big like the *Roanoke* there, but for sure you want bigger than the *Germanic.* Now, look at this one." He lifted his chin toward a middle-sized ship. "She's the *Hosea Higgins.* Ships is always she, even if they got a man's name. *Ja,* for sure . . . The *Hosea Higgins.* That's the ship you want for a voyage around the Horn."

She thought he meant a horn that you could blow until a few days later, when he took her to a store that sold used books. The owner knew her father and asked, "How are you finding Mr. Darwin's tale, Mr. Markuse?"

Her father talked to the shopkeeper awhile. Then he asked to use the store's globe so he could explain to Sadie about continents and how Cape Horn was a place down at the pointy end of South America.

"Now, here is Posen, back in Europe. Who knows what country? Sometimes Poland, sometimes Prussia. That's where your *mutti* and me was born. And here is Brooklyn in North America, where Nathan and you and Hattie was born." With his finger, her father traced a line all over half the globe. "This is the voyage of the *Beagle.*" It sounded important, the way he said it. "But a ship like the *Higgins,* she ain't gonna go so far. She gonna go from Brooklyn here . . . south across the equator. Down the coast of Brazil and Argentina . . . around the Horn, then up-up-up past Chile . . . cross the equator again . . . up some more and then you step off in San Francisco. Four months, it takes. Well, six, maybe. If the weather is bad."

Twice more that week, they went back to watch the *Higgins* discharge her California cargo of wine, smoked salmon, and whale oil. When the ship began to take on westbound

33

freight, her father scooped Sadie into his arms again. "Why not?" he said. "We just go introduce ourselves."

The ship's captain was bearded and gruff. "This is no place for a child, sir! State your business!"

Her father set Sadie down on the *Higgins*'s deck and approached the captain alone. A few minutes later, he beckoned Sadie to come closer. "Captain," he said, "I like to introduce you my daughter, Josephine Sarah. Sadie, say hello to the captain."

She dropped a little curtsy like a girl she saw in a penny play once. "I am very pleased to meet you, sir."

The captain's eyes widened and warmed. A smile lifted his beard.

I did that, she thought. I made him nicer.

The two men moved off a few steps, speaking in low tones again. She craned her neck to watch the sailors up in the rigging and discovered that they were looking down at her, for little girls were rare as rubies in their world and Sadie was an arresting child: small, neat-bodied, with pale white skin and curly black hair and dark brown eyes, her new front teeth coming in nicely. She curtsied to each of the sailors, one after another, turning all around, until she staggered a little, dizzy. And the sailors didn't just smile. They clapped for her and nudged each other and cheered.

She was glad when her father took her back

to the *Higgins* the next day.

"Our secret," he reminded her. "Mutti don't gotta know. Just you and your old papa, eh?"

This time she had to hang on to the hem of his coat. He couldn't hold her hand because he was carrying big stacked trays loaded with samples. Rye, pumpernickel, and soft white bread. Yeast rolls and three kinds of muffins. Cream puffs. Almond macaroons. Crisp strudel. Seven-layer tortes.

This bounty was presented to the captain of the *Higgins,* who shared it with his officers. Grinning, their lips white with powdered sugar, they moaned their admiration for Hyman Markuse's excellence as a baker. Their eyes ate Sadie up, too.

When the trays were empty, nested and tucked under one arm, her father took her hand and they walked, bent-kneed, back down the gangplank.

"Now, what you gonna tell Mutti?" he asked.

"We took samples to a new customer." She felt special to be trusted.

"Good girl. Gotta keep the story straight!" he declared. "Always easier when the story's true . . ."

It wasn't the first time they'd skipped out.

Silently, Sophie Markuse bundled her three children against the January cold and hustled

35

them down the narrow tenement stairs. Nathan was the oldest and he was used to it, but even little Hattie knew what it meant when their mother woke the children before dawn. You had to be very quiet, so as not to alert the landlord. And it wouldn't do to wake the Irish boarder, who was sleeping off a drunk on the kitchen floor. He paid for meals in advance and would want his money back.

Hy already had their bags loaded on a wagon waiting at the end of the block, where the rumble of wooden wheels and the squeal of rusty axles wouldn't give the family away. It wasn't until the driver pulled up by the wharves that Sophie realized this was no ordinary flight from overdue rent.

"Nayn, Chayim! Nayn! Ich vil nit gayen!"

"English, Sophie! We're Americans now! Don't worry, everything gonna be fine," her husband said, mixing encouragement with urgency as he coaxed her off the wagon. "Don't make a *tzimmes* out of it. You gonna upset the children —"

"I'm gonna upset them? Me? *I'm* the one who's dragging them off to the end of the earth? *Nayn, Chayim! Nayn!"*

In the end, Hyman Markuse gave up arguing and simply pulled his weeping wife toward the *Hosea Higgins*. The three children followed like ducklings, their breath forming little white clouds in the first pink light of day.

36

A busy crew wasmaking ready to leave port. "Mr. Marcus, take your family to your cabin!" the captain shouted. Pointing at two of the least soused sailors, he ordered, "You and you, stow their bags below!"

Looking up at his father, Nathan asked, "Mr. *Marcus*?"

"I gonna explain later," Hy promised. "The cabin's very cozy, Sophie. You gonna see. Everything gonna be all right."

Eyes closed, Sophie was shaking her head — *no, no, no* — but she cried out in fright when a sailor stumbled against her, dropped two valises, and apologized with the glassy-eyed solemnity of a drunk trying very hard to show how sober he is.

"You promised me, Chayim!" she wailed as her husband guided her into the bowels of the ship. "You promised! I told you I don't wanna go!"

Sadie tried to take her little sister's hand, but Hattie wouldn't let her.

"Papa musta lied," Hattie muttered, eyes on their weeping mother's back. "Papa always lies."

With his family assembled in their dark little cabin, Hyman Markuse lined the children up in front of the berth they were to share — packed head to toe, like tinned sardines — for the next 158 nights.

Nathan, eleven, was the reason Hy had offered to marry Sophie. She might have hoped to do better than a Brooklyn baker, but at twenty-seven, her chances were dwindling, and with a baby on the way, Hyman Markuse was better than no husband at all. A miscarriage was next, and a stillbirth followed: tragedy piled on irony. When Sadie finally came along, it seemed a miracle. Doll-like and beautiful, she took Hy's breath away. "You spoil her, Chayim," his wife always said, and that was true. He could deny Sadie nothing, for she was lively and demanding, a terror when thwarted and adorable when indulged. Hattie was next. Her mother's daughter. A dour little soul, wary and mistrustful. Glaring at him now, as if daring her father to speak the truth.

"Children," he announced, "today we leave for to seek our fortune in the West! We gonna sail round the Horn to a new home in San Francisco, and our passage is paid, complete, 'cause I gonna be the ship's cook. From this day, our family name gonna be *Marcus.* We gonna have a new American home in a new American city, and we gonna have new American names when we get there."

Nathan made a noise with his lips and left the cabin.

"Just like your father!" Sophie called after him. "Leave! That's the solution to everything!" Red eyes cold with judgment, Sophie declared, "You oughta be ashamed, Chay."

"It's Henry now, and I told you, I gonna pay your brother back."

"Teaching your own children to lie!"

"Whose business is it, we change our name a little bit? You changed your name when you married me. Was that a lie?"

"It's not just the name, Chayim! It's —"

"It's pretending, that's all," Sadie said. "There's nothing wrong with pretending."

Seventy years later, long after memories of Wyatt Earp and Johnny Behan had faded and died, Sadie Marcus could still recall that childhood voyage in moments of crisp clarity.

Her miserable mother dashing across the deck to vomit over the side while seabirds hovered and dove and squabbled for the results.

Her cheerful father's face shining with excitement as he told about a galley fire quickly doused with soup.

The endless Brazilian forest with its uncountable tree trunks — like the masts in Brooklyn harbor!

Whales, rising and falling in vast mounds.

Hordes of seals, sunning on rocks.

Penguins were the best of all, formally dressed for a party that could begin only after they waddled to the edge of the rocks and tumbled into the ocean.

"You see, Sadie?" her father said, lifting a hand toward those awkward, comical birds as they flew through the gray-green water, fiercely graceful and suddenly swift. "Everything changes when you are in your proper element. That's what your *mutti* don't understand."

Sadie stood tiptoe on a roll of canvas, resting her forearms on the rail the way her father did. She was fascinated by his hands and wrists, crisscrossed by shiny pink brands burned into his skin by baking sheets and kettles and ovens.

"Your *mutti,* she wishes we stayed in Brooklyn," he said. "But in America? You can start over. You can change where you live. Change what you do. Change your name even! In America, you just gotta find your proper element and you will succeed."

She was shivering beneath layers of flannel and knitting. Her lips felt thick from the cold, and her face was chapped by wind that had started its own journey in the Antarctic. It was worth mere discomfort to stand at her father's side, listening to his brave words.

"Your *mutti* gonna see. We gonna buy a nice little building on a corner. Corners is always good for a bakery. We gonna live upstairs, and we ain't gonna need no drunk Irishman to share the rent. No more boss who takes the profit! We gonna offer fine pastries and cakes, not just bread and rolls. Lotta money in San Francisco. Lotta rich people gonna want me to cater their parties . . . She'll see.

Everything gonna be fine!"
And it truly was, for a while at least.

Ruin Is Strong and Swift

San Francisco.

It was newer, bigger, brasher, noisier than Brooklyn. San Francisco was willing to give anyone a second or third or fourth chance, and immigrants from around the globe were taking the town up on its offer. Chileans and Chinamen. Bengalis and Brazilians. Jews from all over Europe. Ex-convicts from Australia, ex-Confederates from Mississippi, ex-slaves from Georgia. Mohawks from New York, Cherokees from Oklahoma. Huge Hawaiian laborers, dapper Italian musicians, suave French thieves. Educated or illiterate, dirt-poor or well-capitalized, respectable or on the run — everyone in San Francisco had come for one reason only: to make a fortune in the foggy, chilly city that had mushroomed into existence on top of a boomtown's mud and dung.

When the Marcus family arrived in 1868, the bay was jammed with shipping, and the dockside warehouses were as full as the brothels. New buildings climbed up and over the hills, straining to accommodate a quarter million ambitious men and a few thousand very tired women. Swells with money swanned around town in top hats, frock coats, striped pants, and brocade vests, shoes buffed to a mirror shine twice daily by bootblacks who earned a very decent living from the filthy streets. Watching this swaggering peacock parade, the former Hyman Markuse suspected that every man in town was running from a fuming brother-in-law, or a forlorn fiancée, or a cheated business partner somewhere back in Argentina, or Scotland, or South Africa. But what did that matter? In San Fransisco, anyone could leave a disappointing past behind and *get rich.*

There were, by then, more than a hundred bakeries in town, but after two decades of sourdough, the city was ravenous for soft white bread, elaborate cakes, and fancy pastries. With his pay from the *Hosea Higgins,* Henry Marcus bought a used oven, jammed it into a tiny shack, and sent the kids out with a pushcart to sell pastries. Sophie was mortified and fretted about the children's safety, but nobody came to grief and cash began to accumulate. After six months, he was able to rent a storefront. Sales doubled.

Half a year later, he took a mortgage on a corner lot and built a fine two-story building, just as he had planned. Like Mr. and Mrs.

Marcus themselves, the apartment above the bakery steadily gained bourgeois weight, its rooms filling with heavy furniture, the upholstery well-stuffed, the wood deeply carved. To Henry's immense satisfaction, Sophie's attitude toward their newest home softened along with her widening hips. She loved shopping and not for nothing was San Francisco called the Emporium of the Pacific! Henry took pleasure in his wife's pleasure, never complaining about the expense. Hattie didn't care about clothes, but Sadie! She grew more beautiful by the year, and it was a joy to see what a princess she was becoming. What did it matter if all those pretty shoes and ribbon-trimmed skirts were ruined by San Francisco's mud? The girls were growing. Sophie got plumper every year. They always needed new.

For Henry himself, success meant buying great stacks of books and magazines and newspapers, though he often fell asleep before reading very long. He had to be up well before dawn to make sure that Nathan had the ovens going because . . . Well, admittedly: Nathan was a disappointment. He didn't like working at the bakery but couldn't seem to hold a job anywhere else. He'd come home complaining that he'd been cheated or ill-treated by his boss. After a few weeks, he'd quit in a huff and then mope around the apartment until his mother's nagging became more tedious than looking for a job.

Even so, Henry didn't worry. He was making enough to support them all and even sent money to relatives in Posen — until everything went bust in the Panic of 1873.

"Good times never last, but hard times always end." That was Henry's motto in the early days of the depression. The Marcus bakery remained solvent longer than many more impressive businesses, for there are times when man does live by bread alone. There's always a market for a baker's basics, even if his customers wait until the end of the day to save pennies on stale loaves.

"We gonna be all right?" Sophie asked whenever she heard of another local business going under.

"Sure! Everything gonna be fine!" Henry would say, and then he'd send her and Sadie out shopping, so they wouldn't worry.

By the end of 1875, Henry had laid off all the help. Alone in the shop, he worked the ovens, the counter, the till, the supply room. Too tired to collect due bills, he got into trouble when he failed to pay his own.

Only dour and wary young Hattie saw growing exhaustion beneath her father's resolute cheer. One morning, she got out of bed when her father did — before daybreak — and went downstairs with him.

"What about school?" he asked.

"I can read and write," she said, tying on an apron that went around her twice. "I can add and subtract. What else do I need?"

Before long, he stopped thinking of her as a child. Even when Hattie was small, she had seemed older than Sadie. Now, plain-faced and flat-chested at thirteen, Hattie was everything her beautiful sister didn't need to be: realistic, practical, good with numbers. Give that girl a ledger and she would follow a dime to hell.

When the bakery ran out of flour one morning, Hattie set herself to cleaning up the books. She was determined to figure out how much they owed the mill and why they'd gotten behind on paying for this essential.

"Is this everything?" she asked, waving at the papers stacked in neat, grim piles on the desk. "No other bills? No money hidden somewhere?"

"That's all of it," her father said.

She stared.

"I swear!" he cried. "That's everything!"

"Well, we aren't bankrupt yet but we'll be lucky to make the mortgage payment this month, Papa."

"Hattie, please! Don't tell your mother. She don't gotta know. There's a man — he gonna buy the bakery. He gonna let me rent the apartment. Our name stays on the building. He gonna give me a salary."

"Don't sell," she said. "Not yet, anyway. I

wish I'd known sooner, but now that I do . . ." She looked him in the eye. "You can't spend *anything* without my permission, Papa. You can't say yes just because Sadie pouts. And Nathan has to find work. He brings in money or he moves out."

"He has a job! He works here."

"Now and then," she admitted dryly. "Papa, he's lazy and unreliable. He eats like a horse and drinks like a fish. Would you hire him if he weren't your son?" His hesitation was her answer, and she nodded tightly. "You want to fire him or shall I?"

"All right!" Henry cried. "Do what you gotta do. Just — please! — don't tell your mother."

Nathan was given two days before he'd be kicked out of the house. When he protested, Hattie told him, "You pay room and board or you move out. And if you go crying to Mutti, I'll tell her about that *shiksa* you're seeing." Just to be sure Nate wasn't holding out on the family, Hattie followed him to whatever odd jobs he got after that. "I will pick up his wages," she informed the fools who were willing to hire her brother, and there was something so implacable about that skinny, hard-eyed girl that his bosses handed over the cash.

Sadie moaned and complained about getting up early to help with the baking before school, but Hattie was not above using guilt as a bludgeon. "The Crash hurt the business. Papa can't afford to pay assistants. You want him to die of apoplexy, he's working so hard?"

Give Sadie her due. She'd always been good in the kitchen and had a real flair for the fancier baking. No one who shopped at the Marcus bakery was giving lavish receptions anymore, but a plate of pretty petits fours and iced bonbons could make an afternoon tea more special. Sadie loved decorating the little cakes, but she really shone behind the counter after school, flirting shamelessly with the customers, bringing in mobs of moon-struck admirers. "I was thinking of you when I made these crullers," she'd whisper to a goggle-eyed young man, who'd buy a dozen. Dark eyes flashing, she'd lean over the counter and offer a tiny sample of a torte she'd made. "Here," she'd say. "Try this and tell me what you think." The whole torte would sell.

"That's my Sadie," Henry would say. "She got them eating out of her hand!"

"Idiots," Hattie would mutter, but even she liked what Sadie did for the bottom line.

Slowly, in fits and starts, the economy improved. By 1877, Hattie's ferocious economizing and strict management had placed the business on a solid cash basis. The threat of bankruptcy receded.

If Mrs. Henry Marcus had been kept strictly

ignorant of how and why this had been achieved, she was correct in surmising that Henry's mood and outlook had improved. Which is why she thought it was perfectly reasonable to make a completely ridiculous suggestion on a chilly night in 1878, when she and her husband were getting ready for bed.

"We should buy the girls a piano."

One shoe on, one shoe off, Henry stared. Sophie was as round and sleek as a sea lion under the covers, but her voice was firm with the sort of resolution that every married man recognizes and dreads.

"If Sadie gonna get a husband, she gotta get some *accomplishments,* Henry."

San Francisco's men still outnumbered its women a hundred to one. In Henry's observation, all a female needed to get a husband were two of those and one of the other. Four limbs? Desirable, maybe. Not required.

Stalling, he toed off the second shoe and bent over to pull off his stockings.

"I had a piano," Sophie reminded him coyly, "and such a husband I got!"

Wasn't music got you a husband, Henry thought, but he'd have yanked his own tongue out with pliers before he said as much.

"Both girls should take lessons," Sophie persisted. "Hattie, she gotta get some graces or she never gonna get married. You treat her like a son, Henry."

He slid into bed beside her and made a grave tactical error. "And how you think we gonna get a piano up them stairs?"

Sophie had clearly thought this through. Sitting up, she warmed to her topic, which involved blocks and tackles and windows, and what several ladies at the synagogue had done for their daughters in similar circumstances.

"I'm not listening!" Henry warned, but the very fact that she'd raised this bizarre notion was oddly comforting, so he let her rattle on, thinking all the while, She don't know. Thanks, Gott! Hattie didn't tell her!

"Sophie," he said finally, turning down the light and speaking the truth, "the last thing in the world this family needs is a piano."

"Dora's mother invited me and Hattie to a concert!" Sadie announced at dinner a few nights later. Dora Hirsch was Sadie's best friend at school.

"A piano concert?" Sophie asked innocently. As if she hadn't already talked to Mrs. Hirsch about this. "And who is playing?"

Sadie looked blank. "She told me but . . . I don't remember. Some lady."

"Never mind who's playing," Hattie said. "Who's paying?"

"We're to be Mrs. Hirsch's *guests,*" Sadie said primly. She made a face at Hattie. " 'Guest' means *she* pays, we don't, idiot."

"Sadie!" their mother said sharply. "Don't

call names."

"Can't beat the price," their father admitted. "All right. Why not?"

"I'll tell you why not," Hattie said. "Mrs. Hirsch is a piano teacher, and there's no such thing as a free sample. She's fishing for students."

"So, good!" Sophie said, passing kugel to her husband. "We got two students for her. I told you, Henry. The girls need to play piano so they can get husbands."

"I'm not getting married," Sadie declared, just to stir things up. "I'm going to be an emancipated woman. I'm going to ride a bicycle. And vote."

"And how are you going to make a living?" Hattie inquired. "You think Papa is going to support you while you're out voting and being emancipated?"

"It would be a *mitzvah* for the girls to take lessons," Sophie pointed out. "Evelyn Hirsch is a widow. She needs the money." She waited a moment before adding piously, "Maimonides says the highest form of charity is to help that someone should make a honest, good living."

Henry glanced at Hattie.

She looked at him narrow-eyed, then shrugged. "Fine," she said. It's on your head, she meant.

"They can go to the concert," Henry told his wife, "but that's all."

51

■ ■ ■ ■

So Sadie and Hattie Marcus accompanied
Mrs. Hirsch and Dora to some lady's piano
recital a few nights later. And to her mother's
delight, Sadie came home simply *dying* to
take piano lessons.

Everything about the recital had thrilled
her. That dress! Ivory satin, gleaming in the
limelight. The lady's hair! Sweeping smoothly
upward, adorned with tiny flowers and pearls.
Her creamy shoulders. Those jeweled brace-
lets flashing as her hands moved. The rapt attention of the audience, all eyes on the
performer. The waves of applause! With the
sudden, certain emotion of adolescence, Josephine Sarah Marcus became unalterably
determined to tour the world as a concert
pianist. New York, Paris, London — they
were out there, waiting for her!

All she needed was a piano.

Everything might have turned out differ-
ently if Henry Marcus had simply told her,
"We can't afford it," but he had never been
able to say no to Sadie. What he said instead
was "I don't got time to shop for a piano."

Big mistake.

For the next week, whenever he sat down,
Sadie pounced, and it was "Can we look for
a piano this afternoon, Papa?" He came up
with excuses. He was making inquiries, he

told her. A customer thought she might be willing to sell him her piano. Two days later: "The lady changed her mind." That kind of thing.

But Sadie wouldn't let it go. Her whole future depended on this. Her father was cruel and neglectful. He obviously hated her. Well, she hated *him.* If she could not have a piano, she did not want to *live.*

Every supper ended with hysterical tears, dire threats, slammed doors. Hattie stood it as long as she could before marching Sadie into the back room of the bakery and showing her the books. "We're barely making a living," she said, and she had the figures to prove it. "Papa's killing himself, and you are a selfish pig. There isn't going to be a piano. So quit asking."

Sadie sulked for a few days before shifting the terms of the discussion. "We don't need to *buy* a piano," she told Hattie. "Mrs. Hirsch says I can practice at her house. Can we afford just the lessons, Hattie? Please?"

Hattie had not been thrilled by the concert. She was routinely up at four in the morning to work at the store and had fallen asleep halfway through the recital, bored senseless by a Mozart piece that sounded like an endless repetition of *Deedle deedle deedle deedle.* On the other hand, being asked — please — for permission to do something . . . Well, now. That *was* thrilling. That was not something

Hattie wanted to let go too quickly.

"I'll think about it," she said.

For the next three weeks, Hattie's citadel was stormed. In the end, she agreed to pay Mrs. Hirsch twenty-five cents a week to cover Sadie's lessons but only because she expected that the expense would be short-term. "She'll give up inside a month," Hattie predicted, but to everyone's frank surprise, Sadie kept going to Mrs. Hirsch's week after week, month after month.

When questioned, she rarely remembered what she was working on, but honestly, what was there to remember? Five-finger exercises. Scales, up and down, up and down, with that awful metronome clack-clack-clacking away. On the other hand, she could play simple melodies by ear after she got Mrs. Hirsch to run through them first, "So I'll know how they should sound when they're played beautifully."

Of course, Evelyn Hirsch knew that old trick. Perhaps one student in a hundred was alive to the instrument — pulled forward by the piano itself, not shoved at it from behind. Sadie Marcus had a good ear, but she was the kind who'd never learn to read music well. Eventually her progress would stumble and come to a halt. Until that day arrived, however, Mrs. Hirsch saw no reason to inform Mr. Marcus that his daughter was wasting his money. Evelyn Hirsch was, after all, the sole support of her family, and two bits was two bits.

What she did not expect was the mutually beneficial pact Sadie proposed after it became clear that a career as a concert pianist required considerably more effort than Sadie was willing to devote to the project. "I'll still come over after school, Mrs. Hirsch, but Dora and I will study together, which I really need to do because I'm having a terrible time in school and I don't want my parents to know. You'll still get my twenty-five cents for the lessons, but you can take on another paying student, which will bring that hour's income to fifty cents."

Nobody — in the bakery or above it — need be the wiser.

Evelyn was initially troubled by the arrangement, her need for easy income at war with her ethics.

"It's not *lying,* Mrs. Hirsch," Sadie assured her. "It's just . . . not telling."

You Will Never Be Lovelier Than You Are Now

She did not tell her parents she'd quit piano. She and Dora Hirsch and their friend Agnes Stern spent the time holed up in Dora's room instead. Talking about boys. Poring over illustrated fashion magazines. Studying hats and sleeves and bustles, not music. Or rhetoric or history or mathematics. She never mentioned how she and Dora screamed with excitement when Agnes arrived one afternoon bearing a newspaper announcing that the French actress Sarah Bernhardt would tour America, or how thrilled she was when she realized that she would soon be breathing the same air as the extraordinary Jewess who'd set the world on fire with her boldness and courage on stage.

Soon, however, everyone in the country was talking about Bernhardt. Sadie herself filled a scrapbook with dozens of articles celebrating the Divine Sarah's extravagance, her sexual exploits, her genius, her madness. Bernhardt slept in a coffin. She took lovers. She made no effort to conceal her son's illegitimacy. She traveled with a cheetah, a parrot, three dogs, and a monkey named Darwin. She wore trousers when the very word was unspeakable in polite company. She dismissed bourgeois respectability with the breezy declaration, *"Quand même!"* It's all the same to me!

Condemned by anti-Semites and snobs, Bernhardt said and did anything she pleased, and she didn't just get away with it. She was adored for it!

Bernhardt allowed her astonishing, springlike hair to burst out all around her face; Sadie's own tight curls became a point of pride. Beneath strong dark brows, Bernhardt's magnetic eyes were rimmed by dark lashes; Sadie spent hours gazing into her mirror, practicing intense, dramatic, mysteriously tragic glances. Bernhardt was thin and her breasts were small, like Sadie's still were. The ideal beauty of their times was voluptuous and well-endowed, but — *Quand même!* — the Divine Sarah was the object of every man's lust in Paris, London, and New York. "Kwand meem," Sadie would murmur, imagining herself equally desirable, hearing applause in her imagination.

America had hardly recovered from Bernhardt fever when the nation was stricken with a new mania. Gilbert and Sullivan's *H.M.S. Pinafore* spread like a contagion from the

Fifth Avenue Theater in New York to the Adelphi in San Francisco, infecting thousands of community stages in between. There were children's productions, Catholic versions, Yiddish translations, all-male and all-black and minstrel performances. Suddenly everyone was whistling "We sail the ocean blue," or humming "Poor little Buttercup." Just say the word "never," and you'd be drawn into the patter. "What, never?" "No, never!" "What, *never*?" "Well . . . hardly ever!"

When the Pauline Markham *Pinafore* Troupe arrived in San Francisco, it didn't take much persuasion to get Mrs. Hirsch to accompany Dora, Agnes, and Sadie to a children's half-price matinée. Once was enough for Evelyn Hirsch, but the girls were enthralled and begged to see the operetta again and again. All of them were stagestruck, but when Agnes revealed that Tommy Tucker the Cabin Boy was played by a girl, Sadie was lost.

"You mean she's wearing trousers? Like *Bernhardt*? Agnes, are you sure?"

"I most certainly am."

"In grand opera," Dora informed them, "it's called a *Hosenrolle* — a young man played by a contralto in breeches."

Dora could be a know-it-all.

The next time they went to the theater, Sadie watched for a telltale jiggle beneath the cabin boy's blue jacket that might give a girl away during the sailor's hornpipe. The dancer seemed a bit heavier than when the operetta opened two weeks earlier, but Sadie still couldn't believe it.

"Agnes, you're wrong," she whispered. "That's a boy."

"You'll see soon enough. Tommy Tucker is . . ." Agnes dropped her voice and leaned over to say, ". . . *en famille.*" A lady one row back hissed at them, so Agnes waited a moment before murmuring, "Pauline told me so."

"Pauline? You mean — ?"

"Miss Markham, yes. I met her at a party." Ignoring the insistent *"Shhh!"* behind them, Agnes bestowed her most momentous news in a dramatic whisper. "They're casting for a new cabin boy at the end of the San Francisco run."

Sneaking money from the bakery till and skipping school, Sadie returned to the theater twice more that week to check the choreography. Locked in the bakery storeroom, she practiced the hornpipe madly. When she wasn't hopping on one foot or hauling on imaginary ropes or giving charming nautical salutes, she was upstairs in her room, gazing into a hand mirror and working on her "Mysterious and Tragic but Courageous" expression, while making up a story about being an orphan whose lifelong dream was to join the Pauline Markham troupe and travel the world to earn the applause of audiences everywhere — nonsense that rattled right out of her head the moment she stepped through the stage door at the Adelphi.

Surrounded by a chaos of packing crates, costumes, props, and rolled-up canvas scenery, she waited to be noticed, which she was, but mostly by stagehands who shouted at her to get the hell out of the way.

"Hebe?" a refined baritone asked curiously.

She turned, offended. "I beg your pardon!"

"What part are you auditioning for? Cousin Hebe? The Captain's Daughter? Surely not Dick Deadeye."

She needed a moment to recognize him. The First Lord of the Admiralty was a pompous old man, and she'd paid little attention to that character. Without the ruddy makeup, the admiral's costume, and talc-whitened hair, the actor was much younger than she would have imagined. He had a gallant bearing and tawny leonine hair sweeping back from the kind of forehead she'd learned to call "lofty" from reading novels.

"Come, child! We sail upon the tide! No time to waste!" he cried with merry urgency before adding in the low tones of intimacy, "I do hope you're not trying out for the role of the Captain's Daughter. Miss Markham is herself a 'plump and pleasing person,' but she'll die before giving up the lead to play

Buttercup." His face displayed a kindly expression combining equal parts tolerant amusement and reassuring tenderness. "So, if not Dick Deadeye, then . . . ?"

"Oh. Um, Tommy Tucker. The Cabin Boy."

"Very wise!" the actor declared with twinkling eyes that hinted of shared mischief. "Randolph Murray," he said, offering his hand, kissing hers.

Smiling at her flustered pleasure, he bestowed the complete and practiced attention of his intense brown eyes upon the child before him. Dressed like a schoolgirl in a plaid worsted skirt, a navy jacket buttoned over a crisp white blouse. Tightly plaited hair, wrapped round her head in the Dutch fashion. Seventeen, he judged. And a virgin.

I'll have her, he thought with Richard III's serene confidence, *but I will not keep her long.*

Placing a cool finger under her chin, he lifted the girl's face and turned it from side to side, studying her nose. "A daughter of Abraham, I presume." He could see her wondering if that would help or hurt her chances. She straightened her back and nodded. A Bernhardt devotee, no doubt. "And your name?"

"Sarah Marcus, sir."

He quickly moved his finger to her lips. "The Glorious Pauline despises the Divine Sarah. Professional jealousies are rife in our profession," he confided, knowing she'd be thrilled by that *our.* "Have you a stage name?"

"Well, sir, my first name is really Josephine, but nobody calls me that, and my father always —"

"Oh, but it's perfect! Jo Marcus! Ambiguous! Androgynous! Just the name for a dancer playing Tommy Tucker! Pauline, darling," he called, pivoting on a heel. "We have an ambitious little girl here! Come and tell me what you think of her."

Minimally concealed by a silk wrapper that drifted open to reveal impressive amplitude above and below a loosened corset of sturdy linen, the Glorious Pauline Markham was everything the Divine Sarah Bernhardt was not: tall and blond and soft, with a glowing pink complexion that bordered on the florid.

"This is Jo Marcus, darling," Randolph Murray said smoothly. "She would like to replace Miss McConnell."

"Ah, yes. The *unfortunate* Miss McConnell." The Glorious Pauline gazed meaningfully at the Serene Mr. Murray before turning toward the new girl with an expression that was, apparently, quite friendly. "What an *interesting* little girl! Can you dance, interesting little girl?"

"Yes, Miss Markham. I know the hornpipe by heart already."

"Well? Go ahead," the actress urged.

"Now? Without music?"

"The show must go on, regardless of cir-

cumstance. We play some very primitive ven-
ues."

Hesitantly, she began the dance, but before
she'd completed more than the first few
steps, Randolph Murray stopped her.

"Jo, dear, we cannot see your legs. Lift your
skirt, if you please."

"Look, Randolph!" Miss Markham cried
delightedly. "She's blushing! Isn't that adorable? Rosy little Josie!"

"Theater life requires a certain blithe indifference to bourgeois convention," Mr. Murray said. "No place for decorum here!"

Miss Markham aimed a downward smile at
her own dishabille. "Costume changes in the
wings, you know."

Their unblinking eyes rested upon her.
Curious, expectant, skeptical. A good girl
would have been frightened, nervous, embarrassed. Then again, a good girl wouldn't have
been there at all. And that was how Josephine
Sarah Marcus discovered that she wasn't a
good girl — that she had never been a good
girl, not even when she was six years old,
making sailors smile. She *wanted* eyes on her.
She wanted an audience all to herself, challenging her, daring her to be worth watching.
She wanted to be *seen*.

Reaching behind herself, she unbuttoned
her skirt and stepped out of it. She pulled off
her petticoat as well, tossing garments and
modesty away with a careless theatrical

gesture that became the first figure of the hornpipe. Jaunty now in her navy jacket and calf-length cotton drawers, she did a boy's dance with a boy's grin that got wider as she saw skepticism become surprise, and surprise turn into approval.

The music was so familiar they heard it in their minds. Even stagehands stopped to watch and clap in time. When she was finished, everyone cheered and she took her first professional bow.

I did it, she thought, breathless and exhilarated. I changed their minds! I made them believe!

An instant later, Mr. Murray shouted, "Back to work, everyone! We've got three hours to make the boat to Santa Barbara!"

Equally brisk, Miss Markham said, "You're hired, Rosy Josie. Go home and pack *one* valise — we've no room for more. Be back here in an hour."

She had found her proper element. The wide world beckoned. She could already hear its applause.

She flew home, went to her room, stuffed a few things in a bag, and told her mother, "I'm spending the night at Dora's house!" On the way through the bakery, she gave her father a quick peck on the cheek, as she always did on her way to "piano practice" on school-day afternoons.

She gave no thought to her girlfriends, or to Mrs. Hirsch, or to what her family would think when she failed to come home. Her only moment of doubt came back at the theater, when the fully and elaborately dressed Miss Markham beckoned her close and spoke for her ears only.

"Now listen carefully, Rosy Josie," the actress said in a low, hard voice. "Nobody here gives a 'big, big D' what you do on your own time. But if you do the big, big F with the charming Mr. M.? Be sure he uses a French letter every *single* time! Do *not* get yourself knocked up. Understand?"

On that Thursday afternoon in San Francisco, Jo Marcus had no idea what Miss Markham was talking about, though she knew she was being warned about something.

By Sunday, Randolph Murray had explained it all — that and a great deal more, for he'd always enjoyed developing natural talent and found Jo Marcus a gratifyingly eager student.

"Take your voice down an octave. I want to feel your voice *here,*" he told her, laying a hand on her chest. "It should resonate between your lovely little breasts, not vibrate out your nose."

"Don't flirt like a schoolgirl! Don't be so obvious! You're beautiful, and that will draw eyes. Silence is your tool," he told her. "Stay quiet in a crowd. Smile to yourself — like this! — as though you are amused by the interest your beauty arouses. Lower your eyes demurely. Keep them down, but then bring them up slowly, to meet a man's own. I promise you: The effect will be devastating."

"You have no idea how powerful you can be," he told her. "You can have any man you want. Just look into his eyes. Think, *I want you,* and he'll be yours. But don't be too quick! Let him think about you for a while. Let him wonder."

He taught her how to give satisfaction and to expect it for herself, how to control the rhythm and to tighten at the end. "Most women just lie there like logs. No one has taught them what to desire. You know that now, Jo. You will be able to tell a man what you want and when you want it."

He knew from the start that others would benefit from his instruction. The only thing that surprised Randolph Murray was how soon he was replaced.

Handsome, Woman-Crazed Deceiver

Her Luscious Neck and Ravishing Breasts, the Brilliance of Her Eyes

"Randolph dear, you have a rival!" Pauline observed with a sad gaze that might have seemed sympathetic but wasn't.

The stagecoach depot was surrounded by gray sand flats with low mounds of shattered brown rock in the distance. The entire dismal landscape was disfigured by Arizona's unholy trio of vicious cacti. Wire-wool barrel cactus, like squat satanic footstools. Spiky bouquets of ocotillo, like hell's daisies. Giant saguaro with weirdly human arms that reached toward heaven like the souls of the damned. The heat was demonic as well, without the slightest breeze to dissipate the ammoniac stench of a nearby corral into which months of horse piss had soaked without benefit of dilution. In the meager shadow of a palo verde shrub, a famished little coyote pounced on a scorpion and crunched it up with evident satisfaction, but Randolph Murray's eyes rested instead on the dashing frontiersman who had been paying court to young Josie Marcus since the troupe's performance in Prescott.

"Every living thing in the Arizona Territory has thorns, spikes, or fangs," the actor muttered. "Or pistols."

"Mr. Behan is *very* attractive," Pauline murmured, relishing it.

"Yes. Quite!" Randolph admitted airily. "Pity about his hairline."

Suddenly feeling rather gay, Pauline dabbed a handkerchief at her throat and waved a languid hand toward the unlovely landscape. "Dear God, do the Indians actually want this back?"

"Yes, unlikely as it seems. The Mexicans do as well."

"Whatever for? Really, what is the point?"

"Hearth and home. National pride. Silver. Lots and lots and lots of silver."

"There *must* be nicer places to find silver. Tiffany's, for example." Fanning flies from her face, she noted, "You look weary, Randolph dear."

"Kind of you to notice, Pauline darling."

He was, in fact, sweating, underslept, and in an exceptionally bad temper. The Pauline Markham troupe did not bear his name, but Randolph Murray managed the enterprise and he was responsible for herding, housing, feeding, and transporting — by sea and by land — a cast and crew of eighteen along with luggage, sets, and costumes, all while arranging new bookings, collecting fees, and doling out the payroll. Not to mention singing six numbers in two acts of a comic opera he loathed, seven nights a week with matinées on Wednesdays, Saturdays, and Sundays.

The travel conditions were appalling, but the response from these Arizona audiences to a British musical about sailors had been astonishing. There were week-long sellouts in Prescott and Phoenix and packed houses for one-night stands in half a dozen other little settlements. They'd just closed in Tucson and were moving on to their biggest booking yet: the lugubriously named but famously wealthy Tombstone, where the dashing Mr. Behan was evidently prospering along with his town. A man of many parts, Mr. Behan had given them to understand. Moving with the times. Full of gumption and enterprise.

Pauline sighed and took Randolph's arm. "Poor thing!" she murmured. "It's harder to be left than to leave, isn't it."

"Don't," he warned, but Pauline was always curious about her successors.

"How *was* our rosy little Josie?" she asked archly.

"Eager. Enthusiastic," Randolph replied blithely. "And very . . . athletic."

The actress blinked. The actor smiled. You asked for it, he meant.

Johnny Behan certainly wasn't in the market for a wife in the spring of 1880. In April he'd traveled from Tombstone up to Prescott to sign the papers that would finalize his divorce from the former Victoria Zaff, and he was in no hurry to replace her.

While he was in town, he took the opportunity to see what all this *H.M.S. Pinafore* fuss was about, and by the end of the first act, he had his eye on a couple of girls in the chorus. When he found out the Markham troupe would be coming to Tombstone at the end of their Arizona tour, he leveraged good looks and good tailoring with good humor to get backstage, where he introduced himself to the manager.

"John Behan," he told Randolph Murray, "and I must warn you at the outset that I am a member of that most loathed and feared breed of man: the Irish politician." The actor smiled, so Johnny followed that disarming confession with a few recommendations about Tombstone's best hotels, nicest restaurants, and finest stores, along with a hint or two about where to find the prettiest and most accommodating girls, while letting slip — subtly, of course — that he himself was a mover and a shaker in southern Arizona's exciting new boomtown.

"Just mention my name," Johnny urged, an inherited Dublin lilt adding interest to Missouri's more prosaic tones. "The proprietors will do their very best to make you feel that Tombstone has treated you well, sir. And if you decide to stay at the Grand Hotel, I'd be happy to arrange for an accommodation on the fees. The owner is a friend of mine."

"How very kind," Randolph murmured. He was aware that he was being worked but didn't mind, for it was useful to develop a connection with a local businessman before the troupe arrived in a town. He was also enjoying Johnny's ingratiating performance, for actors and politicians are members of allied professions and often impress one another. "Mr. Behan, we're having a little celebration this evening for Miss Markham's birthday . . ." He dropped his voice before adding, "Though no one would *think* of mentioning the passing of the years within the Glorious Pauline's hearing."

"A slip of a girl," Johnny agreed solemnly. "Hardly out of ringlets."

"Precisely! Perhaps you would care to join us?"

"Well, now, that's real friendly of you, sir. It'll be my pleasure — sometime after midnight, I expect!" Johnny said with a wink.

Randolph smiled back indulgently. They were men of the world, after all.

When you're one of fourteen children, you learn to make an impression fast if you want to be noticed at all. Number three in the Behan brood, John Harris Behan did indeed crave notice, but he and his sisters and brothers had all been sternly taught the perils of getting above themselves. Take momentary pleasure in a small triumph and you'd hear, "There's joy in the spring but sadness in the fall." Brag and you'd be warned, "There's a spoon you'll sup sorrow with yet."

It was better to be discovered than to push yourself forward, so at dinner with the Markham troupe that first evening in Prescott, Johnny listened to the theater stories with quiet appreciation, merely tossing a witty aside into the conversation now and then. Asked a question, he responded with self-deprecating remarks calculated to arouse curiosity. It was only after dessert that he let himself be persuaded to tell the troupe about his frontier adventures.

"Well, I did serve as sheriff of Yavapai County for a couple of years," he admitted, pausing for murmurs of approbation around the table. "That was a lively sort of job, but nothing compared to the time I spent as a representative in the territorial legislature. In Arizona, Republicans and Democrats fight like Kilkenny cats — till there's nothing left but the yowl." He waited for the chuckles to subside. "Now, I'm a Democrat myself," he continued, "but I reckoned there had to be a *few* things we could all agree on. Better roads —" Enthusiastic affirmation. "Education . . ." Insincere murmurs of concurrence. "Keeping the Apaches in check." Shudders, all around.

"Everyone thought I was crazy to try to work with the Republicans, so I played to my strengths," he said with a cocky grin. "Got a bill passed for the humane care and treatment of the insane!" He allowed only a moment before he smothered his smile, almost, and said, "Obviously a madman's self-interest." Which got a laugh from everyone except the girl who was sitting across the table and a few seats down.

Of course, he'd been working hard to remain becomingly modest, but damn if she didn't seem to be ignoring him on purpose. He himself was finding it impossible not to stare at her. What role did she play in the production, he wondered, and why didn't I notice her before? She wasn't conventionally pretty, but she was slim and lively with vivid features and extraordinary dark curls that sprang out around her face, but only grazed her shoulders. He'd never seen a woman with hair so short. It suited her, he decided.

Just then, she raised her eyes and met his own for a moment.

"I see you've noticed Jo Marcus," Miss Markham murmured, leaning close and placing a hand on his thigh. "She dances as Tommy Tucker. The cabin boy?" When his eyes grew round, the Glorious Pauline added, "Yes, she's a wonder, our little Josie. So . . . *athletic*!"

Before she could say more, Randolph Murray interrupted to ask about Geronimo. Yes, Johnny confirmed, Apache raids were a constant threat. They were serious trouble when they occurred, and he told three stories to illustrate the point. Admittedly, he might have played the danger up a bit, for the Apaches were cunning about international politics, living quietly on Arizona reservations while raising merry hell on the Mexican side. Given American attitudes toward greasers, the Indians were welcome to steal livestock in Sonora as long as things stayed peaceful north of the border. Still, why not give the theater folks a thrill? It was just having a little fun. Telling a few stretchers to make the actresses flutter. Sure enough, one of them — though not Jo Marcus — insisted that the gallant Mr. Behan keep her "safe" that night in Prescott. The next morning, the troupe left for Phoenix. Johnny cut overland and waited just north of town. Staying out of sight, he whooped like an Apache and fired off his pistols before riding over the ridge: a one-man cavalry, ready to take credit for saving the girls from a fate worse than death.

His little pantomime worked like a charm on everyone except the Marcus girl. Aloof, she watched him with a small cool smile. Like she knew that he was picturing the way she looked in boy's clothing.

He shadowed the Markham troupe for miles, attending every performance as the show moved south toward Tombstone. He was going that way anyhow, of course, and tried to match the girl's teasing indifference, but he wanted her and bad. Why? he asked himself, and he had no answer except that it was his nature. From the time he was twelve, in any company, he had always ranked the girls: which he'd have first, then second, then third. The world was filled with desirable women. Hell, nearly all of them were desirable! Plump or thin, white or black or brown, young or experienced. Most could be had for a kind word, or a sweet gesture, or a silver dollar. But not this one. Not Jo Marcus.

It wasn't until they got to Benson that he finally broke through and the funny thing was, he'd quit trying by then. They were just passing the time, hiding from the heat in the shadow of the livery stable, trading stories about their families while they waited for fresh horses to be harnessed for the final push into Tombstone.

Her father was a banker, she told him. Her mother was a society lady, active in the community, doing charity work. Theater was just a lark, she said breezily. She loved to dance but expected she'd return to San Francisco and settle down once she'd gotten a craving for adventure out of her system.

"My mother thought you could burn in hell for dancing," he said.

She blinked. "That's absurd. Anyway, Jews

don't believe in hell."

His father would have told her, "You'll believe in hell right enough when you get there, missy!" but Johnny said, "I don't believe I ever met a Jew."

"You have now," she said. "Why would anybody think dancing is a sin?"

"Dancing is the devil's snare," he told her sternly, pulling a long and serious face. "You can't dance without going to a dance hall. You can't go to a dance hall without drinking. You can't drink without sinning."

His mother's folks were teetotal Missouri Baptists who considered fancy meals and store-bought clothes a sinful extravagance but owned slaves who cooked and sewed and cleaned. His father was a Kildare Catholic. "An ex-seminarian, no less, who saw no harm in a drop of whiskey of an evening," Johnny said, briefly mimicking his father's brogue. "Being a drinker was bad enough, but my dad was an abolitionist, too. That was real trouble in Missouri back then."

To her Baptist parents' enduring dismay, young Miss Harris defied them to marry the mick. Fourteen children attested to the couple's passionate love, but the Mason-Dixon Line ran through the middle of the Behan home: a domestic armory packed to the rafters with explosive politics, with a lit fuse concealed in every corner. And it wasn't just slavery or drinking Mr. and Mrs. Behan

78

fought over.

"Christ, but I hated Sundays," Johnny said, bitterness and Ireland creeping into his voice. "No matter where you went to church, you were a heretic for one parent or t'other. And you came home to more strife over the beef — roasted versus corned, y'see. Then there was the potato battle! Mashed with milk and butter or plain boiled? They even argued about how to thank heaven for the food they fought over."

When the larger war broke out, in 1861, John Harris Behan was just nineteen. "Which side did you join?" Josie asked, and she seemed genuinely interested in his dilemma, so he was honest with her. He'd had his fill of rancor. Rather than enlist in either of the armies that were making Missouri a bleeding battlefield, he lit out for California, and he'd done his level best to get along with people ever since.

"I can find common ground with anyone," he told her, and he meant it, though the country was more divided after the war than before it. "There's always a way to make a deal work. Just see to it that everybody gets something and nobody gets everything."

The stage teams were hitched to the wagons by then. Randolph Murray was herding everyone into the coaches, and Johnny helped Josie climb up. He never quite understood what finally brought her around. Whatever the reason, she kept hold of his hand after she settled onto the bench. Then she leaned over and kissed him full on the mouth.

Right there. In front of everyone.

Damn, but she was something! Wire-thin, with an energy that seemed almost . . . What? He had no words for her. Electric, maybe? A glowing face, vivid with mischief, as though she were daring him —

She *wants* it, he realized. He could see it in her. The excitement. The hunger. He sounded courteous, but he could feel his blood rising when he asked if he might visit her in Tombstone that evening after the performance.

"Maybe," she allowed, eyes sparkling. "If no one more interesting takes my fancy."

When he came to her room that night, she pulled him inside, shut the door, and met his need with a bright eagerness undimmed by holy virgins and the threat of everlasting torment. Ten minutes later, stunned and breathless, John Harris Behan truly believed that a lifetime of searching had ended.

At last, he thought. A girl who could go toe to toe with him. A girl who could match him, day and night, and round for round.

Seventy-two hours later, the glorious Pauline Markham was quietly gleeful as she informed the rather grumpy Randolph Murray that rosy little Josie had resigned from the troupe in order to move in with the dashing Mr. Behan.

Her delicious news was greeted with disappointing aplomb, for it had been anticipated. During the balance of their Tombstone engagement, Mr. Murray informed her, the part of Tommy Tucker the Cabin Boy would be played by the lovely Miss May Bell, a chorus girl who had been consolingly eager to step into all of Miss Marcus's roles.

A week later, the Markham troupe concluded its triumphant Arizona tour and set out for the Pacific coast to do a series of return engagements in San Diego, Los Angeles, and Santa Barbara. By that time, everyone in Tombstone was talking about *H.M.S. Pinafore,* excepting only Wyatt Earp.

Wyatt never talked much, but even he had gone to see the operetta twice. Early in the run.

A Man of Many Words

There would come a day when folks would find it ironic that Johnny himself made such a special point of making sure his "wife" met Wyatt Earp, but it would be a long while before that day came.

In the beginning, Johnny had a grand time of it, squiring his exotic Jewish beauty around town, introducing "Mrs. Behan" with a wink and a cocky grin. He savored the envy of other men, and Josie, too, enjoyed the admiration of every male in Tombstone. Even so, when Johnny first called out, "Wyatt! Come and meet the missus!" she had to stifle a sigh.

Johnny possessed that most fundamental of political skills: the ability to recall potential constituents by the thousands. Josie herself had given up trying to keep the names straight and found the men they belonged to nearly indistinguishable. This Wyatt person was in his middle thirties, she judged. Tall and notably well-built, though she was almost too tired to care. After several months of matching Johnny Behan — day and night, round for round — she understood why Irish girls entered the convent. Johnny's thirteen brothers and sisters meant that his mother had been pregnant for ten and a half *years*. It was a calculation that filled Josie with awe and horror, and renewed her gratitude for the existence of the French letter.

"Johnny, I've already met this one," she murmured as Wyatt crossed the street.

"No, honey, you're thinking of Morgan Earp. He's the Wells Fargo guard," Johnny reminded her quickly. "Wyatt's his older brother. Earps are thick on the ground in Tombstone! James is the oldest. He owns a tavern near Chinatown. Virgil's the deputy federal marshal. There's three years between Morgan and Wyatt, but they could be twins. You'll see."

The resemblance was striking. The same handsome well-cut features, the same fair hair, the same broad shoulders, but this brother was thinner in the face and his clothes hung on him badly. Feet dragging, he looked as worn out as Josie felt, but it wasn't until they were close enough to shake hands that she noticed what made him so different from his cheerful younger brother Morgan: those joyless blue eyes.

"Wyatt, I'd like you to meet Mrs. Behan. Josie, honey, this is Deputy Sheriff Wyatt Earp. He made quite a name for himself as a peace officer in Dodge City!"

The deputy looked embarrassed and mumbled something about being pleased to meet her. She smiled prettily and returned the pleasantry. Her new role wasn't much of a speaking part. She just had to stand at Johnny's side while he made small talk about the upcoming county-wide election. Usually these conversations went on at some length, but this man hardly spoke at all and Josie gathered that Deputy Earp had just arrived back in town after transporting a prisoner to the Pima County sheriff's office up in Tucson.

"Johnny, dear," she said, "I think Deputy Earp must be very tired. We should let him go."

Johnny put an arm around her shoulders and pulled her toward him in mute approval. "You're right, honey. How's Mrs. Earp, Wyatt?" Johnny asked, his voice soft with sympathy.

The deputy's eyes slid away. "Haven't been home yet."

"Well, you go on then, but I've got something important I'd like to discuss with you, Wyatt. I have to go up to Prescott this week. When I get back, I'd like to meet with you and talk a few things over."

Wyatt shrugged an assent, knuckled his hat to Josie, and trudged off.

"Be nice to him, honey," Johnny said. "We need to befriend that man."

"What's wrong with his wife?"

"Well . . . let's just say I'm a lucky man."

"Why are we going to Prescott?"

"It'll just be me going, honey. I've got some business to take care of up there," Johnny said vaguely, for no politician enjoys delivering unwelcome news, and he still hadn't mentioned his first wife, let alone the flagrant cheating that had led Victoria to divorce him. Nor had he said anything about having a son, much less the fact that Albert would be coming back to live with Johnny and Josie in Tombstone. "It's a long hard trip, and Geronimo is acting up again," he told Josie. "You're safer here, honey. I'll be back in a few days."

It didn't occur to her to ask for more details. Thank God, was all she thought at the time. I'll finally get some sleep.

Which was exactly what Dr. J. H. Holliday was thinking when he arrived in Tombstone a week later, after far too much time in John Behan's garrulous company.

Sitting on the uncushioned bench of a badly sprung stagecoach was like being beaten with a plank. Being talked at by the voluble Mr. Behan hour after hour had added to the strain. When the dentist finally climbed out of the stagecoach in Tombstone, he made no attempt to find Morgan Earp or his brother Wyatt. Instead, he went directly to the Cosmopolitan Hotel, checked in, and

85

gave Mr. Bilicke exceedingly clear instructions: He was not to be disturbed — by anyone, for any reason — unless the building caught fire. And then only if the flames came within twenty feet of his room.

Exhausted, the dentist slept through his first twelve hours in Tombstone, while Johnny Behan was busy explaining to Josie why he'd waited so long to tell her about the first Mrs. Behan and why he'd failed to mention that his son, Albert, would be living with them from now on. So it must have been another passenger on the coach who started the rumor about what happened between Doc Holliday and Johnny Behan during their shared journey.

Soon, juicy gossip about their brief stagecoach argument over the Anti-Chinese League was circulating. By the time the Earps heard the story, it ended with Doc pulling a knife on Johnny Behan and threatening to gut Albert if Johnny said another word. Knowing Doc, they figured he'd called Behan an ignorant Missouri jackass and told him to keep a civil tongue in his head, but given Doc's reputation, it wouldn't be long before somebody claimed he'd seen Holliday shoot Johnny Behan six times before eating Albert raw in the horrified presence of two Catholic nuns and a sweet little girl named Nancy.

Wyatt and Morgan searched all over town

that night, hoping to find Doc before he got into more trouble. Morgan even asked about him at the Cosmopolitan Hotel, but Al Bilicke was scared of what Holliday would do to him if Morgan woke the gambler up and swore Doc wasn't there. Which meant that Wyatt was still making do with oil of clove for his toothache and felt like hell the next morning.

Johnny Behan, by contrast, had awakened full of energy and rarin' to go on his first day back from Prescott. Josie, who always got a slower start, mumbled, "Johnny, it's too early," but he kissed the back of her neck and reached around to cup her breast and snugged in behind her, murmuring, "It's never too early for some of you, honey!" When he was done, he hopped out of bed and began telling Josie about the deal he planned to make with Wyatt Earp that morning. "It's going to mean a brilliant future for us, and a good one for Wyatt, and it'll deliver far better law enforcement to the citizens of southeastern Arizona. All of that, in one clever move," he crowed. "God, but I do love politics!"

He shaved and dressed while Josie got pancakes and eggs going on the stove. Albert came out of his room, blinking and still half-asleep, just as Josie was putting breakfast on the table. Johnny ate like he was stoking a furnace, and that's exactly how he felt: like a man on fire who needed fuel. When he finished his meal, he kissed his thanks to Josie and ruffled Albert's sleep-mussed hair. "Albert," he said, "if your daddy pulls this off, you're going to be the governor's son someday!"

That was when, hand on the doorknob, he told Josie that he'd be bringing Wyatt Earp home for lunch if their meeting went well. "Bake something special," he suggested. "And make sure Marcelita does a nice job on the house today. Wyatt likes things neat and clean. See you later, Mrs. Governor!"

Spirits soaring, he strode into town, greeting dozens of men, asking after their families or their business dealings, showing that he remembered them, one and all. It was midmorning before he spotted Wyatt hunched over a cup of coffee in a cheap café, and it was right then and there that Johnny decided that he probably ought to marry Josie before the next election cycle. Know a good thing when you've got it, he told himself, for breakfast was still warm in his belly and he was freshly aware of how neglected Wyatt was.

The little bell above the door rang as he entered the restaurant. Sitting across from Wyatt, he leaned over the table. "I just got back from Prescott, and the rumors are true —"

Wyatt winced. "Look, I know Doc can be hard to get along with, but he's —"

Johnny frowned. "Holliday? Oh! That! Forgot all about it," he lied. "No! What I wanted to tell you is, the rumors are right. The legislature is going to split Pima County in two, early next year. And it's because of the sheriff's office!" He paused to order a cup of coffee, putting a friendly hand on a waitress's rump while he did so, chuckling when she slapped it away. He watched her walk back to the kitchen before continuing, "This is no reflection on Sheriff Shibell, Wyatt. Charlie's competent and honest, but everybody knows he's got an impossible job. Pima County's bigger than most states back east. Hell, it's bigger than a lot of European countries! And it's on the Mexican border, which complicates everything. Capitalists have a lot of places they can put their money, and when Mexico makes a fuss over cattle rustling across the border or when the Associated Press runs a story about a barroom shooting in Tombstone, it makes a bad impression —"

The waitress set Johnny's coffee down in front of him, though she stayed on the far side of the table to do it. Johnny winked at her but waited until she left to speak again. "Anyways, the legislature's going to carve a big chunk of Pima County off and put a new sheriff's office right here in Tombstone. The idea is, we get a grip on the crime problem and prove Arizona is safe for investors. Make sense?"

Wyatt nodded. "So?"

"So the new county's going to need a new government. But it takes time to organize a regular election. People have to get registered to vote. You need polling places and election officials, and so on. Both parties have to come up with a slate of candidates. All that might take a year or eighteen months, maybe." Johnny dropped his voice. "Which means the first men to hold county offices will be appointees, right? And Governor Frémont's a Republican, so he's probably going to pick Republicans, right? So when it comes time for the new sheriff of the new county to be appointed, your name is going to come up."

"Yeah. I figured."

"Of course!" Johnny said affably, sitting back in his chair. "You're a Republican, and you're highly thought of up in Kansas, but you were a city policeman in Dodge," he pointed out, careful not to say *only* a city policeman. "Now, me, I'm a Democrat, and God knows that doesn't help me in Arizona! But I've had experience as sheriff up in Yavapai County, and that may count for something when we're getting the new county administration going. I've still got contacts in the territorial legislature, and from what I heard . . ." Johnny leaned over the table again. "From what I heard, we are both in the running for that appointment. Now, frankly, Wyatt, I think either one of us would be a good choice, but I've got a proposal I'd like you to give some consideration."

Johnny laid it out for him, and while Wyatt didn't say yes, he didn't say no, either. Which was exactly what Johnny had expected.

"Just think it over," Johnny urged. "You haven't eaten yet, have you? Why not come on over to the house for lunch? My little Josie is quite a cook, and my son, Albert, would love to meet you."

"I don't know," Wyatt said. "I got a tooth kicking up . . ."

But Johnny wouldn't take no for an answer and filled Wyatt's silence with cheerful gossip about men in the legislature as they walked back to the house, smiling broadly when Wyatt said, "Smells good," for Josie had something wonderful cooking on the stove.

Inside, everything was neat as a pin, except . . . A wash bucket sat in the middle of the floor and Josie was next to it, scrubbing on her hands and knees, her springy hair all mashed down under a kerchief.

"Josie, honey," Johnny asked uneasily, "where's Marcelita?"

The girl sat back on her heels. "I fired her."

"You fired *another* one? But — why?"

"Because clean means clean! It doesn't mean less dirty. It doesn't mean scrub until you're bored. It means *clean.*" Suddenly she was on her feet, balling up the scrub rag, hurling it at him, snarling about Marcelita, and you could tell she'd been rehearsing her speech all morning. "I never should have come here. There's dust all over everything, and pigs in the street, and it's noisy and filthy and it stinks! I found a rat in the flour bin, Johnny. *A rat!* I'm sick to death of this place and everyone in it. Nobody will even talk to me. Anybody who's anybody treats me like I'm a whore. And now *you* come home with your ex-wife's child —"

"Ah, Christ! Josie, I told you why he —"

"I'm not a nanny, John Behan. I'm not some governess who's paid to look after other women's children. He belongs with his mother!"

White-faced, Albert was standing in the corner like a rabbit watching a dog fight: not knowing which way to run and too scared to move.

"Maybe another time," Wyatt mumbled, backing out the door.

"Wyatt! Wait!" Johnny pleaded, but Wyatt never looked back, and that ripped it. "God damn you, Josie, I had him! I was *so close* to making the deal, and now you pull this stunt! Albert, for Christ's sake, stop crying, or I'll give you something to cry about!"

"You didn't even *ask* me, Johnny! You just show up with this boy and —"

"Josie, so help me, you say another goddam

92

word —"

But Josie would never concede. She never quit arguing. Suddenly the manifold pressures of John Harris Behan's life seemed to concentrate in his fist and . . . Yes, he let her have it. No, he wasn't proud of that but he gave himself credit for this much, at least: He left the house before he did worse.

Sprinting down the street, hoping to make things right, he caught up with Wyatt, but before he could say anything, Virgil Earp had come around the corner and told his brother, "We've got some stolen army livestock to deal with, Wyatt. There's a lieutenant in town —"

"The army can't be involved with any criminal arrest," Johnny warned.

Virgil turned to look down at him. All the Earps were big, but Virgil had a couple of inches and probably forty pounds on his brothers. Which gave him eight inches and seventy pounds on Johnny Behan.

"Yeah. We know, Johnny," Virg said in that rumbling voice of his. "That's why Lieutenant Hurst is in Tombstone. He needs a civilian posse." Virgil turned back to Wyatt. "Hurst's getting his men something to eat, but figure three o'clock, at Fred White's office."

"You seen Doc?" Wyatt asked.

"You still ain't found him?"

Wyatt shook his head.

"Well, I'll keep an eye out," Virg said. "See

you at Fred's."

"Wyatt, please! A word with you?" Johnny asked as Virgil set off. "Look, I'm sorry about what just happened back there. I swear, Josie's not usually like that. She must be on the rag."

Wyatt colored up, mumbled something about his tooth, and walked away.

"All right then, I'll let you go," Johnny called. "See you at three!"

Jack Rabbit John, the hookers called him. Johnny Behan dropped by for a quick one the way other men might slug back a drink, or smoke a cigarette, or take a deep breath: to get his temper under control. He'd only been gone from home about twenty minutes, but when he walked in the door, Al was alone in the house and told him that Josie was real mad and said she was never coming back, and then Al started to cry because he was sure it was his fault.

Sighing, Johnny told the boy that wasn't so, but he left again, hoping to find Josie before she got into trouble downtown. When he finally found her crying in the piano room at the Cosmopolitan, he was more than ready to make peace and walked her home, explaining about how Albert was a little deaf and needed some tenderness. She pouted when he said he was needed at the marshal's office but brightened up when he promised they'd go out someplace special that night. All that took time, so it was half past three when he got to Marshal White's office. By then he'd regained some of his morning optimism.

I can still pull this off, he told himself, certain that he could salvage the deal with Wyatt. This is all going to turn out fine.

"Afternoon, Johnny," Fred White said. "What's the problem?"

"Just here to help out, Fred. You must be Lieutenant Hurst." Johnny offered the trooper his hand. "John Behan. Used to be sheriff up in Yavapai County. Virg, I hope you didn't wait for me."

"No, Johnny," Virgil Earp rumbled with good-natured sarcasm. "We felt capable of beginning the deliberations without you. Everything all right at home?"

Behan flushed. "Yeah, well, you know what I'm up against, Virg."

Bluff, good-humored, comfortably heavy at thirty-seven, Virgil Earp nodded and shrugged. Virg was a dozen years older than Alvira Sullivan, but he loved that little girl like a bear loves honey, and getting stung was part of the package. Behan's "wife" was even younger than Allie and apparently more of a handful.

"The mules?" Wyatt prompted, glancing at Hurst.

On the face of it, this should have been

simple. Six army mules had been stolen from Camp Rucker, fifty miles east of Tombstone. Lieutenant Hurst needed a civilian posse to recover the mules for him, but jurisdiction was a tangle. The livestock had been stolen within Pima County and Wyatt was a Pima County deputy sheriff, so maybe he should form the posse. On the other hand, the mules were federal property and they'd been taken from a fort, which was federal as well, so maybe Virgil took precedence because he was a deputy federal marshal. One thing was sure: Fred White wasn't involved at all, for a town marshal's jurisdiction stopped at the town line. And Johnny Behan might have been a lawman a few years ago, but nowadays he was just tending bar at the Grand Hotel, so he had even less to do with the theft than Fred himself, who was simply letting Virgil Earp use his office.

"Where does Hurst fit?" Wyatt was asking. "They're his mules."

"See, Wyatt, that's just what I was trying to explain," Behan said. "The new *Posse Comitatus* law prohibits any military involvement with civilian law enforcement, so this is going to require some finesse. Now, when I was sheriff up in Yavapai . . ."

The youngest man in the room at 29, Fred White was inclined to respect his elders, and ordinarily, he did not mind folks loitering in his office. Being a town marshal was mostly a matter of sitting around, waiting for something bad to happen. Gossip, tall tales, and political speculation made idle hours pass pleasantly. But Johnny Behan could talk the paint off a wall, and no matter how loud Fred yawned, nobody seemed inclined to wrap the discussion up. Except Wyatt. He was staring out the office window, his chair tipped back on two legs, and he didn't seem to be listening at all. Course, it was hard to tell with Wyatt. He never said much, even when he gave a shit.

Fred drifted off, elbow on the desk, cheek propped on his fist, but he snapped to when he heard Wyatt bring the front legs of his chair down with a thump.

Virgil was on his feeet now, and both of the Earps were looking out the office window, watching his younger brother Morgan cross the street.

"Well, fellas," Virg said, "if we sit here much longer, the thieves are gonna cross them mules into Mexico and then the *federales*'ll be involved, even if the U.S. Army ain't. I say we go find the damn animals while there's daylight, and sort the legalities out later."

Hurst said, "Suits me."

"I understand how you feel, boys," Johnny Behan said quickly, "but you can't play fast and loose with jurisdiction that way. It's hard enough to get a conviction when you've done due diligence."

Johnny started in on another story about blown arrests and criminals going free, but the Earps were done listening and headed out the door with Lieutenant Hurst.

Glad to see the backs of them, Fred yawned again and was about to select the least bad jail bunk for a nap when Morgan Earp stuck his head into the office.

"Fred, do you know Doc Holliday?"

"Heard of him. Gambler. Why?"

"Wyatt's got a tooth that's giving him hell, and Doc's a dentist —"

"A dentist! I didn't know that!"

"Yeah. Good one, too. Anyways, Wyatt's got a bad tooth and Doc came into town to take care of it, but we haven't run into him yet. If you see him, let him know we'll be back in a few days. And, Fred . . . look after him, willya? Doc is a friend of ours."

Morgan left the office and joined his brothers outside.

"You find McMasters?" Virgil asked him quietly.

Sherman McMasters, he meant. They never said Sherm's name out loud. McMasters ran with rustlers, but he was an ex–Texas Ranger, playing both ends against the middle. That would likely get him killed one day, but in the meantime, Sherm made a tidy income selling information to lawmen.

"Old Man Clanton's youngest boy stole

'em," Morgan said. "The mules are in Sulphur Springs Valley now. Prolly at the McLaury place."

"All right, we'll try there first. Go home and get your gear," Virg told his brothers. Then he called, "Hurst! We leave in twenty minutes."

HOT THY LOVE,
HOT THY HATE

"The canteen's full," Allie told Virgil as he packed. "There's apples, and I made roast beef sandwiches for you and the boys."

Wyatt was almost thirty-three and Morg was twenty-nine. Both of them were a good deal older than Alvira Sullivan, but they were still "the boys" to her because that's what Virg always called them.

"Thanks, Pickle," Virgil said. "Nice of you to think of them."

"And if I don't, who will, I'd like to know!"

Morgan was batching it while his girl, Louisa, was off visiting relatives. Lou was a honey, but Wyatt's woman . . . Well, Allie felt sorry for Mattie Blaylock but had no illusions about her. Mattie was slovenly and down at the mouth most of the time, and hell would freeze before she lifted a finger for the man who put a roof over her head.

In the beginning, Allie had blamed Wyatt for Mattie's cheerlessness, for his silence seemed cold and mean.

"Why don't Wyatt ever say nothing?" Allie asked Virgil one time.

"Well, now, Pickle, I'll tell you," Virg had said. "Wyatt's steady in a fight and he's got a real way with horses, but he can't hardly read and he's ignorant. He's afraid if he talks, people will find out."

Allie wasn't much for books herself. "Lots of folks can't read. Don't stop 'em from talking!"

"Yeah, well, maybe it oughta," Virg said, laughing when Allie laid into him with small fists and not entirely comic ferocity.

Wyatt was all right, Allie had decided after she got to know him. And Morgan was as sweet as men come. She liked the boys' older brother James, too, but Alvira Sullivan was sure of one thing. She got the pick of the Earp litter.

Virgil was fitting a box of cartridges into his saddlebag.

"Don't mash them sandwiches," she warned. "How long'll you be?"

"We're pretty sure we know where the mules are. Day or two, if everything goes right."

He finished buckling the flap and looked up. Allie was bustling around their little house. Clearing dishes off the table, wrestling bolts of tent canvas into neater stacks, wiping cotton fluff off her sewing machine. She always got extra busy when he had to ride out like this.

Pickle, he called her, because that's what she was eating when he first laid eyes on her, up in Iowa. He was driving freight. She was a waitress at a stage stop. Not much bigger than the gherkin she downed in two bites, but damn if she didn't hoist a heavy tray right up onto her shoulder, carrying half her weight in crockery to the kitchen. He caught her eye and he could tell she liked the looks of him, so he struck up a conversation and learned pretty quick that she was an orphan. Father gone. Mother dead. Sisters and brothers scattered. Sharp-tongued and independent, Allie had shifted for herself since she was twelve. He respected her before he loved her, and he loved her before he finished his lunch that first day.

"How'd I get to be so damn lucky?" he asked now, voice low and soft.

She came to him, and he bent almost in half to receive her wiry arms around his neck. When he straightened up, she shrieked a laugh as he lifted her off her feet. "Maybe I'll just stick you in my saddlebag and take you along!" Virg said. "How'd you like that?"

"I'd like to see you try!"

He set her down, planted a kiss on the top of her head, threw his saddlebag over his shoulder, and grabbed his hat off a peg by the door. Allie followed him outside and stood on the porch, shading her eyes with her hand.

She'd seen two men killed by Virgil Earp in the line of duty, and she knew what every cop's wife knows: The next time shots are fired, it could be her man staring empty-eyed at the sky.

"Be careful!" she hollered.

Virg didn't look back, but he raised his hand in acknowledgment.

There was a time when Mattie Blaylock looked forward to hearing Wyatt's footsteps on the porch. She'd been walking the streets in Dodge when he took her in, and she was grateful in the beginning. Wyatt seemed glad of her, too, for a while.

He hardly looked at her when he came in now. Mattie didn't say anything either. She just sat there in her chair, rocking in the shadows.

He reached past her and yanked the drapes open. She turned her face from the sunlight.

"Place stinks," he said, raising the sash to air it out. "It's past four. Why ain't you dressed?"

"Why do you think?" He could be so damn stupid. "Headache."

"We got a posse," he told her and went into the bedroom to collect what he needed.

"How's your tooth?" she asked. Making an effort.

"Same."

103

"You find Doc?"

"Not yet."

"Huh," she said.

Tombstone was the biggest place she'd ever lived in. Not finding a person who'd been in town for a whole day was an idea that took getting used to.

Wyatt came back into the front room, a bedroll under one arm, the rest of his gear in a saddlebag. Hand on the doorknob, he paused to look around the house, making a list of her sins. Dust. Clothes on the floor. Dishes waiting. Chamber pot unemptied.

"Clean this place up," he said. Then he added, "Clean means clean, Mattie. It don't just mean less dirty. It means *clean*."

"Go to hell," she muttered, but she waited until he was gone to say it.

She waited a good deal longer before she got out of the rocking chair. She tried to pick a few things off the floor, but leaning over made the migraine worse. So she poured herself another dose of laudanum, pulled the curtains closed, and went back to bed.

■ ■ ■ ■

WHEN STRIFE
FIRST APPEARS,
SHE IS SMALL

■ ■ ■ ■

TROY, A CITY
BUILT ON RICHES

Of all the witless, obtuse questions addressed to John Henry Holliday in his short, unlucky life, the one he currently despised most was a simple rhetorical pleasantry: How are you? He'd never been to Tombstone before, but he was known to about half the gamblers in town, and every one he met had opened the conversation with "Well, if it ain't Doc Holliday! How the hell are you, Doc?"

"Just fine, thanks," he always said, but producing that genial reply required iron self-control, for what he wanted to ask in return was "Are you blind or stupid? *Look* at me." Skin like parchment. Hair half-grayed. So thin, he looked like a beanpole wrapped in cream-colored linen. Not content with destroying his lungs, tuberculosis was now eroding his vertebrae, two of which had collapsed in a stunning explosion of pain one evening when he attempted to pull Kate's chair out for her after dinner. That small act of gallantry had cost him two inches in height, and he'd yet to find a tailor capable of concealing the resulting hump.

John Henry Holliday had recently turned twenty-nine. On a good day, he looked fifteen years older. On a bad one, he felt about three weeks shy of a hundred.

How are you, Doc? I'm miserable, jackass. How are you?

The constant gnawing ache in his chest became briefly worse when he emerged from a quiet restaurant on Third Street. Squinting into the fierce glare of Arizona's afternoon sunlight, he took shelter under the broad brim of a panama hat, though not before the sudden brilliance set off a violent sneeze. Leaning on his walking stick, he bent at the waist, rendered motionless by the sharp, familiar pain of tearing pulmonary adhesions. Laughter could cause this, or an unusually intense coughing fit. Sneezing was the worst, for it ripped his lungs away from the chest wall with a pang that could only be endured, not countered.

"Jesus, Doc! Damn, you look like hell!"

He turned at the sound of that dear, familiar voice and straightened as much as he could. "Morgan," he said, offering his hand, "I feel even worse than I look, but it was worth every moment of that wretched journey to see you again."

Grinning, Morg lifted the lapels of Doc's coat and whistled at a pair of pistols. "You carrying two now? Hell if that hardware don't weigh more'n you!"

"Luke Short tells me Tombstone is about twice as dangerous as Dodge, so I have come prepared."

"Luke's not lying," Morgan admitted. "Thanks for coming. Wyatt's gonna be real glad. Where you staying?"

"The Cosmopolitan, of course."

"Was I right about that piano? Nice one, ain't it!"

"The best I have ever played. I am perishin', Morg. Let me buy you a drink — assuming Wyatt hasn't turned you into a temperance man."

"Doc, he don't even try anymore. And listen to this! My fine, upstanding, teetotal-Methodist brother has a quarter interest in the Oriental Saloon's gambling concession! He don't drink up the profits, so he's making enough to bank faro games in a few other saloons, too. Him and Mattie own their house. And you ain't gonna believe this: He's wearing a badge again. Deputy sheriff. Working for Charlie Shibell."

Doc coughed his surprise. "How did he talk himself into that?"

"Long story, and I ain't got time to tell it. Him and Virg and me got a posse going out. Stolen livestock. Wanna come?"

"I believe I will decline the offer, but I appreciate the invitation."

Morg glanced at the cane. "Hip giving you trouble again?"

"It'll be better after I've had a little more rest."

"Well, I gotta go," Morgan said, moving off with a backward skip. "Hot damn! Wyatt's gonna be real happy to see you! Soon as we get back, we'll come by the Cosmopolitan."

"Take care, y'hear?" Doc called, leaning on his cane as Morgan Earp trotted off, dodging horses and wagons and foot traffic with thoughtless, easy grace.

"You, too," Morg yelled back. "I mean it, Doc! This place is dangerous."

At least eighty professional gamblers had converged on Tombstone in its first year: wolves drawn to a herd of highly skilled hard-rock miners who got paid a stunning four dollars a day. Nearly two thousand men were working in a dozen silver mines, and competition was fierce among those who wished to feast on their wages.

John Henry Holliday was still living up in northern Arizona when he ran into the famous gambler Luke Short in a Prescott saloon. Luke had warned him off Tombstone, for the town was being snarled over by two groups of loosely organized sporting men. "There's easterners like us, but then there's a bunch from the California slope, west of the Rockies. Vicious young bullies. It's not like working in Dodge, Doc. I won big one night. Four of the Slopers came after me and took the cash before I could get back to my hotel. I went to the town marshal — Fred White, his name is — but they all had alibis for each other."

Luke had been on the gambling circuit a long time and he backed down to no one, but he was a small man with no taste for quarreling. "There's a mountain of money in Tombstone," he told Doc, "but it's not worth the risk. Seems like somebody gets killed damn near every night."

"Word is," Doc said quietly, "you were called upon to add to the tally."

"Charley Storms." Shaking his head at the memory, the spruce little gambler sat back. "Took a dislike to me after he lost, and got loud about it. Bat Masterson was there, and you know Bat. He always tries to sweet-talk an idiot before things get physical. He settled Storms down and got him to leave, but ten minutes later, Storms comes back with a pistol. He was drunk and he was slow. I was sober and fast enough. Grand jury decided not to indict, but afterward . . ."

"Couldn't stand the sight of the place?"

Luke shrugged. "You and Mike Gordon?"

"What have you heard?"

"The usual dime-novel horseshit. Insults, a showdown, and another notch on the deadly dentist's gun!"

Doc closed his eyes and pulled in as deep a breath as he could — always a mistake. When the coughing passed, he drank off the last swallow of bourbon in his glass and waited a moment for the warmth to help. "You know Miss Kate and I had a saloon over in New Mexico?"

Luke nodded.

"Well, one evenin', Mr. Gordon got it into his thick-boned, liquor-addled, hayseed head that one of our bar girls would enjoy spendin' some private time with him. He was not an attractive suitor, and Miss Lucy was disinclined to accept his very insistent invitation. Mr. Gordon became cross, and Kate was on him like a duck on a June bug. Most men would have had the sense to get out and stay out."

"But not Gordon."

"He left but — like your Mr. Storms — it was only to find himself a gun. Came back shootin' at Kate and Lucy. I stopped him."

"Jesus. Justifiable homicide?"

"That was the judgment, but afterward . . ."

"You couldn't stand the sight of the place."

They both fell silent for a time.

Luke shook the mood off first. "Bat Masterson gave up on Tombstone, too. The Earps are still down there, last I heard. Course, there's always three or four of them around and even one Earp by himself is fearsome enough to inspire courtesy. Me? I look like easy pickings. I'm going back up to Dodge."

He didn't have to spell it out. Tombstone would eat John Henry Holliday alive.

Luke left Prescott the next day. A few weeks later, Doc left as well. Drifting south. Looking for warm, dry weather. He settled in Tucson, a little mountain town with a good climate and enough cash in circulation to support a small fraternity of professionals. He did all right for himself, too, making a decent enough living at the poker tables. There wasn't a reason in the world to visit a mining settlement so dangerous it scared Luke Short. Then he received a letter from an old friend.

Wyatt has a bad tooth, Morgan Earp wrote. *He dont say so but he is nervis to go to another dentist. Can you come to Tombstone? We are doing good here. There is a liberry and they got a real nice piano at the Cosmopoliten hotel.*

Ordinarily, the dentist would have told Wyatt to come to Tucson for treatment, but before making up his mind, he telegraphed a single question:

IS PIANO A STEINWAY STOP

Morgan's reply came about two hours later:

CHICKERING SQUARE GRAND STOP

Close enough, Doc thought, and bought

himself a ticket to Tombstone. He wanted to play a first-rate piano before he died.

This ambition he had fulfilled in the company of the pathetic child who was currently being called Mrs. Behan. As for her "husband," Doc had taken a dislike to the man before they even boarded the coach at the Tucson depot. John Behan was a talkative, pushy, self-important little jingo who misinterpreted courteous murmurs for genuine interest. His enthusiasm for Tombstone was tiresome and at the end of their shared journey, Doc had seen no reason to stay in the city for more than a week. His agenda was uncomplicated: take care of Wyatt's tooth, host a party for his friends, and stamp the dust of Tombstone from his feet before anyone got a chance to kill or rob him.

Now, however, he had begun to reconsider his plans.

For one thing, he'd underestimated how punishing the journey here would be. Climbing back into a stagecoach when the bruises were still fresh held no allure. Seeing Morgan Earp — albeit briefly — had lifted his spirits. And after a night's sleep, he found himself receptive to the exuberance of a mechanical engineer with whom he'd just shared a restaurant table.

"We, sir, are sitting on what may be the richest silver strike in world history," the engineer informed him as they lingered over a well-prepared meal in a very decent restaurant. "Tombstone will dwarf the Comstock strike before it's over. The ore assays at over forty-five hundred dollars' worth of silver to the ton and we're hauling a good twelve tons out of the works every day. Drilling still has to be done by hand with a steel and a hammer, and the ore is broken up with picks and extracted by the shovelful, but from that point on, processing is completely mechanized!"

There were underground tram systems. Sixty-horsepower hoists. Stamping mills, roasters, dryers, and retorts. Ironworks, lumber mills, cartage companies. Capitalists were pouring hundreds of thousands of dollars into the operations, but with refined silver at $1.20 an ounce, they were extracting millions. In the engineer's opinion, Arizona would produce enough wealth to bring the whole nation back to prosperity.

"All Tombstone needs is water and some good people," he declared, "and it'll turn into a garden spot!"

The same might be said of hell, Doc thought, though it seemed unkind to say so in the face of such confident optimism.

Doc himself was too familiar with the natural history of these western boomtowns to be quite that sanguine. A handful of men would stake out a grid in the wilderness and place gloriously deceptive advertisements in

115

eastern newspapers, touting the location's business potential. Empty lots would be sold to the first hardy settlers, who arrived with the tools of their trade or a wagonload of stock. Soon, crudely lettered one-word signs leaned against tents or raw board shacks. BLACKSMITH. BARBER. GROCERIES. LIQUOR. AMMUNITION.

Often, that was the end of it. Cattle drives went elsewhere; a railroad surveyor chose a different route; a promising seam of ore narrowed and disappeared. Tents were stowed. Shacks were abandoned. Folks moved on.

Sometimes, however, a local industry flourished and a second wave of boomers would arrive. Proper walls went up around wooden floors. Roofs were shingled. Window glass was shipped in. Proprietors' names were emblazoned upon elaborate signs painted on false fronts, and it didn't matter that no one was fooled by those phony second stories. Even the pretense of impressive architecture could be gratifying in the middle of nowhere. A few men might make money in astonishing quantity for a while, but more often than not, the boomtown would dwindle into a mere village or disappear altogether within a few years.

Would Tombstone be different? It was too soon to tell. The streets remained unpaved. Wandering pigs snuffled through horse manure. Horseflies were a plague. Stray dogs fought for restaurant scraps in the alleys. The afternoon wind sent alkaline dust stinging into the eyes, and John Henry Holliday was not the only man in town with a chronic cough.

Even so, a stroll through Tombstone was impressive. There were dozens of restaurants. Several good hotels. A pharmacy. Two chartered banks. Three local breweries. A pair of ice factories. Saloons, gambling halls, and brothels were certainly in evidence, but families had settled here as well, and there were shops that sold them groceries, dry goods, clothing, and furniture. A sign on a vacant lot announced plans for a school. The Episcopalians and Methodists already had churches; the Catholics were building one. At the edge of town, on a street called Toughnut, the foundation of a hospital had been laid near the pitheads, and . . . There it was!

The library.

He couldn't remember the last time he'd seen so many books. Five hundred? Six? At first he simply sat in one of the upholstered chairs, catching his breath and gazing at the shelves. Then he browsed the collection and borrowed a copy of Trollope's *The Way We Live Now.* If I don't finish it before I leave town, he told himself, I can mail it back from Tucson.

Book in hand, he returned to Allen Street, where he noticed some very fine gabardine on display at a haberdashery. Between his new hump and the most recent loss of weight, nothing he owned fit, but if he had one of those new double-breasted suits made, the additional fabric might give the impression of a few extra pounds.

My own false front, he thought as he walked on.

Admittedly, after Tucson's peace, Tombstone's industrial noise was wearying. The miners worked two ten-hour shifts, with time between to let the dust settle and the fumes dissipate. At any given hour, half were off duty, and Luke Short was right: There was a mountain of money here. *But why compete with the Slopers for play against miners?* he asked himself as he read the signs on office windows.

Tombstone had attorneys and physicians, bankers and accountants. Surveyors, geologists, metallurgists, hydrologists, chemists. At least six kinds of engineer. Intelligent men, literate men. Men capable of conversation, not just vulgar, repetitive, ignorant bombast. Men who gambled in quiet, carpeted rooms with crystal chandeliers and silk-upholstered chairs, where attentive waiters provided good cigars and excellent liquor to a clientele unlikely to assault or rob the player who won a game.

All around him, buildings were going up. The scent of raw pine boards reminded him of Atlanta after the war, when the city was

118

getting back on its feet. The streets and boardwalks of Tombstone teemed with people in a hurry, people with big plans and great expectations. He found himself smiling at the bustle, stepping more quickly, feeling less hobbled and enervated, more lively and mettlesome. It was as though he'd laid down a burden —

He stopped. And took a step back. And stumbled into a stranger, to whom he apologized without hearing his own voice. Hardly knowing what he was doing, he moved away from the crowds and noise and light and into a strange private silence where he was even more alone than usual.

When did it happen? he wondered. When did I give up?

It must have been sometime after he left the sanatorium.

He had done well with rest and decent meals, but the doctors said he needed a year or more of care, not just a few months, and he was running out of cash. "We'll buy our own place with the money we got left," Kate decided. She would run the business; he would preside over the tables. They'd build a saloon up and sell it off at a profit. Then Doc could stay in the sanatorium until he had this damned disease beaten.

That was the plan until Mike Gordon all but demanded to be shot down in the street like a rabid dog.

It *was* justifiable homicide. He did not regret doing what he had to, but . . . afterward, simply walking in the front door of the saloon was unnerving.

Kate couldn't understand what was wrong. She would argue with him — coax and cajole and rail at him — but he found it increasingly difficult to concentrate and started losing money at the tables. One morning, he went to a lawyer, signed the property over to Kate and got on a train without saying goodbye.

He had drifted ever since. Just waiting to die, really. But now . . .

A piano. A library. Morgan and his brothers to keep the wolves at bay. Why not deal faro in Tombstone for a while? Build up a stake. A few big poker games and he'd have enough to spend a year at the sanatorium. Longer, if he had to.

Hope, long missing from his life, came rushing back. The silence around him shattered, and he stopped a passing stranger to ask, "I wonder if you can tell me where I might find the Oriental Saloon?"

"Two blocks down," the stranger said, "at the corner of Allen and Fifth."

John Henry Holliday would have no recollection of his first step on the twisted road that led him — and the Earps and the Clantons and the McLaurys — to a vacant lot behind a photography studio near the O.K. Corral, thirteen months later.

He would remember asking for directions to the Oriental. He would recall that he expected to be welcome in a saloon where Wyatt Earp owned 25 percent of the gambling concession. Everything else would remain fragmentary and muddled, apart from a single clear and terrifying memory: regaining consciousness in a room he did not recognize, one eye blinded by blood.

He would not remember shooting two men, nor did he have the slightest idea why he might have done such a thing, though Fred White tried to explain it several times. Later, he found a receipt in his wallet: He'd paid a $20 fine for disturbing the peace and $11.25 in court costs, but he did not know if his plea was innocent or guilty.

He would not remember making arrangements to have his belongings shipped from Tucson to Morgan's house, where he stayed while he recovered, and could only hope that he gave the delivery boy a decent tip when the trunk arrived.

Slowly, the annihilating headache would recede. Gradually, the mental fog would lift. But by then, it would be far too late to change what was going to happen on October 26, 1881.

CATTLE CAN BE HAD
FOR THE RAIDING

In Frank McLaury's observation, modifying a brand on livestock benefited from a certain amount of artistry. A lot of people didn't understand that. They thought it was simple to turn *U.S.* into *D.8.* Connect the ends of the *S* and you've got your *8.* Square off the left-hand bottom of the *U,* close off its top, and you're done. But Frank wasn't the kind of man who settled for good enough. An altered brand looked more convincing if he added a little extra curving bit at the top and bottom of the *D*'s straight line. It wasn't easy either, not when the artist's canvas was an unhappy mule who preferred to be elsewhere. Frank had only finished with the third animal when his younger brother Tommy started to pace.

"C'mon, Frank. Doesn't have to be perfect!"

"Don't rush me. Go make supper, willya?"

"This's a federal crime. Billy's gonna bring the army down on us."

Frank shoved the iron back into the fire. "The army can't come on private property, and they can't arrest anyone without an act of Congress. That's *Posse Comitatus.*"

Tommy knew Frank was right, too. They'd both read law for a year, and their oldest brother, William, had stuck with it. Will had a practice in Fort Worth and gave them advice whenever Frank asked questions. *For a friend,* Frank always wrote.

"Soldiers can't make an arrest," Tommy allowed, "but they can shoot people. Billy Clanton's gonna get us killed."

"Tommy," Frank reminded his brother patiently, "down here, people can get killed just for wearing a new shirt."

Tommy knew that was true, too. A few days ago, they'd heard how a man by the name of Waters went into a bar wearing a new shirt his sister had sent him. The shirt had blue and black checks, the likes of which nobody'd ever seen before. Any sort of novelty was liable to get noticed, and everyone in the bar started ribbing Waters about his fancy shirt. Waters got mad, and then he got drunk, and then he swore he'd beat the hell out of the next sonofabitch who said anything about his damn shirt. Which he did. The matter seemed settled until the fella he beat up came back with a gun and shot Waters four times. Killed him stone-cold dead. Spoiled the shirt for further use, as well.

In a world like that, why worry? That's how Frank saw it. You could never think up all the ways a bullet might find you. No point trying.

He finished the lower serif and let the mule go. "Anyways, we're no worse than anybody else in this valley."

"No better either," Tom muttered before he trudged off to the house.

Folks had a hard time telling the McLaury brothers apart, but they had their differences if you paid attention. They were both good-looking, blue-eyed brunets, but Frank had six years on Tommy, who'd just turned twenty-seven. When Frank took his hat off, you could see that his hair was beginning to go. And Tom McLaury wasn't just good-looking. Tommy was so pretty, he attracted more attention than he liked, from women *and* men. It embarrassed him and always had, ever since he was a little kid.

Both brothers were slender and short, but Frank held his head high to put every inch on display. Tommy did what he could to avoid notice, keeping his eyes on the ground and sort of hunching over as he hurried along, especially when they went into town. Of the two, Frank had more ambition. He wanted to build up to a big cattle spread and get rich and hire men to do the work. Tommy liked farming. Plowing and planting and harvesting suited him fine. He didn't see the need of a place bigger than they could manage on their own.

Frank enjoyed having a little excitement to spark up the workday now and then. Tom wasn't timid exactly, but he didn't like trouble. "Where's your sense of adventure?" Frank would ask him, but Tommy was a worrier.

The funny thing was, moving down here was Tom's idea in the first place because Arizona acreage was a lot cheaper than farmland back in Iowa. They'd invested everything they had in this spread before they found out what kept Arizona property values low: Geronimo's Apaches were still up in the Chiricahua Mountains, a few miles away, and the Indians were none too happy about seeing their hunting grounds plowed up. Tommy was already concerned about the potential for mutilation and murder when Old Man Clanton came by on his first visit. Frank himself was not inclined to give his little brother's fear a great deal of consideration. It only encouraged Tommy to fret. Besides, everybody in Sulphur Springs Valley was pasturing Old Man Clanton's stolen Mexican stock.

"Greasers let their cattle roam free instead of husbanding them," Mr. Clanton explained. "Damn beaners don't deserve to keep stock they don't care for, so there's no harm in a quick trip to Mexico for a few strays. That's how *Americans* see it."

And it seemed like pure patriotism to agree.

The problem was, Mexican beeves were long-legged and the meat was stringy. "Used to be, you could only sell 'em to Indian reservations," Mr. Clanton said, "but now we got a couple thousand miners who like meat, and plenty of it. There's a big market right there in Tombstone, not to mention all the mill towns and lumber camps. You can get army contracts for beef at Camp Rucker and Fort Huachuca, too, but civilian stockyards give you the best price, and they want the cattle fattened some."

So Mr. Clanton had the rustling trade all organized. His operation wasn't just amateurs sneaking across the border for a couple of strays. No, sir! Clanton's Cow Boys would dash into Sonora, round up a few hundred head, and run them over the border. "That's where most *rancheros* give up the chase, lazy bastards, but if they come after us," Mr. Clanton said, "we just drive the stock deeper into the mountains and wait 'em out."

Soon as it was safe, the Cow Boys pushed the herds into grassy valleys like Sulphur Springs, where small ranchers like the Mc-Laurys were perfectly positioned to act as middlemen. "Turn a steer into a steak, nobody asks where it came from," Old Man Clanton said, by way of summary. "You graze the cattle till they put on some weight. Then you drive 'em into Tombstone or sell 'em to the army. We split the cash. You get twenty percent."

"I don't know," Tommy said doubtfully. "Can we think about it?"

Mr. Clanton's eyes went small, and he had his big horny hand around Tom's windpipe, fast as a rattlesnake strike. "I wasn't askin' you a question," he pointed out. "I was tellin' you how this works, peckerhead."

Tommy was ready to pack up and head back to Iowa the moment Clanton left. Frank was shook, too, but couldn't see turning and running. Besides, they'd put every penny they had into this land — you couldn't just walk away from an investment like that.

So Frank asked around to see how their other neighbors handled Clanton. If you co-operate, folks told him, you can be sure your own livestock won't disappear in the night. And sometimes the Cow Boys would let you keep a few head of cattle for yourself — like a tip, sort of. Or let's say you needed help building a barn or something. The Cow Boys might lend a hand if they were nearby. The money was good, too.

"I look at it this way," one man told Frank. "Break the law, and you *might* have trouble. Cross Old Man Clanton, and he *will* come down on you. The sheriff's office is way up in Tucson, son. The Clantons live next door."

That settled it for Frank, and he had no regrets. Old Man Clanton's Cow Boys didn't stay at the McLaury spread long, but they always seemed nice enough, and Frank admired their style. They wore doeskin trousers tucked into tall boots with fancy designs on the shanks, and he liked the look of their big Mexican sombreros, which were sensible because the sun was so fierce down here. They wore fancy silk neckerchiefs and brightly colored shirts, and nobody joshed *them,* by God. The Cow Boys got respect.

Tommy being Tommy, he tried not to have much to do with any of them, but even he liked Curly Bill Brocius. Curly Bill was personable and lively and always seemed to have a joke going in his eyes. He could generally keep the rest of the boys in line and when they went on a spree, he made sure they just shot up little places like Galeyville or Charleston.

Course, Johnny Ringo was different.

But he was only trouble when he drank.

KNOW WHEN SPEECH IS PROPER AND WHEN SILENCE

It was close to sunset and supper was nearly ready when Tom McLaury looked out the window over the stove and saw eight armed men approaching on horseback.

An army officer. Four troopers. Three civilians.

"Oh, Lord," he whispered. "I knew this would be trouble."

He moved the stewpot off to the edge of the stove top, wiped his hands on his shirt, and went outside to warn Frank with a shrill whistle that they had visitors. Frank straightened and put a hand to his forehead to shade his eyes. When he saw who was coming, he tossed the straight iron behind a shed, let the last mule up, and started toward the house, mad as hell.

"Goddammit! I know our rights!" he hollered. "They can't come on our property —"

"Let me handle it!" Tommy yelled back.

Frank planted his feet and glared but did as he was told for once. Tommy was better at keeping his temper, and this might get ticklish.

A few hundred yards away, Virgil Earp watched a figure dog-trotting down a line of wagon ruts toward the fenceless gate that sketched the McLaury property line. Short. Slight. Head down, shoulders slumped. "Which one's that?" he asked Morgan.

"That's Tommy. He's harmless. Frank's the one working the iron. He can be a handful."

"Your call, Lieutenant," Virgil said.

Lieutenant Hurst swung off his horse and tossed the reins to one of his men. "Stay back," he told the Earps. "I'll handle this."

Though Joe Hurst was a good soldier, he — like Tom McLaury — preferred diplomacy to conflict, and that was exactly why his superior had chosen him to recover the mules.

Just two years earlier, a dispute over who could sell dry goods in Lincoln County, New Mexico, had blown up into a shooting war. When cavalry troops were dispatched to restore order, one gang holed up in a store and refused to surrender, so the soldiers set fire to the building, expecting to smoke the civilians out and end the stand-off. Instead, there was a fair-sized battle that ended with a lot of dead, burnt civilians.

The whole bungled mess stirred up a hornets' nest of ex-Confederates who hated the federal government in general and anyone wearing a blue uniform in particular. An outraged Congress passed the *Posse Comitatus* Act, forbidding the army to have anything to do with law enforcement, and from the nation's capital to the remotest frontier fort, standing orders came down to this: For the love of Christ, don't make anything worse.

So when Tom McLaury arrived at the gate and shook hands with Joe Hurst in the pink-and-orange light of an Arizona sunset, the pair of them were quite possibly the two most reasonable men in Arizona, and they were united in their hope of working things out sensibly.

The facts were not in dispute. The mules were stolen; Frank McLaury had been seen tampering with their brands.

"I am barred by law from going onto your land," Hurst admitted, "but Virgil Earp is a deputy federal marshal, and he has the legal authority to recover federal property. His brother Wyatt is a deputy sheriff who can arrest you and your brother, if I decide to press charges."

"Please, don't do that, sir," Tom said. "Me and Frank just moved down from Iowa. Two of our brothers fought for the Union and one of them died, but we're just about the only ranchers in this valley who weren't rebels. We're kinda caught in the middle here. We want to obey the law, but we gotta keep peace

131

with our neighbors, and that's not easy, sir. They are not peaceable men."

After some discussion, an acceptable compromise was reached. The troopers and the Earps would withdraw. No one would be arrested, but Tom McLaury would see to it that the mules were returned to Camp Rucker in a few days. The matter would then be closed. No questions asked, none answered.

"Lieutenant, with all due respect," Virgil said when Hurst informed him of the terms he'd agreed to, "that might be the stupidest thing I've heard since Christmas. There is no way in hell that Tom McLaury can make good on that promise, and we'll look like idiots for believing him."

"We should go in there right now and enforce the law" was Wyatt's opinion, but Morgan held up a hand. "Lieutenant, if we arrest the McLaurys now," he said, "they can tell Old Man Clanton we caught them dead to rights, so they had to give the mules up. You can drop the charges later. Everybody wins. You get your mules back, and Tom and Frank'll be off the hook with Clanton."

You could see it on everyone's face. *Damn. That's a good solution.* Even Lieutenant Hurst thought so, but it was too late now.

"I gave my word," he said, "and that's the end of it."

■ ■ ■ ■

They made camp in the dusk and split up in the morning, the troopers heading back to Rucker, the civilians returning to Tombstone.

Virgil was polite enough when Hurst offered his hand and thanked the Earps for their time and aid, but as soon as the lieutenant was out of earshot, he muttered, "Pigs'll fly before he sees them mules again."

Morgan and Virgil finished the last of Allie's sandwiches as they rode. Wyatt didn't eat. "What's going on with Behan?" Virgil asked, to take Wyatt's mind off his tooth. "Why's he sticking his nose into your business?"

"Offered me undersheriff if he gets sheriff."

Virg snorted. "What makes Behan think Frémont is going to appoint a Democrat?"

"Not in the mood, Virg."

Even if a crumbling molar weren't sending lightning bolts of pain through his jaw, and even if he'd been allowed to arrest the McLaurys for a crime that anybody with a single working eye could see they were guilty of, Wyatt couldn't have told his brother exactly what Johnny Behan was proposing, though it had mostly made sense to him while Johnny was talking. "Only about half of a sheriff's job is law enforcement, Wyatt. That's where your experience is," Johnny had said. "The other half is administrative." That half involved a lot of political horseshit. Going to parties, being chummy, making small talk. Which is what Behan was good at. "But, see, if we divide the work up," Johnny told him, "we'll each be playing to our strengths. I take care of the political end of things, you take over enforcement, and the sheriff's office as a whole does a better job for the citizens. Make sense?"

"So far," Wyatt admitted.

"Now, in my experience," Johnny had told him, "the worst part of a sheriff's responsibility is visiting every property in the county once a year and coming up with a valuation for taxes. Everybody wants county services, Wyatt, but nobody wants to pay for them. And since the sheriff keeps a percentage of what he collects, everybody figures you're jacking up their taxes for your own gain. Mining companies have lawyers to fight every penny of their assessments. And when you show up on a man's ranch, he hates you on sight! That part of the job means soft-soaping people — seeing their side of things. It takes finesse and patience."

"But it pays," Wyatt pointed out.

"Yes, indeed. It surely does." Behan dropped his voice. "Did you know Sheriff Shibell is pulling in upwards of twenty thousand a year?"

That was news — and by the sound of

Johnny Behan's grim laughter, the look on Wyatt's face must have shown it. Of course, Wyatt knew Charlie Shibell was making a good buck but . . . twenty *grand*?

Until that very moment, Wyatt had thought he himself was doing well. He was getting three times his salary as a Dodge City policeman. His house wasn't much, but he owned it outright. He could feed and stable Dick Naylor and Roxana and their colt Reuben. He was banking faro games, and that was a steady stream of money, too, but . . . twenty grand a year!

Across the table, Johnny Behan had fallen silent. With the patience of a Missouri fisherman, he simply watched Wyatt Earp think about that big round number. Then he flicked the line just a bit. Twitching the bait.

"What are you making, Wyatt?" he asked. "Five hundred a month? I don't call that fair! Do you?" He waited until Wyatt's eyes met his. "Now, if I get the appointment, I'm prepared to make you —"

"No deals," Wyatt snapped.

"— an *offer,*" Johnny continued, unruffled. "If Governor Frémont appoints me sheriff of the new county, we'll split the responsibilities *and* the income. Fifty-fifty."

Wyatt frowned and looked at Behan sideways.

Then he swam back, still drawn toward that nice big number.

"Now, then, if you get the appointment," Johnny went on, "you could appoint me under-sheriff, and we could still split the responsibilities, just the way I figured. You can pay me whatever you think is fair. I won't hold you to fifty-fifty."

"I don't know," Wyatt said cautiously, but he was thinking that even half was ten grand a year.

And that was when John Harris Behan set the hook, for he had learned something important from his father, that ex-seminarian from Kildare: To understand a man, you must identify his besetting sin. Wyatt coveted the wealth of the men who owned things and ran things, but what he truly craved was the deference accorded to those men. It was not greed or envy that drove him. It was pride.

"It's not just money, is it, Wyatt. It's freedom. It's a future. It's *respect,*" Johnny said in a low, tight voice. "I've seen how those big shots look right through you. They pass you on the street and don't even say hello. Uppity sonsabitches walk around town like they own the place, but if anything happens? Who do they come running to? Whose help do they want then, eh, Wyatt?"

"You got that straight enough," Wyatt muttered.

"I'll be honest with you, Wyatt. I am an ambitious man. I see the sheriff's office as a stepping stone to bigger things. I want to show Washington that I can work with Demo-crats *and* Republicans, and that there are federal appointments I might be worthy of. Now, then . . . what does all this mean for you?"

Wyatt waited, and the Missouri fisherman readied the net.

"It means," Johnny said, "that no matter which of us Governor Frémont appoints, we can work together for the first twelve to eighteen months. I'll teach you what I know, and then I hope to move on to bigger things. And that leaves you free to run for sheriff unopposed in 1882."

Wyatt frowned. "I don't know . . . If I'm appointed, I'd probably go with Virg or Mor-gan for undersheriff. I have to look out for my brothers."

"I understand, Wyatt. I come from a big family myself," Behan said easily, letting the line play out a bit. "But my offer stands. I believe we'd make a good team that could serve the county well. And I believe both of us would benefit in the long run. Just think it over." He smiled then and sat up straight. "You haven't eaten yet, have you? Why not come on over to the house for lunch? My little Josie is quite a cook, and my son, Al-bert, would love to meet you."

Wyatt was still thinking it over on the way back to Tombstone from the McLaury place.

Truth be told, he hadn't understood how much went into sheriffing until Johnny Behan explained it. Assessing property values. Dealing with appeals and lawyers. It probably made sense to learn that part of the job from Johnny. In the meantime, he'd still make a real good buck as undersheriff.

He'd keep the little house on the edge of Tombstone, he decided, but maybe rent it out and buy something nicer in the good part of town. And he could invest some cash in the mining claims he'd won from idiots who'd put their properties on the faro table. Silver didn't lie around waiting to be panned out of a riverbed. It had to be extracted from the ore. That required a lot of equipment and men who knew how to run it . . .

Prolly oughta sell off the mines, he decided as he rode. Use the cash to buy a spread right here in Sulphur Springs Valley.

The land east of Tombstone was green, with streams and lakes. Best grazing in Arizona, everybody said. He'd always wanted to own a horse farm. Most of the racehorses down here were thoroughbreds. He could buy breeding stock right here. Build on what Dick Naylor and Roxana and Reuben had in them . . .

He could use some experience, he guessed. And he liked what Behan said about the two of them showing how Democrats and Republicans could work together. "It's up to our generation, Wyatt. Men who fought in the war — they'll never lay down those old grudges. We don't have those memories, and it's our responsibility to make the nation whole again."

By the time he and his brothers got back to Tombstone, he'd pretty much decided to throw in with Behan. Even so, he told himself it might be better to wait a couple of days before he said yes to Johnny. Could be he wasn't seeing everything he should. Because that molar was killing him. He hadn't slept well in weeks. He was stupid with fatigue, but Doc was in town now. The tooth would be out soon and he'd finally get some good rest.

A stable boy came over to take the horses off their hands when they dismounted at Dexter's. The kid was new. Wyatt shook his head when the boy reached for Dick Naylor's lead.

"I take care of him," he told the kid. "He bites."

He was unsaddling Dick when Fred White came jogging over and started talking to Morgan. There was something apologetic about "I was at the office when it happened." Morg was frowning, but Wyatt finished brushing Dick down and then called to the kid, "You can feed and water him. Go easy on the grain."

He was carrying his saddle to the racks,

trying to decide if he'd go see Doc Holliday about the tooth right away or try to get some sleep first, when he heard Morgan give a shout of dismay.

Hell, it's always something, Wyatt thought, but he was not prepared for what he heard next.

"He's dead?" Morg cried. "Doc is *dead*?"

Few Words, But Very Clear

A moment later, Fred White was looking at three Earps standing shoulder to shoulder to shoulder. All of them tall, all of them broad, all of them fair-haired and mustachioed. All of them staring at him like it was his fault somehow.

"What happened?" Virg wanted to know, his voice low and wary.

"Who did it?" Wyatt demanded.

"Was he sick again?" Morgan asked. "Coughing blood?"

"Calm down and let me finish! First I heard, somebody was yelling about how Doc Holliday just got killed over at the Oriental. He's gonna be all right, but Milt Joyce clobbered him pretty good."

Morg slumped in relief. "Jesus, Fred!"

"It's not all good news," Fred warned. "When Holliday came to, he pulled a pistol out and emptied it inside the saloon. He hit Milt, and a bartender, too."

"Christ," Virg sighed. "How bad?"

"Milt's hand is a mess. They might have to amputate. And his bartender's gonna be lame. Lost the big toe on one foot. They both pressed charges. Assault with a deadly weapon."

"Shit," Morgan whispered. "That's prison."

"So Doc's under arrest?" Virg asked.

"No, he was in court already this morning. Told the judge he couldn't remember a thing about it, and I gotta be honest, he looked kinda lost, like he didn't understand what anybody was saying. Morg said he was a friend of yours, so I got him a lawyer, and he told the judge that Doc was only exercising his First Amendment rights when Milt assaulted him. Milt had seventy pounds on him, which the judge could see for himself, and Doc wasn't in full possession of his faculties when he fired the gun. They bargained down to guilty of simple assault. Doc got off with a fine and court costs."

Virgil was rubbing his eyes. "Start over. Why did Milt hit Doc in the first place?"

"I was down at the office, remember, but from what I heard, Doc went into the Oriental and asked Milt Joyce about getting a game going. Johnny Tyler and a bunch of them California fellas was in there, and Tyler comes up and says that the Slopers run gambling in the Oriental, and easterners like Doc ain't welcome —"

Wyatt bristled, but Morgan put a hand on

his arm.

"So, Tyler and Holliday get into it pretty quick. You know Tyler — he's a blowhard. But from what I hear, Holliday's got quite a mouth, too."

"I swear," Virgil muttered, "that man is like one of them yappy little Mexican mutts with no idea how small it is. He's gonna get himself killed one of these days."

"Yeah, well, he came pretty close this time," Fred said. "He tore into Johnny Tyler, and the Slopers all made a move on him, so Milt tells 'em to take it outside. Tyler and his boys left, but Holliday didn't see as how he done anything wrong. And, hell, it woulda been five to one outside. I don't guess Holliday was in a hurry to get jumped. So he starts mouthing off at Milt, and you know Milt — he don't take no lip. Picked Holliday up off his feet and threw him into the street."

Morgan put his hands over his eyes.

"Yeah," Fred said grimly. "Holliday comes charging back inside and he's madder'n hell, and that's when Milt buffaloed him. Holliday went down like he was killed. Head laid open, blood all over. Somebody went to get me, but in the meantime, Holliday comes to and starts shooting. When I got there, Milt and Parker was both bleeding, and I made the arrest."

"Where's Doc now?" Morgan asked, but what Wyatt wanted to know was "Where's

Tyler?" And that was when Fred White decided it was a good time to roll a cigarette and think things through. The fact was, Fred wasn't entirely sure what to make of Wyatt Earp. Wyatt didn't drink and he went to church a lot, too, but everybody knew he had damn near beat a shopkeeper to death up there in Dodge City. And while Fred wouldn't have shed a tear if somebody took the starch out of that swaggering sonofabitch Johnny Tyler, the notion of arresting Wyatt for felonious assault afterward did not hold much appeal. So, as he lit up, Fred looked to Virgil, who met his eyes and inclined his head ever so slightly in Morgan's direction.

Pretending he hadn't heard Wyatt's question, Fred answered Morgan's. "He's over at the Cosmopolitan. He threw up a couple of times and I didn't want it stinking up the jail, so I took him back to his hotel room and told him to stay put. One eye's all swole shut and Doc Goodfellow says he's got a concannon or some damn thing like that, but he'll be all right."

The hotel room was darkened. The curtains were closed. He had pulled a pillow over his head, but the persistent banging on the door was shattering.

"Kate?" he called. "Please! The door!"

There was no answer. He lifted his head to look for her. The nausea got worse. Heart pounding, he recognized an impulse to get a gun. He was scared, but *why* stayed just beyond his reach. After a few moments, he'd forgotten what he wanted to find.

"Doc? It's Morgan! Open up! Wyatt's here, and Virgil, too. Doc? *Doc!*"

He drew back the bed linens and sat up, trying not to cough. Or vomit. Morgan hollered again, which reminded him that he meant to go to the door. "I must look a sight," he said when opened it and saw the Earps' shock. "I fear I am not properly dressed for visitors."

Questions, then. Too loud. Too fast. Too many.

"My apologies," he said. "I do not seem to have my wits about me. I believe this must be the worst headache I have ever had."

Wyatt left. Virgil went after him. Morgan seemed torn between staying there and following his brothers.

What's that all about? Doc wondered briefly. Then the fog rolled back in and his curiosity dissipated. He wanted to lie down and go back to sleep, but he could hear his mother's voice. *Now, sugar, it is very kind of the gentleman to come and visit you.* With a mighty effort, he concentrated on his guest's face and attempted to make conversation.

"Well, now, Morgan," he said. "What brings you to Tucson?"

"Some men never look angry, but they never forget a slight."

That's what Mayor Dog Kelley once told Wyatt Earp back in Dodge City, but the warning did not stick, for Wyatt Earp was a man without guile and could not imagine it in others. He did not anger easily or often. When he did, there was no subterfuge, no nurturing of grudges, no waiting for the right moment to strike back.

Within fifteen minutes of leaving Doc Holliday's room, Wyatt had located Johnny Tyler, flung him against a wall, and uttered a single short sentence making it plain to Tyler and the rest of the Slopers that they would be unwise to venture back inside the Oriental Saloon. Ever again.

As intended, word got around: Anyone who laid a hand on Doc Holliday would answer to Wyatt Earp. Among those to whom Wyatt gave notice of this directly was the owner of the Oriental, Milton Edward Joyce.

Milt was back in his saloon by then, wearing a fresh white apron. His old one had been discarded, so badly stained with blood that it was no longer fit for use, not even as a rag. Some of that blood had splashed off Doc Holliday's head. A little of it came from the bartender's toe, though his bleeding mostly leaked into his shoe and onto the floor as he hopped around the room, yelling. By far, the greatest portion of the blood that soaked the apron was Milt's own.

His torn and broken hand now throbbed beneath yards of bandaging. A constant ache reached high into his arm. He was still light-headed. Dr. Henry Matthews had strongly urged bed rest, but Milt preferred the distraction of activity and with his bartender laid up, he couldn't afford to take time off from the business. He had overhead to support and demanding customers to keep. The Oriental stayed open day and night, no matter what.

The days when you could thump a mug of beer on a bar and call it done were long gone. Modern drinkers expected ornate mirrors, sparkling crystal, gleaming mahogany, and polished brass. They wanted a free lunch, too, or billiards, or music. Or all three. A free lunch wasn't just food. It was a kitchen and a cook and a waiter; it was dishes that got broken and cutlery that was stolen. Billiards meant an expensive table and cue sticks that idiots broke over one another's heads. Music meant a fiddler, or a piano and somebody who could play it, and if your man was any good at all, other saloons would try to hire him away, so you had to pay the bastard well.

All that added red ink to the ledgers, but when Milt Joyce sold his San Francisco place in '79 and traveled down to Tombstone, he was determined to build a saloon so elegant it would attract and hold the classiest clientele in a boomtown that was supplying the New Orleans Mint with all the silver it could use. He commissioned a beautifully carved, white-gilt bar and twenty-eight gas-burning chandeliers to light his place like a palace. He purchased a heavy walnut billiard table, ivory balls, and walnut cues with a matching rack. He paid top dollar for a corner lot at Fifth and Allen because it had the best view in town. He freighted in plate glass for the windows so his customers could look southward over their drinks and rest their eyes on wave after wave of rolling silver-stuffed hills or gaze at the lumber-rich Huachuca Mountains, lovely and lucrative in the distance.

There was no beer on tap at the Oriental, for Milt Joyce did not cater to filthy miners from Cornwall or Pennsylvania, no matter how well-paid they were. The Oriental served imported whiskeys, brandies, and cordials in cut glass. He didn't just plunk a jar of pickled eggs on the bar and call it lunch, either. The Oriental had oysters, crabs, and shrimp, packed in ice and delivered daily, with hours to spare before the seafood went off. The overhead was staggering, and there was only one way to get ahead of the game, so he brought in another source of steady income: gambling. To set the tone high, he walled off a club room at the back of his building and covered its floor with a Brussels carpet so beautiful that even a drunken lawyer would hesitate to spit on it. There were poker tables, a faro layout, and a roulette wheel, but Milt added upholstered chairs to each corner, and sold fine cigars, and provided newspapers and magazines as well, so his customers might tarry an hour or two longer, sipping an expensive cognac as they read.

He'd begun to turn a decent profit when the California Slopers showed up. They favored the Oriental because Milt was from San Francisco, and he appreciated their business at first, but it wasn't long before the Slopers were more trouble than they were worth. Foul-mouthed and loud, they were poor losers who chased out all the high-class play. Within weeks, he was losing business to the Crystal Palace, across the street.

To keep the troublemakers in check, Milt brought in a minority partner with a reputation for keeping the peace in such establishments: Wyatt Earp, late of Dodge City, Kansas.

Wyatt Earp, who got 25 percent of the club room's take for his services.

Wyatt Earp, who had *not* been in the Oriental last night and who was therefore unavailable to prevent or defuse an altercation between Johnny Tyler and Doc Holliday.

Wyatt Earp, who nevertheless had the unmitigated gall to dress down Milton Ed-

149

ward Joyce in *his own saloon* for cold-cocking an obnoxious, belligerent, consumptive sonofabitch who happened to be a friend of Wyatt's.

Already today, Milt had put up with being joshed about how lucky he was to have escaped slaughter by the notorious Doc Holliday, who was said to be a lightning-fast and deadly accurate gunman.

"Musta been an off day for Doc!" the wags cried. "He just winged you!"

Milt accepted the gibes with a smile, though he would not know for weeks if his hand could be saved. If Wyatt Earp was not the kind of man who angered easily or often, Milt Joyce could go him one better. Milt was not the kind of man who got angry at all. He would, quite simply, get even — with Doc Holliday and Wyatt Earp, both.

No matter how long it took.

Women of Troy

Wretched, Headstrong Girl!

"Come on, Josie!" Johnny urged. "Try again. You're not hurt —"

"How do *you* know? I might've broken something!"

"The best thing to do when a horse throws you is to get right back on."

"No!"

Head down, Johnny Behan planted fists on hip bones and stared at the soft sand of the raked corral, trying to get a grip on his reaction. Josie hadn't really been thrown. To be thrown, you have to be mounted and get tossed off. Josie had her boot in the stirrup and was on her way into the saddle when the pony pivoted away from her. She hit the ground, but it was just plain falling, and not very far at that. She might have been a little shaken up, but Josie could make Greek tragedy out of burnt toast.

"You said you wanted to learn to ride, honey," he reminded her. Admittedly, an edge might have come into his voice then because she hadn't just *said* she wanted to learn to ride. She announced it. She declared it. She proclaimed it.

First she told him, weeping, that she had "lost the baby." He was properly sympathetic but knew they'd been careful and reckoned it was more likely that she was just a few days late. She mooned around for a week before informing him that learning to ride would console her and cure her melancholy. Soon "the baby" — if indeed there had ever been such a thing — was forgotten and all conversation in the Behan household began to focus on Josie's sudden need for a horse. A pretty little bay pony had come up for sale at the Dexter Stable. Josie wanted it. She would need a handsome tailored riding habit, as well. And the charming veiled hat that went with it. And boots and a sidesaddle.

She wheedled. She begged. She stormed and sulked. He had not enjoyed a moment's peace — or a single toss in bed — until she had it all. And now it was "Well, I changed my mind!"

Why, John Harris Behan asked himself, *why* does this kind of argument always happen in front of Wyatt Earp?

Face expressionless, eyes on the horse he was cantering on a line in the next pen over, Wyatt was doing his best to make it seem that he was unaware of the Behans' argument, but Josie had briefly understudied for a speaking role in the Markham troupe and she could make her voice carry.

"Come on, Josie," Johnny said. "Try again."

"*No!* I don't *want* to," she insisted, brushing sand off her skirt, "and you can't *make* me!"

"Listen to yourself!" he whispered fiercely. "You sound like a child!"

"And you," Josie replied, loud enough for the back row of a theater in Chicago to hear, *"you* sound like a *mean old man!"*

Wyatt smothered a laugh.

"You want the little brat, Wyatt?" Johnny called. "She's all yours!"

It was more a threat than an offer. He didn't mean it, but Josie went off like a mine charge, and then it was "Lincoln freed the slaves," and "I don't belong to you, John Behan," and "You can't give me away." He shot back, "That's right — because nobody would take you!" Finally, rather than listen to more of her nonsense or hit her in public, Johnny dropped the pony's reins and walked away.

Stamping her foot, Josie yelled, "Stand and fight, you coward!" But Johny didn't even glance over his shoulder, and she snarled in exasperation, *"Oh!* That *man!"*

"It's a bad match," she heard Mr. Earp call.

She turned, glowering at him. "I'm sure that's what my mother would say!"

He looked confused. Then he said, "Oh. Well, maybe. I guess. But . . . I meant the

155

horse." He let his own animal slow to a walk and came to the fence between them. "A small rider isn't necessarily better off with a little horse like that," he told her, his voice quiet and factual. "A bigger mount can be a better fit."

She joined him at the fence and looked up, neck craning. He was nearly a foot taller than she was, and a good six inches taller than Johnny Behan. Eyes mischievous, she tilted her head. "Is that so?" she asked. Bold as brass.

It took him a moment before he got the joke. "I — I didn't mean it like that," he stammered. "Honest, I — I'm sorry if you thought — It's just that little horses can be more skittish, and . . ."

She would have teased another man mercilessly, but she could see that this one was genuinely mortified. And in what was, perhaps, the first truly adult moment of her life, Josephine Sarah Marcus realized that joshing was more likely to wound Mr. Earp than prod him to banter.

"That's a beautiful stallion," she said to change the subject. "What's his name?"

It was an innocent question, but he stood mute for a time, as though he were trying to decide what to tell her. She expected a lie and, indeed, his eyes slid away.

"It's — His name . . . His name is Dick."

"Oh, my," she said, blinking. "This just

keeps getting worse!"

"I — He was already named. When I got him. A Texan named him . . . that."

"Just the sort of vulgarity I've come to expect from Texans," she said lightly. Glancing at the horse again, she added, "I believe I'll call him Richard, if you don't mind."

He smiled at that, and she felt as though she'd accomplished something, even if she wasn't quite sure what.

"A horse'll move away from pressure," he told her, lifting his chin toward her pony. "That's why you fell."

"I don't understand."

"When you put your foot in the stirrup, you took too long getting on. The saddle started to haul down on her from the left, so she moved off to the right. Johnny shoulda gave you a leg up."

Tying *Richard* to the fence rail, he ducked under it and said, "C'mon. Try again." Standing next to her pony, he leaned over, linking his fingers. "Just step into my hands like they're the stirrup."

He didn't seem embarrassed or self-conscious about this, so she did as she was told. An instant later, she was sitting four and a half feet off the ground.

He bent to guide her left foot into the iron, careful to hold her boot by its heel. A hint of his previous discomfort reappeared. "Now, I guess . . . you hook your, um, knee around

157

that pommel."

She tried, but the skirts of her riding habit were bunched beneath her. In an effort to re-arrange the fabric, she stood up a little on her left foot, which was in the stirrup, but quickly sat down when the pony started to pivot.

"Away from the pressure," she observed, and then she went still, struck by a thought. "That's why fences work! I always wondered why such big animals don't just push these flimsy little fences over and escape, but they'd feel the pressure and move away from it!"

He looked impressed. "Never thought about it, but you're prolly right."

He watched her struggle to balance her weight while attempting to straighten her skirt and helped as best he could without being too familiar.

"Sidesaddles are foolishness," he decided. "Johnny should take this thing back and get you a regular one. My sister Adelia rides astride. No reason why you shouldn't. And you should prolly just wear, um, trousers. Like you did. When you danced. In that play."

He could feel the blood rise in his face. To change the subject he handed the reins to her. "Don't haul on the horse's mouth. Just put pressure on the neck —"

"Of course! To go right, you pull the reins toward the right because that puts pressure on the left side of the neck, so she'll move to the right, to get away from it."

He liked that she caught on quick. Saved him a lot of words. He liked how she lit up when she got the hang of something, too.

He kept her on the horse for almost an hour. Then he said, "That's enough for now. Let it sink in some."

She followed him as he led both horses back into the barn. "You are remarkably chatty this afternoon, Mr. Earp! I don't believe I've heard you say more than a few words before."

He flipped the stirrup leather up to unbuckle the girth. "I had a bad tooth. Been bothering me since June. Doc Holliday pulled it. I feel better now it's out."

She watched him lift the saddle off her pony, admiring the easy way he propped it against his hip and carried it, one-handed, to the rack. "Johnny says Doc Holliday is dangerous and ought to be run out of town."

"He won't say that if he gets a toothache! You see a brush around here anywheres?" he asked. "If people would just put things back in the same place every time . . ."

She stepped up onto a stool and looked around. "Over there," she said, pointing. "On the shelf by the harnesses."

"Doc's a real good dentist," he told her when he came back with the brush. "My teeth used to hurt all the time, but Doc fixed me up good, back in Dodge."

She hopped off the stool and sat down to watch him brush her pony down. Long, slow strokes, firm and rhythmic. She liked the way he moved.

"People always seem to get the wrong idea about Doc," he was saying. "Brings some of it on himself, I guess. Thing is, he's not strong, and gamblers have to carry a lot of cash, so . . ."

He stopped brushing and looked to see if she understood.

"So if you look easy to rob . . ." she said.

He nodded and went to work on the pony's mane.

"Why doesn't he just be a dentist then?"

"Too sick, most of the time. Consumption. He can still pull a tooth or something quick like that, but he can't make dentures or do fillings or anything, like he did up in Dodge." To her astonishment, he pulled his front teeth out to show her the bridge. "Thee?" He put the teeth back in. "He used to do things like that, but it's finicky work and his cough got real bad. Winter in Kansas was hard on him. His cousin Robert's a dentist, too. Doc's still hoping to get better and go back home to Atlanta so's they can work together, but . . . I don't know. He's worse than when I saw him last. And getting hit on the head set him back."

"I heard about that. You like him, then?"

"He can be hard to get along with, when

his chest hurts. But he's quality." Finished with her pony, he led the little horse into its stall. "Him and my brother Morgan are friends. They're readers," he said, as though that explained it.

"How is Doc now?"

"Side of his face is all bruised up, but he's thinking straighter."

"He gave me a piano lesson once. I'm afraid it was wasted on me. I'm just a dunce about music, I guess."

He stood motionless for a time, and when he spoke again, his voice was soft with remembered awe. "Doc played piano at a party this one time, up in Dodge . . . Never heard anything like that before. It was real pretty."

Thoughtful herself, Josie watched him brush Dick down, his motions calm and unhurried, the animal drowsing beneath his hands. "Johnny and I still owe you a dinner. Do you like cake, Mr. Earp?"

"Sure. Everybody likes cake." He looked away for a moment, then back at her. "You don't have to 'mister' me. Wyatt's fine."

"Friday, then," she said "Come by around sunset. Wyatt."

"We all have our vices," Dr. J. H. Holliday had observed during Wyatt's first visit to his Dodge City dental office. "Sugar is yours."

There are a lot of ways a tooth can go to

161

hell in the utter absence of dental care; in 1878, Wyatt Earp's mouth provided horrifying examples of most of them. It took six weeks of steady work to deal with years of accumulated damage: pulling teeth too decayed to salvage; filling those that were still fundamentally sound; fabricating a bridge to replace the missing upper centrals. Wyatt's father had knocked those out when Wyatt was seven, but most of the destruction was self-inflicted, for if an opportunity to sweeten any kind of food or drink presented itself, Wyatt Earp took it. He mixed molasses into every spoonful of breakfast oatmeal. He poured maple syrup over his pancakes *and* his bacon. He drank a lot of coffee and loaded every cup with sugar. He carried rock candy with him and sucked on it while he was out exercising his horses. Nearly every evening, he visited a soda fountain or an ice cream parlor. And in the autumn of 1880, the assault on his enamel got worse.

The Behans' kitchen window looked out over the street, and whenever Wyatt happened to walk by, the seductive fragrance of baking sugar reached out to him. Josie often noticed him passing, and it was natural that she would offer him a taste of whatever she had cooling on a rack. Orange jelly cake, sponge cake, spice cake, honey cake. Apple cake in layers. Sometimes she fried crullers or dough-nuts, and she always dusted them with powdered sugar. She baked cookies, too. Ginger-bread, hermits, and Boston creams. And every morning, there was fresh bread. Thick, warm slices dripping with butter, fragrant with cinnamon, crusty with sugar crystals.

There was nothing secretive about this. Johnny Behan knew and approved. A successful stint as a southern Arizona sheriff was key to achieving his ambitions; Josie understood that it was important for Wyatt to trust Johnny's judgment and to believe in his goodwill. That autumn, Johnny himself often urged, "Come by for supper, Wyatt."

The answer was nearly always yes, for Wyatt found it close to impossible to say no to Josie's cooking. He liked Johnny, too. The older man was friendly and helpful and never made Wyatt feel awkward or ignorant, the way Wyatt's own brothers could sometimes.

Mostly Johnny talked about the things a sheriff needed to understand. "Tombstone's townspeople was industrialists and merchants. Northern Republicans, like you and your brothers," he said. "They want law and order on the streets. That means getting guns and drunks off them." Out in the rest of the county, it was independent ranchers, and most of them were ex-Confederates and southern Democrats. "They're all citizens, Wyatt," Johnny said. "And southerners don't like anybody pushing them around or telling them how to do things."

Wyatt knew that. Hell, he knew Doc Holliday and how touchy the Georgian could be, but he didn't see how that justified letting somebody get away with breaking the law. Just look at what happened with those mules! The McLaurys never delivered them, which showed the Cow Boys they could get away with rustling and act however they pleased and nobody would do anything about it. Curly Bill Brocius was getting bolder and Johnny Ringo was more belligerent all the time, and they were always backed up by five or six other toughs. When Fred White or Wyatt or Virgil arrested a Cow Boy, a lot of judges dismissed the charges. Even if a judge wasn't intimidated or on the take, half a dozen men and a couple of whores would cheerfully perjure themselves to provide an alibi. Wyatt just wanted the law taken seriously, but Johnny always argued for moderation.

"Tombstone isn't Dodge, Wyatt! You were dealing with transients back in Kansas. You could buffalo drovers and they'd wake up with a headache and ride back to Texas. A county sheriff deals with local folks. They're taxpayers, Wyatt. They're voters! You have to be more respectful."

Wyatt could see Behan's point. Even so, he'd think, I don't care who they are. If they're breaking the law, they're breaking the law.

Mostly he let Johnny's talk roll off him, except one night when Johnny got on him about Doc Holliday. "It wasn't sensible to go after Milt Joyce like that," Johnny told him. "Milt's an important businessman, and he's talking about running for city council. Doc Holliday's an outsider, Wyatt. He's a gambler and a troublemaker, and he can only hurt you politically —"

"Doc saved my life in Dodge," Wyatt said. "I stand by them that stand by me." And he walked out, right then, to make sure Johnny got *his* point.

But he came back the next night anyway.

Because it was nice to watch Josie while she cooked. It was interesting how she'd stand still when she was getting started and talk to herself. "Scalloped potatoes in the oven. Steak in the fry pan. Stewed carrots in the pot." She'd squint then and decide, "Scrub the vegetables first." Sometimes she'd laugh to herself and say, "Oy! I sound just like Mutti!" Then she'd get the water into the pot so it would heat up while she sliced the potatoes and put them into a buttered pan and sprinkled bread crumbs over the top and put more little bits of butter over the crumbs so they'd brown up. After the potatoes went into the oven, she'd put the carrots into the boiling water with butter and eight spoons of sugar. Ten, if she noticed Wyatt was watching. She'd start the steaks last, and while the

165

first side of the meat fried, she'd get the dishes ready. A few minutes later, it would all go out onto the table at the same time, hot and delicious. And there was always something sweet for dessert.

He liked how she talked to little Albert, too, and let him help in the kitchen. She wasn't hardly more than a kid herself, so maybe she remembered what it was like — wanting to be helpful but not knowing how. She always had reasons for why she did things a certain way, and he liked how she explained them to Al in a kind voice, instead of expecting the kid to figure it out on his own and then smacking him if he was slow or got something wrong. She'd say, "Try to make all the cookies the same size, or some of them will still be raw when others are done." Or "Cut an X across the top of the bread dough. Otherwise, the crust will bubble up when it's baking. Careful with that knife, sweetheart." That's how a parent oughta talk to a child, Wyatt decided. And it came to him that his own mother might have been like Josie, if Virginia Cooksey hadn't married a mean sonofabitch who thought it was right and proper to beat the daylights out of everyone in the house, from his wife on down.

Josie would read to everyone after supper, the way Morg did before bed when the brothers were growing up, but this was even better because Josie used different voices for the people in the book, so it was like listening to a play. Sometimes Al would ask questions about things in the books, and Johnny would answer them because he knew a lot about the world.

Wyatt was a little embarrassed about how often he ate with the Behans, but not enough to turn an invitation down. Going home to Mattie Blaylock got harder and harder. It was just kind of an accident that he'd let Mattie start living with him. Mattie seemed to think he was stupid for allowing that to happen, and maybe she was right . . .

Anyway, it was always nice being at Johnny Behan's house. It was the kind of home any man might like to have.

"Wyatt's lucky to have you as his friend, Johnny," Josie said one night when their guest had left, and Albert was asleep, and Johnny had rolled off her. "I'm glad you invite him over. He obviously never gets a decent meal at home. And did you see the shirt he was wearing this evening? Why, it's never been within half a mile of an iron! It's sad to see a man so uncared for."

"Mmm," Johnny agreed, for he and his son Al *were* well cared for, and he was smart enough to appreciate it.

"I think he liked the brisket," Josie added thoughtfully.

"Me, too," Johnny said sleepily. "The

167

candied yams were good, too."

"Nice to see him filling out a little."

"Not so thin in the face," Johnny agreed, turning over and going to sleep.

Another man might have found it surprising that a girl from a prosperous San Francisco family was so good in the kitchen, but Johnny Behan was not one to inspect the mouth of a gift horse who was young, pretty, and (he always heard the words in Pauline Markham's voice) *so athletic.* And as much as he enjoyed his private life, Josie's public esteem was of even greater value to him. Victoria had never understood that part of being a politician's wife, but Josie's conspicuous admiration encouraged others to believe that the territorial governorship was within the grasp of John Harris Behan, Democrat though he might be. Yes, Josie was snubbed by the wives of the mining executives and business owners and professional men Johnny was trying to impress and influence, but really — what did that matter? Women couldn't vote, and Josie had their husbands wrapped around her little finger.

The funny thing was, Josie had stopped nagging about a wedding, even though Johnny was now inclined to make an honest woman of her. In fact, she'd waved the notion off the last time he'd brought it up, declaring angrily that marriage was old-fashioned and an offense to a modern woman's love of independence. "I'd have no rights at all! A girl who marries is legally dead!" she informed him with a venom that seemed to hold him personally responsible for this outrageous state of affairs. Johnny didn't know what to make of that, but he expected she'd change her mind as soon as she found a pattern she liked for a wedding dress.

In the meantime, he saw no reason to rock the boat, for everything was going his way. He was especially pleased that — after a bad start — Josie and Albert had forged a fine and genuine affection. Better yet, attention to the son did not come at the father's expense. Even Albert's partial deafness now seemed lucky, for they never woke him up at night, or in the early morning. Of course, until the school building was finished, Al's presence in the household would be a problem in the daytime, but there were plenty of bordellos in town if a man felt the urge at noon, say, or three.

When supper was over and the dishes were cleared away, Johnny liked the way Josie sat at his side reading to the family or listening as he and Wyatt talked about politics or history. He liked the feel of her small hands around his strong right arm and enjoyed the warmth of her slender body leaning against his own.

If he suffered from any sort of uneasiness, it was the occasional feeling that there ought to be a theater placard outside their home announcing, *Miss Josephine Marcus, starring in the role of the Good Little Housewife!* Of course, Josie could've expressed her flare for the dramatic in worse ways, so he never thought too hard about that. He had forgotten that this was a girl who understood audience sight lines and knew how to hit her mark onstage.

You Are Right to Blame Me!

Johnny Behan might have been blind to what was happening in his own home, but it was plain as day to the women who lived with James, Virgil, Wyatt, and Morgan Earp.

"Biscuits ain't good enough for him now," Mattie Blaylock told the others. " 'Why don't you never make a cake?' " she asked in a whiny voice, like it was Wyatt whining. "He's always got some mean thing to say when he comes home, too. It's 'Fix a button, can't you?' or 'Clean this place up!' "

Morgan's girl, Lou, kept her gaze on the tie-down she was whipstitching for the corner of a nearly finished tent, but Allie Sullivan glanced up from her sewing machine for a moment and met Bessie Earp's eyes. *A little housework wouldn't hurt you none.* That's what they were thinking.

Allie cleared her throat and lifted her chin toward the puddle of canvas she was working on. "Mattie, straighten that out for me, will you?" she said, mostly to get the woman to quit complaining and do something useful.

"Oh, all right!" Mattie snapped.

She made it sound like it was the tenth time Allie had asked her to do something instead of the first. Mattie always did what you asked, but she acted like it was a big chore, so you couldn't hardly feel grateful. The other three women took the brunt of her moods, but since they worked together most days, keeping the peace was important, especially when they were putting in a lot of hours to fill a big sewing contract.

Lou got up to run the iron over another set of tie-downs. Bessie was having a bad day — tumors, the doctor said — and she was just rocking in the corner, but Allie pedaled away, attaching a floor to a tent wall while Mattie held the heavy fabric out so the layers would feed smoothly into the sewing machine. Everywhere you looked, bolts of canvas leaned against the walls. Allie had thought about asking the boys to put an addition onto the house just for the tentmaking, but that might cause hard feelings, for she and Virgil already had the biggest place and had ever since the Earps arrived.

So many boomers had poured into Tombstone in 1879, you couldn't get a house for love nor money, so at first the Earps had lived out of their wagons. Then early one morning, Morgan spotted some Mexicans moving out of a four-room adobe with a dirt floor. Virgil

172

and James stood guard over the house, scaring off squatters. Wyatt and Morg found the owner before the place could be let out to somebody else, but the monthly rent rocked them back on their heels.

"Forty dollars!" Wyatt cried. "That's six times what a *nice* place back in Dodge fetches."

"Feel free to return to Dodge, sir," the landlord said. "Forty dollars is what a mud hut costs in Tombstone."

"Why, the roof ain't even solid!" Morgan objected.

"It's a desert. It doesn't rain here," the landlord lied. "Throw a tarpaulin over the hole, if you like."

The brothers fixed the roof themselves and stretched out the wagon sheets like awnings, to make a sort of canvas veranda. All eight of them lived together, which was a trial. By and by, other houses opened up nearby. Everyone had their own place now, though the girls still came to Allie's to sew.

There had been considerable debate about hauling Allie's sewing machine down to Arizona. The brothers only had two wagons to transport four households. Each woman had furniture and dishes and clothing she hated to give up. Toward the end, they were arguing about whose rolling pin was better. There just wasn't any room left for a sewing machine.

"You're gonna hafta leave it, Pickle," Virg told Allie.

"Fine," she said. "I'll leave that machine here, and you can leave *me* — sitting right next to it."

"I guess we can get it in somewheres," Wyatt muttered, though he added, "Hell if I know where."

It took two days to repack but they fit the machine in somehow, and a good thing, too. None of the boys could find work when they first got to Tombstone, so the girls started making prospectors' tents with double rows of tight machine-stitching that held up real well in the wind. They took in mending, too, and charged a penny a yard for thread and use of the machine. It added up.

"I don't think he's screwing the bitch," Mattie was saying. "Not yet, anyways. Hell, he still goes to church twice a week!"

Bessie snorted. "Honey, if it weren't for ministers and married men, half the whorehouses east of the Mississippi would be outta business."

You oughta know, Allie thought.

Allie still wasn't quite sure what to think about Bessie Earp. Virgil's older brother James had married Bess fifteen years ago, but Bessie ran bordellos even after that, and she'd kept working until her tumors got bad last year. James didn't seem to mind, Virg said, but Allie found it all pretty strange.

174

"None of the other Jews in town will talk to her," Bess was telling Mattie, in a consoling sort of way. "And the quality know she's just a floozy who calls herself a *actress* — like that's any better'n a whore! You know that theater society they got? She went to one of their meetings and said, 'Why don't we do *Pinafore*?' They cut her dead. Went home with her tail between her legs, I heard."

"That's why she's got so much time to do all that fancy baking Wyatt talks about," said Allie. "Nothing else to do." Pedaling furiously, Allie scowled at the endless line of stitches emerging beneath the needle. "I was buying thread at the mercantile t'other day, and she went by with her nose in the air. Out in daylight with her bosoms half-nekkid. Shameless, I call her, parading around on Johnny Behan's arm, and all while she's playing up to Wyatt."

"Mattie, honey, you ain't the first, and you sure as hell won't be the last," Bessie told her. "You want to know why a man cheats? Because he can. Simple as that. Anyways, why do you care? I should think you'd've had enough of that side of life when you was on the street. Twenty-five years was enough for me, Lord knows, but James is only forty. I hope he *is* goin' elsewhere."

"Bessie!" Allie cried.

Bessie shrugged. "It's true. I'm sick of the whole business."

Bess was trying to make Mattie feel better, but the whole conversation was making Allie angry and scared. She was pretty sure Virg stayed out of the brothels when he was transporting prisoners and whatnot, but he had a legal wife up in Iowa somewhere. Nobody would say a thing about it if Virg decided to get himself somebody prettier or nicer or more educated than Allie Sullivan.

She glanced over at Louisa Houston to see how she was taking all this. Lou was a quiet little thing, fragile-looking and sweet-tempered. She was a good match for Morgan, who doted on her, but Morg rode shotgun for Wells Fargo and he was out of town as much as Virg and Wyatt.

Lou rarely joined in when the others gossiped, and when she finally spoke of Josie Marcus, she just sounded curious, not angry or spiteful. "I wonder where she learned to bake like that. Morg heard her father's a banker. Seems odd she'd be so good in the kitchen. Wouldn't a family like that have servants for chores like cooking?"

"Well, it don't seem fair to me," Allie muttered, pedaling again. "There's her, out having a nice time, and here's us, working our fingers raw." Allie stopped and looked at the three women who were her sisters-in-law, for all practical purposes. "Why should that woman have all the fun? That's what I'd like to know!"

Gradually the idea took hold. If Johnny Behan's hussy could do it, then why shouldn't the Earps' women fix themselves up and go downtown? For almost a year, they'd heard wagons rumbling past their homes and wondered at the contents of the passing freighters' crated cargo. Where was the harm in doing a little window-shopping at Tombstone's splendid stores? Why not see the town's grand hotels and fancy restaurants for themselves? It was a free country, wasn't it?

Still, they hesitated, for this was a greater insurrection than they had ever previously contemplated, fraught with danger and the possibility of disgrace. They'd listened to their men remark upon the rapid progress downtown, but what did the brothers talk about most of the time? Crime, that's what. Stabbings and shootings and holdups. Fistfights and arrests and prisoners. James wasn't a lawman, but he ran a tavern for Chinks on the edge of town and white men would come in sometimes just to start a brawl. Even Doc Holliday had been assaulted! And that was in the Oriental, where Wyatt Earp's name should have protected him! Who was safe in a town like that?

And while they did not wish to fall to the level of "Mrs. Behan," none of them had more than the sketchiest notion as to what constituted respectability in Tombstone, Arizona. As the wife of a tavern owner, Bessie was one step from the bottom of the social ladder, so long as no one outside the family knew about her past. Mattie Blaylock was a former hooker. It was a rare john who looked at a whore's face, but either of them might be recognized by one of thousands of men who'd used them in the old days. Lou had never turned tricks, but she was working in a dance hall when Morg met her. They were living together without the state's sanction or a clergyman's blessing — a fact Lou's father belabored in weekly letters, calling her a harlot, begging her to repent and return home. As for Allie, well, if Virgil Earp hadn't stopped by the restaurant that day, she'd have been fired for insolence soon enough. Where would she have been then? On the street, is where.

In all those months, these four women had not once breached the unseen walls of what they believed to be propriety, but a question had been asked and lingered unanswered: Why should that Marcus woman have all the fun?

Days passed. Then weeks. Finally, the stars aligned. Wyatt was in Tucson, talking to Bob Paul about running for sheriff. Virg was up in Prescott, delivering a prisoner to the feds. Morgan was on a stage run for Wells Fargo.

James would be at the tavern until three or four in the morning.

Neat in ironed shirtwaists with snug, high-buttoned jackets, the Earp women clinked chipped china mugs and drank two fingers of Dutch courage before tying bonnet bows under nice, clean faces. Gathering their nerve and their long full skirts, they set off for town with heads held high, as though they had every right to be out on their own and needed no man's permission or protection.

"Lordy! Will you look at that!" Bessie cried when they got to the corner of First and Allen. "It's like Nashville before the war!"

"Bigger than Council Bluffs, that's certain," Allie said.

"Bigger than Topeka, too," Mattie breathed, awed.

Buoyed by the energy and bustle of the crowds that jammed the boardwalks, they linked arms to keep from getting separated and moved down Allen Street, admiring the merchandise in each store window. They actually went into a furniture shop for a few moments, but the proprietor scared them off, chattering about "Eastlake" and "the Ee-setic movement." Even if they'd had the cash to buy something, new furniture would have been impossible to explain when the brothers got home, so they retreated back outside.

"This sun is killing me," Mattie muttered, squinting into the glare. Bright light seemed to bother her more and more these days, making her eyes water and nose run. Her arms were starting to itch, too, and rubbing them didn't seem to help. "I think I need to go home," she told Lou.

"Oh, not yet!" Lou cried. "Is it a headache, Mattie? I have some laudanum in my purse."

"You are a lifesaver! It's so hot!" Mattie complained, dabbing at her dampening face with a hankie while Lou dug through her purse. "Is this all you have?" she asked, frowning at the little brown bottle Lou offered.

"I never use much," Lou told her, adding in a whisper, "It binds me."

Mattie turned away from the street and drained the contents, closing her eyes to concentrate on the warmth of the opium-infused alcohol: always a welcome sign that relief was on the way.

"Mattie's feeling a little faint," Lou told the others. "There's an ice cream parlor over there. That'll cool us off."

They spent a nickel each on dishes of vanilla and sat at a little table by a window, spooning in the cold, creamy treat while taking note of the new fashions. Faces were shaded by parasols, not sunbonnets. Fancy little hats perched on hair that was swept back and piled up. Sleeves were tight. Skirts were narrow across the front now, ruffled and swagged in back. Everything was decorated with tassels, bows, and lace.

"Well, I reckon we can fix our things up with doodads, too," Bessie said. "We can tell the boys we saw it in a magazine."

"Hell, none of 'em'll notice doodads," Allie said.

"Wyatt wouldn't notice if I grew another arm," Mattie grumbled.

"Feeling any better, Mattie?" Lou asked.

"Yes. Yes, I am," Mattie said. The itching had stopped, and she wasn't perspiring anymore.

"You should be careful when you clean your hairbrush," Allie advised. "If birds use the hair to build a nest, you'll have headaches for the whole year."

This notion provoked a lively discussion. According to Allie, it was a well-known fact. Not being Irish, the others had never heard of such a thing.

"You can cure a headache with a piece of sheet that's touched a corpse," Allie informed them. "Tie it just above your eyes."

"I'd rather have the headache," Bessie said, but Mattie told her, "If you had them like I do, you'd try anything."

Finished with their ice cream, they returned to the boardwalk and started back the way they came. They'd all had enough excitement for one day and were ready to go home, but Allie slowed down and stopped in front of the Occidental Hotel's restaurant. There, chalked on a blackboard out in front of the Maison Doree, was the longest menu she had ever seen, even back when she was a waitress.

"Lou, what does all that say?" she asked.

Morgan's girl was the only one among them who had more than a passing acquaintance with the alphabet, but even she had trouble reading the impressive list aloud.

Chicken Giblet and Consome, with Egg
Columbia River Salmon, au Buerre et Noir
Fillet a Boueff, a la Financier
Leg of Lamb, sauce Oysters
Corned beef and Cabbage
Lapine Domestique
Peach, Apple, Plum and Custard Pies
California Fresh Peach a la Conde

"Damn if I know what half them words mean," Bessie said.

"There's more," Lou told them. "At the bottom, it says, 'We will have it or perish. This dinner will be served for fifty cents.' "

"All that for fifty cents?" Mattie wondered.

"I'm not sure," Lou admitted.

"We could buy one dinner and all four eat parts of it," Allie suggested.

"Or, perhaps you will do me the honor of bein' my guests."

They turned at the sound of that soft Georgia voice and saw Doc Holliday, leaning on his cane.

"Ladies," he said, "it would be my very great pleasure to take y'all to dinner this eve-nin'."

The Peer of Murderous Mars

Inside the Maison Doree, gaslight chandeliers gleamed and oil paintings in big gilt frames hung on wallpaper that shimmered like silk. Crystal sparkled on big round tables covered with white damask, and there was silver *everywhere.* Silver vases, silver platters, silver pitchers, silver teapots, silver coffee urns, and silver cutlery that clinked quietly against white bone china decorated with wide silver bands.

"Everybody's dressed up like it's a wedding," Allie whispered.

"Except that one," Bessie whispered, lifting her chin toward a man wearing a black suit with a starched white shirt who was hurrying toward the door to meet them. "He oughta be runnin' funerals."

Doc kept a straight face as he removed his hat and requested, "A table for five, please. Toward the back."

The man bowed and said, "Very good, sir," and made a sweeping gesture when he said,

"Follow me, ladies, if you please."

"Well, I guess we *do* please," Bessie said, sashaying a little, but she didn't say it real loud.

Everything seemed hushed and special as they made their way down the length of the long, narrow dining room, their steps cushioned and quieted by carpets. Over in a corner, a fiddler was playing something slow and soft, and all around them there was a murmur of conversation.

"That's Doc Holliday," someone whispered, but only after the little party was out of earshot. And if anyone in that room was inclined to disdain clean calico and dowdy hats, he wisely kept his remark inaudible to the thin man with the refined face who accompanied four unfashionable ladies to the far end of the room.

Doc took his place with his back to the wall, silent while he caught his breath. Exclaiming over the elegance of their surroundings, the girls had barely settled into their seats when a man with a white towel wrapped around his middle arrived at the table.

"Champagne Perrier-Jouet for the ladies," Doc told him. "Bourbon, neat, for me."

"Very good, sir," the man replied, giving a little bow before he turned on his heel and swanned off toward a huge walnut bar.

"Well, I never!" Allie whispered. "A man waitress?"

"And him wearing an apron!" Mattie cried softly.

"Girls, we need to get us one of those at home!" Bessie declared. "I should think a fella like him would be awful handy to have around."

"Look how pretty these candlesticks are!" Lou exclaimed. "Do you suppose all this silver comes from right here in Tombstone, Doc?"

He'd started to answer when the door banged open at the other end of the room. Three men sauntered in like they owned the place, and though the fiddler kept playing, conversations ended, one by one, around the room.

Allie twisted in her chair and sized up the newcomers. Drunk, all three of them, she noted with an ex-waitress's automatic disapproval of difficult customers.

The cleanest and soberest was smiling broadly and acting like everyone in the restaurant had been waiting for him to arrive so the party could begin. Black trousers were bloused into knee-high tooled boots, and his spurs dragged big brass rowels across that nice carpet. Still, he appeared to have had a bath recently. Clean black curls sprang out beneath a sombrero, which he now removed and used to knock the dust off his clothes.

Which might have been nice of him, if he'd done it outside.

The loudest and dirtiest was bearded and coatless. A red shirt, faded to pink, gray with dust where it wasn't wet with sweat stains. Battered leather vest. Filthy canvas trousers with a pistol jammed into the waistband at the small of his back. He was talking a lot but seemed nervous, too. Showing off, but not really sure of himself.

He'll probably break something before he leaves, Allie thought sourly.

The quietest stayed by the entrance, swaying slightly. Cleaner than the dirty one, drunker than the clean one. Two guns, a knife in his boot, and the look of a man who'd welcome a reason to explode.

That one's trouble, Allie thought. And Doc Holliday must have been thinking the same thing, for she heard him say, "Miss Allie, I wonder if you would move your chair a little to the left."

With his view of the room clear, Doc unbuttoned his coat and drew a flat silver case from an inside pocket. Eyes on the quiet man at the door, he removed a slim black cigar from the case, which went back into his pocket. He left his coat open.

The loud one was at the bar now, leaning over a large brass tray, poking at odd-shaped items displayed on ice. "Waddya call *them* things?" he was asking the bartender. "Huh? Huh? Waddya call *them*?"

"Those are oysters, sir, iced and shipped in

daily, direct from —"

"Oysters? *Oysters,* you call 'em? Well, damn if they don't look like elephant boogers to me!"

It was a joke his friends had heard before. The curly-haired one smiled indulgently. The quiet one looked away, bored. The nice people in the restaurant pretended not to hear him, but that just made him laugh louder at his own cleverness.

Moron, Allie thought.

He was driving business away, too. A pair of new customers took a step or two inside the restaurant and turned right around when they heard the loudmouth holler, "Just like elephant boogers! I swear!"

Just then, the waiter returned with a little table only big enough for a silver ice bucket with a heavy green bottle in it. As he pulled the dripping bottle out of the ice and wrapped it in a white napkin, Allie jerked her head toward the three drunks and asked, "Who in hell are those idiots?"

That startled a laugh out of Doc, who'd been lighting his cigar. Smoke and amusement set off a coughing fit, but he was smiling behind his handkerchief when a second waiter arrived with four tall, narrow glasses and Doc's bourbon in a cut-glass snifter on a silver tray.

"Cow Boys. Old Man Clanton's boys," the first waiter told Allie. "The comedian is the old man's son — Ike. The chummy one is Curly Bill Brocius." He glanced over his shoulder and turned back toward Doc Holliday to warn, "The one by the door? That's Johnny Ringo."

Who was staring at Doc.

While the second waiter placed a glass in front of each lady, the first one removed the little wire cage from the green bottle's cork, which he gripped and twisted. He had just about eased it out of the bottle when it suddenly came loose with a *pop!* that made Allie and the other girls jump.

When they finished exclaiming over the startling noise of the uncorking and how the champagne fizzed in their mouths, Doc helped them with the menu. ("The French is more ambitious than authentic," he told them.) Everybody was trying to pretend that things weren't getting worse down at the other end of the restaurant. Curly Bill was wandering around the dining room, his manner offensively friendly as he leaned over tables, asking, "How is that? Any good? Would you recommend that dish?" Ike Clanton was still talking about the elephant he'd seen at a carnival one time.

Ringo had not taken his eyes off Doc Holliday since the coughing fit, but now he turned his head slowly. "Ike," he said, dead-eyed, "shut up."

Ike's face went slack. He covered his unease

with a nervous laugh, like what Ringo said was a joke. Curly Bill changed the subject by reaching across a table and taking something off a stiff-faced mining executive's plate. "Now *that* is real damn good!" he declared, chewing. "We should have us some of that, Juanito! C'mon, Ike!" he called, beckoning his companions toward a table near the front window. "Let's get something to eat."

Conversations around the room resumed, and yet another waiter arrived at the table in the back, bearing little cups filled halfway up with brown water.

"Might be I could worry some of that down," Allie said, "if it didn't have them little weeds in it."

"That would be parsley, Miss Alvira," Doc told her. "It is meant to add color without harmin' the soup very much."

"They got some nerve callin' this soup," Bessie said, frowning at the novelty. "Nothin' much in it."

"*Consommé* is French for 'broth,' " Doc told her. "It is meant to arouse the appetite without layin' it to rest."

"It's nice," Lou said after an experimental taste. "It'd be easy to make, too."

"I admire your new suit, Doc," Mattie said. "It's very *becoming*."

Allie noticed Mattie said that like it was some kind of private little joke between her and Doc. The dentist's eyes warmed up, like

Mattie'd done good, but he sounded doubtful about the judgment.

"It is very kind of you to say so, Miss Mattie. I am disappointed in it myself. Martha Anne — she is a very dear cousin of mine, Miss Alvira, back in Georgia — Martha Anne asked me to send my photograph. I thought a double-breasted suit might bulk me up some, but I fear she will receive the picture and think it a portrait of an unusually sturdy ghost."

"Well, *I* think you look nice," Mattie said. "Are your headaches better?"

"Infrequent, and not so severe as your own," Doc said, reaching over to squeeze her hand briefly.

"Morg and I miss having you at the house," Lou told him.

Allie's ears pricked up at that, for she knew Lou was glad when Doc's head cleared enough for him to move into a boardinghouse nearby.

"Miss Louisa, there is no plumb that could sound the depths of your hospitality, but I expect you two are relieved to have your home to yourselves again."

"You were no trouble at all," Lou assured him.

Another lie, Allie noted. I guess *Miss Louisa* ain't so pure as she looks!

"How is your new place, Doc?" Mattie asked.

191

"Clean, quiet, and entirely suitable to my small needs. Mrs. Fly is a very competent cook who is determined to fatten me up. I wish her well in this endeavor, though I don't imagine she will succeed."

"I heard she's a photographer, too," Bessie said. "Not just her husband."

"A photographer?" Allie cried. "Her own self?"

Doc nodded. "Yes. Mr. Fly travels a good deal and Mrs. Fly does much of the studio work in his absence. She's the one who took my picture."

The waiters arrived again. Soup cups were removed to make room for the main course.

"The rabbit is real tasty," Bessie said after a few bites. "How's that lamb, Mattie?"

"Better'n elk. More like venison but not so chewy."

Allie was staring suspiciously at the fish on Lou's plate, and Lou didn't look much happier.

"Salmon is supposed to be that color," Doc told them. " 'Try one bite, sugar.' That's what my mamma used to say, Miss Louisa. If you don't like it, we shall send it back and order you something else."

Lou picked up her fork and carried a little piece of the strange pink fish toward her lips. "Kind of a strong taste," she admitted, "but I like it enough to keep going."

"And how are you findin' your corned beef

and cabbage, Miss Alvira?"

"Good," Allie said, then held her tongue.

Doc Holliday was always so polite Allie suspected he was making fun of people, even if she couldn't quite work out how. Sometimes he didn't talk at all, but when he did, he talked a streak, and a lot of it was hard to understand. The other girls knew Doc from when they were all living up in Dodge, but Allie had only met him here in Tombstone after he got hit in the head. The clerk at the sundry store told her about how dangerous Doc was, but when she asked Virg about him, Virg just smiled. "Well, now, Pickle, tales are told that Doc Holliday has murdered men and committed crimes around the country, but when you ask a fella how he knows all that, it's just gossip and hearsay. Wyatt checked into it back in Dodge, but nothing much could be traced up to Doc's account. And Morgan thinks highly of him." Bessie liked Doc, too, but what caught Allie's interest was the way Mattie brightened up and got sort of shiny when Doc was around.

Of course, all four of the girls were feeling pretty shiny by the time they finished their main courses, for they were working on their second bottle of champagne. Doc himself just sipped at his bourbon whenever his cough got bad. He didn't eat much either — no wonder he was so skinny! But when the waiter asked about dessert, Doc said, "Let's have one of everything for the ladies to try. And I myself would like to see how a California peach stacks up against the Georgia variety."

"When was you home last, Doc?" Bessie asked, sounding a little wistful.

"Mercy . . . Must be seven years now." He stared at nothing for a time, then shook the mood off. "You ever consider a trip back to Nashville, Miss Bessie?"

"No kin there. None who'd care to know me, anyways."

"Yes. And if my family ever finds out what *I* do . . ." Doc left that hanging. "We had an acquaintance from Charleston back before the war — he was from a very good family, but a thing or two happened and his fortunes changed. When it became known that he was reduced to gamblin' for his livin' " — Doc paused to draw his silver case from that inside pocket and removed another slim black cigar — "no one in society would so much as speak his name. I fear my fate would be the same."

"What's wrong with gambling?" Allie asked. "Everybody gambles!"

"It's not gamblin' *per se* that is objectionable, Miss Alvira. It's professional gamblin'. I do for a livin' what respectable folks do for recreation."

"Like a whore," Bessie said. "Most women do it. Some of us get paid, is all."

Doc had barely puffed on the little cigar to

get the burn started before the smoke set off a nasty coughing fit. Allie herself didn't mind a pipe of tobacco now and then, but she reckoned she'd have the sense to give it up if smoking made her cough herself blue that way.

"Should I get you another?" Mattie asked, glancing at Doc's empty glass.

Still coughing, Doc nodded, handkerchief over his mouth. Mattie turned toward the bar, holding up Doc's empty and waggling it at the bartender.

Once again, folks in the restaurant were starting to go quiet. Allie reckoned that was because of the disgusting, croupy noise of Doc's cough. You could tell he was sorry for making this ugly racket, for he'd turned away from the table to face the wall, but when the violinist stopped playing in the middle of a tune, Allie looked behind her and saw why.

At the other end of the long room, Johnny Ringo was on his feet and headed toward the table in the back.

He was handsome, almost. Tall, slim. Boyish features. Mussed-up red-brown hair. But he was really drunk now. Mumbling to himself. "Lunger. Pathetic lunger. Die and be done with it, why don't you?"

Halfway along, he staggered against a table. The gentlemen sitting there moved quickly to catch their glasses before their drinks spilled. A few steps later, he almost banged into the waiter who was bringing Doc another bourbon. The waiter hesitated, but Ringo didn't. He just snatched that heavy crystal glass right off the silver tray and carried it himself to the table at the back of the room.

"Come out here for the dry air, did you?" he asked Doc.

Handkerchief still over his mouth, John Henry Holliday turned.

"Won't help," Ringo told him. "Sunshine won't help. Rest won't help. This won't help." Ringo lifted the glass high. "Nothing's gonna help you, lunger." He drained the bourbon in three long swallows before tossing the glass at the wall. "Nothing's gonna help you. Nothing but a gun. Pain'll get so bad, you'll want to die. It'll get worse, and worse, and worse, until you blow your own head off. Bony old skull, making everyone remember death. Walking *momento mori,* that's all you are."

"It's *memento,* not *momento,*" Doc murmured, "but I suppose the metaphor is apt."

Ringo didn't even pause. "Every day is *el Día de los Muertos* when a lunger's around! Why don't you just put a gun to your head? Pull the trigger, and the pain'll end — just like that!" Ringo said, snapping his fingers, his voice rising now. "Why don't you just be *done* with it? Too scared? Too scared to do it yourself? I'll put you out of your misery, lunger. Say the word. I'll shoot you, and it'll be over — just like *that.*"

196

"Careful, Juanito," Curly Bill called, making his voice jolly. He was on his way to the back of the room, with Ike Clanton trailing him. "That's Doc Holliday."

"Yeah, Johnny, that's Doc Holliday," Ike repeated, smiling uncertainly.

"Doc Holliday?" Ringo's dead eyes glittered. "Well, now . . . I've heard of you, Holliday! I'm Johnny Ringo. You heard of me, Holliday?"

"I cannot say that I have had that pleasure, sir, though I must confess that I was not listenin' attentively."

"Well, I've heard of you."

"So you mentioned." The coughing had stopped. Laying his handkerchief on the table beside his plate, Doc sat back in his chair. Allowing the drape of his coat to slip back. Letting a brace of pistols become visible.

"Oooh, now, lookit *them*!" Curly Bill said, with fun in his voice. "I heard Doc Holliday's *real* fast, Juanito! I heard he dropped Mike Gordon over in New Mexico! Single shot, straight through the heart!"

"Yeah?" Johnny said, eyes still on Doc's. "Well, I heard he emptied a gun in the Oriental and only hit a bartender in the toe."

"In the toe!" Ike Clanton repeated, cackling.

Ignoring Bill and Ike, John Henry Holliday kept his eye on Ringo. "I have no quarrel with you, sir, but if you insist on makin' one," he

197

said, his voice mild and musical, "let us choose a time and place when there are no ladies present to have their evenin' spoiled by a boorish, drunken, belligerent cracker."

"Ladies?" Ringo sneered. "I don't see no —"

In an instant, Doc was on his feet, cane in hand, ready to beat the man to the ground. Mattie half-stood, crying, "Doc! No!"

That was when Fred White arrived, alerted by the restaurant staff to an impending fracas. He and Curly Bill shouldered in between Holliday and Ringo, pushing the pair apart, staying between them until it was clear that the two didn't propose to make a shooting matter out of it.

"Don't mind Ringo, Marshal," Curly Bill said with good-natured smile. "He's just drunk. No harm done, right?"

"Dammit, Bill, you told me you'd keep him out of Tombstone!"

Curly Bill's smile was rueful now. "I do my best, Marshal. I truly do." He clapped Ringo on the shoulder and said, "C'mon, Juanito! Time to go."

"Yeah," Ike said. "Time to go, Juanito!"

Looking vaguely in Ike's direction, Ringo seemed to lose his train of thought. Then, without warning, he buried his fist in Ike's belly, doubling the man over.

There were small cries of surprise and dismay around the room. Ike dropped to his knees, windless and bug-eyed.

"Ike," Ringo said as he moved toward the door, "if you had half a brain, you'd be twice as smart."

Arms over his chest, Fred White stayed where he was, blocking Holliday's way. Curly Bill — smiling and murmuring encouragement — got Ike to his feet and steered him out of the restaurant.

When all three of the Cow Boys had left the building, Fred called out, "It's over, folks. Enjoy your meals."

The fiddler began a sprightly tune. Conversation began to buzz.

Fred took a step back from Doc Holliday so he could study the man. The Earp brothers all vouched for Holliday. They claimed the dentist never started anything. He was trembling after that little dustup, and Ringo was always looking for a fight, so could be Holliday hadn't started the trouble, but some men just seemed to draw it, like shit draws flies.

"It's over," Fred said. "Right, Doc?"

"Never started, Marshal," Holliday replied softly.

"Well, see that it don't," Fred said.

The marshal left, but Doc remained on his feet until Mattie put a hand on his arm. Blinking rapidly, he didn't seem to recognize her for a few moments. He came to himself at last and sat down, using his arms to control the drop into his chair. "My apologies for the unpleasantness, ladies."

"Wasn't your fault," Mattie said firmly.

"You got some kinda history with him?" Bessie asked.

"Never saw him before in my life."

"Well, something set him off," Allie said.

"The coughing, I think," Lou said.

Presently a team of waiters returned to the table: one with a whisk broom to clean up the shards of crystal on the floor; another bringing a replacement drink to Doc; a third carrying a large silver tray laden with sweets, which were distributed and shared. The girls concentrated on their pie, but Doc didn't touch a thing. Not even his peach.

It was Lou who brought him around. "That man is wandering in the wilderness," she said quietly. "He is angry because he is lost. And . . . he's afraid."

Doc's eyes came to rest on Lou's. "Well, now . . . ain't you somethin'."

For a time, he was thoughtful, simply gazing at each of his companions. Apart from Allie — wary but fearless, he judged her — these women had seen him at his lowest, back in Dodge: all but naked, trying not to drown in the blood rising in his eroded lungs. Terrified, and so near to death that he himself did not expect to see the morning. He had no secrets from Mattie and Bessie and Lou.

Back in control, he squeezed Lou's hand

briefly before addressing them more generally. "Perhaps it would be best if we do not
mention any of this to your menfolk."

"No argument from me," Allie said.

One by one, her co-conspirators nodded
their agreement.

■ ■ ■ ■

Clanless, Lawless, Homeless Men

■ ■ ■ ■

Beneath the Sun
and Starry Skies

Curly Bill Brocius was feeling pretty satisfied with the day's accomplishments as he shepherded Ike Clanton and Johnny Ringo out of Tombstone that evening. True enough, Juanito had gotten a little out of hand at the end, but Fred White was a good old boy. As long as you didn't make *too* much trouble right inside town limits, the city marshal was willing to turn a blind eye. Course, Fred understood that Bill Brocius couldn't really order anyone to stay out of Tombstone, Johnny Ringo least of all. All Bill could do was encourage the boys to seek their entertainment in Charleston, about eight miles south, where no federal, territorial, county, or town officials were around to spoil the fun. That was logic even liquored-up youngsters could understand.

Curly Bill himself rarely dealt directly with customers, so he was surprised when Old Man Clanton sent him into the city.

"I'm buying a place in New Mexico," Mr.

Clanton had told Curly Bill last night. "Go into Tombstone in the morning and sell off that new herd. I want better'n five dollars a head and I want cash. Take Ike and Ringo with you."

One by one, Old Man Clanton was buying up a string of ranches from the Mexican border to the mining towns of southeastern Arizona. The idea was to turn the entire length of the transport route into private property. *Posse Comitatus* would take the army out of the calculation. Then all you had to do was buy off the Pima County sheriff and your business was secure.

Curly Bill admired the old man's thinking and was determined to bring equal acumen to his own task. Riding from the Clanton ranch to Tombstone, he'd spent hours in careful consideration of which buyer he ought to approach and how. By the time the city came into view, he had settled on the mining district's second-biggest meat supplier, for the top man would be satisfied with his status and not inclined to try anything new, whereas the next man down might aspire to improve upon his position and would be more open to strategy.

"Now, Mr. Clanton says I can offer you a real good price on a herd that's just come in, direct from Mexico," Curly Bill told Number Two that morning, "but you gotta make up your mind right now. He's in a hurry to make this deal, and there's others I can take it to."

You could see the man thinking. The cattle on offer would not enjoy their customary stay in Sulphur Springs Valley for fattening. Their meat would be stringy and tough. "I don't know," he said cautiously. "If the customers complain about quality, it could cost me a contract."

"Just work the cheap meat into the mix," Bill suggested. "The miners might grouse about a meal or two — or maybe one man's stew is fine and his friend's is chewy. They won't be able to tell what's going on."

"They won't be able to tell!" Ike said cheerfully.

Ike tended to repeat things that way. It made him sound stupid, but Ike had his reasons, which were good and sufficient, in Curly Bill's estimation.

"Since you're getting the herd so cheap," Bill went on, "you could maybe drop your price to the chow houses a little. They get a sweet deal now, and maybe you get a bigger slice of their business next year. In the meantime, you pocket the difference."

"Pocket the difference," Ike said.

Bill waited patiently, watching the decision come closer. "Everybody wins," he said with an amiable grin, "except the miners!"

"Except the miners!" Ike said.

You could see Number Two wondering if Ike had been born dumb or if his old man made him that way. Then his eyes fell upon Johnny Ringo, who was standing over at the shop window like he wasn't paying any attention, and Curly Bill's smile widened. Old Man Clanton was a shrewd one, all right. Ike's face almost always sported the kind of yellowing bruises that reminded you how it was ill-advised to make the old man unhappy. And Ringo? All he had to do was stand there and a sensible person would take a herd that still spoke Spanish.

"Four dollars a head," Number Two tried. Half the going price.

"Five twenty-five," Bill countered.

"Four fifty."

Over at the window, Ringo blew a little noise of annoyance.

"Four seventy-five," Two said firmly. "Best I can do."

Ringo turned and stared with those dead-snake eyes of his. It was about then that Number Two started to sweat. Granted, the day was warming up.

"All right," he said. "Five fifteen."

"Toss in an extra twenty for me and the boys," Curly Bill suggested, upping the ante, "and you got yourself a deal."

"You got yourself a deal!" Ike said happily.

"Ike," Ringo said, "the devil himself is going to recommend you to God, just to keep you out of hell."

Ike's mouth worked a bit. You could see he

was trying to decide if that was good or bad, but he shut up while he figured it out.

"I'm going to the library," Ringo said on his way out the door.

"Always reading," Bill said, shaking his head. "Juanito's a strange one." Smiling brightly, he returned to the business at hand. "Mr. Clanton requires cash, sir. That won't be a problem, will it?"

It was, but Number Two came around on that as well. Afterward, Bill and Ike met up with Ringo again and they had themselves a time in the bars and brothels out past Sixth Street before heading over for a real good meal at the Maison Doree.

It was too bad Fred White got drawn into that little standoff with Doc Holliday — what in hell was *that* all about? — but Ringo didn't shoot anybody and only broke a glass. Ike's belly would stop hurting in a few days, and Bill himself was pleased to have something cheerful to report to Ike's old man.

Yep, he thought as the Clanton ranch house came into view in the moonlight. It was a damn fine day, all around.

If old man Clanton had a first name, nobody living used it. As far as anyone in Arizona knew, he'd been born with a week-old beard and iron-gray hair. Mean, straight out of his mamma's womb.

His wife called him "sir." Once, just after

Ike was born, she tried to run away, but the old man tracked her down and brought her back bleeding. "Try that again," he told her, "I'll nail your feet to a four-foot plank. That'll stop you running."

It was about that time the old man quit shaving himself and started making his wife do it. Once a week, in honor of the Sabbath, he'd lie back and let her take a straight razor to him. He smiled once a week, too, when she scraped that razor's edge over his neck. It amused him to know that she was that close to killing him but didn't have the sand to do it.

She was weak. That was the old man's opinion. She came of weak stock, and she was a bad breeder. Most of her brats lived, but they were worthless, all of them. Except maybe the youngest — Billy was the best of the lot. Alonzo, though . . . There was something wrong with that one, right from the start. The night that ugly little toad was born, the old man took him to a horse trough, meaning to drown him, but Ike came running up, sniveling and promising to take care of the brat.

"Take him then," the old man said. "Cryin' little babies, the pair of you."

Alonzo was feeble-minded and seemed happiest with dogs. Cows liked him, too. They'd walk right up to him, let him pat their noses. He had cow eyes — calm, quiet, stupid eyes

— but sometimes he'd panic, the way cattle panic. He'd run in big circles, screaming and screaming with those cow eyes open wide, flapping his hands like chicken wings.

Ike was the only one who cried when Alonzo died.

"Figures," the old man said. "That just figures."

When the war broke out, Old Man Clanton took his three oldest boys — Joe, Phin, and Ike — traveling across the South to enlist in one regiment after another. They'd stay in camp just long enough to get the signing bonus, take off in the middle of the night, and then do it again in the next state over.

The old man didn't give a damn about abolitionists or the Cause. "Not our fight," he told his sons. "Fight for niggers or fight for planters and either way, you're a damn fool. Damn fools deserve what happens to 'em."

The old man's drinking got worse when his wife died. Ike was nineteen by then. He might have gone off on his own like his older brothers had, but Ike stayed and that was his misfortune.

True to his watered-down nature, he took his mother's place, trying to keep the littler kids fed and out of trouble. Billy was only four and he was a handful, but Ike took special care of him.

211

"Do as you're told, and don't never talk back," Ike always warned Billy. "Just say whatever the old man says, and you'll be all right." But Billy never listened to Ike. Billy never much listened to anybody. And what puzzled Ike was, the old man seemed to admire Billy for that.

After the war, the old man took the family to California for a while but he couldn't make a go of it there, so they doubled back in 1877 and settled in a portion of nowhere called the Arizona Territory. The old man staked out a townsite, called the place Clantonville, and prepared to become rich. He put ads in newspapers, expecting to draw settlers who'd buy parcels of empty land off him and make him mayor. Nothing much came of the scheme, but he didn't blame himself. His failures weren't for want of trying, and that's what infuriated the old man about his son Ike.

"No gumption," he'd mutter. "No *try.*"

Course, all of Ike's *try* went into keeping the old man happy, but there's no pleasing some people. Ike opened a little restaurant for miners in Millville, and he did pretty well, but then it was "Getting ideas now? Getting above your old man, are you? I'll teach you to act high and mighty! I brought you into this world, and I'll send you to hell whenever I please."

It wasn't until the old man got into the cattle

business that the family really made good. Billy was only sixteen on his first raid, but the old man liked how he handled himself. "Best of the lot," the old man always said. "Good-looking, too, with a temper and some real guts." Ike, on the other hand, was useless. That was the old man's opinion.

Nobody was inclined to argue the point with him, not even Ike, who generally took things as he found them. The old man was just part of a world that included rattlers, scorpions, and a hundred kinds of cactus. You had to be careful in a world like that. You had to know what to watch for, what to listen for, what to avoid. Ike had made a particular study of his old man and knew when bad spells were coming on. After their mother died, Ike taught Billy and the girls how to see them coming, too.

"It's like thunderstorms," he told them.

The old man would get quieter and quieter, like that heavy, windless heat before a storm. Then there'd be a rumble of orders and threats, like thunder in the distance. *Shut your goddam mouth, or I'll shut it for you! Don't speak till you're spoken to! Do as you're told, God damn you, and be quick about it!* The old man's mood would get darker and darker, like clouds piling up, and he'd get angrier, like wind rising. Then he'd explode. Lightning would strike the nearest target. *Give! Me! My!*

Due! the old man would yell over and over, a blow landing with each word, until he'd spent his fury on that week's unlucky child. Muttering would signal an end to the storm. *That'll teach you to talk back, you mouthy little bitch.* Or *Shoulda put you in a sack when you was born and drowned you like a sick pup, you worthless little bastard.* Then it was over, like a storm blowing itself out or passing on, out of sight.

You could learn to live with rage like that. It was predictable. You could see it coming and take cover. That's what Ike tried to teach his sisters and his little brother Billy. *Do as you're told. Don't talk back. Say whatever the old man says.*

Mostly the girls took his advice, but when they didn't, Ike stepped in and took the beating for them. He was proud of that, but there'd been a price to pay.

"How long you worked for him?" Sherm McMasters asked Curly Bill once.

"Old Man Clanton? Must be a coupla years now," Bill said.

They were bringing a herd north after a raid into Mexico. The younger boys were settling the animals into a draw for the night while the older ones made camp. Ike had the cook fire going, with the beans heating in a kettle. There was a Dutch oven in the embers.

214

Biscuits tonight. Say what you would, Ike was a damn fine cook.

"Pay's good," Sherm acknowledged, "but he's a tough man to deal with."

That made Curly Bill smile. "Sherm, the old man's easy as pie. Right, Ike?"

Ike nodded. "Do what he tells you. Say what he says."

Ringo was lying on his back, head propped against his saddle, holding a book up to make the best of the sunset and the firelight. "The old man's like everybody else out here. Nobody goes west except failures, misfits, and deluded lungers."

"Failures, misfits, and lungers," Ike said, adding chilies to the beans.

"That may be stretching things some," Sherm said, but he was real quiet about it. He wanted Curly Bill to hear but wasn't taking a chance on setting Ringo off. Old Man Clanton might take a horsewhip to you, but Ringo would kill you.

"I think Juanito may have the right of it," Curly Bill decided after a time. "A fella's doing well back east, he's likely to stay put. I wager there are very few men who wake up in Philadelphia, say, or Cincinnati and look into their mirrors and think, I'm prosperous and my life is wonderful. I guess it's time to turn my back on all this good fortune and head west!"

"Head west," Ike said.

Ringo's book went down against his thighs. "Ike," he said wearily, "we could replace you with a goddam parrot and nobody'd notice the difference."

"Parrots can't cook," Ike pointed out. "They can talk, though. I saw one at a carnival once. And an elephant, too."

"Jesus," Ringo said, and went back to his book.

The boys came straggling in for supper, but later that night Curly Bill's mind returned to Ringo's notion, for Bill was getting on toward forty and past the age when sleeping on the ground is easy.

Take the inhabitants of Texas, he thought, staring up at the stars. A man might wind up in Texas for any number of reasons, but few of them were based on solid achievement elsewhere. In Texas, your Pilgrim Fathers were leftover Mexicans, a bunch of land-hungry German immigrants, and hard-scrabble Scotch-Irish backwoodsmen. After the war, you added your white trash and bankrupt planters driven off their land by Yankee troops and carpetbagger taxes — all of them resentful about the way the war had ended. Course, there were Yankees in Texas, too. They were apt to be cheerful about the outcome of the conflict, but generally arrived in Texas just as broke. The past fifteen years had not been easy ones, what with the depression and the droughts and so on. Round the population out with orphans and runaways looking for others of their kind to gang up with — Johnny Ringo was a fair example of that. Anyway, "failure" might be too hard a word for those who'd come west. Unlucky, maybe.

If things had turned out just a little different, Bill himself might've been a ranch foreman by now. As it was, he held a similar sort of position, standing between Old Man Clanton and the boys. Settling disputes. Defusing fights. Keeping the business running, day to day.

Still and all, it was true enough that most men went west in search of a fresh start after a poor showing elsewhere. They might even go so far as to adopt a new name in an attempt to restore an unblemished record — a circumstance with which Curly Bill himself was familiar, for while he'd stuck with "William" after moving to Texas, he had so recently and so abruptly shifted from Graham to Bresnaham to Brocius that he was still unsettled as to how to spell his newest surname.

There were those who said Johnny Ringo's name was really Johann Rheingold. Juanito had denied that with a certain amount of heat, declaring that he had no love for Dutchies and sure as hell wasn't one himself. As far as Bill knew the story, Ringo got his start in Texas during the Mason County War, when the sons of German settlers ran afoul of the great-grandsons of Ulster clansmen, who considered cattle raids an old and honorable form of enterprise and entertainment. Mexican cattle were fair game for rustlers, but the Dutchies of Mason County objected to their well-bred European short-horns being run off and branded as mavericks. When Ringo got arrested for cattle theft, his young friends sprung him. The Rangers caught up with him later on and when they did, they had him on a murder charge. In those days, however, frontier jails were still in the experimental stage, hardly capable of holding a stray dog captive if it spotted a rabbit a few yards away. Ringo got loose and lit out for Mexico, where he picked up a little Spanish while drinking and lying low. That's where Curly Bill noticed him in a cantina and recruited him for a raid on a Sonora herd for Old Man Clanton.

Seemed like a good idea at the time.

Juanito wasn't like the rest of the boys. Juanito was intricate. He was sick a lot. Headaches. Stomach pains. He was fine when there was action to take his mind off his troubles, but when things got peaceful, Ringo got moody. When he got moody, he drank. And when he drank, Lord have mercy!

Once, in a bar up north near Prescott, Ringo offered to buy a man a whiskey. All that fella said was "No, thanks. I've got a beer." Ringo shot him in the neck. Just like that. Walked away like he'd swatted a fly. And he had this trick where he'd smile at a new kid who was looking to get into the gang. "You're all right," Ringo would say. "I like you. You're all right." Then he'd slug that kid in the gut with no warning at all. The new kid would drop to his knees, sucking air, and Ringo would walk away like nothing had happened.

The first time Ringo did that, it was so sudden and over so quick, nobody had time to react. Now, though, the boys all expected it, so they'd wait, grinning, and laugh their heads off when it happened. The new kid would be kneeling in the dirt with his eyes bugged out, and when he got enough breath back to ask what in hell he'd done to deserve *that,* the others would tell stories about how Ringo did the same thing to them once. Juanito always felt better afterward. And the kid who got punched was probably used to getting hit back home.

The moon was setting by the time Curly Bill was ready to drop off. He listened for a time to the cattle and the horses, to the night birds and the breeze. Fished a couple of stones out from under his bedroll. Turned onto his side.

Boys will be boys, he thought. His crew were just boys with fists, knives, pistols. And Johnny Ringo wasn't the only one with a warrant or two tied to his tail.

THIS RECKLESS COURAGE
WILL DESTROY YOU

"You seen these?" Frank McLaury asked his brother, slamming a collection of torn and crumpled papers onto the table.

Tommy smoothed out the least-damaged flyer and read it with growing dismay. Lieutenant Joseph Hurst was offering a reward for information leading to the arrest, trial, and conviction of the thieves who'd stolen six army mules, which were last seen in the possession of Frank and Thomas McLaury.

"They're tacked up all over the county," Frank told him. "I found one on our own damn fence post out front!"

"Well, it doesn't say *we* stole the mules," Tommy pointed out, but if Hurst's careful wording skirted a straight-up accusation of theft, the nuance was lost on Frank. "I promised him I'd bring the mules back and I didn't, so what was he to think?"

"That wasn't your fault," Frank countered, for Billy Clanton had shown up early the next morning, paid Frank for changing the brands, and taken possession of the animals again. "You couldn't have returned them."

"True," Tommy admitted, "but that would be hard to explain to a judge. And the fact is, we received stolen property. That's aiding and abetting, Frank."

Frank knew that was true, but he was the kind who just couldn't stop picking at a scab until it bled again, and the longer he thought about Hurst's flyer, the angrier he got.

All through supper, he fulminated about abuse of federal power and the army's interference in decent citizens' lives. While Tommy washed the dishes, Frank found paper and a pencil and stayed up late that night, composing an essay on the subject. Tom entertained some hope that this might get it out of Frank's system, but the next morning, Frank woke up with the phrase "damnable despotism" on his tongue and added it to the piece before he even went outside to take a piss. Later on, while he was fixing the roof of the horse shed, he came up with a line about how his honor had never been impugned before and he didn't propose to start tolerating it now. That sounded good, so he dropped the hammer, climbed off the shed, went back inside to rewrite the whole thing, and made Tommy listen to the essay again.

This was tedious but not alarming until later that day, when Frank managed to talk himself around to the notion that Lieutenant

Hurst had stolen the mules himself.

"He stole 'em and he sold 'em for his own gain," Frank declared, "and now that army sonofabitch is trying to pin the crime on us!"

"Billy Clanton stole those mules, and you know it," Tommy cried, boggled by this turn. "Frank, there are *witnesses* who *saw* the mules out in our coral!"

"Well, it's their word against ours!"

Tommy sighed, for there are people — his brother among them — who can become so convinced of their own rendering of events that believing something is tantamount to proof. Arguing only makes them dig in deeper. So Tommy stopped talking and hoped the whole thing would blow over, but Frank not only added the accusation against Hurst to his essay, he copied it all out again neatly. Then he saddled up and rode to town, determined to get it published.

Frank's first stop was at the office of the *Tombstone Epitaph*. He expected the editor to be sympathetic to the interests of one of the few Republican voters who lived outside Tombstone, but John Clum read the essay and handed it back.

"Mr. McLaury," he said, "in my opinion you would do well to forget the whole thing."

"I didn't ask your opinion," Frank said. "I told you to print mine."

"I will be happy to print it on flyers and

you can tack them up wherever you please, but nothing goes into my newspaper unless I decide to put it there."

"Are you saying you won't print it?"

"My decision is in your own best interests, Mr. McLaury. Your speculation could be construed as libel. Lieutenant Hurst could take legal action against you."

"Well, I read law for a year and I'll by-God decide what my best interests are," Frank told him. "There are other newspapers in this town, you know. I can take this letter to the *Nugget.* Harry Woods might be very happy to accommodate an honest citizen's protest against governmental tyranny!"

This was not exactly news to John Clum. It was a frustrating fact of life that however well reasoned and factually correct the opinion he published in the *Tombstone Epitaph,* Harry Woods over at the *Daily Nugget* would print the exact opposite with similar confidence in the irrefutable logic of his own editorial.

"Do as you see fit, sir," Clum replied. "I'll have no part in this."

Frank loitered in the office for a while, denouncing damnable despotism. He even declared his intention to turn Democrat over the issue, but not even that threat swayed John Clum, whose mind was closed to all reason, as far as Frank could see.

What happened next did not seem important to Virgil Earp at the time. He happened to be walking past the *Epitaph*'s office when Frank McLaury came stumping out, so intent on his own righteous indignation that he slammed straight into the federal officer. Frank's hat hit Virgil about chest-high. Virg caught it before it could fall to the ground. Another man might have snapped, "Watch where you're going!" but Virgil handed it back with a good-natured "Whoa, there!"

Another man might have said, "Sorry," but Frank McLaury was the kind who often confused *I am short* with *People look down on me.* And that afternoon, he was in no mood to be reminded of his size by someone who was nine inches taller, even if Virgil Earp couldn't exactly help that.

"Were you in on it with that sonofabitch Hurst?" Frank demanded.

"In on what?"

"Don't play innocent with me!" Frank warned, his neck cranked back so he could glare at Virgil. "You ever come out to our ranch again, you'll have a by-God fight on your hands."

Living with Allie Sullivan should have made Virgil Earp wiser about advising small, excitable, angry people to calm down. Such a suggestion is rarely taken well, but the words were out of his mouth before Virg thought better of them, and that was when Frank McLaury started hollering about "malicious liars" and how "this matter will be ventilated," adding other memorable phrases that were fresh in his mind from having worked on his essay so much.

While that was going on, somebody went around the corner to the Oriental and told Wyatt Earp that his brother and Frank McLaury were putting on a good show over by the *Epitaph.* Wyatt finished out the deal, shut down the faro table, and went to see what was happening.

"Don't think you can gang up on me!" Frank warned when he saw Wyatt. "I got a brother, too! I got friends who'll stand by me! You sonsabitches come near my ranch again, you'll answer to the Cow Boys!"

"What was that about?" Wyatt asked, watching Frank go.

"Hell if I know," Virgil replied. Eyes narrow, he turned to Wyatt and asked, "Did that sound like a threat to you?"

Circulation of the *Daily Nugget* went up almost 15 percent when Harry Woods printed Frank McLaury's essay, for the notion that Lieutenant Hurst had stolen those army mules himself caused quite a stir in Pima County. Republicans in Tombstone and Tucson considered Frank's charges absurd. Democrats in the countryside thought that was just the sort of thing a damn Yankee might do.

In Sulphur Springs Valley, ranchers who'd

been standoffish when the Iowans arrived suddenly found it in their hearts to drop by the McLaury place and express their support. Frank enjoyed the attention, and Tommy hoped his brother would be satisfied now. But no such luck.

Everything Frank's eye fell upon reminded him of the mules, or Lieutenant Hurst, or the Earps, and he'd start in again on injustice and honor impugned. At first, Tommy tried agreeing with him, just to keep the peace. Frank could tell he didn't mean it, though, and kept arguing until Tommy finally said, "Frank, I am done with this. I am not going to listen to another word." For the next few days, Frank tested Tommy's resolve. Tommy continued to ignore him, which might have been a mistake, looking back on it, for that was when Frank started seeking companionship among the Cow Boys.

Whenever they came by with livestock after a raid, Frank would work himself up enough to throw down his tools or walk away from a half-milked cow. He'd pick a fight with Tommy and end by hollering, "I already got the reputation of a rustler, so maybe I oughta get the good of it, too!" Then he'd ride off with Curly Bill and the boys to have a few drinks at Frank Stilwell's saloon down in Charleston.

Leaving Tommy to finish the chores.

■ ■ ■ ■

Even before the mule incident, Frank Mc-Laury had been hinting around that he'd like to go along on a raid into Mexico, but Curly Bill had always discouraged the notion.

"I am due for some excitement!" Frank would declare, casually mentioning four or five times that he'd like to investigate that side of the cattle business himself.

"Frank," Curly Bill would say, "you are overestimating the romance of the profession."

Sure, cattle raids could be fun, especially if the *federales* gave chase on the way out of Mexico, but once you were north of the border? Rustling was just chasing half-wild beasts through cactus in sun glare and heat. Sleeping on stony ground under thin blankets in the desert cold. Eating dust by day and beans by night. "You only see the end of the trail," Curly Bill would tell Frank, "when the boys are finishing up and ready for a good time." He was trying to be nice about it, but the truth was, Curly Bill had enough trouble keeping his crew sweet without adding a bantam rooster like Frank McLaury to the mix. So Bill did his best to change the subject whenever Frank asked about joining the gang and in the autumn of 1880, that was easy.

All you had to do was pour a couple of

whiskeys into Frank McLaury and say, "Mules!" It was like touching a match to a fuse. Frank would spark and sputter, telling everyone about how "I read law for a year!" and "I know my rights!" And then he'd holler about how his brother Tommy might be content to trudge along behind a plow horse, letting himself be slandered and abused by the likes of a lying Yankee thief like Lieutenant Joseph Hurst, but Frank himself would not let such things slide, by God.

This was always a good show, and Curly Bill would pretend to share Frank's outrage and indignation, just to see how excited the little man could get. Which was plenty. And it was interesting to Bill how the target for Frank's outrage began to shift. Joe Hurst was stationed way over at Camp Rucker, whereas there were four Earp brothers right there in Tombstone. And though Frank had crossed words with Virgil in front of the *Epitaph* office, his animosity seemed to settle on Wyatt, for Morgan was always pleasant and James Earp just sold beer to Chinks, but Wyatt! Hell if he'd ever said a single *word* to Frank McLaury!

"Last time I was in town to buy supplies, he passed me without so much as a nod!" Frank cried one night. "It's about time I show that arrogant, stuck-up sonofabitch a thing or two!"

"You're gonna have to climb a ladder to do

it," Sherm McMasters pointed out. Everybody laughed, which made Frank hot up worse.

"Well, then, I'll get myself an equalizer!" he declared. "Wyatt Earp ain't too tall to shoot!"

Even Frank got tired of the mules after a time, but as the 1880 Pima County elections approached, he found a new hobbyhorse to ride, for hadn't Wyatt Earp been appointed deputy sheriff by Charlie Shibell, who was a Democrat? And wasn't Wyatt now supporting Shibell's Republican opponent, Bob Paul? What kind of perfidious, back-stabbing Yankee ingrate would do such a thing?

"And what kind of name is Bob Paul anyways?" Frank wanted to know. "Why doesn't he have a last name?"

Ever since the *Nugget* printed his letter, Frank had been practicing up on being a Democrat. To hear him talk now, you'd have thought he was from South Carolina, not Iowa, what with all his "damn Yankees" and "no-good carpetbaggers." Curly Bill always found that funny as hell.

"Frank's right! It is a crying shame!" Bill said one afternoon in Frank Stilwell's bar. "These Republicans move into Tombstone because of the silver, and now they want to take over Arizona. Why, it's just like after the war, when those sonsabitches took over the South!"

He was aiming at Frank McLaury, but it was Johnny Ringo that Curly Bill hit, for Ringo read newspapers and took a lively interest in politics. He'd even won an election once when voters in a Texas township made John Peters Ringo a constable, figuring an outlaw might be just the man to deal with others of his kind. The job didn't last, but Juanito knew his way around a ballot box.

"We have to do something about this," he said, and there was no fun in his voice. "I am damned if I will be run out of Arizona! By God, there'll be no Brownsville here! Bob Paul will not become the McNelly of Arizona!"

That was when the mood changed, for all the freelance cattle importers in the Southwest knew that Captain Leander McNelly's Texas Rangers had killed a dozen rustlers down near Brownsville and stacked their bodies like cordwood in the town square to show that cattle thieves were no longer welcome in the Lone Star State. Word was, Bob Paul planned to clean the Cow Boys out of Pima County if he got elected, and if Bob Paul was sheriff, Wyatt Earp would likely be his undersheriff, with all the inflexible, humorless intolerance that implied.

"How many of you are registered to vote?" Ringo asked the boys, and he did not hide his disgust when it turned out that Ike Clanton and Ringo himself were the only ones.

"That is a damn disgrace," he told them. "No damn Republican is going to be sheriff of Pima County," he declared, banging his shot glass on the table. "Ike, you and me are going to get ourselves appointed poll watchers, and we are going to see to it that the votes of our precinct's citizens are recorded, even if they have not observed all technicalities."

"What kinda name is Bob Paul anyways?" Ike asked. Sometimes it took him a while to catch up. "Why don't he have a last name?"

"God damn him," Frank Stilwell muttered then. "Don't matter how far you go. Don't matter what miserable shit hole you live in. The goddam Yankees are right behind you, looking to take over." But Stilwell wasn't talking about Bob Paul. He was looking out the window of his saloon, glaring at a tall man riding by on a black horse.

"Hell if that ain't Wyatt Earp!" somebody said, and the boys started ragging Stilwell about how he better watch out because there were a couple of warrants out for him and Wyatt Earp might arrest him.

Frank McLaury said, "We'll make short work of him if he comes in here."

"We?" the boys yelled. "Waddya mean *we*, Frank?"

Ringo got that queer look in his eyes then, the one that always appeared when he was about to slug a new kid. "Well, now, Frank, if you're gonna be a rustler, I guess it's about time you cut your teeth on something. I hear Wyatt Earp sets great store on that horse of his."

Frank frowned. "You mean steal it?"

"Nah, he ain't got the sand," Billy Clanton scoffed.

"Hell if I don't!" Frank declared. "Why, I'll steal that horse right now!"

"I like Frank," Ringo told the others then, like he was defending the little man. "Frank's got all the sand he needs."

Stay Your Anger and Keep Clear from Fighting

Frank Stilwell wasn't the only wanted man in Charleston, but Wyatt Earp wasn't in town to arrest anyone. He was on his way to talk to Mr. Richard Gird at Johnny Behan's urging.

"Wyatt, if you're gonna run for sheriff in '82, you would do well to get Richard Gird on your side," Behan told him. "Gird's a partner in the Tombstone Mill and Mining Company and might well be the most important man in the new county." Wyatt hesitated. Johnny pushed harder. "You've got to get used to asking for votes, Wyatt. Go out there and introduce yourself. Shake hands. Look men in the eye. Find out what the voters are thinking!"

When Wyatt told his brothers and Doc Holliday about Behan's advice, Virgil snorted. "Find out how much you'll hate running for office, he means. He thinks you'll take your name off the governor's desk now and settle for undersheriff in '82."

"Maybe so," Wyatt admitted.

Morgan said, "I think Behan's deal makes sense for you, Wyatt. He'll be the politician and you'll be the lawman. What do you think, Doc?"

Doc was playing something nice on the piano. "Mr. Behan has unusually fine teeth," he said, his hands still moving. "Of course, 'one may smile and be a villain, at least in Denmark.' "

"What's Denmark got to do with anything?" Virgil asked irritably.

"Oh, hell, Virg. Don't ask," Wyatt said because, a lot of times, if you asked Doc to explain something, you'd just get more confused.

Took about three days before Wyatt was ready to take Behan's advice. This year at least he wouldn't be asking for votes for himself. He'd be asking for Bob Paul. And that got easier after Johnny helped him with the words. "You can say, 'Bob Paul and Charlie Shibell are both good men. I'm proud to work for Charlie, but Bob Paul means to enforce the law no matter who breaks it. Will he have your vote, sir?' "

Wyatt practiced that until it felt natural and spent a lot of October riding through Pima county, canvassing voters to see how the election for sheriff was likely to go. Which was why he rode past Frank Stillwell's bar that day: He was on his way to Millville to talk to Richard Gird. Then he'd speak to the workmen about how they might vote in November.

Millville was directly across the San Pedro River from Charleston. A bridge connected the two towns, but Dick Naylor wouldn't cross it. Wyatt found the horse's reluctance understandable. The mill noise was fearsome, what with tons of rock and water crashing through heavy timber frameworks, and huge iron lifters dropping eight-hundred-pound heads onto the ore, and gravel sluicing out the other end. What baffled Wyatt was why men chose to work in that hell. A moment of distraction, and you'd pay with a limb or your life.

It was plain prudence to ban alcohol in Millville, for accidents were common enough without adding drunkenness to the mix. Mr. Gird was a temperance man, too, intent on saving souls from Demon Rum and a Republican, of course. So it was no surprise that he intended to vote for Bob Paul.

The surprise was that the millworkers were going to vote for Bob, too. They lived on the Charleston side of the river, where there was a lively local market for whiskey, gambling, and fornication, but they all seemed to agree with their boss. Strict law enforcement was good for the mining industry, and that was good for their jobs.

It was late when Wyatt finished the canvass. He decided to stay in Charleston that night and went to bed feeling pretty good about things. With less than a week until the election, he calculated that Bob Paul would win by more than a hundred votes. And Mr. Gird had encouraged Wyatt to run for sheriff next year when the new county was declared. That was good news, too.

Wyatt was having breakfast in the hotel café before starting back to Tombstone when a boy came in and handed him a note in Sherm McMaster's handwriting. *Your horse is taken for a prank,* he read. *Dont get too mad. But watch out for Frank Maclowery he is making threts.*

"Hell," he said. He gave the kid a nickel and told him, "Keep your mouth shut."

The cook agreed to pack him a lunch, and while that was being done, Wyatt walked down to the telegraph office to send a wire to his brother James:

DELAYED STOP SEE TO MB STOP

James would understand that this meant "Keep an eye on Mattie Blaylock," for Mattie was getting worse all the time, and as much as Wyatt disliked being with her, he didn't like to leave her on her own.

Dont get too mad, Sherm wrote, but horse theft was no prank. And on top of the crime, and the inconvenience, and worrying about Mattie, he'd have to hire a horse. Which

236

added expense to insult.

The livery owner was nowhere to be seen, having left a stable boy to face Wyatt Earp's displeasure. "I'm sorry, Mr. Earp," the kid said. "They had guns and they was drunk."

"Not your fault," Wyatt said. "Which way'd they go?"

The boy hesitated. "I have to live here, sir."

Wyatt kept looking at him.

The boy lifted his chin toward the road to Sulphur Springs Valley.

"That's what I thought anyways," Wyatt told him. "Don't worry. They won't trace it up to you."

Or to Sherm McMasters, either. Sherm always worried that the Cow Boys would find out he sold information about them, but you didn't have to be an Apache to follow the trail. Dick Naylor had a clubfoot. Years of steady training and patient stretching had leveled it and the horse ran well. Still, his shoe wore a little light on one side of that hoof. The track was distinctive. Easy to find, easy to follow.

There looked to be ten or eleven other horses in the party. One rider was so drunk, he fell out of the saddle about a mile out of Charleston. Two of his friends dismounted to get him back on his horse. One of them fell on his own ass in the attempt. The other must've laughed himself sick at that. There was a fly-covered puddle of puke a little ways off.

For the next couple of miles, the road was bordered by vegetable gardens that belonged to the Chinese farmers who supplied the restaurants in Tombstone. Some people objected to Chinks owning American soil. Wyatt didn't see anything wrong with it. They bought their land and paid their property taxes like anybody else. He wasn't sure what he thought about Chinamen in general. A lot of white men thought they drove wages down, and there were rumors about Chinese gangs kidnapping white women and making them prostitutes. Johnny Behan kept pushing Wyatt to join the Non-Partisan Anti-Chinese League, but then Doc Holliday reminded him about China Joe back in Dodge.

"Jau Dong-Sing was an honorable man," Doc said, "and he was very kind to me when I was ill, Wyatt."

Which was true enough. But China Joe was just one man. And he had a laundry business. That was different from what went on in Tombstone.

Mattie had been using laudanum for headaches for as long as Wyatt had known her. It was opium dissolved in alcohol. He got it for her from the pharmacy and she called it "my medicine." Wyatt would say, "Medicine shouldn't make you sicker." She'd just look at him like he was so stupid, it wasn't worth trying to explain. Lately, she'd been sneaking off to Chinatown to smoke opium whenever he was out of town. Maybe she was better off using a pipe — at least there was no liquor involved — but one of these days, she was going to get into real trouble.

He could just see the headlines in the *Nugget:* DEPUTY SHERIFF'S WIFE FOUND DEAD IN OPIUM DEN. Or maybe: MRS. WYATT EARP ARRESTED FOR PROSTITUTION IN CHINATOWN. Assuming the *Nugget* did him the courtesy of calling Mattie his wife.

How in hell did I get myself into this? That's what Wyatt had asked himself a thousand times. But if he was honest — which he tried to be — what he really wanted to know was, How can I get myself out of this?

Once he'd asked the pharmacist, "Can you die from drinking too much laudanum?" When the answer was yes, he was tempted to ask, "How much would it take?" He even thought about buying twice as much as usual and leaving the bottles where Mattie could find them.

He wasn't proud of himself for thinking that, but there was no denying that the idea had crossed his mind.

By midday, it was pretty clear that the men he was following were headed for the Clanton spread, not the McLaurys'. An hour later, he paused to study the ground with a grim little smile, for the sign was easier to read than a book.

Dick Naylor had checked up and jerked loose.

Two of the drunks went after him . . .

Another drunk followed them . . . That one was good with a rope.

Dick had always hated being led, and for the first time since getting McMasters's note, Wyatt could feel the potential for anger coming on. He'd bought Dick Naylor off a Texan back in Dodge when the animal was a skinny, frightened, mistreated three-year-old. It had taken a long time and a lot of work to earn Dick's trust. The idea of drunken idiots undoing everything he'd accomplished with that horse was intolerable.

Don't hit him, Wyatt warned the thieves in his thoughts. You hit that horse, there will be hell to pay.

Johnny Behan's careful civic tutelage had borne some fruit. Wyatt was willing to keep in mind that Old Man Clanton was respected in Pima County and had a lot of influential friends. He understood as well that the ranchers of Sulphur Springs Valley were citizens and voters, but that didn't change the facts as Wyatt saw them.

Theft is theft, he thought. That's what Behan forgets. Moving stolen goods across a border don't make possession legal. The Cow

240

Boys are thieves.

And that was why Wyatt was backing Bob Paul over Charlie Shibell. Charlie had done him a good turn by appointing him deputy, and Wyatt was grateful, but Charlie made allowances. Bob Paul was determined to enforce the law, no matter who he had to arrest. You don't want trouble with the law? Don't break it. That's what it always came down to for Wyatt, though even his brothers argued with him.

"There's room for some discretion, Wyatt," Morg would say, and Virgil would add, "Use some common sense, kid!"

All right, then, Wyatt thought. If Dick Naylor is returned unharmed, I won't press charges. That's discretion. As for the common sense part . . . Well, it probably wasn't real smart to ride alone into the Clanton stronghold, where there were perhaps two dozen rustlers, several of whom were known killers.

He dismounted before he crested a rise that gave out onto the Clanton ranch house and hobbled the hired horse off by a patch of grass in the shade of a good-sized cottonwood. Hunched over, he climbed the hill and bellied down at the top, hoping Dick Naylor was in plain sight, the way the mules had been.

He couldn't see Dick, but the wind brought Old Man Clanton's voice to him in broken

snatches. "God damn" was being used liber-
ally, and "fools," and something else that
must have been "drunken idiots."

Johnny Ringo was sitting in a beat-up
wicker chair on the veranda, rocking it onto
its back legs and smiling, but the rest of the
Cow Boys were hanging their heads — just
taking it from the old man, like they knew
they deserved what they were getting. Even
Curly Bill Brocius looked ashamed when
Clanton pointed toward Charleston and
yelled, "Take that goddam horse straight —"
Back to Charleston, he must have said. One
of his sons — the youngest one, Billy, his
name was — Billy must have answered back.
The old man swung around, head lowered
like a bull, horse whip in hand, and . . .

Everything slowed down.

The old peculiar deafness settled in, the
way it always had when Nicholas Earp
rounded on one of the kids. Suddenly, Wyatt
was seven years old again, with his vision narrowing until all he saw were hands.

A big hand, rising and falling, black leather
snaking away from it. Small hands raised to
parry the blows. His own hands, reaching out
to grasp the lash as he stepped between his
old man and his little brother and took the
beating meant for Morgan —

Except it wasn't Morg. It was Billy Clanton, and the one taking the beating for his
brother was Ike Clanton, but that didn't seem

to matter.

Stop him, Wyatt was thinking. I have to make him stop.

Time snapped back to its accustomed pace.

He was on his feet, and it was five long steps downhill to the hired horse. Jerk the hobble off. Swing into the saddle. Kick toward the crest. Pull the rifle from its scabbard. Fire into the air.

Old Man Clanton's arm went down. He turned to see Wyatt Earp on the rise. Coiling the horse whip, the old man pointed it at Frank McLaury, who bobbed his head *yessir* and ran for the barn, with Billy Clanton right behind.

A minute later, they brought Dick out. Frank led the animal, glancing over his shoulder repeatedly, trying not to let the horse get too close.

Billy was already puffing up, putting on that "I don't care" toughness that frightened boys will fake, but Frank was hungover and Old Man Clanton had taken him down a peg, and now he could see Wyatt Earp at the top of the hill. Just waiting.

Which was when Frank remembered two important things: Wyatt was a deputy sheriff, and horse theft was a hanging offense.

Frank faltered, trying to think what he could say that would get him out of trouble. When he came up with a serviceable lie, he started toward the lawman again, pulling the black horse along behind him.

"We found him," Frank ventured, drawing near. "Horse musta got loose."

Wyatt stared. Frank's eyes dropped, but Billy Clanton was willing to work with the story.

"You oughta be more careful with your property," Billy said, "cause we ain't gonna catch him for you next time. Sonofabitch bites!"

"He get you?" Wyatt asked.

Billy nodded. So did Frank, rubbing his arm where the shirt was torn.

"Serves you right," Wyatt told them.

He dismounted and looked Dick over. When he was sure the horse was unhurt, he shifted his saddle off the hired animal, for he meant to ride Dick home. Cinching up, he jerked his head toward the rental. "Take that gelding back to the Charleston stable. I will know if you don't."

They mumbled agreement. Wyatt swung up. Dick wheeled twice, feeling his rider's intention to ride away, but Wyatt reined him around instead and looked toward the Clanton ranch house.

Everyone was standing on the veranda, watching the show, but Ike Clanton was watching hardest of all, ready to move if Billy needed him.

Wyatt raised a hand. Ike returned the

gesture, though you could see he was uncertain about it.

Wyatt's gaze shifted downward.

Billy Clanton wasn't even in his twenties yet. Frank McLaury was old enough to be balding, but he seemed like such a child . . . Maybe it was because he was so short. Maybe it was because he was so foolish.

"You two keep running with the Cow Boys," Wyatt warned, "you're gonna get yourselves killed."

Frank and Billy watched him ride away. He was over the rise when Billy Clanton asked, "Did that sound like a threat to you?"

BETTER FOR ME TO DIE

Lights and Shadows of New York Life was the fattest book Morgan Earp had ever seen, except the Bible. He'd been lugging it around for almost two whole months, but every one of its 850 pages had something that surprised him, and he often felt compelled to tell somebody about what he'd just read.

"Listen to this, James! Says here, there are six hundred brothels in New York. That don't even count the streetwalkers. There are five thousand of them." Or: "Listen to this, Wyatt! Even a regular patrolman on a beat gets twelve hundred a year. Maybe I should move to New York." Or: "Listen to this, Virg! Says here, every burglar has his own style of breaking in, so New York detectives can tell who hit a house. I wonder what gives it away?"

Morg understood how this kind of thing could get on peoples' nerves, but Doc Holliday liked talking about books. The moment the dentist took his hands off the keyboard, Morgan said, "Listen to this, Doc! Says here, they got one single store in New York with two thousand people working in it. That'd be like all the miners in Tombstone working just one —"

"Damn your eyes, Morgan! It is hard enough for me to concentrate without you rattlin' on about department stores."

"Sorry. I'll be quiet."

On the outside, Doc was over the concussion, but his mind still wasn't working like it did before. He had a job at the Alhambra dealing faro for a few hours in the evening, but Doc wasn't sharp enough to play poker at all, and that scared him. You could tell. Playing piano was the only thing that seemed to make him feel better, but this week Doc had gotten it into his head to learn something new, just to see if he could. The dentist would go over and over some little chunk of music until he had it perfect. Problem was, when that took longer than Doc thought it ought to, it nerved him up worse.

Doc generally practiced in the afternoon, when the Cosmopolitan was mostly empty, so folks wouldn't get tired of him playing the same damn thing a hundred times. Morgan himself knew to be patient because eventually Doc would put all the little bits of music together and then . . . there would be *beauty*. That was worth waiting for.

In the meantime, Morgan read.

"Hey, Doc," he said when Doc finally

closed up the keyboard and seemed to be in a better mood. "You ever notice? You don't hardly cough at all while you're practicing."

"I'll be damned . . . You're right," Doc said thoughtfully. "Must've been the same for Chopin. He gave recitals almost to the end."

"Maybe it's because you don't talk while you play."

"Yes, that's possible. Steadier respiration, I suppose."

"Anyways, what kinda name is Show Pan?" Morg asked. "Sounds Chinese."

Which made Doc laugh, and cough, and ease up a little. "It's French, though Chopin himself was born in Poland . . ." His voice trailed off as he looked past Morgan toward the music room door.

Morgan got to his feet. "What's wrong, Virg?"

"Either of you seen Wyatt?"

"He was down in Millville to talk to Richard Gird," Morgan said, "but he sent James a telegram this morning saying he was delayed. Why?"

"It's Mattie," Virgil said. "Real bad this time."

Many things had become clear to Mattie Blaylock while she waited for Wyatt to come home with her medicine. He wanted to kill her. He wanted her dead so he could run off with that Jew slut.

And he'd put bugs under her skin. She could feel them crawling.

"Bastards. Awful little bastards," she muttered, scratching, scratching, scratching.

"Wyatt, please!" she wailed. "I need my medicine!"

The pillows! She hadn't looked there. She seized them, one by one. Gripped the ticking. Tore them open.

Feathers flew. Sticking to her face, pricking her skin.

Nothing. Nothing. Nothing!

"Where did you hide my medicine, you bastard?" she screamed. "Where did you hide it?"

Dropping to her knees, she peered under the bed again. Maybe she hadn't looked hard enough before. She dragged the china chamber pot out and dumped its contents on the floor. "You ruined my life!" she screamed, throwing the pot at Wyatt and his Jew slut.

It shattered against the wall.

"Oh, Jesus. Oh, Jesus. Gentle Jesus, save me!" She wanted to weep, but her mouth was so *dry.* She was crumbling to powder. Why had they ever left Kansas? Kansas had grass and flowers. Arizona is dead, she thought. He wants me dead, too. Dead and dry and crumbling.

"Christ!" she snarled, ripping off her blouse, her nails digging for the bugs under her skin.

Lurching to her feet, she yanked the drawers out of the bureau, throwing clothes on the floor. Too tired to stand, she sank onto the wet carpet and laid her body on the dampness, moaning in pleasure. It was cool and wet. So good. So *good*! Better than anything she'd ever felt. Better than any man ever made her feel.

"Oh, Jesus," she cried. "Wyatt, please, where did you hide it? I need my *medicine*!"

The other girls were waiting outside Wyatt's house, their arms wrapped tight over their bosoms, their faces stiff. You could hear Mattie yelling, all the way out on the street.

Winded by the run from the Cosmopolitan, Doc gasped, "When did this start?"

"About an hour ago," Allie told him.

"She chased us out," Bessie said.

"Morg, it's different this time," Lou said. "I've never seen her like this."

Doc leaned against the veranda post, coughing into a handkerchief. When he got his breath back, he nodded and Morgan opened the door.

The house had been ransacked. Chairs overturned. Tables knocked over. Clothing everywhere. Mattie was half-naked, feathers stuck to her sweat, arms bleeding from long ragged scratches.

One step into the front room, the stench hit them.

Piss. Puke. Crap.

"My God," Morg gasped, his own coughing as bad as Doc's.

The dentist handed him a handkerchief and Morg held it over his nose and mouth as he moved from window to window, shoving them open one-handed.

"Where have you *been*?" Mattie screamed. "You were humping that Jew slut, weren't you! I need my *medicine*!"

Breathless and white, Doc knelt next to her on the filthy carpet. "Mattie, honey, that's Morgan. Wyatt's been delayed. He'll be home soon."

"Oh, Jesus," she wailed, fingers raking through her tangled hair. "Oh, Jesus. Oh, Jesus. I need my medicine, Doc! Where did he *hide* it?"

Empty brown bottles were lying all over the house. Doc handed one to Morgan and said, "Take this to the pharmacy. Tell Mr. Rabinovich that I have a patient who needs three six-ounce bottles, right away." When Morg hesitated, Doc said, "It's all right. Mattie and I will be fine, won't we, Mattie honey."

"Oh, Doc!" she wailed. "Oh, Doc! He wants me dead. That bastard brought me here to die."

Ashen, Morgan went back outside. "When did she get so bad?"

Lou and Allie looked away, but Bessie said, "She's been using it all along. I warned Wyatt

251

back in Dodge. I told him she was just looking for a meal ticket, but he took her in anyways. And this is the thanks he gets."

"I need my medicine!" Mattie was yelling.
"God damn you! I need it *now*!"

By nightfall, the story was all over Tombstone.
Nobody said anything, but Wyatt could feel
eyes on him as he rode through town. All the
good feeling he had from getting Dick Naylor back left him. He worried that something
bad had happened to one of his brothers, so
it was a relief to see Virg and Morg waiting
for him outside the Dexter Stable.

They told him about Mattie while he took
care of Dick Naylor.

"Doc wanted to bring her to the hospital,"
Morgan said, "but we figured you didn't want
more gossip than there already was."

Virgil said, "We've got her at our place.
She's sleeping now."

"Doc had two Mexican women come clean
your house," Morg said. "They scrubbed the
floors and walls and washed the curtains. We
had to burn the carpet. The mattress, too."

"Jesus, Wyatt!" Virgil cried softly. "How
long've you been living like that?"

"Hell. I don't know," Wyatt said, halfway
between misery and anger. "It just sorta
creeps up on you." He closed Dick's stall,
and they walked outside. "I thought I left
enough for her. She's going through it faster

than she let on, I guess."

He scrubbed at his face with both hands and was about to say something more when they heard a small boy calling, "Dad? Dad!"

A moment later, Josie Marcus came down the stable's center aisle by herself, a shawl around her shoulders. When she saw the Earps, she said, "Al, go see if your daddy's horse is in the corral." She waited until the boy had run outside before asking, "Have any of you seen Johnny? He was due home for supper hours ago."

"I just got back to town," Wyatt told her.

Virgil and Morgan exchanged quick glances before looking at their feet.

Men were often tongue-tied in her presence, but Josie knew the difference between a shy reticence and a kindly reluctance to tell an unkind truth. "Oh," she said, and there was no drama in her voice. The brothers had simply confirmed what she suspected. And what all the whores in town knew. And what the former Mrs. Behan could have told her to expect.

"Thank you," she said, straightening her shoulders. "You've saved me the trouble of looking for him any further."

Tugging her shawl tighter, she turned toward the doorway and called, "Albert! Your daddy's at a meeting! We'll wait for him at home, sweetheart."

The boy came to her side. Josie sketched a smile.

"We'll be on our way, then," she said. "Good evening, gentlemen."

"You two shouldn't be out alone at night," Wyatt said. "I'll walk you home."

"Evening, ma'am," his brothers said, touching their hats.

Side by side, Virg and Morgan watched Wyatt disappear into the darkness with Johnny Behan's son and mistress.

Virgil spat tobacco juice into the dirt by way of commentary.

"Could you blame him?" Morgan asked quietly.

"I guess not," Virg admitted. "But *that* is gonna be trouble."

The boy skipped ahead, excited to be out so late, secure in the protection of two adults who hardly spoke at all, each alone in a misery that was deeply private and humiliatingly public.

"I heard about your wife," Josie said after a couple of blocks.

"She's not . . . I mean . . . Not really."

"Oh. I see. She's Mrs. Earp the same way I'm Mrs. Behan."

When they reached the Behans' house, Josie told Albert, "Say good night to Mr. Earp, Albert. Then go on in to bed." The boy did as he was told. Josie offered her hand. "Thank you for escorting us home, Mr. Earp."

"Wyatt," he reminded her.

"Wyatt," she said, and went inside.

Sheer habit took him back to the corner of First and Fremont. The Mexican and Chinese neighborhoods nearby were quiet. It was cold, and everyone was tucked up inside. For a time, Wyatt stood out on the street, just looking at the place he called home.

Hell, he thought.

The door opened. Doc came out, his woolen cloak pulled close, like a blanket. "I expect someone has told you what happened."

"Yeah. Morg and Virg."

"I will hear no word against Mattie Blaylock," Doc warned. "She has had a hard life. I fear it will be harder yet, before it is over."

Leaning on his cane, the dentist stepped off the porch, grunting softly when his meager weight hit his bad hip. A gunshot wound had nearly killed him back in '77. If he sat still for long, the scarred-up muscles stiffened.

"Thanks, Doc," Wyatt said. "I 'preciate what you did."

The dentist nodded and put a hand on Wyatt's shoulder as he passed.

Alone again, Wyatt walked through the open door. The little house was neat and nearly empty, everything scrubbed and spare.

It reminded him of the place he'd rented back in Dodge.

When he was living on his own. Before Mattie Blaylock moved in.

He never meant that to be permanent. From the start, he had reason to regret letting Mattie cross his threshold. At her best, she was not easy to get along with, and he could hardly remember her at her best. It came to him then: He could saddle up and ride away. Leave her behind. Just . . . disappear. But Wyatt Earp had never run away from anything before, and he couldn't see doing it now.

Besides, he had a future in Tombstone.

The Earp brothers all lived within a few hundred yards of one another, but they didn't get together all that much. Virg and Wyatt traveled a lot, transporting prisoners mostly. Morgan rode shotgun for Wells Fargo whenever a strongbox was being hauled to or from Tombstone. James couldn't afford to hire help, so he tended bar at his tavern from dusk until three in the morning. Even so, the four of them were on Virgil's front porch a couple of nights later. Smoking in the starlight. Talking things over.

"You ever do anything legal about Mattie?" Virgil asked Wyatt.

"I let her use my name, is all."

"Well, kid . . . time to fish or cut bait."

Morgan kept quiet. He knew how unhappy Wyatt was, but Morg himself had found things to admire in Mattie Blaylock. She'd been thoughtful about cooking soft foods when Doc was working on Wyatt's teeth back in Dodge. And when Doc himself was so sick that winter, Mattie was a good nurse to him.

"That's a hell of a thing to ask!" Virg cried, bringing Morgan back to the present.

"I'm just trying to figure it out!" Wyatt was saying. "Don't make sense to me why a man would cheat if he had a fine woman at home."

"Well, I can tell you why *I* don't." Virg jerked his head toward the house. "Allie would know I'd been up to something before I took two steps into the house and she'd strip the bark off me. What about you, Morg? You ever get a little something on the side when you're up in Tucson?"

"Well, I suppose I could if I cared to," Morg admitted, "but I'm not a good liar. And it's like . . . like I'd have to pull some kind of shade down between me and Lou. Maybe that's how women know if you're tomcatting. They can tell when you pull that shade down."

"Yeah," Wyatt said. "Fine. That's why men *don't* go to whores. What I'm asking is why men *do,* if they got quality right there in their own bed."

"Just don't know when they're well off" was Morg's opinion.

"James?" Virg said. "You're the expert, I guess."

James Cooksey Earp was the first of the five sons born to Nicholas and Virginia Earp and the most conventional of the brothers, in a thoroughly unconventional way. Nineteen when the war began, he'd enlisted in the Union Army and lost the use of his left arm for his trouble. James had lingered near death for a full year in an army hospital. When he finally turned the corner and began to heal, he counted himself a lucky man, for he emerged from that travail as husband to a Nashville madam named Bessie Ketchum. Overseeing a big, busy brothel like the one she and James had run back in Dodge City was beyond her now. Bessie had retired. Serving beer for a nickel a glass to Chinks and drifters certainly wasn't what James had expected when he and his brothers set out for Tombstone, but if anybody had asked him about how things had turned out, he would have shrugged with his good side and said with genuine cheer, "Can't complain! It's a living."

"Why would a man with a fine woman go to whores?" he asked, repeating Wyatt's question. He followed with one of his own. "We're talking about Behan, right?"

"No! Well, maybe, but . . . Just in general, is what I want to know."

"Lots of reasons." James stood, stretched,

258

and spit over the porch railing. "Sometimes a man can't get all he wants at home. Or he might like things his wife don't. Or maybe she's sickly, like Bess. Or she don't want more kids, so she lets him know it's just as well if he looks elsewhere for his needs, long as he keeps quiet about it." He sat down again. "And sometimes, things look good to visitors, but it's a different story when the door closes. People get tired of each other. Or maybe it was just bad from the start and when they figured that out, it was too late."

For a while, they all just sat there, smoking in the darkness.

"How's Mattie now?" James asked.

"Sleeps a lot. But when she's awake . . ." Wyatt shook his head.

In fifteen years of tending bar in bordellos, James Earp had seen a lot of whores come and go. Many died young. Suicide. Disease. Murder. Some just sort of disappeared into the alleys, sucking off cowboys and soldiers and miners for drink money or drugs. A few, like Mattie Blaylock, managed to find a man decent enough — or stupid enough — to take them in. They'd set up housekeeping with him before he knew what was happening.

"Wyatt," James said quietly, "you've kept her off the street for a couple of years. That's gotta count for something."

Everyone's life was hard, one way or another.

That's what Curly Bill Brocius had observed. People found ways to soften things a little. Some ways were better than others. In Bill's experience, opium was the best of all.

The first time he lifted the canvas flap and peered into Ah-Sing's hop joint, he was surprised to see a white woman lying full-length on one of the low, quilt-padded pallets. Her eyes were vague as she gazed up at him, and he wondered if she was among the services on offer.

Ah-Sing beckoned to him. "You new, yes? Come in! Come in!"

The woman touched Bill's leg when he ducked inside, passing near her. "It's so good," she warned, "don't even try it once." Bill looked down at her, confused, but Mattie Blaylock was too far gone to say more.

If he'd cared to, Ah-Sing could have explained — though in Cantonese, not English: "Euphoria is the poppy's first gift, gently vanquishing the soul's distress, mercifully muting the body's pain. What follows is a gorgeous floating languor. *Be warned:* To experience that sensation even once is to desire it again and again, forever. To be deprived of opium's beneficence is to endure first longing, then anguish, and finally torment."

Of course, Ah-Sing said no such thing. He was a businessman. Repeat customers were the main source of his income. "She crazy," he told Curly Bill. "You only addict when you smoke three pipe a day."

After that first amazing night, Bill tried not to visit Ah-Sing's tent more than once a month. Well, twice a month sometimes. It was hard to keep track, for rustling did not run to a schedule, and Bill Brocius was a busy man. Organizing the crew for Old Man Clanton. Leading the raids if the old man did not take charge himself. Getting the cattle distributed to the most cooperative ranchers. Paying off the boys. Keeping the peace among them, and keeping them out of Tombstone while they drank and gambled away their cut of the profits. It was a wearisome sort of life, marked by constant belligerence and endless strife.

All burdens of responsibility fell away when Curly Bill entered Ah-Sing's world. Even before he lit the pipe, its warmth in his hands was enough to calm him. Soon, he felt like he was wrapped in soft down pillows, though he lay on a hard wooden pallet. His limbs grew heavy even as he seemed to float, dissolving into the air, mixing with the smoke.

Bliss was best experienced without the distraction of companions, so it became Curly Bill's policy to visit Chinatown only when he was alone. Everything might have turned out different if he'd held to that rule the night Fred White got hurt.

Looking back, Curly Bill himself was inclined to blame Little Willie Claiborne for what happened. Claiborne was eighteen, same as Billy Clanton, and when those young fools got to be friends, Old Man Clanton hired Claiborne to handle the remuda. Claiborne was pretty good with horses, but Curly Bill had taken a dislike to the young braggart from the start.

"Well, now," the little redneck had drawled, "this gang's already got itself a Billy Clanton and a Curly Bill. I'm the youngest, so I reckon y'all can call me Billy the Kid!"

It was presumptuous, giving yourself a nickname like that — trying to make out like you were a famous outlaw when you were just an obnoxious young cracker who thought highly of himself.

"Billy the Kid?" Ringo scoffed. "You mean Billy the Baby Boy."

Claiborne bristled and started talking about how tough he was. There was laughter in response, so he said he'd killed lots of men, but anybody could see he was making it up as he went along.

"I killed as many as Billy Bonney, by God," Claiborne hollered, "and I'll kill more if anybody says different!"

"Little Willie," Ringo decided. "We're gonna call you Little Willie."

The nickname stuck because it was fun to see how stirred up Claiborne got whenever you called him that. Which Frank McLaury did as often as he could, because he wasn't the low man anymore. To get some of his own back, Little Willie Claiborne started ragging Frank McLaury and Billy Clanton about going into Tombstone after they'd stolen Wyatt Earp's horse.

"You gonna let that sonofabitch scare you?" Claiborne would say. "Why, he ain't so tough! I killed me lotsa men tougher'n Wyatt Earp!"

Didn't take much of that before Claiborne had the boys ready to ride into Tombstone and dare them law-dogs to do something about it. Curly Bill couldn't order Old Man Clanton's kid not to go. He also knew that if something happened, he himself would get the blame, so he decided to go along and keep those young fools out of trouble. He figured he'd corral the boys over at Ah-Sing's place and put a pipe in their hands. Next morning they'd all ride out of Tombstone without Fred White ever knowing they were in town.

God's honest truth: What happened that night was just an accident.

■ ■ ■ ■

PORTENTS
OF BATTLE

■ ■ ■ ■

ALL BEGUILEMENTS
AND LOVELINESS

It was almost midnight but Albert Behan was sitting on the edge of the bed, watching his father's girlfriend get ready to go out. She had a tiny glass jar with pink stuff inside and ran the ball of her little finger across it. After she dabbed some on her lips and cheeks, she turned her head from side to side to judge the effect.

"War paint," she said, winking at his reflection in her mirror. "Hand me that hat, sweetheart. The one with the blue feathers."

He hopped up and brought it to her. She put it way over on the side of her head and had to use a fancy pin to keep it from falling off. Leaning toward the mirror, she adjusted the little curls around her face. When she was satisfied, she stood and smoothed the wrinkles on her skirt and slipped into her jacket.

"What do you think?" she asked, tugging her sleeves down.

Dumbstruck, he nodded his approval. She

looked nice even when she was just cooking or something, but when she was all fixed up, she was the prettiest lady Albert had ever seen. A lot prettier than his mother, who had lines in her face from frowning so much and never said anything kind to a person.

"It's really dark out there, Sadie." That was the name he used when he wanted to remind her that he was her most special friend. "I could go with you. If you like. We could protect each other. Like when we went out looking for Daddy."

She smiled, pulling on her gloves. "Albert, you are the dearest thing, but I really need to go alone. Are you sure you'll be all right by yourself?"

"Sure, Sadie. I'm nine now," he reminded her.

He was, in fact, a little nervous. Snakes sometimes came into the house because it was warmer inside at night.

"Sadie?"

"Yes, sweetie?"

"I love you, even if Dad doesn't."

It just sort of came out. He thought it would make her feel better, but her face crumpled. "I'm sorry," he said quickly, ready to cry himself, but she came close and bent to put her arms around him.

"Never!" she said fiercely. "Never be sorry for loving someone, Albert!" She pulled back to look him in the eye. "I love you, too. I always will, no matter what."

But then she left. Just like his mother.

And walked out into the darkness, determined to show John Harris Behan that two could play his nasty game. She had, briefly, savored the notion of cornering Johnny in a cathouse with Albert at her side, but the past six months had made a realist of her. Fatherhood had not kept Johnny from flagrant infidelity to Victoria, whose legal status was not enough to keep her husband home. So Josie Marcus was going to fight fire with fire. Let Johnny worry about her, for a change! Let him think about where she might be, and with whom.

That was the entirety of her plan when she left the house. Just . . . be gone when he finally came home that night. That new Chinese restaurant was open all night. She'd pass the time at Kee's Can Can Café, then she'd waltz into the house at dawn and refuse to answer questions.

Let's just see how *you* like it, John Behan!

Downtown Tombstone didn't seem all that far away in daylight, but she hadn't walked far when she began to feel uneasy. Clouds were rolling in. The moon kept disappearing. She could hear the noise of the mine engines half a mile away, but the houses she passed were quiet, their doors and curtains closed against the desert's nighttime chill.

The only sound nearby was the crunch of her own feet on the gravelly roadside until something rustled in a clump of mesquite she was passing.

A dog, most likely. Or a coyote. Maybe a pig.

Not a snake. It was too cold at night for snakes to be active.

Probably.

She picked up her pace and hurried past the mesquite, but that was when she really grew nervous, for the soft rustling was behind her now. She turned quickly and looked back, thinking Al might have followed her, but nobody was there.

Nobody she could see, anyway.

She had never before gone out at night without a male escort, even if he was only a nine-year-old boy. If somebody snuck up and grabbed her arm and dragged her off, there'd be no sympathy. Everyone would say she asked for it, going out alone like that.

She considered turning back. Maybe she should get Albert to come with her, after all. Or just take off her hat and stay home with him.

Except she was a lot closer to town than to the house now.

She kept walking, but moved to the center of the empty street.

If she were back in San Francisco, she could have gone to Dora Hirsch's house. Or Agnes

Stern's. Dora would have bucked her up and told her that a *shegetz* like Johnny Behan wasn't good enough for her. Agnes would have told her to pack her things and leave that *putz*. But she wasn't in San Francisco, and she hadn't sent a word to her friends since she ran away. She stopped writing to her parents after she got an answer to her letter telling them she was Mrs. John Behan. Her father didn't exactly say it, but she could read between the lines. We didn't raise you to marry some mick gonif. I am disappointed. You broke your *mutti*'s heart. And that was his reaction to the idea that she'd *married* outside the faith. The truth was a bigger *shanda.* If her parents found out she was simply shacked up with a man whose first wife had divorced him for constant, remorseless philandering, they'd declare her dead and sit *shivah* for her.

So. Here she was, walking down a dark street in Tombstone, Arizona. Nine hundred miles from home. Living with a man twice her age who cheated on her routinely and publicly. She had no friends. Not one woman in Tombstone would speak to her. Nobody but Albert really cared about her. Several men in town would have been happy to take her as a mistress, but she wasn't drawn to any of them. Even her schoolgirlish crush on Wyatt Earp had faded for lack of the slightest encouragement from him.

She understood those joyless eyes now. Wyatt had troubles of his own. She'd probably only fallen for him because he was everything Johnny wasn't. Tall, blond, blue-eyed. A *goyische* god, Agnes would have called him. True, he was awkward as a guest, but she'd never forgotten that day in the corral when she'd seen him in his proper element: outdoors, working wordlessly with horses. There was something about that quiet, self-contained competence . . .

Johnny, on the other hand, wanted to be your best friend the minute he met you, but he was a politician to the bone. Once he had your vote, it was on to the next man. Or woman. And the talking! Say yes to Johnny Behan, and he was still making his case an hour later, as if he knew you'd only given in to him so he'd shut up. Wyatt didn't have a syllable of cajolery in him. The only time he'd said more than a few words to her, it was about horses.

And dentistry, for heaven's sake!

It was then that she remembered the slow southern voice, inflected by an eerie musical malice. *If you ever decide to leave that presumptuous, third-rate, overdressed Irish bigot, ask at the desk for the envelope, y'hear?*

Fifty dollars . . .

I could go anywhere, she thought. Chicago, maybe. Or New York! Stay at the Cosmopolitan tonight. Get on a stagecoach tomorrow,

272

and *go.* I can buy new clothes when I get there and start over.

Leave, she thought. That's the solution to everything.

Albert was forgotten in a rush of optimism, along with humiliation and anger, discouragement and fear. Eyes on the future, she hardly noticed the drunks who came to a sudden, swaying stop to stare at her.

The oldest among them swept off his wide-brimmed hat, revealing a luxuriant mass of dark, curling hair as he bowed with elaborate courtesy. "Show the lady some respect!" he snapped, slapping at his younger charges with the sombrero.

"Evening, ma'am," they mumbled, pulling their own hats off.

Cheered by this frontier gallantry, she smiled her acknowledgment with a confidence bred for daylight.

"C'mon, boys!" she heard the curly-haired one urge after she passed. "You're gonna love it! One pipe at Ah-Sing's, and everything's just *grand . . .*"

A hophead, she thought, for she'd read the lurid stories in the San Francisco press and knew the Chinatown lingo. Feeling worldly, she sailed on toward Allen Street, her head full of plans and possibilities, and after that first friendly encounter, she wasn't the least bit concerned when she saw a knot of miners jamming the boardwalk.

"Please," she began politely, "Let me —"
Let me pass, she was going to say.

"I'll let you do anything you like, little lady!" one said. "What do you like, little lady?" He grabbed her hand and pressed it against his crotch. "How 'bout this? You like this?"

Startled, disgusted, she snatched her hand away amid gales of laughter and gripped her skirts, lifting the fabric slightly when she stepped into the street to go around the men. Setting her face, she kept her head down after that, minnowing through the crowds in front of every saloon, hoping to go unnoticed the rest of the way to the Can Can.

She made it to Allen before someone jostled against her and she stumbled into a man who caught her before she could fall. She started to thank him. Then she saw the look on his face.

"Excuse me," she said stiffly. Moving left, then right.

Grinning, he matched her moves, stepping from side to side, blocking her way. "You wanna dance, sweet thang? C'mon, I'll dance with you!"

All around her, men got closer. Remarks got uglier. A callused hand reached around from behind and closed over her breast. She shrieked, twisting to get loose, only to be gripped by someone else who smelled so bad, she gagged and pushed against his chest. "Let me go! I'm not — I'm not what you think!"

"What? You mean you ain't female?"

Frantic, she began to scream for help, but her struggle only amused the miners and ranch hands. It seemed a miracle when three young women elbowed their way to her side, their painted faces contorted by fury as they forced themselves between her and the laughing, leering drunks.

"Thank God! Thank *you*! I am so grateful," she began, only to be silenced by the glittering hatred in the eyes of a Chinese girl who couldn't have been more than fourteen.

"This our corner," the girl snarled. "You go now!"

"But I'm not — Really, I wasn't trying to —"

"God damn, I tell you! You go now!" the little hooker yelled, shoving hard.

With a dancer's grace, she managed to keep her balance, but she was no longer sure which way the Allen Street crowd was moving her. West, toward the hotels and restaurants? Or east, toward the brothels? Tamping down panic, she scanned the street, hoping to see something familiar and get her bearings, but everything looked so different at night and —

"There!" she cried, voice cracking, when she identified the brightly lit lobby of the Cosmopolitan through its plate-glass windows.

"Out! Of! My! Way!" she shouted with the

imperious disdain of Miss Pauline Markham correcting a foolish ingenue who'd upstaged her in rehearsal.

Cowed by her ersatz courage, the drunks let her through, and she entered the lobby with her head held high and stood still, blinking in the gaslight's flaring brightness, waiting for her heart to stop hammering.

"Evening, Mrs. Behan," Mr. Bilicke said. "I'm afraid Johnny's not here."

Still rattled, she needed a moment to understand what he was talking about. "I — I know," she said, coming to the desk. "Doc Holliday left me something and —"

"Doc's right in there," Mr. Bilicke informed her, lifting his chin toward the piano room.

She was pleased to have the opportunity to tell the dentist he'd been right about Johnny Behan all along and that she'd be leaving Tombstone in the morning. But it wasn't music she heard now. It was gusts of deep male laughter.

Peeking through a gap in the slatted swing doors, she saw a dozen men smoking cigars and drinking, enthralled by a story about a horse and a whorehouse, and she was about to turn away — to ask at the desk for Doc's envelope and check in for the night — when she recognized the storyteller.

Wyatt? she thought. *Wyatt* is telling a funny story?

Doc Holliday was coughing and wiping

tears off his thin cheeks. "No more, Morgan! Please! I'll hemorrhage!"

Oh! That's *Morgan,* she realized. And that older man — that must be Virgil.

Shifting slightly, she caught sight of Wyatt in the corner, and her mouth dropped open again, for Wyatt Earp had been at her table a dozen times or more this autumn, but he had never so much as smiled, let alone laughed like this: great, gasping sobs of laughter.

"Did I ever tell you fellas the elbow story?" Morgan asked.

"Morgan, don't!" Doc pleaded. "I swear! You'll kill me!"

"C'mon, Doc! They gotta hear this one! Now, this was a coupla days after Johnnie Sanders' wake, right? And Doc was just about broke after that, remember, so he needs some cash to get a faro game going again. So I says, 'Well, I got some money saved,' and he says, 'No, son — just come along to Eddie Foy's show tonight, and I'll show you how it's done.' So I stop by the theater on my rounds, and Doc sees me, and goes over to Eddie, and it's . . ."

Morgan made himself grave and still — Doc Holliday's poker face, Josie presumed — while miming a whisper into somebody's ear.

"So now Eddie calls out to the crowd, 'Quiet down, boyos! We have a wee wager on the table, so we have!' And now five hundred Texas cowpunchers are —" Morgan paused to look stupid and drunk and curious by turns. "And Eddie says, 'There's a fine gentleman here offering a bet of one thousand dollars that nobody can lick a smear o' jam off his own elbow. Let's see yer cash, boys!' So these dumb sonsabitches are *falling* over themselves to get in on this bet, and Doc's standing there, watching this stampede to give him money, right? Because everybody's thinking, 'Well, hell, my elbow's right *there* . . . and my tongue's right *here* . . .' "

You could see that Wyatt was thinking the same thing, which made his brother Morgan point at him, and Virgil howled, and Doc Holliday was coughing so hard he could barely speak, though he managed to gasp out a threat to have Morgan arrested for assault if he kept this up. But the others were beckoning, *Come on, come on! Keep going!*

Behind the swing doors, Josie was smiling as well, for she was enjoying Morgan's story as much as any of them. But it was Wyatt to whom her eyes returned again and again. It was amazing how boyish he looked. Untroubled, unburdened, utterly at ease . . . And she was swept by a kind of sadness then, for there was such a difference between what Wyatt was and what he might be — if only someone loved him enough.

"So now Eddie's got a grand collected," Morgan was saying, "and there's this *parade* of idiots coming up to the stage and, one by one, they push up their sleeves, and Eddie's got this big ole jar of jam, which Doc just *happened* to bring that evening —"

"Strawberry," Doc choked out, wet eyes shining.

"And Eddie smears a dab of it on each cowboy's elbow, and then it's —"

Morgan broke off to demonstrate their efforts. Neck twisting, elbow sawing up and down next to his ear, just out of range of his tongue. Face earnest, and determined, and angry, and flummoxed by turns. Which had everyone wailing and breathless.

"Can't . . . be done!" Doc said, behind his handkerchief. "Anatomically . . . impossible!"

Wiping his eyes, Virgil declared, "Maybe so, but 'impossible' won't stop a Texan from trying!"

"Half an hour later," Morg said, wrapping the story up, "Dr. John Henry Holliday was back in business, dealing faro at the Lady Gay!"

Bright-eyed but white-faced, the dentist sounded as though he'd run for miles when he said, "I can . . . only get away with that . . . trick once in every town. I . . . save it for . . . emergencies."

Wyatt leaned over and poured Doc a drink, which was another shock, for Josie had never seen Wyatt touch liquor.

"You need another?" he asked when the dentist drained the glass.

Doc nodded and was about to say something when Wyatt went still.

And so did all the other men in that room as they followed Wyatt's gaze and saw Johnny Behan's girl standing at the door.

It was only a moment — with everyone around them hushed and motionless — but for that one moment, Josie Marcus and Wyatt Earp were all alone, eyes locked, smiles fading to a deeper kind of recognition.

I *knew* it! she was thinking, jubilant. I knew it all the time!

No, he was thinking. No, no, no.

But he knew, too. He always had.

Doc Holliday reacted first, reaching for his cane, determined to be on his feet in the presence of a lady. "Why, Miss Josephine! If you don't look a picture! Will you join us?"

"Please, gentlemen, don't get up," she said, giving Doc some cover and favoring all of them with a sort of generalized smile.

Breaking out of his trance, Wyatt asked, "You looking for Johnny?"

"Why?" she asked. "Do you suppose he's worth finding?"

There were hoots of surprise and approbation. Doc Holliday beamed like he'd just won another thousand-dollar bet. Even Wyatt reacted, snorting and looking away.

They *all* think Johnny treats me poorly, she realized. It's not just Doc —

That was when they heard the gunshots.

"Hell," Wyatt said wearily. "Now what?"

Virgil rubbed his hands together like he was about to tuck into a good meal. "C'mon, boys! Let's go see what the idiots have for us tonight!"

They did not hurry, but neither was there any discussion of jurisdiction. Wyatt, Virgil, and Morgan Earp headed out the door, followed by several men Josie did not recognize. Doc belted down the second shot of bourbon before he hobbled toward the lobby, tipping his hat as he passed.

Josie herself stood still for a time. Thinking about what had just happened. Reconsidering her decision to leave town. Then she, too, left the music room and crossed the lobby to the hotel doorway.

The gunfire seemed to have stopped, but Mr. Bilicke came to her side. "Don't go out there, ma'am," he warned. "It's just drunks shooting at the moon, I expect, but the bullets can come down anywhere. I once saw a girl killed that way in New Orleans."

Out on Allen, the crowd was quiet, so it was easy to hear Marshal White shout, "I am an officer! Give up that pistol!"

The answer was clear as well: "Fred, I swear! That wasn't us shooting! We was just on our way over to Ah-Sing's place —"

"Give me that pistol! *Now,* damn you!"

The report of a gunshot echoed off the

buildings.

There was a stunned silence. A strangled cry of "I'm hit!" Shouts of outrage.

Virgil Earp roared, "Back away! All of you! Back *away*!" And the injured man began to scream.

Josie clutched at Mr. Bilicke's arm. "Who is it? Who's been shot? Please!" she begged. "Please! Go find out who's shot!"

He took off and she turned from the door, hands pressed to her lips. Pacing the lobby. Listening to that awful high-pitched, inhuman wail. "I'm hit!" she heard over and over in her mind, but the voice was so distorted, so crazed with pain. "Not Wyatt," she prayed. "Not Wyatt. Please, God. Not Wyatt."

"Josie!" she heard, but she was weeping with fear by then, blinded by tears, and only felt Johnny Behan take her arm.

"Josie, why did you leave Albert alone? What are you doing here by yourself? Tonight of all nights! My God! Don't you see how dangerous —"

"Who is that, *screaming*?" she cried. "Who's been shot?"

"Fred White," Johnny said, bewildered now. "What are you so — ?"

"Oh, thank God!" she sobbed, sinking to the floor. "Thank God. Thank God."

"Jesus, Josie! What a thing to say! What'd Fred White ever do to you?"

But the girl was hysterical, and there was

no point talking to her. "Never mind," he said patiently, lifting her to her feet. "Come on, honey. Albert's waiting for us. Let's go home."

BLACK BLOOD FLOWED
FROM HIS WOUNDS

You do not get used to it, Morgan Earp thought.

The shit stink of ripped intestines. The flare and smoke of clothing set alight by a muzzle flash. The sound of a man's screams rising higher as you try to beat the flames out with your hands . . .

This was the second time Morgan had seen an officer gut-shot at close range. Three years ago, up in Dodge City, it was poor Ed Masterson. Now it was Fred White. Two men his own age. Both gunned down by drunks.

Screaming in the dirt. Writhing in agony on a public street.

Ed had died within the hour, but Fred was lingering, and that was bad luck. There's nothing worse than gut pain, that's what the doctors said. And poor Fred was suffering a special kind of horror. Somehow, one of his balls had been torn off by the bullet as it passed down and out of his body.

When the sky began to lighten a few hours

after the shooting, Morg sat up and swung his legs over the side of the bed.

Lou whispered, "Did you sleep at all?"

He shook his head.

"Is it your hands?" she asked. "Do the burns hurt?"

He ignored the question and pulled in a shuddering breath. "Help me get dressed, will you? I'm going over to see if . . ."

To see if Fred was dead yet. To find out if the suffering was over.

Across the street and down the block, Doc Holliday had lain awake all night as well. Lame and breathless, he'd arrived just after the shooting. Wyatt already had Curly Bill Brocius under arrest. Attention had shifted to the excitement of a potential lynching. Virgil and Morgan backed the drunken crowd off and the Earps were making it clear that Fred White's assailant was going to reach his cell alive, but the mob went with them toward Tombstone's jail, leaving Fred on the ground in the darkness.

Only a slack-jawed young miner remained, watching blood well out of the marshal's belly. "Go to the hospital," Doc said slowly and firmly. "Get Dr. Matthews or Dr. Goodfellow. Go, son. *Now.*"

The boy's eyes focused and he took off.

"Help me," Fred was saying, his voice as small as a child's now. "Please. Help me."

285

Planting his cane, John Henry Holliday lowered himself, kneeling at the side of another healthy young man he had not expected to outlive. "Squeeze my hands," he told Fred. "Hard as you can. Harder! That's right. Do you have family, Marshal? Is there someone we should tell?"

"Help me," Fred begged. "Make it stop. Help me."

That's all he would say, and that's what John Henry Holliday would hear long after Fred was lifted onto a stretcher and carried away.

Help me. Make it stop. Help me.

At dawn the next morning, the dentist sat up and coughed and poured himself a drink. Then he lit a cigar, staring at his bruised and aching hands while he smoked.

Virgil Earp slept that night, but there was no rest in it for him.

When he jolted upright a little past dawn, Allie was awake and sitting in her rocker. She had learned to get out of bed as soon as Virg started to mumble, for he would soon begin to thrash about, and he was a big man whose unconscious blows could be dangerous. He'd bloodied her nose once, and another time, he tried to strangle her while tangled in a nightmare about Fredericktown. Of the battle itself, she knew only that James had been wounded there and that Virgil had carried his brother off the battlefield, arriving at the hospital tent so soaked in blood, the surgeon thought Virg was wounded, too. The boys made the story sound like that was a good joke, but Allie knew better.

Slowly Virg lost that awful look of frightened confusion. Blinking, he saw her in the corner and rubbed his face. "Sorry, Pickle. Fighting the war again."

"I'll put the coffee on," she said.

Morgan came by a little while later, dark circles under tired blue eyes.

"Still alive," he reported.

"Christ," Virg said.

Allie asked, "You want breakfast, Morg?" He shook his head, so Allie just poured him a cup of coffee. "I'll be over with Lou," she said and left the house, knowing the brothers would want to be alone.

Elbows on the table, they stared into their mugs. It was a long while before Morgan spoke. "Maybe Wyatt's right. Maybe prohibition ain't such a bad idea."

Sitting back in his chair, Virg looked out the window, toward town. "It's not just drunks," he decided after a time. "It's drunks with guns."

Things were very quiet in the Behan household that morning. Which, in Johnny's experience, was not a good sign. Usually Josie yelled her head off when he stayed out late. This morning she was acting like he was invisible. Elaborately busy in the kitchen. Keeping her back to him as she worked. Her eyes elsewhere if she had to turn in his direction.

When he tried to find out why she'd gone downtown alone last night, all she said was "I don't want to talk about it." I don't want to talk to *you,* she meant, and to make her point she was chirpy and affectionate with Albert, ruffling his hair when he shuffled into the kitchen rubbing sleep crust out of his eyes.

"What would you like for breakfast, sweetheart?" she asked the boy.

"Pancakes, please," Al mumbled.

"Sounds good to me!" Johnny said heartily, but Josie gave no indication that she'd heard him. "Get dressed and run uptown for the newspapers, son," Johnny said, handing Al a dime. "Marshal White was hurt last night. I want to find out how he is."

As soon as Al left the house, Johnny came over and wrapped his arms around her. "C'mon, honey!" he whispered, rubbing himself against her backside. "We've got just enough time."

She went stone-still. He let her go. She started pouring pancake batter without a word.

"Guess I'll go get dressed," he said.

When he returned from the bedroom, Al was back, wide awake with exciting news to convey. "Marshal White's still alive, but everybody says he's hurt real bad. There's a big crowd outside the jail, and everybody's mad. Mr. Earp and his brothers are guarding the door."

"Wash up, Al," Josie said.

Johnny busied himself with the papers, laying the *Epitaph* out on top of the *Nugget.* He liked to know what the opposition was saying about any given topic before he read something that might more closely reflect his own opinions.

Josie brought a crock of butter and a can of syrup to the table. Albert's stack of pancakes was neat, symmetrical, and perfectly browned. Johnny's were, predictably, a little burnt.

I suppose I've got it coming, he thought.

Josie sat down across the table. Posture perfect. Eyes on her plate.

"John Clum has some very flattering remarks about Wyatt," Johnny told her, for it was his policy to acknowledge good things about his political rivals, and that was still how he thought of Wyatt Earp on the morning of October 29, 1880.

Laying her fork aside, Josie reached for the *Epitaph* and read the lead article. When she finished, she looked up and met his eyes. "That's not flattery. It's just accurate reporting."

This was Johnny Behan's first real clue, but it didn't quite sink in.

■ ■ ■ ■

Over at the jail, Wyatt Earp had spent the night guarding the five prisoners arrested in connection with the shooting of Fred White. Four of them were jammed into the main lockup, but Curly Bill Brocius was in a cell by himself and he kept asking, "What have I done? I have not done anything to be arrested for! Why am I in here?"

Wyatt didn't bother answering. Brocius wouldn't remember the answer and didn't seem to know he'd asked before. That was interesting to Wyatt, for he'd buffaloed his share of idiots up in Kansas but hadn't spent time with them afterward. He didn't know about this kind of befuddlement until he saw how fogged up Doc Holliday was after Milt Joyce hit him.

"Jesus," Brocius moaned, face in his hands. "Why'd you hit me like that?"

That was a new question, so Wyatt answered it. "Because I decided not to shoot you."

Which would've been within the law. Better than two hundred men heard Fred White identify himself as an officer and order Brocius to hand over his weapon. Bill raised his pistol — not handle first but with the barrel toward the marshal. Shot him, point-blank.

Brocius was stupid with drink, and just stood there looking at Fred on the ground, like he didn't know what to make of it, but the gun was in his hand, still smoking. Any officer could have killed Bill on sight and it would've been justifiable, but in all his years as a lawman, Wyatt Earp had shot only one man, and he'd regretted it afterward. Disarm, subdue, arrest. That was Wyatt's policy. Let the law take its course.

"Jesus," Bill said again. "Why'd you hit me like that?"

History would remember John Philip Clum as the mayor of Tombstone who sent the Earps and Doc Holliday striding toward the O.K. Corral on the afternoon of October 26, 1881. On the night of October 28, 1880, however, Clum was merely the twenty-nine-year-old owner and editor of the *Tombstone Epitaph,* mortgaged to the top of his prematurely bald head and teetering on the brink of a second ignominious business failure.

He was in bed when he heard the gunfire down the street. Staring at the ceiling. Wondering how he was going to avoid yet another bankruptcy. He had, in fact, just told himself, firmly and resolutely, "The Lord will provide," when the terrible eerie wailing began.

Two minutes later, he was dressed and out the door. Two hours later, he was back in the press room, composing as he set the type and working as fast as possible. The town marshal was unlikely to live past noon and John Clum intended to wring every penny he could from the poor man's death throes.

Twenty-four-point type for the headline, he decided. Back it down to eighteen for the second deck.

MARSHAL FRED WHITE
PERHAPS FATALLY WOUNDED!
Arrest of Shooter
and His Companions.

Pausing to wipe sweat from his face, the editor raised his eyes toward heaven, for this was the very sort of crime he'd been predicting for months. And he thanked God for it.

John Clum was not a callous man. He was a newspaperman, which is similar but not identical. He was also dead broke — a related condition, but one he had reached as a result of a long series of unusually principled decisions. Dewy with idealism, he had come west when the elders of his Dutch Reformed congregation prevailed upon him to accept a post as Indian agent on the San Carlos reservation. Disastrously ethical, he failed to line his own pockets in that capacity and had resigned in protest of the government's ill treatment of the Chiricahua Apaches, whom he'd found intelligent, congenial, and worthy of respect. Still determined to serve the

Indians, he borrowed money from relatives, bought the *Arizona Citizen* in Tucson, and used its editorials to demand fair treatment for the Apaches, to criticize the army, and to condemn the venality of the Bureau of Indian Affairs.

What he had not taken into account was the fact that very few Apaches bought newspapers. White folks, who did, were frightened of Geronimo's renegades and grateful to the army for its protection. They considered John Clum's screeds unpatriotic and wrongheaded. Not to say annoying. And stupid.

Subscriptions fell off. Advertising dried up. When he sold the *Arizona Citizen* to a less morally combative man in February of 1880, he cleared barely enough to pay his debts, but he had big plans for a fresh start in journalism in the silver boomtown that had sprung up seventy miles south of Tucson. This time, he vowed, he would avoid topics that antagonized people and pay more attention to advertisers. When he boarded the stagecoach, he already had a name and a wonderful motto for the newspaper he planned to found: "Every Tombstone Needs an Epitaph."

God will provide, he told himself, and his faith was rewarded when Millville's ore magnate Richard Gird agreed to underwrite the venture with a $7,000 loan. A fellow New York Republican and an ardent anti-saloon reformer, Gird had admired John's crusading Tucson editorials and was happy to back an uncompromising Dutch Reformed non-drinker whose principles aligned with Gird's own.

The business did well for a few months. Then Frank McLaury showed up with his screed about those army mules. The *Daily Nugget* benefited from John's refusal to print that, while John Clum's own newspaper lost subscribers and advertisers. This time, however, he understood what he needed to lure business back. Something to hammer on daily. Something that would make readers worry, so they'd feel compelled to protect their interests by being in the know.

Crime, for example.

Even before Fred White was shot, the *Epitaph* had played up Tombstone's wickedness: the drinking, the gambling, the prostitution, the violence. "A dead man a day, served up with breakfast every morning!" his editorial proclaimed in June. He was proud of that memorable phrase, though the town wasn't really that bad. Carousing was generally confined to the vice district out past Sixth Street, but his primary investor was an ardent prohibitionist, so it didn't hurt to emphasize the role of liquor in every form of criminal behavior, whether actual or potential. At the same time, he had to be careful not to criticize the nicer saloons, like the Oriental and the Crystal Palace, or they'd withdraw their ads. Day after day, he had walked this narrow line. Night after night, he prayed for the Lord's grace and mercy.

And that was why John Phillip Clum lifted his face to heaven and gave thanks to God when Curly Bill Brocius shot Fred White. The incident would crystallize the region's politics just days before an election. An honest Republican lawman had been gunned down while defending Tombstone's law-abiding citizens from the enemies at her gate: a few hundred Democrats, many of whom were known criminals and none of whom subscribed to the *Epitaph.*

Hand flashing between the case and the chase at a veteran typesetter's thirty words per minute, John muttered to himself as he composed the article.

Blame for the crime must be placed on a cowardly lot of drunken Texas Cow Boys who disturbed the peace early this morning with gunfire. When Marshal Frederick White intervened to stop violation of town ordinances, he was ruthlessly shot by one of their number.

Here he paused, trying to remember how to spell Wyatt Earp's name. Was it W-I or

W-Y? Eliminate the problem, he thought briskly.

> Deputy Sheriff W. Earp, ever at the front when duty calls, arrived in time to see the Marshal fall and knocked the assailant down with the man's own six-shooter. With the assistance of his brothers Virgil and Morgan, Deputy Earp arrested the shooter's companions. All five were jailed.
> Much praise must be given to our fallen Marshal White for his gallant attempt to arrest the outlaws, and to Deputy Sheriff Earp and his brothers for the energy displayed in bringing the murderer and his accomplices to arrest.

John paused there. Technically, the crime was still assault with a deadly weapon, but nobody ever survived a wound like Fred's. Let it go, he thought. It'll be murder soon enough.

As John Clum locked the form and inked up for his next edition, events in town moved quickly. At nine A.M., the Tombstone Village Council met in emergency session. Assuming that Fred could not survive, Council called for a special election to decide on a new town marshal. In the meantime, Deputy Federal Marshal Virgil Earp would serve in that capacity. Sworn in, Marshal Earp urged immediate passage of ordinances forbidding the carrying of guns within city limits, citing precedent in Dodge City. No action was taken.

Council adjourned to Judge Michael Gray's courtroom for arraignment of the five men arrested in connection with the shooting of Fred White. Amid rumors that vigilantes were preparing to lynch Curly Bill Brocius as soon as Fred White died, Virgil Earp deputized his brothers Wyatt and Morgan as city policemen, along with several other townsmen he considered game to stand against a mob. The suspects were brought before Judge Gray under heavy guard.

Four were accused of misdemeanors, and their pleas were heard first. Each defendant expounded in turn on the general theme of "We was just having some fun, Your Honor." Their testimony was consistent. They'd become rowdy under the influence of liquor. Curly Bill Brocius told them to behave themselves and had in mind to take them down to Chinatown. It was somebody else, down the street, who starting shooting at the moon. Fred White just thought it was the defendants, which wasn't so, honest to God, Your Honor. Fred getting shot was a pure accident, and they were all real sorry.

Judge Gray imposed fines on the first four defendants for being drunk and disorderly. Leaving open the question of who had started the trouble, he ordered them released. The fact that the judge's son was friendly with several of the Cow Boys became the subject of vigorously expressed commentary. This discussion was gaveled into silence. With decorum reestablished, the court turned its attention to the felony case.

The charge against William Brocius remained assault with intent to murder. Fred White was still alive and might recover — though that notion persisted only among those who had not seen the hole blown in the man's abdomen a few hours earlier. Mr. Brocius asked several times why he was in court. He was reminded that he'd shot Fred White in the gut and that he was accused of attempted murder. He seemed surprised each time and said, "I guess I better get me a lawyer."

The court ruled that Mr. Brocius would be given time to secure an attorney and that the case would be moved to Tucson. Any jury impaneled in Tombstone would likely convict regardless of the evidence presented in Mr. Brocius's defense, assuming that the Cow Boys didn't show up sooner to bust Bill out of jail before he could be tried. The prisoner was therefore to be transported without delay to the new railway terminus in Benson, some twenty-five miles northwest of Tombstone, and thence by train to Tucson.

Deputy Sheriff Wyatt Earp now swore in

his brothers Virgil and Morgan as county deputies, along with the other townsmen who'd guarded Curly Bill on his way to Judge Gray's courtroom. Armed to the teeth and determined to thwart any attempt — by a lynch mob or the Cow Boys — to interfere, this party left immediately for the Benson depot.

Nothing much was said during the railway journey from Benson to Tucson. Wyatt Earp was never much of a talker. Curly Bill Brocius, who was, had a hellacious headache.

"I feel sick," Bill announced after a while, rubbing his face with hands held close by iron shackles. "Jesus! Why did you hit me like that?"

The answer was still "Because I decided not to shoot you," so Wyatt didn't bother repeating it.

About an hour later, Bill asked, "Can you recommend a good lawyer in Tucson?"

"James Zabriskie," Wyatt said.

"Zabriskie's in Arizona now?" Bill cried, eyes scrunched up against the light. "Damn. He prosecuted against me back in Texas."

Wyatt shrugged. "That's who I'd go to."

They couldn't have known it, but even before they reached the Tucson jail, Curly Bill had been exonerated.

When Fred White failed to die as soon as

expected, a delegation from the Tombstone Municipal Court went to his bedside to take a deposition from him. Fifteen hours into his ordeal, Fred was too weak to scream and too strong to die, but he was still clear-headed and confirmed that the shooting was an accident.

"My own damn fault," Fred told them. "Never shoulda . . . grabbed his gun like that. Shoulda told him . . . throw it down."

Sobered and shaken by what they'd seen, the delegation filed out of the dying man's room. It was Judge Gray who asked the doctors, "Can't you fellas do anything for him? Whiskey? Laudanum, maybe?"

"He can take nothing by mouth," Doc Matthews said regretfully.

"It would only leak into his belly," Doc Goodfellow explained, "and that would make the torn tissue even more painful."

"Jesus," Judge Gray said.

"Yeah," the others agreed.

Frederick George White's suffering ended at ten A.M. on October 30, 1880, some thirty-three hours after Curly Bill's pistol discharged.

An autopsy performed by Dr. Henry Matthews revealed extensive immediate damage to the large and small intestines caused by the passage of a .45-caliber bullet through the abdomen. After traveling through the soft tissue, the bullet's path led it to a particularly dense region of the pelvic bone, which deflected the slug downward, destroying one of the organs of generation upon its exit from the deceased's body. The cause of death was judged to be acute infection, widely spread throughout the abdominal cavity, with consequent heart failure.

"I don't know how he lasted as long as he did," Dr. Matthews said.

Poor Fred, John Clum thought, but the Bard was right: It's an ill wind that blows nobody good. In just three days, John had published and sold out five special editions, picking up over two hundred new subscriptions. Back aching, legs stiff, feet swollen, hands battered and blackened, John Philip Clum was an exhausted but happy man as he typeset coverage of Fred's funeral.

The services were held in Gird Hall, a spacious building crowded to its utmost capacity. The cortège following our murdered marshal to the grave was the largest ever seen in Tombstone. It embraced all classes and conditions of society, from the millionaire to the mudsill, and numbered fully 1,000 persons.

By then, of course, Fred's deathbed testimony had made it clear that the shooting was unintentional, but John couldn't resist the alliterative allure of "murdered marshal," especially when he could hammer that beauty home with a phrase like "millionaire to mudsill."

Tomorrow he'd begin coverage of the presidential election with the *Epitaph* already decisively solvent. And the contest for sheriff was of great interest locally, so sales would remain good, even with Fred White in his grave.

Lord, John prayed that night, Thou hast made me glad through thy work. I will triumph in the works of Thy hands.

MEN STEEPED IN
QUARREL AND CONTENTION

When Dr. J. H. Holliday registered to vote in Tombstone in the fall of 1880, he handed the completed form to a deputy registrar for the Pima County recorder's office and muttered, "For all the good it will do."

"Democrat?" the registrar asked, grinning.

"Born and bred," Doc said with a sigh that ended in a cough.

Like all white southerners of his age and era, John Henry Holliday had grown to manhood when the very air around him was filled with loathing for Abraham Lincoln and the entire Republican Party. He himself was only thirteen when the war ended, so he had not been disenfranchised during Reconstruction, but Union veterans — Republicans almost to a man — had dominated the government for fifteen years of increasingly venal rule. At the age of twenty-nine, John Holliday had never yet voted for anyone who'd managed to win an office.

This state of affairs was not devoid of

amusement. Back in June, for example, he'd followed press coverage of the Republican convention with a quiet, bitter glee. Hundreds of delegates and thousands of observers crammed into Chicago's Industrial Exposition Building and screamed themselves hoarse over which as-yet-unindicted criminal might best disserve the country in their name. In the end, the field narrowed down to two men who were disliked and mistrusted even by their fellow Republicans. Ulysses Grant had left the White House three years earlier under a dense cloud of scandal; he was now ferociously backed by Roscoe Conkling, arguably the most corrupt politician in the nation. Which was saying something. Grant's opponent for the Republican nomination was James Blaine, a man so sensationally consumed by the desire to attain the presidency that even his friends admitted he'd sacrifice anything — including honor and his firstborn child — on the altar of his ambition.

After thirty-six ballots, the Republican convention remained deadlocked, whirling between corrupt Scylla and vainglorious Charybdis. Fistfights broke out on the convention floor. Baroque insults were traded. There were threats and deals, betrayals and reprisals, high dudgeon and low comedy. As entertainment, it was hard to beat.

Just when it seemed the Democrats would

win the White House by default, James Garfield emerged out of nowhere as a candidate and was nominated by acclamation. "Who in hell is James Garfield?" people asked, and the answer was: a former college professor who'd taught Greek and Latin at Hiram College in Ohio and who'd risen to the rank of general in the Union Army. Quiet, ethical, and brilliant, Garfield tried repeatedly to dissuade the delegates, warning that he would do nothing to gain the office if they forced the nomination on him. He'd kept his word, too, traveling no farther than his own front porch during the campaign.

Instead of capitalizing on their opponents' disarray, the hapless Democrats sabotaged their first postwar opportunity to regain influence in national politics by nominating Winfield Scott Hancock, a man known primarily for his willingness to hang a woman for her very doubtful part in Mr. Lincoln's assassination. Which had left John Henry Holliday to wonder what he might have done if he'd had to choose between a well-educated, reform-minded Republican and the cynical, unprincipled mediocrity served up by his own party.

He was delivered from this extremity by circumstance. Arizona was a territory, not a state; its residents were barred from voting in the national elections. Only Pima County and City of Tombstone offices would be on the ballot in November. The decision to cross party lines felt no less consequential, however, for men he knew were involved in the local elections. Virgil Earp was running for town marshal. Virgil's opponent was the late Fred White's deputy, Ben Sippy. Ben was a nice enough fellow, but he lacked Virgil Earp's experience in law enforcement, not to mention Virgil's sheer physical presence. For John Henry Holliday, it came down to this: If I were being beaten and robbed in an alley, which of the two candidates would I feel most relieved to see? The answer was clear, though he half-expected his hand to shrivel and turn black when he voted for a Republican. His X went next to Virgil Earp's name.

He was willing to go no further. James Earp was on the ballot for village assessor, but if James was going to win that office, he'd have to do it without a Georgian's support. John Henry Holliday had too many memories of kin and neighbors thrown off their properties when carpetbagging Yankees jacked up real estate taxes beyond the owners' ability to pay. He would not place that financial weapon in the hand of any Republican, not even a friend's.

Which left the Pima County sheriff's office. And that was his most difficult decision, for Morgan Earp was dear to him, but Wyatt . . .

Well, the truth was that Wyatt often seemed stupid. Or, more charitably, rigid in his thinking. Wyatt himself wasn't running for sheriff — not yet, anyway — but his support for Bob Paul was exactly what made Doc hesitate. Bob Paul and Wyatt Earp shared many strengths and weaknesses. Both had demonstrated admirable moral and physical courage, and Doc had no doubts about their competence and honesty, but they also shared a propensity to see the world in black or white. Charlie Shibell, by contrast, was more flexible in his thought, as demonstrated by his willingness to deputize a Republican like Wyatt Earp. Furthermore, a Democrat like Charlie Shibell understood that Pima County's ranchers and farmers would respond to a Yankee push with a Confederate shove. Pin a sheriff's badge on Bob Paul — or Wyatt himself, one day — and you could end up with a shooting war like the one in Lincoln County.

Grateful for the sacred secrecy of the ballot box, John Henry Holliday cast his vote for Charles Shibell and did so in the knowledge that Wyatt would probably be out of a job if Charlie was reelected. That was regrettable, but Wyatt must have known that campaigning actively for his boss's opponent was a risk.

One vote won't make the difference anyway, Doc thought as he folded his ballot and tucked it through the slot. There were so many Republicans in the county now, the lat-

307

est odds were on Bob Paul to win with a
spread of sixty votes.

HIS SLAVE GIRL OR
HIS WEDDED WIFE

"Those figures are wrong," Wyatt insisted when Johnny Behan finished reading the newspaper to him a few days later. "The numbers don't add up."

"I tried to warn you, Wyatt. I knew the race would be closer than you expected, but . . ." Johnny Behan shrugged his helplessness in the face of the younger man's stubborn disbelief.

Johnny himself had seen the results coming from a mile away. James Garfield would be the next president. Sheriff Shibell was re-elected. Virgil Earp's defeat was decisive, and James had lost by an even wider margin. The prospect of two Earps holding two important city offices had galvanized the opposition. Democrats all over the county — and even some Republicans in town — were deeply opposed to putting so much power in the hands of one family, especially when a third brother was a deputy sheriff who didn't seem to recognize that his badge was a political gift, graciously bestowed. Democratic turnout was heavy, particularly in Sulphur Springs Valley.

His brothers' losses stung, but it was Bob Paul's defeat that had stunned Wyatt — a state of mind evidenced by the cruller left untasted on a plate next to the coffee Josie had poured for him.

"Anyway, the election's over," Johnny said. "We have to accept the results."

Wyatt shook his head mulishly. "The numbers from Precinct Twenty-seven can't be right. A hundred and four ballots cast, and all but *three* of them for Charlie Shibell? That precinct don't have more than thirty registered voters, total!"

Josie paid very little attention to politics, but she came out of the kitchen when she heard that, wiping her hands on a dish towel and frowning.

"Wyatt," Johnny was saying, "the votes have been certified."

"It's fraud," Wyatt snapped, and without another word or so much as a glance at Josie, he left the Behans' house.

Johnny shook his head and reached across the table for the abandoned cruller. Josie went to the doorway, watching until Wyatt was lost to view.

"You knew Bob Paul would lose," she said. "Didn't you."

Chewing, Johnny brushed crumbs off his

waistcoat. "Everybody knew Bob Paul was going to lose — except Wyatt, I guess."

"But you told Wyatt to support him!"

"I did no such thing." Johnny wiped his mouth with the back of his hand and swallowed. "Wyatt was going to support Bob no matter what I said. I just told him he oughta talk to voters and find out what they were thinking. It's not my fault if Wyatt can't read people any better'n he can read a newspaper." Josie was staring at him, mouth open, and he laughed — gently — at her innocence. "Wyatt has many fine qualities, honey, but he's smart about politics only on Tuesdays and Fridays in months that begin with Q. The sooner he figures that out, the better off he'll be. Sometimes people have to learn their lessons the hard way."

"What do you mean, 'the hard way'?"

"He gambled and lost." Johnny cleaned his hands on a napkin and pulled a piece of flimsy yellow paper from his pocket, holding it out to her. "Charlie Shibell is going to replace him."

She read the telegram and looked up. "With you."

"I've got the experience. I've got the skills. And *I* didn't campaign for Charlie's opponent."

"But if it hadn't been for that one precinct, Bob Paul would have won. And if those results are fraudulent, then Bob Paul did win."

"The results are whatever the Board of Elections says they are, and the board says Charlie Shibell was reelected by forty-two votes." Johnny sat back in his chair, crossed his arms over his chest, and smiled with pure satisfaction. "Pick out your wedding dress, honey, and start thinking about the big new house we're going to build! This's going to mean forty grand a year —"

"Forty . . . But, Johnny, you told Wyatt his half would be ten."

"And he'd be happy to get it, too. Anyway, it was only an estimate. A lot depends on how Charlie and I assess the mines."

"But if there's a new county . . . does your offer to Wyatt stand?"

"Of course," Johnny said comfortably. "If Frémont appoints me sheriff, I'll make Wyatt undersheriff. The deal still makes sense for both of us."

She was frowning at him, trying to put it all together. He could see that she suspected he was pulling a fast one on Wyatt. Which would be — God knew — easy enough. "I know you like Wyatt, Josie. So do I, and I'll do what I can for him, but he's his own worst enemy and dumb as shit to boot."

"At least he's *honest.*"

Refusing to rise to the bait, Johnny reached for another cruller.

312

Josie snatched the plate away. "Those are for Albert."

It was that coldness that did it. The contempt. She had hardly spoken to him since the night Fred White was shot. Day after day, he had been conciliatory and understanding.

"Put that back," he said.

The threat was clear: in his voice, his eyes, his fist. But Josie never gave in, and she was still child enough to fling the plate against the wall rather than do as she was told.

The noise of his chair hitting the floor came an instant after the plate shattered. What happened next was over quickly, almost before the powdered sugar had settled out of the air. He gave her the back of his hand. Spun her around with the force of it. Clamped a hand over her wrist. Twisted her arm behind her. With the ancient anger of men defied, he pushed her facedown over the table, shoved her skirt up, and taught the brat a lesson she needed to learn.

When he was done, he leaned close to her ear and said in a voice soft with warning, "You will do well to keep in mind who's buttering your bread, princess." Then he left the house.

Alone in the sudden silence, shocked, almost disbelieving, she looked around her. A table she'd served meals on. Plates she'd washed. Curtains she'd ironed. The familiar, weirdly

313

changed.

Shuddering now, reaction setting in, she went to the kitchen, worked the pump, washed her face. Her first impulse was to go straight to the Cosmopolitan. Collect that fifty dollars and leave town, but . . . there were practicalities to face.

Johnny hadn't used a French letter. What would she do if she got pregnant? Go home? Face her parents?

Break their hearts. Shame them.

Go to Chicago! Try to brazen the situation out. Bernhardt got away with it, but the Divine Sarah was famous and rich and adored. The Unfortunate Miss Marcus was unknown and talentless. Fifty dollars wouldn't last long. What would she do when the money ran out?

Johnny was on her night and a day. How much harder could whoring be? At least she'd get paid, but how long would that last? Who'd want a pregnant whore?

All right, an abortion then. But where would she get one? Chinatown?

Or . . . or maybe she should just pick out a wedding dress.

She told herself, There are worse things than living in a big house with an important politician who might be governor someday.

She told herself, He'll make it up to me. He always does.

She told herself, Nobody's perfect. Most of

the time he's very nice.

She told herself, It was my own fault. He has a temper, and I know that. I shouldn't have made him mad.

Albert would be home from school any minute now. She had to pull herself together.

For a moment, she considered telling Wyatt. No, she thought. He'd kill Johnny. It was strange, how sure she was about that.

"All men are capable of savagery." That's what Bob Paul told Wyatt Earp over coffee, back when they first met. "I learned that lesson in 1855, Wyatt. I was undersheriff during the Ranchería riots. You probably don't even remember them."

"I was seven," Wyatt said.

Bob snorted and shook his head. "Damn, I'm getting old. Anyway, a gang of liquored-up Mexicans started it. Went from one Chinese camp to another. Robbing stores. Stealing horses. Killed a white woman and her kids. An Indian. A couple of Chinks. Word got around fast. Really brought the community together," Bob said cynically. "White miners and Chinese shopkeepers and the Indian's relatives rounded up all the beaners they could lay hands on. Lynched eight of them."

Before nightfall, entire families had been convicted of being Mexican and driven from their homes. More than fifty houses were burned to the ground, along with a Catholic church.

"Course, some of those 'Mexicans' turned out to be from Chile," Bob said, "but they spoke Spanish and that was by-God close enough. Meanwhile, the real killers were twenty-two miles south. My posse ran them down. I shot two myself. We hauled the others back to jail and locked 'em up, so I thought it was safe to go home and get some rest. While I was asleep, another mob broke into the jail and dragged out the man they thought killed that woman back in Ranchería. Ran him up three times."

"Ran him up?" Wyatt asked.

"Half-hanged him. Brought him down, revived him — twice! Wanted to make sure he suffered before they finally killed him," Bob explained. "*That* is what happens when people take the law into their own hands: Crime is compounded by vengeance and brutality. The law and its strict enforcement are all that separate civilization from barbarism. That's why I'm running for sheriff, Wyatt, and I'd like to have your support."

There were very few men Wyatt Earp looked up to, morally or physically. Robert Havlin Paul was among them. Standing six feet, six inches tall in his stocking feet, a massive 260 pounds in meaty maturity, Bob had placed his own huge body on the line between civilization and barbarity for two and a half decades. That such a man had been defrauded of the sheriff's office was, simply, not to be borne. And Wyatt Earp meant to do something about it.

He got Morgan to compose a letter of resignation, copied it out in his own hand, and signed it. Ignoring Morgan's questions and Mattie's, he packed a valise and left Tombstone on the evening stage. Changed to the train in Benson, arrived in Tucson the next morning, and went straight to the sheriff's office. Told Charlie Shibell he was resigning and why. Told him he was going to Bob Paul next with his suspicions about Precinct 27.

Charlie rubbed his face with both hands. "Bob will appeal, I expect."

"Yes, sir," Wyatt said. "I expect so, too."

Charlie stared at him. "You don't think I had anything to do with this, do you? That I rigged the election?"

"No, sir, I don't." But he wasn't willing to work for a man who'd accept such a tawdry victory.

"Well, I'm still sheriff until it's decided," Charlie said. "No hard feelings, Wyatt, but under the circumstances, I've hired Johnny Behan to replace you as my deputy."

"Yes, sir. I figured that would happen."

And if that's the price of honesty, he told himself, I'll pay it.

He went to Bob Paul next and laid out what

he knew about the fraud in Precinct 27. Bob listened without comment and when Wyatt was done, he said, "You're a good man, Wyatt. I owe you."

They didn't make any deals about who'd be Bob Paul's undersheriff, but if appeal of the Precinct 27 results went in Bob's favor, Wyatt was pretty sure Bob would remember his help.

He caught the next train back to Benson and got some sleep on the way. He was waiting for the stage to Tombstone when it came to him that his own affairs might work out better with Johnny taking over as Charlie's deputy. Johnny liked to be in the thick of things. He might move to Tucson where the Sheriff's office was. After the county got split up, Johnny might stay up north because Pima County would be controlled by Democrats and he'd have more of a chance at higher office if he had a base there.

Which would make it likely that Governor Frémont would appoint Wyatt himself sheriff of the new county in southeastern Arizona. Which meant collecting taxes in the Tombstone Mining District. Ten percent of which would set him and his brothers up for life. In the meantime, Wyatt would be free to look after his business interests.

Nights, he had faro tables in several saloons — four that he banked now, plus the one at the Oriental that he ran himself. Mornings, he took one of the horses out for exercise and did a little prospecting while he was at it, for it had not escaped his notice that a man could stake a claim, dig a hole, announce a strike, and sell the pit for $50,000 to some fool with more money than sense. Doc Holliday had him thinking about water rights, too. People kept talking about piping water down from the Huachucas, but so far only one small line was operational. "Everything in Tombstone depends on water, one way or another," Doc had said. "If this town is goin' to grow, that is where the money will be." So Wyatt was thinking maybe him and his brothers ought to ride out to the canyons west of the San Pedro River and stake some water claims. Doc, too. It would do the dentist good. Get out in the sunshine. Build himself up some. And if he had an income from water rights, he could go back to that sanatorium sooner and stay a while.

When a handsome, broad-backed sorrel came up for sale over at Dunbar's in early December, Wyatt looked her over. Duchess, she was called, and she was cheap because the idiot who broke her had scared the animal senseless from the start, probably slamming a big, heavy Mexican saddle onto her and sawing at her mouth. She'd flinch at a blanket and frog around for a time after she was saddled, but once she was moving, she had an easy gait that wouldn't wear the dentist out before they got halfway to the mountains. Wyatt had gentled horses like that before — look how well Dick Naylor had turned out! It was time to start training Reuben, too. The colt hadn't inherited as much leg from Roxana as Wyatt had hoped, but Reuben would do well in the mile.

That's what he was thinking about after he closed out his faro table at dawn one day in mid-December. About how good things were going. About how satisfying it would be to work with Duchess and Reuben — salvaging one, bringing the other along the right way.

The sun had just started to climb as he walked home, and the town was quiet. Shops still closed. Dogs gnawing on fleabites or asleep in the dirt. Mountains, blue in the distance. A cold wind was carrying the noise of the mine engines away, which made everything seem peaceful.

"Mr. Earp?" a soft voice called.

Two of them. No weapons visible. Ike Clanton and a young stranger who asked, "You're Wyatt, right? Not one of the others?"

"Who wants to know?"

The boy looked around, then backed away, beckoning Wyatt into the vacant lot between Fly's photography studio and the O.K. Corral. They'd be out of sight there, which is exactly why Wyatt didn't follow him.

A movement caught his eye, above and to

his left. Corner room, second story of Mrs. Fly's boardinghouse. Doc Holliday was standing at the window, coat off. His hands were on his shirt buttons — he was getting ready for bed — but he lifted those arched brows high as if to ask, Everything all right?

Wyatt met Doc's eyes, then returned his attention to Ike and the fidgety kid with him.

"My name's Jim Johnson, sir," the boy told him. "But I — I said I was Henry Johnson, when — Look, I'm the one who certified the votes in Precinct Twenty-seven, but it was Ringo's idea!"

"It was Ringo's idea," Ike confirmed.

Wyatt waited while the kid gathered his nerve. That cost the boy some work, but once he started, the words came out in a rush.

"Ringo, he told me to say there was a hundred and four votes for Charlie Shibell, but there warn't, sir. They was mostly for Charlie, that's true, but there warn't more'n a coupla dozen real votes. Ringo told me what numbers to put down and said I should sign the paper. He's acting like he's boss now. Curly Bill never bossed us, but ever since Ringo took over — You never know what's gonna set him off, and he'll kill you if you cross him."

"He's a mean sonofabitch," Ike said, "and I know mean when I see it."

Wyatt and young Johnson turned to stare. There was real conviction in that statement,

321

and they both knew why.

"My daddy's in Mexico," Ike said. "Ringo thinks he's in charge when the old man's gone."

"We want Curly Bill back," the boy said.

"What do you expect me to do about it?" Wyatt asked. Bill Brocius was still in jail up in Tucson for shooting Fred White, even though Fred had said the shooting was accidental. "It's in the courts now."

"So's the election, sir," Johnson said. "It's in the courts, right? Because Bob Paul's trying to get the results declared a fraud. Well, you was there when Fred got shot. If you testify for Curly Bill and he gets off, I'll by-God say in court what I know about the vote in Precinct Twenty-seven."

"What makes you think Ringo won't kill you for that?" Wyatt asked.

Johnson lifted his chin, like a little kid sticking up for himself. "Well, he might. So I want fifty dollars and a train ticket, too. I'll testify, then it's me for Memphis. I got kin there."

"Why not just go home to Memphis and be done with it?" Wyatt wanted to know. "Why do you care if Curly Bill gets out?"

"Because Bill was always kind to me, sir, and Ringo —"

"Ringo is a mean sonofabitch," Ike said.

"He can't just hit people for no reason!" the kid cried, sounding aggrieved. "If Ringo don't want Bob Paul to be sheriff, then by

God, that's why I do! Because that'll show him!"

"Lemme think about it," Wyatt told them. "Come by the Oriental on Friday. I'll give you an answer."

Satisfied, they bobbed their heads and hurried off.

Wyatt glanced up. Doc was still standing at the window, ready to help if he was needed. Wyatt nodded his thanks. Then he finished the short walk that took him back to a house that passed for a home and a woman who passed for a wife.

■ ■ ■ ■

The Ache of
Longing Mounted

■ ■ ■ ■

No Joy for Us in the Sumptuous Feast

The year-end holidays of 1880 were glittering in Tombstone. Hardly an evening passed without a choral concert or an ice cream social, a costume party or a dance. There were horse races and prizefights, and a shooting contest in which Doc Holliday tied for tenth in a field of fifteen. He blamed the abysmal showing on the cold weather but earned no mercy from the Earp brothers, who ragged him relentlessly about not being able to hit a barn door with a shovel full of horseshit. Then Dick Naylor came in dead last in the Christmas quarter mile. For that stunning defeat, Doc smugly blamed the jockey: Wyatt himself, who'd gained weight and lost another tooth owing to a dramatic increase of baked goods in his diet.

A variety of amateur theatrics debuted in December, but the Nellie Boyd Dramatic Company lit up the season when it came to town with costumes, sets, a four-piece orchestra, and a repertoire of twenty-two plays. The theater was packed for three weeks of riveting dramas and diverting comedies, but this entertainment paled in comparison to a dazzling display of sheer criminal audacity. Doing business as the Tombstone Townsite Company, Jim Clark and Mike Gray laid claim to the entire city's real estate. Even in a boomtown where survey lines were honored mostly in the breach, extorting "payment" for properties built before the village was incorporated was pretty startling. Civic discord escalated when Messrs. Clark and Gray began to expand their property lines by sending men out at night to move fences. And occasionally an entire building. The practice was violently contested, most notably on the evening when a Nellie Boyd performance was attended by a large group of men who, not wanting to miss the show, carried loaded shotguns into the theater in anticipation of being called upon to defend their stores and houses at any moment.

Through it all, work at the mines went on, stopping only on Christmas Day. Glum geologists who'd predicted a speedy failure of Tombstone's limestone-embedded silver deposits were mocked by rich men who had every expectation of becoming even richer in the New Year. Why, the Contention alone had paid out $600,000 in dividends in its first seven months! Its stock was going for $80 a share, and if the silver veins were indeed pinching out, well . . . no one was inclined to spoil the fun by mentioning that to new investors.

In the privacy of boardrooms and drawing rooms, there may have been a moment or two when the wealthy wondered if they were lying or merely keeping their own counsel, but who was to say? Seven years after the Crash of 1873, many found it difficult to distinguish between canny business practice, sharp dealing, and plain deceit.

Do what works. That was the motto. Grab what you can when you can. That was the plan. It was not a golden age, as Mr. Twain had recently pointed out, but a cheap and flashy gilded one. A time of fakery and exuberant corruption, of patronage and cronyism and every species of shameless self-seeking. In such times, even honorable men give up trying to draw the line. It's different now, they always think. Everything is different now.

In spite of it all, because of it all, the work of government went on, from the corridors of power in Washington, D.C., to the dusty streets of Tombstone, A.T.

At church on Christmas Day, President-elect James Abram Garfield was a man besieged. Wherever he appeared, office seekers crowded around, pressing requests for political appointments in the new administration. One strange little man in a threadbare suit stood out, even among such throngs. Approaching with an odd mixture of antique formality and modern intimacy, Charles Julius Guiteau took Garfield's hand and held it just a little too long for comfort.

"I have had a change of heart about accepting the ambassadorship to the Austro-Hungarian Empire," Guiteau confided. "I think I should prefer Paris to Vienna, and I believe I shall be satisfied with a consulship."

"Mmm," the president-elect replied.

Mr. Guiteau withdrew, serenely certain that he was personally responsible for the pleasing outcome of the national election and that he'd soon be rewarded with a lovely apartment in France.

Two days later, and two thousand miles away, Wyatt Earp placed his hand on a bible in the Tucson Municipal Court and swore to tell the truth, the whole truth, and nothing but the truth. He testified that he'd witnessed the shooting of Tombstone city marshal Frederick George White by the defendant William Brocius. Yes, he agreed, there was a rumor that Mr. Brocius had pulled a gun trick called the border shift on Marshal White, but it was his own belief that while attempting to disarm Mr. Brocius, Marshal White had given the defendant's pistol a quick jerk, causing the gun to fire. Counsel for the defense then called a gunsmith, who testified that the trigger mechanism of that weapon was damaged and liable to go off under such circumstances, whether Mr. Brocius intended to shoot or not. Taking into account the marshal's own deathbed statement, the court ruled Fred White's death accidental. Mr. Brocius was released after eight weeks in jail.

As Curly Bill passed Wyatt Earp on the way out of the courthouse, he spat at the lawman's boots. Which surprised Wyatt, for he hadn't expected thanks, exactly, but he sure hadn't seen *that* coming.

The next morning, a young man named James Johnson took the oath in the Pima County Superior Court and testified that he was the mysterious "Henry Johnson" who'd certified 104 predominantly fictitious votes for Charles Shibell in Precinct 27. On the basis of this testimony, Robert Havlin Paul was ruled to have won election as sheriff of Pima County. Mr. Johnson took the first train out of town and was not seen in the Arizona Terrority again.

Charles Shibell immediately filed an appeal of the decision overturning his election, which would require some months to work its way through the courts. In the meantime, Bob Paul took a job with Wells Fargo, riding shotgun on stagecoach runs carrying silver bullion and company strongboxes, splitting shifts with Morgan Earp.

Down in Tombstone, John Philip Clum announced his intention to run for mayor in the January 4 municipal election. His platform was to "defeat corruption while bringing peace and prosperity to our city by taking on the audacious depredations of the Townsite cabal of Clark and Gray." With clean government, Clum promised, Tombstone's underground riches would attract the investment capital needed for continued growth. "Tombstone," he wrote, "will become the city upon the hill: a beacon as bright as ancient Rome."

Reading this declaration in the *Epitaph,* Dr. John Henry Holliday was heard to murmur, "Ah, the glory that was Rome! Tiberius. Caligula. Nero. Domitian. Commodus. Elagabalus . . ."

This sally was met with blank stares.

Kate would have gotten that joke, he thought.

The gaiety of New Year's Eve often feels a little forced. After six weeks of parties beginning in late November, a general weariness of festivity sets in, replaced by a yearning for plain food and a more ordinary routine. When he reserved the Cosmopolitan's music room for December 31, Doc had modest expectations for the evening. He simply meant to give the Earps' ladies a chance to dress up and step out on the town. He would play piano for them and see the New Year in with friends.

In retrospect, his last-minute decision to include Josephine Marcus might have been more carefully considered. He had noted Deputy Sheriff Behan's departure from town on the thirtieth, realized Miss Josephine would be alone the next night, and hoped that she might renew her study of the piano. So he'd invited the young woman and Sheriff Behan's son without anticipating the attitude of the other ladies at the party. The results were mixed. Allie was a bit stiff, but Morgan and Lou were always taking in orphans — Doc himself among them — and Lou seemed pleased to spend time with someone new and interesting. She and Josie passed much of the evening talking and giggling in the corner, apparently unaware that Mattie Blaylock was looking daggers at them.

Josie and Wyatt rarely came within three yards of each other, though at one point, Doc noticed them approach the buffet table at the same time.

Standing at Wyatt's side as she lifted an hors d'oeuvre, Josie turned away to face the rest of the room. "Suppose I were to leave Johnny . . ."

Wyatt's eyes remained on an assortment of sweets. "There's still Mattie," he said, his voice quiet with resignation.

At midnight, a magnum of champagne was shared around. Josie asked for her cloak a few minutes later. Morgan and Lou said they'd walk her and Albert home, and left with their hands entwined, a more private celebration on their minds. Virgil and Allie went home as well, similarly inclined, followed by Wyatt and Mattie, who were not.

Alone again, John Henry Holliday played half a nocturne, paid the bill, and made his solitary way back to Molly Fly's boardinghouse. There, he lowered himself onto the front stoop to catch his breath before he climbed the stairs to his room.

The cacophony of the steam engines down at the mines and the routine carousing east of Sixth Street were occasionally loud enough to be heard out here on the northwest corner of town. Most of the time, however, wind carried city sounds away. Pay attention to the hush of a breeze passing through a nearby stand of palo verde, and there was a certain solace to be found. Gaze at the glittering intensity of the Milky Way in this desert air, and a useful clarity of thought could sometimes be attained.

His first four months in Tombstone had gone well, apart from that early unpleasantness at the Oriental. As the effects of the concussion dissipated, he had established a sensible daily routine. Mrs. Fly served up regular meals and he was getting enough rest in her house, for she was strict about noise and selected her boarders with an eye to their manners. He was dealing faro on commission at the Alhambra, and John Meagher was kind enough to allow him to break the work into three-hour stretches. He took short walks to stay limber and practiced piano to stay sane.

At Wyatt's urging, he'd begun riding again. His stamina was improving, though his damaged hip gave him trouble — a problem that would recede as his legs strengthened. Wyatt wanted him to buy that sorrel Duchess, but it made more sense to rent her for a few hours a week. Miss Kate would be proud of me, he thought, for Mária Katarina Harony had always been the one to keep expenditures in check when she and Doc were together. With a fairly reliable income from faro, he was building up a decent stake. At this rate of savings, he could retire to a sanatorium at the end of '81, though he'd begun to wonder if that was really necessary.

His breathlessness was permanent — once cavitated, lung tissue is gone forever — but it wasn't getting worse. His cough was drier. With the chest pain diminishing, he was drinking less. Why not settle in Tombstone? The winter climate was close to ideal. Sunny, pleasant, with occasional rain that kept the dust down. Why endure the sterile boredom of a sanatorium if he could stabilize his health right here? He had friends in Tombstone. He had music and books. He had even accepted a few patients who could be helped with quick extractions; there was a great deal of

335

satisfaction in that, though hardly any money.

Objectively, it was as good a life as he'd managed to construct for himself since leaving Dodge City. And yet, as 1880 drew toward its close, he had grown increasingly melancholy. Emptied out. Hollow at the center.

Easing to the edge of the stoop, he gripped the porch rail with one hand, pulled himself to his feet, and let himself in. The stairway to the second floor was steep, but he was not yet reduced to pausing with both feet on each tread.

Once inside his room, he lit the oil lamp and sat on the edge of a narrow monastic bed. Only then — when he was settled and calm — did he lift the latest letter from his cousin Martha Anne from its place on his bedside table.

Congregation of the Sisters of Mercy
St. Vincent's Convent
Savannah, Georgia

The return address wasn't a surprise. She had entered the novitiate some time ago. He had thought himself accustomed to the idea, but until this letter, there had always been a possibility that . . .

That *what?* That he would find a cure and go home someday? That Martha Anne would still be there, waiting for him? That the life he'd left behind when he was twenty-two would somehow resume, as though seven years had not passed for anyone but himself?

"Idiot," he muttered. "Sentimental, self-important, self-deluded fool."

Even if the progress of his disease stopped tomorrow, there was nothing left for him in Atlanta. There would be no marriage, no children, no prosperous dental practice to support a growing family. That ghost life had been consigned to its grave by an unfamiliar signature in a dear and familiar handwriting: *Sister Mary Melanie.*

From the day he left home in 1873, loneliness had been nearly as constant as his cough, and it now felt just as permanent. The only time it had ever lifted was when he and Kate were together.

Was that it? he asked himself. Was that what all this enervated despond came down to? He tested the idea like a man with a broken tooth, tonguing the jagged surface, and . . . Yes. He missed Kate.

He missed the intimacy of their partnership, the way she found a town's best poker games for him, and rolled his cigarettes, and kept his shot glass filled with honeyed tea while he was playing well and with bourbon when the cough was bad enough to break his concentration. He missed her childlike glee when he won, her tough confidence when he lost, and even her snappish annoyance when he played poorly. He missed the husky contralto rasp of her voice when she tossed off a Greek quotation or a Latin proverb, or murmured French in bed. He missed the back of her neck, the ripe-peach softness of her hips. He missed her energy and her impatience, her decisiveness and her practicality. She was difficult, profane, abrupt, and unsettling, but she gave his days and nights color, shape, taste, surprise.

"I will never leave you," he had once promised her.

He had given his word, and he had broken it.

The weeks after he killed Mike Gordon were filled with discord and misery. He told himself that Kate would be glad to see the last of him, but even then, he knew she would not take it as a kindness. Indeed, when they met again — briefly, in Prescott — her fury was searing. He was a no-good lying goddam sonofabitch who'd slunk out of town while she was asleep and when he went to hell where he belonged, she would by-God dance on his grave.

He turned down the lamp. Lay back against the pile of pillows that made breathing in bed a little easier. Stared out the window toward a sky lightening on the first day of 1881. Spunk up, he told himself. Apologize. She may not care, but now is the time to try.

■ ■ ■ ■

Twelve months later, John Henry Holliday
would spend New Year's Eve sitting at Virgil
Earp's bedside, waiting for Virg to die. In a
state of melancholy deeper than any he had
ever experienced, he would go over and over
everything that had led to the gunfight in
October, hoping to identify some moment,
some decision, some choice that might have
made a difference in the way things had
turned out. There was plenty of fault to
splash around. Wyatt, Ike Clanton, Frank
McLaury, Little Willie Claiborne, John Clum,
Kate Harony . . . All of them bore some
responsibility for what happened. And Doc
himself? His involvement could be traced to
a wholly innocent event. He went to the
library. He struck up a conversation with a
fellow reader. Who could have seen the harm
in that?

Curious about the landscape around him,
he was leafing through a battered copy of Lyell's *Principles of Geology* when a well-dressed
young man of perhaps twenty-three years
entered the room. Each nodded pleasantly to
the other. That might have been the end of
the encounter, if Doc hadn't noticed that the
book being returned to the shelf was Anthony
Trollope's *The Way We Live Now*.

"Did you enjoy the novel, sir?" he asked.

"It was a little close to home," the young gentleman admitted. "I feel as though I am surrounded by Melmottes and Longestaffs and Carburys these days. Sometimes I wonder if we learned anything at all from the last crash."

"Yes, there seems to be a great deal of money ridin' on a great deal of optimism. This time it's silver mines instead of railways, but . . ."

"It's still cash chasing dreams." The young man offered his hand. "Edson Waffle," he said, sounding resigned.

"Belgian, I presume."

Waffle laughed, the tension leaving him. "Yes, and a lifelong victim of jokes about pancakes! My wife and I arrived last month from Ohio. I'm a teacher. I just started work at the new school down in Charleston."

"John Holliday, from Georgia. I am a dentist, though my health prevents me from takin' on as active a practice as I would like —" He stopped. "Pardon me, did you just say there is a *school* in Charleston?"

"Yes, indeed! Drunken rustlers shoot out the lights and murderers walk the streets with impunity, but Mr. Gird employs a number of professional men at the stamping mills. They have families and want their children to be educated. I've been hired to do the job."

"Well, sir, that is good news for the future of Arizona!"

They exchanged a bit more small talk, and once again, that might have been the end of it, had young Mr. Waffle not decided to broach a more difficult subject. "Dr. Holliday, if you don't mind my asking, I wonder . . . how are you finding the climate? You see, my wife also suffers from . . ."

"Chest complaints?"

"Chest complaints," Waffle repeated, grateful for the euphemism. People hesitated to speak the name of the disease, as though to say "tuberculosis" or "consumption" would cede to the illness additional power over the lives it blighted. "That's why I took the Charleston job, you see. The snow and the cold in Ohio were undermining my wife's health. We believed Arizona would be more salubrious."

"I have not been here long enough to have a firm opinion, I'm afraid. Dust can be a problem, but there may be something to the idea of heliotherapy. I have had no episodes of pneumonia or pulmonary hemorrhage durin' my time here."

They chatted about the treatments each sufferer had tried and what the outcomes had been, and about what else might help. Edson Waffle was heartened to discuss this with someone who was both knowledgeable and realistic, and it was only natural that the young teacher would want to introduce this pleasant, soft-voiced gentleman to Mrs.

Waffle. "Would you consider visiting us in Charleston?" he asked. "I think Clara would love to meet you, and it would be so helpful for her to talk to someone who has dealt with these problems for so long."

Doc's first visit to their home was in mid-February. "There is a difference between stamina and strength," he told Edson's pale little wife. "Bed rest harms both, in my experience. No alternative durin' a crisis, but invalidism is not inevitable, Mrs. Waffle." As evidence he offered the young woman his own presence at her table. "When I started ridin' back in November, a mile was all I could manage. Now, here I am in Charleston, all the way from Tombstone!"

He had continued to gain ground physically in early 1881. His mind, too, seemed to have recovered, but there remained one last mental hill to climb. He had not played poker since Milt Joyce laid two and a half pounds of iron against the side of his head six months earlier. When he visited the Waffles, they often played cards and he could feel the old skills returning. The concentration and patience. The capacity for strategy.

"Dr. Holliday," Edson said one Sunday, "I wonder if you would be interested in filling an open seat in a weekly game of five-card stud. One of our regulars is going to be out of town." It was a ten-dollar ante, the teacher warned. The opponents would be men of substance. An accountant, a hydraulics engineer, and the owner of the biggest store in Charleston. Even young Mr. Waffle had more money than one might have expected, for he had used his teacher's salary to invest in a successful livery stable and was doing quite well for himself.

A ten-dollar ante was serious poker, but John Henry Holliday felt ready. The Charleston game could be an entrée to high-stakes play at the level of society he'd hoped to join in Tombstone before the unpleasantness at the Oriental. And so he had agreed to play poker in Charleston on March 15, 1881.

The Ides of March, Doc would think, looking back on it. That should have been a sign.

A Virtuous Man

Farmers are like gamblers in many ways. There's a lot of chanciness in the way they make their living. Like John Henry Holliday, Thomas Clark McLaury was a quiet, thoughtful person who found comfort in routine.

Each evening before bed, Tom would grind some coffee, draw water for the pot, and gather kindling for the morning. He'd clean up the supper things, putting pots and dishes in their places. He swept the floor, too, for moving each day's dust and grit outside made him feel like he was putting that in its place, as well. Before shutting the door, he'd look for signs of rain. At dawn, he'd roll out of his bunk, pad over to the stove, bring up the fire, and move the coffeepot to the hottest plate. While that came to a boil, he'd go outside to take a piss and study the sky again to see if he'd been right about the rain.

Weather down here took some getting used to. When it was winter up in Iowa, Arizona was warm and dry. Then in summer, when Tommy expected things to get even drier, it rained so much Frank joked about building an ark. On any given day of the year, the afternoon heat might be worse than a farmer could imagine up north, then water might freeze that very same night. These were strange conditions and a challenge to agriculture. What kind of crop could you grow in a place that might have summer and winter, both, inside a single day? What should you plant in a desert that was liable to turn into a swamp a few months later?

Not knowing any better, the McLaurys put in sixty acres of corn their first year. Most of the crop withered before it came near to tasseling, and the rest rotted in the summer wet. After seeing their work and investment come to nothing, Frank was happy to shift his sights toward livestock when Mr. Clanton came around to explain things, but Tommy couldn't quit on the idea of being a real farmer. After the corn failed, his next thought was cotton, though he didn't know much about that, except you needed field hands to pick it. Even after the brothers started taking money for fattening Mr. Clanton's stolen cattle, the McLaurys weren't in a position to hire a crew.

Well, Tom told himself, look around you. What likes to grow here?

Cactus covered the high, sandy slopes.

Cottonwood edged the streams. Grass grew in the valley. That natural pasturage was good enough for the local beef market, but when Tom heard that big ranchers like Henry Hooker and Texas John Slaughter were breeding up better cattle, he asked Mr. Hooker about his business plans, just from friendliness and curiosity.

"Chicago meat packers are paying premium prices for premium beef," Mr. Hooker told him. "I've got the stock — if I could get better fodder, the beeves'd be worth a good deal more up north."

"What kind of feed would you buy, sir?" Tom asked.

"Rye. Or alfalfa." Then, seeing what Tom was driving at, Mr. Hooker told him, "Grow either of those, son, and I'll take as much as you can bale."

Frank was unenthusiastic. "Why in hell would we want to work like mules on a crop when plain old grass just grows itself?" He was against it something fierce when Tommy borrowed money from Mr. Hooker to give rye and alfalfa a try. Tom put in eighty acres of each anyway, just to see.

Rye survived, but alfalfa really *liked* the valley. Tom was able to pay off the loan at the end of 1880 and still had enough left over to make improvements to the farm. Ranchers who'd seen how well Hooker's stock did on good feed placed orders for the next season.

Tom planned to skip the rye and go with alfalfa in '81.

It was nice to make decisions without having to argue with Frank, though Tom was saddened about their falling-out. Looking back, it seemed a surprise that the brothers' partnership had lasted as long as it did, for Frank was a real McLaury. Prickly and combative. Ready to go to law over the least little dispute. "I know my rights!" was the McLaury battle cry. You could trace the clan through Irish history just by looking at generation after generation of lawsuits. As far as Tom could see, all they'd ever won in court was hard feelings among their neighbors and bad blood within the family. Nobody but Tommy ever said, "Let it go." He'd always been the odd man out. A stranger, almost, in his own family.

When Frank announced that he wanted an end to their business association in January, it was kind of a relief. Frank got everything done legally. That was fine with Tom. The farm was his idea anyway, and he preferred a clear title, for he expected to finish 1881 in the black and wanted no cause for future grievance.

After a few weeks alone, Tom realized that he didn't miss his brother. He wasn't even sure where Frank was living now. Charleston, maybe. Or with the Clantons. Frank was drawn to companions who would lead him down the wrong path. Tommy couldn't do anything about that, except worry. It was better not to know.

Tommy liked things quiet, too, and Frank had always got right to talking the moment his eyes opened. It was a wearisome start to the day, especially when Frank had a dream about some floozy. He liked to tell Tommy about such things and show him the stain on his drawers. Which was disgusting. Then he'd nag Tommy about going to a cathouse. "We have earned ourselves some fun!" he'd say.

Tom had tried that a few times, but the girls pawed at him and called him "sweet face" and "handsome." It was embarrassing, and he couldn't get any pleasure from what they wanted to do with him. He kept thinking about the awful pictures the pastor back in Iowa had showed all the boys in the congregation when they got to be of age. You could get horrible diseases that would cover you in pustules and make you go crazy.

"Keep yourselves clean for the one true love the Lord has ordained for you," the preacher told them. "She is out there somewhere, waiting for you."

Now, at last, Tom McLaury found her: his one true love. Standing in a rocky little square of dirt around a small adobe house, she looked like a lily growing up through a patch of cactus, but she had a shovel leaning against her veranda steps and she was planting a pair of cutback shrubs with heart-shaped leaves. That's how Tommy knew she was meant to be a farmer's wife.

"Those are lilacs, aren't they," he said, sitting high up on his buckboard, the wagon bed filled with a month's supplies.

She straightened and clapped the dirt off her gloves and shaded her eyes with her palm. "My sister sent them. They do well by her door."

"That's may be," he allowed, "but her door isn't in Arizona, is my guess."

"You're right. She lives in Utah."

"Are you a Mormon then?"

She hesitated. A lot of people hated and feared Mormons, but she didn't like to lie — he could see that. He wanted her to know that he would never hate or fear her, so he said, "Seems to me, Mormons are uncommonly handsome people. That's why I thought you might be one. You are the prettiest person I ever saw." She looked startled and he could feel himself go red. "I — I'm sorry. I'm a farmer. Now that my brother moved out, I don't hardly talk to anybody but the animals. I forget my manners with people, I guess." Shut up, he told himself. You sound like Frank, talking so much.

She didn't seem to take offense. She just turned her head a little, to let the breeze blow a curling strand of straw-colored hair from

her face. "I don't believe we've been introduced."

"I'm Tom McLaury, miss." He rubbed his
palm on his trousers and leaned down to offer his hand.

She pulled off her gloves and came closer
to take his hand briefly, then stepped back
right away. "I'm Louisa Earp," she said, as if
in warning. "Mrs. Morgan Earp."

"Oh," Tom said.

This was a sharp disappointment, though it
should not have been a surprise. All the
women in Arizona were either somebody's or
anybody's. He wanted to tell her right then
that she was with the wrong man, but he
remembered his manners just in time. "I am
very pleased to meet you, Mrs. Earp." He
glanced at the lilacs. "Might be you could
find a place in Tombstone where a lilac could
take hold, but that place is not by your door.
It's better to plant something that likes to be
where you want something to grow. I could
bring some flowers that will do well for you
there. If you like."

Before she answered, her eyes shifted away
to someone behind him. He couldn't be sure
of what he saw in her face. Relief, but a little
bit of nervousness, too. Tommy turned and
saw an older fella. Skinny and a little bent
over — a city man, bundled up in the chill.

"Miss Louisa," he said in a slow southern
voice, "is this gentleman disturbin' you?"

"This is Mr. McLaury, Doc. He is a farmer, and was giving me some gardening advice. Mr. McLaury, this is Doc Holliday. He is a dentist and a friend of the family."

Neither man recognized the other's name. Tom didn't read the papers and hadn't heard about what happened in the Oriental last year. Thoroughly addled, Doc Holliday had missed all the excitement about the mules. So the sweet-faced farmer from Iowa nodded to the soft-spoken dentist from Georgia, who inclined his head. There was no quarrel between them on that bright blue day in early March, nor would there be when they met again on the cold and blustery afternoon of October 26, 1881: the day John Henry Holliday was going to blow a four-inch hole in Tom McLaury's chest.

Gathering the reins, Tom put his foot up against the wagon brake, getting ready to release it. "Anyway, I don't believe lilacs will grow here," he said, "but I do wish you good luck with them, ma'am."

"How was your walk today?" Lou asked when the farmer had driven off.

"Splendid!" Doc told her with a little flash of pride. "Two miles, without stopping to rest."

Something in the dentist's thin, lined face made her eyes go narrow and speculative. "Oh, Doc!" she cried when she realized that she was seeing happiness. "You heard from Kate! Has she agreed? Is she coming to visit?"

The funny thing was, Lou didn't much like Kate Harony and certainly didn't think the woman was right for Doc. It wasn't that Kate was a whore. After knowing Bessie Earp, Lou could not condemn such women out of hand. What Lou found difficult to understand was why a gentle man like John Holliday was drawn to a woman who seemed as crude and harsh as Kate. "I don't understand it either," Morgan said once when he and Lou were talking about the couple back in Dodge. "But if she makes Doc happy, that's good enough for me." And now it was good enough for Lou, for it was such a welcome change to see Doc's eyes alight, Lou would have kissed Kate and hugged her neck if the little Hungarian suddenly appeared in Tombstone at that moment.

The dentist unbuttoned his coat, drew a carefully folded telegram from his breast pocket, and handed it to Lou. Smiling, she took it from him, but after she read its brief message, she looked up and frowned at Doc's sunny mood.

"I know," he admitted ruefully. "I know . . . But it is progress! At least this time, she sent an answer."

That morning in Globe, Arizona, a Western Union telegrapher had received the latest in a long string of wires sent by J. H. Holliday. Ordinarily he maintained a professional attitude toward transmissions he conveyed, but the terse, compressed messages often told of emergencies and sicknesses, deaths and births. Despite his best efforts to remain aloof, a telegrapher could get caught up in an unfolding drama. This was one of those times for the Western Union man in Globe. He had not simply taken an interest in a serialized story. He had taken sides.

There was some confusion at the beginning, for the first of J. H. Holliday's telegrams were sent to M. K. Harony. No such person lived in Globe; after some inquiries, it was established that the intended recipient was now going by the name of Katie Elder, and that she was proprietress of a boardinghouse populated by a dozen silver miners. Miss Elder was, the telegrapher presumed, the injured party in what seemed to be a lovers' quarrel, for the first telegram was simply:

I AM SORRY STOP FORGIVE ME STOP

There was no reply.

NO EXCUSES STOP I WAS A FOOL STOP

Again, no reply, and the next few messages were in some kind of foreign language.

ERRARE HUMANUM EST STOP

LA COEUR A SES RAISONS QUE LA RAISON NE CONNAIT STOP

SINE AMOR NIHIL EST VITA STOP

CURA QUID EXPEDIAT PRIUS EST QUAM QUID SIT HONESTUM STOP

Maybe she doesn't know what any of this means, the telegrapher fretted. The sender went back to English a few days later.

LET ME MAKE IT UP TO YOU STOP

Despite J. H. Holliday's evident and sustained contrition, Miss Elder did not bend. The telegrapher was increasingly impatient with her intransigence, and he had found this morning's message particularly poignant.

LET ME LOVE YOU STOP I ASK NOTHING IN RETURN STOP

"If that doesn't do the job, I don't know what will," he muttered, handing the flimsy yellow paper to the messenger and sending him to Miss Elder's place.

The boy came sprinting back a few minutes later. "She's coming!" he cried, with something close to alarm in his voice.

Eager to see the goddess who had inspired such devotion, the telegrapher was taken aback when a blond woman entered the office, strode to the counter, grabbed a pencil, and scribbled three words on the reply form. From the persistence of her admirer's pursuit, he had imagined someone young and beautiful; Miss Elder was nigh onto thirty, thin-lipped and thick-waisted, with a face that failed to charm. He was, nonetheless, struck by a fearsome intelligence blazing in eyes the color of Indian turquoise when she thrust the form through his grate.

"Send that!" she snapped.

"Yes, ma'am," he answered, flinching when the office door banged shut behind her. He sighed when he read her message, then dutifully tapped it out.

GO TO HELL STOP

Moments later, a message came back — not from J. H. Holliday but from the Western Union man in Tombstone to his counterpart in Globe: DAMN SHE MUST BE SOMETHING STOP

I GUESS came the reply from Globe, BUT ANGER IS A HORSE THAT WOMAN CAN RIDE FOR DISTANCE.

"She'll come around," Lou said, handing Kate's telegram back to Doc. "Tell her about the piano here. Tell her you'd like to play for her again."

"You think that would help?"

"Doc," she assured him, "after that night in Dodge, Kate would have to be made of stone to say no to that."

Looking doubtful, Doc said, "She won't back down in front of the Western Union man."

"Well, then, send a letter!" Lou cried with brisk practicality.

"Why didn't I think of that?" he wondered, genuinely puzzled.

Because you are a hopeless spendthrift who wanted an immediate answer, she thought. "Because you care so much," she said, laying a hand on his bony shoulder. "Clean up, and come on back for supper. I hate to eat alone, and Morg's not due home from Benson until late."

I Wish I Were the
Wife of a Better Man

"I'm sorry, Honey," Johnny said. "I know I missed New Year's Eve, and now I'm going to miss Valentine's Day, too, but it's county business. I can't help it."

Josie had been on her best behavior since he'd pounded some sense into her last November. "Duty calls," she said. "How long do you think you'll be gone?"

"Hard to tell. I need to find Curly Bill Brocius and settle things down."

Freshly acquitted of murder, Curly Bill might have preferred the dreamy peace of opium, but folks in Tombstone were still pretty sore about Fred White's death. Unable to visit Ah-Sing's hop joint, Bill was making do with liquor — a lot of it. Under its influence, he and his friends were making a good deal of trouble in Charleston and Contention. Deputy Sheriff John Harris Behan's cordial relations with Bill and the boys were well known; both small towns were asking for his help in dealing with the crime spree.

"As long as I'm down near the border, I'm going to ride over to Bisbee and introduce myself. That copper find has been confirmed," he said. "The executives are moving in already, getting the new mines started."

"I understand," she said. "The papers say electricity is the future. Copper wire is the next big thing."

"Bigger than gold or silver," Johnny agreed.

"There'll be a lot of votes down in Bisbee," she said, and wished him safe travels when he left later that afternoon.

The trip went well, though it took longer than he'd expected. Curly Bill agreed to quiet things down; no arrests were necessary. Johnny continued on to Bisbee, where he made a good first impression on the movers and shakers in Arizona's next boomtown. He stopped in at ranches along his route, making sure the voters were happy with his work. All of them promised loyalty in '82. He was looking forward to telling Josie his good news when he got home.

In his absence, a great deal had changed. As anticipated, the city of Tombstone had been named the seat of government for the newly created Cochise County, though the governor's appointees had not yet been announced. What Johnny Behan did not expect was to be greeted at his own door by a stout and scowling Mexican woman of middle years, who happened to be cutting up vegetables at the time.

"Who are you? *¿Quién es?*" he asked.

"Me llamo María Elena," this formidable person told him. "The lady, she say you pay me one dollar a day. You owe me eighteen dollar already. I cook. I look after *el chico.*" With her paring knife pointed at him in emphasis, she made her meaning very clear when she added, *"¡No más!"*

"Where's Al?" he asked. *"Mi hijo — dónde está?"*

This brought a shrug. Reassurance, not indifference.

"*Con la* lady," he was told. "He come back later. You eat now."

Across town, just west of sixth, the bellboy of a small Tombstone hotel was knocking on a door at the end of a second-floor hall. It was a hesitant and quiet knock, not an insistent pounding or a businesslike rap, for the bellboy had just turned fifteen and he was new to this job, the nuances of which were full of mystery. The hotel was on the border between the vice zone and the nice part of Tombstone; like the hotel itself, the women who lived here were on the edge of being bad. What they did wasn't illegal, but it wasn't respectable, either.

The bellboy couldn't decide what to call this new one. He'd had enough church back in Illinois to know that she wasn't a good girl, but whore didn't seem right either. Sometimes she only went to dinner with men, or she just went dancing with them. She didn't always . . . entertain them in her room.

Was she alone, the bellboy wondered, or was somebody else in there?

That was another problem. He didn't know how to refer to her visitors. They weren't miners or cowboys. They dressed nice and had manners, and they tipped well, too, so he didn't want to do anything to annoy them. Were they gentleman callers? Clients?

He knocked again, a little louder this time. "It's the bellboy. There's someone downstairs wants to see you."

"Tell him to come back at eight."

"No, ma'am — I mean miss — I mean . . . It's not that kind of . . . person. It's that little kid again."

A silence. The sound of bedsprings creaking. He waited, trying not to imagine what she looked like before she put on her dressing gown.

She came to the door and opened it a crack.

"He's crying," the bellboy told her, doing his best not to look . . . *down.*

She closed her eyes, and lifted her face, and stood very still for a few moments. "Tell him, 'Sadie says you have to go home.' "

Her only regret was leaving Albert. Otherwise, life as a demimondaine suited her admirably, so far. She was Becky Sharp, in *Vanity Fair.* She was *La Traviata* — the Lady of the Camellias — except she had no intention of dying tragically at the end of her story. She was certainly not a whore. She just . . . took lovers. Like Sarah Bernhardt.

In her first two weeks, she'd seen a mining executive, a lawyer, and a very sweet geologist. They were grateful and generous. She enjoyed their company and their admiration. She liked the look on their faces when she stepped out from behind her dressing screen and dropped her wrapper. She liked to be seen. She liked sex, too. Not as much as Johnny did — it was a sickness with that man — but enough to enjoy what she was doing.

"You can have any man you want," Randolph Murray had told her the night after the Markham troupe left San Francisco. "Just look into his eyes. Think, *I want you,* and he'll be yours."

She hadn't quite believed him then. Now she knew that it worked like a charm, except with the one man she really wanted.

She had imagined it a thousand times. The knock on the door. Wyatt standing just beyond it, twisting his flat-brimmed hat around and around in his hands.

"This is wrong," he would say. "I shouldn't be here."

She would pull him inside and change his mind. She would make him forget that woman he lived with. Even in her imagination, he would finish too soon the first time. She would make allowances: the long waiting, the urgency.

"You're rushing," she would tell him. "It is more tender when you take your time." Then she would teach him what a woman wants.

When they were done — both drowsy, both satisfied — she would ask, "Wyatt, are you sorry?"

"No," he would say. "No."

The next day, they would leave Tombstone together. She would send Albert a letter to explain everything. *Your father needs women,* she would write. *Wyatt needs* me.

Over and over, she thought: I want you. Come to me.

But the knock on the door was never Wyatt's.

MY HEART IS BALANCED BETWEEN TWO PATHS

It wasn't like he didn't know. At New Year's, Josie had told him straight out that she was thinking about leaving Behan. He'd figured she was just mad at Johnny again. Fighting was part of what kept the fire going for couples like Doc Holliday and Kate Harony. The Behans were battlers, too.

Besides which, the governor still hadn't announced his appointment for sheriff of Cochise County, and if Johnny Behan got the nod, Wyatt could be working for him soon. That was a $10,000-a-year bridge he didn't want to burn.

He had no intention of getting tangled up with a flighty girl who changed her mind four times an hour. Sure, there was a spark — he wouldn't deny that. But he was used to keeping a tight rein. It was a mistake to let your feelings get away from you. Look what happened when he let himself feel sorry for Mattie Blaylock! He ended up living with her, and they were miserable, but he didn't see

364

any way out of it. He had enough trouble at home without borrowing any from Johnny Behan.

So he'd stayed well clear of the Behans' mess until the afternoon he found young Albert standing in the middle of Sixth Street with his little head cranked back and his face all smeared with dirt and tears.

"Sadie? Sadie! Come home!" the kid was hollering up at a second-floor window. "Sadie, *please*! Come *home*!"

Wyatt had worked all night at the Oriental. Then he'd taken Dick Naylor out for a few hours of exercise. All he wanted was to go to bed, but he couldn't just ride by like he didn't see the kid.

"What's the trouble, son?" he asked.

The question seemed to make things worse. Snot running, mouth wide, the child was gripped by soundless sobbing until he pulled in a big, gasping breath and wailed, "It's n-n-ot my fault! It's my f-f-father's fault!"

"What is? What's your father's fault?"

"Everything!" Al yelled, rage trumping sorrow. "He's a cheater! A-a-and he *cheats,* and I *hate* him! A-a-and now he made S-S-Sadie go, too!"

Confused, Wyatt asked, "Who's Sadie?"

"She's *Josie*!" Al screamed, as if Wyatt had misunderstood on purpose. "Sadie is her se-e-cret name, and you can only use it if you love her, and she's up *there,* and she won't

365

come home!"

Hell, Wyatt thought. What's she doing in a hotel like that?

He knew the answer but couldn't dwell on it — not with Albert gulping and hollering and crying so hard he could hardly breathe. Wyatt had all but raised Morgan, and he knew that when a kid gets that worked up, all you can do is wait it out — unless you're the kind of grown man who'd belt a child until he's hurt too bad to whimper.

Wyatt Earp had spent his whole life trying not to be that kind of man, so he dismounted, and got Al out of the street, and made him sit on the boardwalk, and sat down next to him, and tried to patch the story together. Al seemed to think that the problem started after Fred White was shot, though the boy didn't understand why that was so.

"Sadie stopped talking to him," he said, still weepy. "And Dad *knew* he was in trouble and he was trying to make it up to her, but then — it was like she was *scared* of him. And I *knew* everything was getting ruined, because that's what happened before my mother left! He stays out late, and they cry, and then they get scared, and then they leave! And it's his fault!"

It took some work not to laugh when the boy called Johnny "a no-good son of an itch," which was probably Al's first attempt at vulgarity. Another man might have bawled the boy out because the Bible said to honor your father. But some fathers don't deserve it, and nobody knew that better than Wyatt Earp.

"You like ice cream?" he asked when Al ran out of steam. He nudged the boy with his elbow. "Course you do. Everybody likes ice cream, right?"

"And cake." Al wiped his nose on his sleeve and sucked in a shuddering breath. "You love Sadie, too. I know you do." He started to cry again, but it wasn't anger anymore. It was sadness. "You know what I wish?" the boy asked. "I wish you were my father and Sadie was my mother."

Wyatt set his jaw and looked away. Then he cleared his throat. "Al, that's the nicest thing anybody ever said to me." He stood then and unwrapped Dick's reins from the post. "Wanna ride him down to the stable?"

"Sure," Al said, brightening up. "Ice cream after that?"

Wyatt nodded, though his face was still. "Sure," he said. "Ice cream after that."

It took three dishes of peach before the boy was willing to go home. He was still mad at his father, but what choice did he have? His mother had a new husband and a new baby. She didn't want him back. "Sometimes you just have to make the best of things," Wyatt told him. He took Al home, and when they got there, he had to sit and listen to Johnny tell how he was fed up with Josie and glad she'd left, and how she was more trouble than she was worth, and so on. Course, Johnny always said everything about six times, so it was well after dark when Wyatt finally got back to his own place.

And there was Mattie, sitting in that rocker of hers.

Waiting for him, like a rattler.

"Last," she said, her voice low and tense, like she'd been patient all this time and was just beginning to lose her temper. "I'm always last."

He hung his hat on the peg and kept his back to her, afraid of what he might say if he looked at her.

"Everything comes before me," she said, still quiet. "Your brothers. Your friends. Your investments. Your horses. Your *whore.*"

He turned at that. "If you're talking about Josie —"

"Yes, I'm talking about her!" Mattie said, getting louder. "Yes, I'm talking about that Jew bitch! She was always a tramp, and now she's your whore."

And you were a two-bit streetwalker before you moved in on me, he thought, but there was no point in pouring kerosene on a fire.

He took off his coat and hung it next to his hat. "Mattie," he said wearily, "I have never laid a hand on that girl. Hell, I haven't laid eyes on her since New Year's."

"You expect me to believe that? You must think I'm as stupid as you are. Behan's *using* you, Wyatt! It's just like up in Dodge, and you're too dumb to see it. Behan and that little Jew tramp. You think I don't know what you're doing, but I know. I see what you're doing." She was hitting her stride now. "You leave me alone for days, but you never leave me any money. Why do I have to go begging for my medicine? You want me to crawl, don't you. You want me to beg that Jew at the pharmacy for my medicine. Goddam Jews — they're all in on it! They're trying to kill me, so you can marry your little Jew whore."

In years to come, people would say he'd stolen Johnny Behan's girl, and that was the reason for the bad blood between them. They'd say he abandoned poor Mattie Blaylock for that hussy Josie Marcus, that he'd jumped from one woman's bed into another's. But on the night he left Mattie, all he wanted was *quiet*. An orderly home. A pleasant word when he got there. A decent meal. Was that too much to expect? Was that too much to want?

"You're probably turning Jew, too." Mattie was saying. "You're such a goddam tightwad, you'll fit right in."

It came to him: He could afford to walk away from this house. He had mining interests. Gambling concessions. Good prospects of an excellent political position. He could take a room over at the Cosmopolitan, where maids kept the place clean. Restaurants would be glad of his business, and he wouldn't have to pretend to like the food. He could come and go as he pleased, without all this endless, hopeless, pointless strife.

Silent, almost in a trance, he went to the bedroom and reached up for the carpetbag slumped on top of the wardrobe. Out in the front room, Mattie kept on about the Jews and her medicine and how stupid he was, but when he didn't come back out into the sitting room, things got quiet.

She was right behind him. He could hear her breathing.

"Don't you dare leave me," she said, her voice low and mean.

He wondered if she'd stab him. That's how bad things were between them. He thought she might pull a knife and stab him in the back.

Turning, he said, "Mattie, I can't live like this anymore. You can stay here. I'll give you money to live on. But I'm going to leave."

Her face was white. "You bastard," she whispered. "You cold, rotten, heartless bastard."

He didn't even shrug. He went back to packing while she yelled and wept. When his bag was full, he returned to the front room for his coat and hat.

"Go on, then! Leave!" she snarled. "Go to

your Jew bitch! That's what you've always wanted, isn't it! You *never* wanted *me*!"

"I kept you off the street for a while. That's gotta count for something, Mattie."

Her face crumpled, and she began to cry. "But . . . *why?* Why did you bring me here if you never wanted me anyways?"

He paused, one hand on the doorknob. When he had an answer for her, he opened the door and spoke the only truth he could offer.

"Mattie," he said, "I am damned if I know."

"I told you so," Allie said, standing at the front window. "Maybe now you'll believe me when I tell you what's in the cards."

Virgil hauled himself out of his chair with a groan and came to her side. Wyatt — carpetbag in hand — was walking away from his house. Mattie was standing on the veranda, face contorted, hands fisted. You could hear her cursing through the window glass.

"Hangman, upside down," Allie reminded Virgil, for she'd been casting tarot all afternoon. "I told you Wyatt was due for a change."

Well, hell, Virg thought. That could mean anything! A change of shirt. A change of job. A change of luck. A different haircut. Anything.

"I'll tell you something else," Allie added smugly. "Morgan needs to tend to his business at home."

Virg looked at her sharpish.

"I laid the cards for Lou," Allie said. "Lovers, reversed. She's got someone on her mind, Virg. And it ain't Morgan she's thinking about."

That winter, Tom McLaury went for days at a time without another human being to speak to, but it was no hardship. He enjoyed the quiet companionship of his draft horses, Peggy and Bob. He talked to the dogs, too, and to a pair of Mexican pigs he'd bought recently.

"Your babies'll be meat someday," Tommy told the pigs when he fed them, "but I'll give them a good life until then. That's about all a pig can ask for."

As the weather warmed, Tom got out into his fields every day, keeping track of the growth and taking note of wildflowers growing along the edges of his fields. Later he would dig them out and pot them up in old coffee cans. Lifting each plant from the earth, gently teasing the roots loose, he would talk to Louisa Earp in his mind, planning what he'd say when he saw her next.

He would tell her, "Most folks here take what they want from the land and move on. I love you because you are trying to make things better."

He would tell her, "The Lord meant you

for me. I know you're married, but you are with the wrong person." If she disagreed, he'd say, "I will be patient and wait for you. A good farmer knows how to do things by littles."

One day he would load the buckboard with sand verbenas and primroses, with lupines and gold poppies and larkspur, and drive to Tombstone and knock on her door. "You see?" he'd say. "I have brought you a wagon filled with spring and love."

■ ■ ■ ■

AMID
JUTTING CLIFFS AND
STEEP RAVINES

■ ■ ■ ■

BETTER THAN NIGHT
FOR A THIEF

"Listen to this, Budd!" Morgan Earp said around a mouthful of lunch.

Budd Philpot was a patient young man, but everyone has his limits and Budd was reaching his. "Jesus, Morgan! Lemme eat in peace, willya?"

"You'll like this," Morg promised. "It's in a book, but it's just like what we do."

Morgan was the second of the Earp brothers to serve as the shotgun guard on the stages Budd drove between Benson and Tombstone. Most folks liked Morgan better that Wyatt, but Morg could be a talker and a lot of the time, he talked about books. Worse yet, he would *read* to you from the books, like you were just as interested in them as he was. Which was not the case.

"There's a stagecoach called the Dover mail, see, and it's in England a long time ago, but it carries passengers and the mail just like we do. There's a driver like you and a guard like me because —" Morgan held up

377

the book and began to read aloud. "Robbery was 'the likeliest thing upon the cards.' And then it says that the guard had an arms chest with 'a loaded blunderbuss' and 'six or eight loaded horse-pistols, deposited on a . . . a substratum of cutlass.' See? That's just like our box, except I've got a shotgun and revolvers. No cutlasses, though."

"What in hell's a stradum?" Budd asked irritably. He motioned to the waitress for more coffee.

"Beats me," Morg admitted after a few moments. "We can ask Doc Holliday when we get back to Tombstone."

"I don't want anything to do with that sonofabitch."

"C'mon, Budd! Doc's not so bad."

Budd grunted. He was friendly with Milt Joyce and not inclined to be forgiving about what happened in the Oriental last September. Milt hadn't lost his hand to Holliday's bullet, but his fingers were never going to work right again. Morgan claimed the shooting was a misunderstanding, but Budd Philpot knew what he knew. Holliday was a bad-tempered, argumentative drunk who left bodies in every town he got run out of, and Budd didn't give a damn if all the Earps in the world thought different.

Morg went back to reading aloud about the Dover mail coach, and even if Budd didn't say so, it *was* kind of interesting. He admired how the book talked about horses, for example, especially about how the lead horse would shake his head and rattle his harness because he was "an unusually emphatic horse, denying that the coach could be got up the hill." That was pretty funny. Budd liked another part about how the horses drooped their heads when they were pulling uphill and how "they mashed their way through the thick mud." Mashed. That was good. That said it just right. That was just how it was, getting a team over the hills between Benson and Tombstone where the road skirted the San Pedro River near Drew's Station. The track was sandy there and washed out whenever it rained. Gullies crosscut the road, and there were ditches on either side and steep little rises. Budd Philpot had earned his reputation as the Kinnear Stage Company's best driver, but he hated that part of the run as much as anyone. You were between towns, a long way from the law in either direction. Those hills and gullies provided plenty of cover for robbers on horseback, so Budd listened with more interest than usual to what Morgan was reading that day, until lunch was over.

They had a full coach for this run. Two salesmen, a lawyer, and another batch of whores on their way to Tombstone. The girls were all aflutter because Morgan was a good-looking sonofabitch, though if Morg ever took advantage of that kind of thing, Budd never saw it. Word was, Morgan Earp had raised his share of hell when he was younger, but now he said he was as good as married, and that seemed to be the case.

"Will you protect us if there are robbers?" That's what passengers always asked a shotgun guard, and Morgan always said, "I will do my best." Which was sort of a lie. Drivers like Budd worked for the stagecoach company, but Morgan worked for Wells Fargo. His job was to protect the strongbox. Kinnear's passengers were a secondary consideration at best. Truth be told, passengers were in a lot more danger when the stage was carrying a Wells Fargo shipment, which everybody could see when they did. Put a man with a heavy, short-barreled shotgun across his knees up next to the driver, and you might as well paint a big sign on the side of the coach that said, "There's something worth stealing on board." Silver bullion, payroll for miners, bank deposits. If they unloaded the strongbox at the Benson train station and if there weren't many passengers, Budd would ask the guard to sit inside on the way back to Tombstone so thieves would see there wasn't any money and leave the coach alone.

Once he was up on the bench, Morgan wasn't any chattier than Wyatt, which is why it was a surprise, and an unwelcome one, when they were a few miles out of Benson and Morgan said, "Well, now . . . what d'ya spose these boys want?"

Budd glanced at him.

"Left side," Morg said. "Just past that white thorn."

Budd squinted through the late afternoon dust and swore.

"Two more, right side," Morgan said.

"Give 'em the goddam box," Budd suggested. He wasn't joking, either.

"Where's the fun in that?" Morgan was grinning, but his eyes were on the horsemen. "They call halt — you drop down into the boot, but hang on to those ribbons, y'hear? I'll take the ones on the left first, and then I'm gonna swing right and put the other barrel into that pair. Stay low till I tell you different."

"Oh, Jesus," Budd said. "Oh, Jesus."

But he gripped the reins more firmly and got himself ready for trouble.

Now that Wyatt was living in the Cosmopolitan Hotel, his brothers would come by the hotel restaurant two or three nights a week to share a meal with him. Sometimes other friends joined them. Turkey Creek Jack Johnson or Texas Jack Vermillion, maybe. Fred Dodge or George Parsons, sometimes. Ordinarily, Morgan would have made a good story out of what happened that afternoon, but on March 10, it was just Virg and Wyatt

381

and Doc Holliday, and while some of what Morg told them *was* pretty funny, nobody was laughing.

"I don't know who was whiter, Budd Philpot or them poor damn Mexicans. I never saw hands in the air faster," Morg was saying. "They was out looking for a string of remuda horses that got loose and wanted to ask if we'd seen 'em, so they was standing by the track, waiting for the coach. All of a sudden they're staring down the wrong end of a shotgun with me ready to put half a pound of buckshot into 'em. And you shoulda heard Budd! One minute he's telling me to hand over the strongbox, and the next he's cussing 'em six ways from Sunday for scaring him shitless."

"Idiots," Virg rumbled. "Standing in the road like that, they was asking to get killed."

Morgan shook his head at the memory. "Innocent men just don't think like guilty ones, I guess. They didn't think they was doing anything wrong —"

"And they weren't," Doc noted. "I don't imagine they realized how that would appear to someone who was expectin' trouble. And a lawman is always expectin' trouble."

"Damn straight," Virgil snapped. "The day you drop your guard is the day they get you."

"Pardon my elbows," Doc murmured, pushing his plate away so he could rest his forearms on the table and take some pressure off his chest. "What would've happened if Morgan had opened up on unarmed men?"

"Prolly woulda been some kinda investigation," Virg said, "but he'd have been within his rights, is my opinion."

"Performance of his duty," Wyatt confirmed, "but it's a hell of a thing."

"Bad day for them," Morgan said, "and a bad night for me."

"More'n one," Wyatt said quietly.

"You know," Morg said after a time, "when we came over that little rise and I saw those fellas, I'd have sworn it was a holdup. They had bandannas over their faces 'cause of the dust, and my heart's going like a steam engine, and I've got both barrels cocked, and poor Budd's there next to me, yelling, 'For crissakes, shoot those sonsabitches!' I was *this close* to firing when I realized they weren't armed. If they'd been a little slower about raising their hands . . ."

"They'd be dead tonight," Doc said, "instead of just startled."

Virgil snorted. "Better them than Morg."

"Better nobody dead," Wyatt countered. He leaned back in his chair and lit a cigar. "Just remember, Morg. Anybody with a gun on you is likely drunk, or nerved up, or both. So take your time. Make a judgment."

"I don't know, Wyatt. That was so, in Dodge," Morg allowed, "but down here, it's not a bunch of liquored-up young drovers.

Here, you got robbers laying for you. Come around the corner, and there they are, and it's them or you. Take your time . . ."

". . . and it'll be you," Doc supplied softly. He laid the price of his meal on the table, got to his feet, and coughed for a while. "Well, gentlemen, I do not envy you such decisions. A bad tooth can kill a man in the long run, but I never had to decide on the proper treatment between one heartbeat and the next. These days?" He gave them that crooked grin of his. "Life is even simpler. I just deal cards on commission. And I am late for work. Evenin'."

The brothers watched him go.

After a time, Wyatt broke the silence. "Go home, Morg. Get some sleep."

Nodding, Morgan pushed himself upright and shuffled off, feet dragging.

"Hell of a day," Virgil observed, watching Wyatt watch Morgan.

They looked out for one another that way. There were enough years between them that each brother could remember the day the next younger had been born. A sense of responsibility had lingered, long past when any of them believed he needed protection.

"You tell Morg yet?" Virgil asked.

"He had enough on his plate. Nothing to do with him anyways."

At long last, Governor Frémont had announced his interim appointments for Cochise County's offices, and the news wasn't good. Frémont was a Republican presidential appointee, but the territorial legislature was dominated by elected Democrats. They could override anything they didn't like, so Frémont had threaded the needle. Until the formal election in November 1882, Democrat Johnny Behan would be the sheriff of Cochise County, with all the political power and immense income that entailed. Wyatt had always understood that this might happen. The blow came when Johnny Behan appointed Harry Woods to the position of undersheriff.

"My opinion? You're well out of it," Virg told him. "It's gonna be a thankless job."

Cochise County was sixty-two hundred square miles of bad land. Five mountain ranges to hide in, a desert in the middle, a convenient border to cross. If you didn't run a man down in the first few days, the wind would scrub the tracks away, and you'd lose him.

"Let Harry Woods bust his nuts patrolling this wretched slice of hell," Virgil said. "You've got better things to do."

Wyatt tapped ash off his cigar. "Behan gave me his word, Virg."

"Yeah, well . . . he's a politician."

Good one, too, Virg thought. Harry Woods was not just a Democrat, he was a member of the Arizona House of Representatives —

so influential in the creation of the new county, he'd provided its name. Harry was also the editor of the *Tombstone Nugget,* so press coverage of Johnny Behan's tenure as interim sheriff would be lavish and fawning. When Behan ran for the office in the '82 election, Harry Woods would be an effective counterweight to John Clum's influence as mayor of Tombstone and editor of the *Epitaph.* You had to admire the thinking.

"Saw you and Behan this afternoon," Virg said. "What'd you say?"

"Not much. Just told him I'll run against him next year."

Virgil managed not to sigh. After his own loss to Ben Sippy, Virg was pretty sure Wyatt would never be sheriff of Cochise County, but Virgil wasn't going to be the one who told him so. Instead, he yawned and stood and stretched. "I gotta get home, or Pickle's gonna sic the dogs on me." He clapped Wyatt on the shoulder. "Don't let it get you down, kid. A lot can happen between now and that election."

Wyatt nodded and Virgil almost left, but then another thought struck him. He waited until his younger brother looked at him. "Wyatt, it's none of my business, but . . ." Virg jerked his head in the direction of Sixth Street. "Don't rush into anything." Leave that girl alone, he meant. It'll only complicate things.

386

"You're right," Wyatt said. "It's none of your business."

Not far away, at that very moment, during a private dinner in a secluded room at the back of the Maison Doree, over a multicourse supper that included many delicacies described in bogus French, Mr. Richard Gird of Millville sat across a damask-covered table from John Philip Clum, the freshly elected mayor of Tombstone, discussing the ramifications of Governor Frémont's appointments to the offices of the newly constituted Cochise County. They had opinions about all of the appointees, but the conversation had primarily focused on the Republican candidate with whom they hoped to replace Sheriff John Behan some twenty months in the future.

"No matter how you cut it, our man's going to help," Mayor Clum said. "Wyatt has determination and integrity, but it'll take more than that to beat John Behan at his own game. It will take money and influence."

"And yet, it is my firm belief," Gird replied, "that if we yoke the power of the press to the power of finance, and harness both in the service of the public, there is nothing that men of good character cannot accomplish."

Having delivered himself of this pronouncement, Mr. Gird laid aside his fork and knife, which had been unceasingly busy during the past two and a half hours, and lapsed into a thoughtful silence. Across the table, stuffed almost to insensibility, John Clum discreetly unbuttoned his waistcoat and eased back in his chair, while awaiting his patron's next utterance.

Amid a population of whip-thin, weather-toughened men, Richard Gird seemed as soft and ductile as the metal that had made him rich. His large, rounded body was testimony to the lavish diet that immense wealth afforded, *quod erat demonstrandum;* on an Italian barber's recommendation, his tightly curled and graying goatee was sharply trimmed to approximate a spade, though it failed to provide much definition to a bland and boneless face. What gave Richard Gird shape was his capacity for large-scale organization of money, men, and matériel; what gave him hardness were his principles and his insatiable intellect. He was also the most systematically ambitious person John Clum had ever encountered.

At nineteen, Dick Gird had left a good New York family during the California gold rush, but instead of panning or digging for the mineral, young Mr. Gird had learned assaying and apprenticed himself, as well, to mechanical and civil engineers. While still in his early twenties, he sought further experience with a mining concern in Chile, where he studied hydraulics and business management. When he returned to North America a few years later, he took a relatively menial job preparing topographical maps of the Arizona Territory based on the geological studies of Professor J. D. Whitney. It might have seemed an odd choice at the time, but a year of hand-coloring such maps provided Dick Gird with an encyclopedic knowledge of the region's geological formations.

Everyone in Tombstone knew what happened next: One day, a half-starved prospector named Ed Schieffelin brought Gird a black lump of silver ore the size of a hen's egg.

When Ed and his brother Al returned for the assay results, Gird asked, "Where did you find this?"

"Oh, south of here," Ed said, unwilling to say more.

Gird produced paper and pencil and began sketching little mountain ranges. "The Dragoons," he said quietly. "The Whetstones. The Huachucas." Within the space thus delineated, he drew a series of parallel lines, quickly shading them to look like wales of corduroy. "Long limestone hills, eroded and gullied." He looked up. "This is where you found the float. Am I correct?"

Ed glared at his brother, who cried, "I swear, I didn't tell him!"

"I assure you, Mr. Schieffelin, your brother revealed nothing. Now, as to my results. At this morning's price for silver, this ore assays at better than two grand to the ton. That is exceedingly high. In my opinion, you will do well to return here" — he tapped the center of his little map — "to establish your claim without delay." Gird held the piece of paper out to Ed. "Would you like to keep this as a memento, sir? Or shall I burn it? Either way, your secret is safe with me."

That display of acumen and rectitude led to less guarded discussions. By the end of the week, the men had a handshake agreement. All three of them would journey to the source of the ore, a place so desolate and dangerous that soldiers warned, "You'll find nothing out there but your tombstone." Two years later, the Tough Nut, the Goodenough, the West Side, the Defense, the Owl's Nest, the East Side, the Tribute, and the Lucky Cuss mines had made them millionaires.

Ed and Al sold their thirds early on. They were prospectors with no interest in organizing the complex interlocking industrial processes that transformed raw ore into progress and wealth. Richard Gird by contrast, had spent his life preparing to do exactly that. He brought California investment capital into the business. He initiated logging in the Huachucas to provide lumber for company buildings. He recruited, hired, and housed hardrock miners from Pennsylvania and Cornwall. He found experienced managers to oversee the daily operation of the mines. He negotiated with suppliers of steam engines, explosives, hammers, bathtubs, canned goods, and coffee. He had a road to the San Pedro River graded, established Millville, and supervised the construction of a two-hundred-foot dam that would funnel thirteen million gallons of river water over a one-thousand-foot flume that powered twenty-five massive reduction stamps to crush the ore for smelting. Finally, he retained Wells Fargo to ensure the delivery of payroll cash for thousands of employees and the export of millions of dollars in silver ingots to the New Orleans Mint.

All that, barely three years after Ed Schieffelin's lump of ore was dropped into Richard Gird's palm. All that, in jeopardy now because of a rootless gang of thieves who called themselves Cow Boys.

The editor of the *Tucson Star* had wasted no words on subtlety when he wrote, "These outlaws are worse than Apaches. They should be hunted down and shot." Throughout Arizona, newspapers were calling for a territorial police force like the Texas Rangers. Unlike Geronimo's Chiricahuas, the Cow Boys no longer confined their depredations to the Mexican side of the border. They were stealing from American ranchers now. Shooting up small towns. Taking whatever they wanted from stores and restaurants. Taunting local lawmen, daring them to do something about it. Scaring off investors.

"Civilized society requires law and order," Gird said, dabbing at his lips with a heavy linen napkin. "We cannot tolerate drunkenness and thuggery and violence on our streets. And Sheriff Behan is, I fear, a tolerant man."

"Too tolerant," John agreed.

"He is playing a long game, Mr. Clum. Behan wants to be governor one day. Perhaps even president . . . In the meantime, he thinks the sheriff's office will serve his ambitions. I myself believe he will find his new job a mixed blessing. We have a year and a half before the first election. That is plenty of time to hold Sheriff Behan accountable for every unsolved crime in Cochise County."

"I'll do my best," John promised.

Mr. Gird smiled mildly. "I'm sure that you will."

John Clum still owed him $5,720, and they both knew it.

Gird nodded to their waiter, who snapped his fingers at a boy, who rushed to retrieve the gentleman's topcoat from the cloakroom. The mayor stood and steadied the chair as the mining magnate hurled himself onto small, neat feet with a grunt and a shove. Gird was helped into his coat and handed his hat and walking stick.

John waited deferentially as the fat man lumbered toward the door. There was always one last thing at the end of such a meal. One last order, one last remark. Sure enough, Gird paused before leaving the room.

"John," he said with the kind of quiet delicacy that meant something unpleasant was about to be discussed, "it has come to my attention that there are certain of Wyatt's associates who do not reflect well on him."

John cleared his throat. "Yes. That unfortunate woman he brought here from Kansas . . . I believe Wyatt has broken with her."

"But . . . there are others. That Holliday fellow, for example. He has been seen in Charleston lately. He is a southerner. A Democrat. A notorious troublemaker. Even if he isn't in Charleston to make common cause with the Cow Boy element, he will harm Wyatt's chances."

"Yes, sir. I understand your concern," John said. What he didn't understand was what Richard Gird expected him to do about it.

RUMOR WENT BLAZING AMONG THEM

It snowed on the ides of March that year: a light frosting of white that made the desert landscape glitter. By John Henry Holliday's Georgia-bred standards, it was bitterly cold when he set off on Duchess for that big poker game down in Charleston, but it was nothing compared to what Bob Paul remembered from his New England childhood. Standing at a café window that evening, warming his hands with a tin mug of coffee while waiting for the stagecoach team to be changed, Bob could still recall thigh-high snow in temperatures so low, your lips thickened and the hairs in your nostrils froze together.

That chilly childhood was long gone. When he climbed up beside Budd Philpot on March 15, 1881, Robert Havlin Paul was fully half a century old. His big old bones were arthritic, his personality brusque on good days, crotchety on bad ones. This was among the latter.

He was losing patience with the slowly grinding wheel of justice. Charlie Shibell was within his rights to appeal when his election was overturned, but three months had gone by and there was Charlie, sleeping in a nice warm bed up in Tucson, still turning a blind eye to crime, still raking in 10 percent of Pima County taxes. And here was Bob himself, on another Wells Fargo night run with a shotgun over his knees, for the princely sum of $125 a month.

Budd slapped the reins. A team of six leaned into their harnesses, straining to start the stage moving over the rutted, stony track dignified as the Tombstone-Benson Road. They had a full load tonight. Luggage and salesmen's sample cases crammed into the front and rear boots. A heavy canvas bag of mail. A massive iron and oak strongbox with $26,000 in cash and coin. Nine passengers, one of whom had to sit on top of the coach behind the driver's box.

In the dark, in snowy weather like this, a momentary miscalculation by the driver could send a heavily laden coach skidding into a ditch, but the trip went smoothly until about two hours out, when Budd hunched over and let out a groan.

"What's wrong?" Bob hollered above the noise of the team and the harness and the coach springs and the wind.

"You eat that chili back in Watervale?"

Bob shook his head. "Why?"

Budd didn't answer; nor did he slow the

horses when he leaned over the side to puke. The only indication that he'd let that chili fly was a string of outraged curses from a passenger next to the window on the driver's side of the coach.

"Sorry," Budd called.

"Feel better?" Bob asked.

Budd shook his head. "Belly cramps, still."

"Want me to drive?"

"Yeah. Maybe. I don't know."

"Can you wait until we get to the next stop?"

Budd didn't answer that time either, but he did manage to shout, "Roll down the curtains!" before he loosed a second gout of vomit.

Bob twisted on the bench and caught the eye of the passenger who'd been sitting on the roof. "What's your name, son?"

"Roehrig," the young man yelled back. "Peter Roehrig."

"Peter, I'm gonna change places with the driver. You hang on to this," Bob said, handing him the shotgun. "Don't worry. This won't take long."

They were moving fast in the starless dark on an awful road with patches of ice in the ruts, but there didn't seem to be any plan to pull up while the switch took place. Holding his breath, Peter watched the guard grip the railing around the rooftop, stand up backward in the box, and make a Roman arch of his

396

body. The driver kept the reins until he'd scooted over on the bench, then gave them to the guard, who pivoted face forward and sat down with a bump as the coach hit a rock. The maneuver was neatly done and completed in just a few seconds. Good thing, too, for the driver was clearly in misery: stiff-faced, eyes closed, hunched over.

Grinning, the enormous guard winked over his shoulder and held out a huge hand for the shotgun, laughing when he saw Peter trembling. "Cold?"

"Freezing!" Peter yelled back, grateful not to be mocked for his nerves. "I'm from Wisconsin, but I didn't bring a winter coat. I didn't expect it to be so cold this far south."

"Lie down flat on that roof," the big man hollered, eyes on the team now, the shotgun gripped between his knees. "Stay out of the wind!"

"How much farther to the next stop?"

"Not long, son. You can warm up there."

So young Peter Roehrig of Kenosha, Wisconsin, bellied down and gripped the rail with both hands. He was chilled to the bone and scared by the bad road and the swaying coach, but the giant guard seemed competent and that poor, sick driver was having a much worse night. At least I'm not throwing up, Peter consoled himself as he lay his head on his outstretched arm to cushion the jarring ride.

"Christ, Bob, I'm sorry," the driver said, "but I gotta take a shit."

They were on a steep grade, the team mashing their way toward the crest of a draw where the track skirted the San Pedro River. It was a stretch of road that Dickens might have recognized. A long way from the law in either direction.

Intent on the turmoil within, Budd Philpot didn't notice the three men in the road. He might have seen the first muzzle flash but did not live long enough to hear the gunfire that followed, for the second slug hit him square in the heart. He was dead before he toppled out of the driver's box.

Peter Roehrig saw the driver fall and heard the shouted order: "Hold!"

The big guard yelled, "I hold for no man, damn you!"

A third bullet hit the seat next to Bob Paul, and the fourth tore through young Roehrig lengthwise, entering the top of his shoulder and tumbling through his left lung toward his spleen.

Later, one of the passengers inside the coach would tell everyone about the gasping, wet cough he heard that night. "It came from somewheres outside and above the coach," he'd say. "Sounded like somebody with consumption."

The men at Drew's station were in bed when

they heard the gunfire just after ten at night. Pulling on pants, they grabbed their rifles, rushed outside, and were nearly run over for their trouble, for by then the team was at a dead run, and the big man with the reins was yelling, "Hyah! Hyah! Hyah!" The coach went flying past them and disappeared into the darkness, headed toward Benson. They sprinted for the top of the hill and arrived in time to see four mounted men racing off in the other direction, toward the river.

A few minutes later, one of the boys found Budd Philpot's body lying on the side of the track and asked, "Who in hell was driving the stage?" But Mr. Drew himself decided that this wasn't the important part and sent the kid to Contention City to tell the Wells Fargo agent there'd been an attack on the Kinnear stage.

Western Union didn't have an office in Contention yet, so the agent rode to Tombstone with the news. By that time, Bob Paul had reached the telegraph office in Benson and his wire had thrown Tombstone into a state of alarm.

Roused from bed at eleven P.M., Mayor Clum dispatched members of the Citizens Safety Committee throughout the city to spread the alert. When the Wells Fargo agent finally arrived half an hour later, men on foot and men on horseback were rushing in all directions, ready to take action — but against whom?

Garbled, embellished, made up out of whole cloth: All night long, the stories circulated. Another stage holdup, and this time a man's dead! No, two fellas, that's what I heard. No! It was three passengers and Bob Paul.

Bob Paul was killed? Wait, it couldn't've been Bob Paul! He sent a telegram from Benson about the holdup.

It was Budd Philpot! A fella from Drew's Station said Budd was gut-shot, just like poor Fred White. Musta been Curly Bill again!

Anybody know a fella named Rorig? Bob Paul's telegram said a passenger named Rorig was killed. Wasn't he the fiddle player over at the Maison Doree? Hell, they killed a *fiddler*?

They got eighty grand from the Wells Fargo strongbox, I heard. Took the mail pouch, too. Jesus, they stole the mail? Nobody ever tried that before!

This time, jurisdiction was clear, if interwoven. The murders were a county affair. Sheriff Behan was organizing a posse that would leave at first light. An attack on a stage carrying the U.S. mail was a federal crime, so the posse would include Deputy Federal Marshal Virgil Earp, and he had deputized his brothers, Wyatt and Morgan. Wells Fargo would be represented by an armed agent named Marsh Williams.

By five in the morning, this posse had assembled at the sheriff's office, waiting for their tracker, Buckskin Frank Leslie, to appear.

"What's the plan?" John Clum asked Johnny Behan.

"Am I addressing the mayor of Tombstone or the editor of the *Epitaph*?" Sheriff Behan asked in return, understandably wary after weeks of bad press.

Clum considered the question and answered honestly. "Both."

Eyes on the lightening sky, Behan settled his hat, shrugged deeper into a sheepskin jacket, and pulled on his gloves. When he answered, his tone was civil and unstressed. "We're heading for Drew's Station. We'll track the killers from there." He spoke slowly then, to make sure Clum quoted him correctly. "The cold-blooded murder . . . of two men . . . during the attempted robbery . . . of the Kinnear stagecoach . . . requires the sheriff's direct involvement."

"Who's in charge of the office while you're gone?"

Behan put a foot in the stirrup and swung up. "Undersheriff Woods."

"Any notion yet about who was involved?"

"Nothing reliable."

It was Williams — the Wells Fargo agent — who said, "According to the Benson police, a passenger told them one of the robbers had a bad cough. Probably a lunger."

"Bill Leonard, maybe?" Morgan suggested.

"He hangs with the Cow Boys," Wyatt agreed.

At last, Johnny's deputy Billy Breakenridge came around the corner with Buckskin Frank. They made an odd couple. Small, spruce, and bespectacled, Billy Breakenridge would not have looked out of place in the business district of Chicago or New York. Hungover and bleary-eyed, Frank Leslie was something out of a Wild West show. Long, blond hair lank beneath a wide-brimmed hat, an eagle feather stuck in its beaded leather band. Indian-style fringes fluttering on his buckskin jacket and leggings. Their arrival was the signal for the rest of the riders to mount up, and Mayor Clum stepped back onto the boardwalk, though not so far away that he did not overhear a quiet exchange between Wyatt and Morgan Earp.

"You find Doc?" Wyatt wanted to know.

"He's out of town," Morgan said. "I left a note for him at Molly Fly's."

"Let's go," Johnny Behan said.

"Good luck," the mayor called, and he led the cheering as the posse left town.

By dawn, Clum was in the pressroom, composing the morning's special edition. It was easy to write the editorial, for he'd been beating this drum all year, in print and in City

Council meetings. Tombstone was an island in a storm-tossed ocean of crime. Dire consequences could be expected when the tide of violence began to rise. Sheriff Behan and Undersheriff Woods were themselves southern Democrats who seemed reluctant to take action against the Cow Boys. There'd been shootings and stagecoach robberies within a few miles of Tombstone and a number of break-ins right in the city. Were Behan and Woods inadequate to their tasks, the *Epitaph* asked, or actively colluding with the outlaws?

In response to his own paper's editorial urging, Mayor Clum himself had organized a one-hundred-man vigilance committee in anticipation of riotous lawlessness that might break out in the city at any moment. Among its members were Tombstone's most prominent citizens. All Yankees, all Republicans, all likely to back a political candidate who'd serve their interests in Prescott, or perhaps even in Washington . . . Gratifyingly, the murmurs had already begun. Who better to succeed Governor Frémont than the crusading editor and incorruptible mayor of the territory's largest, wealthiest, and most important city? Who better than John Philip Clum, a progressive Republican reformer after President Garfield's own heart? A man who could be counted on to serve the mining industry's interests.

A man who had Richard Gird's blessing, and wanted to keep it.

Mrs. Fly was making breakfast for her boarders when John Clum knocked on her door. "Terrible thing about the stagecoach robbery," she said, drying her hands on her apron. "Is it true they killed a woman?"

"I believe that is merely a rumor," the mayor told her. "There are a lot of unfounded stories going around. Mrs. Fly, is Doc Holliday in?"

"No, sir, he's been gone since yesterday morning. Why?"

"Did he mention where he was going?"

"Well, he said he'd been invited to a card game in Charleston and that I shouldn't expect him until today sometime. Probably in the late afternoon."

"I wonder if I might leave a note for him in his room."

"Why, of course you can, Mr. Clum! Morgan Earp just did the same."

Flattered to be visited by the city's chief executive and proud to show off the quality of her rooms, Mrs. Fly led the mayor up the stairs, pulling a chatelaine's key chain from her apron. "Try not to touch anything," she warned, stepping aside to let the mayor enter alone. "Dr. Holliday likes his things just so."

There were two books on the table by the bed. *L'éducation sentimentale,* by Gustave Flaubert. *Principles of Geology,* by Charles

Lyell. A framed daguerreotype of a mother with her small, solemn-eyed child. On the bureau, several issues of *Dental Cosmos: A Monthly Record of Dental Science* in a neat-edged stack. A bundle of letters tied with a blue ribbon from St. Vincent's Convent, of all places! A gold watch. Sheet music for the Piano Concerto No. 1 in B-flat minor, transcribed for solo piano, composed by someone whose name was a typesetter's nightmare: Pyotr Ilyich Tchaikovsky. There was a hand-written message on the cover page. *My dear John, Father Erbarth says you really ought to study something composed after you were born! Blessings, Alex.* Morgan Earp's note was in plain sight as well, left on a tall pile of bed pillows. *Doc, we are gone with a posse. Look after the women.*

"I scrub the floors, wash the windows, and do his laundry," Mrs. Fly said, still standing in the hall, "but he always leaves his room neat as a pin."

"Is he often out of town?" the mayor asked.

"Well, recently, he's been visiting friends in Charleston. He usually stays overnight. It's a long ride for him. He's not well, you know."

He was, in fact, Molly Fly's best boarder. Quiet and clean, John Henry Holliday always paid on time, didn't eat much, and was unfailingly courteous. He was also unlikely to want anyone snooping around in his room, and Molly Fly was beginning to think that there was something not quite right about the mayor's visit.

"Would you like a piece of paper, Mr. Clum?"

The mayor turned. "Sorry?"

"You said you wanted to leave Dr. Holliday a note."

The mayor looked blank for an instant, as though he'd forgotten he'd said anything about a note earlier.

"Thank you, Mrs. Fly, I'll speak to him when he gets back to town. No need to tell him I was here," Clum said pleasantly. "It was nothing urgent."

He had not expected a dangerous, dissipated gambler to be so tidy. It gave him pause — seeing the man's life laid bare in a few surprising possessions — but the pause was brief. Whatever John Holliday might be in private, in public he was an albatross hung round Wyatt Earp's neck and one that Richard Gird wanted removed.

Clum headed back to the newspaper office by a circuitous route, stopping along the way to interview a few chatty citizens about the stage robbery, though no one in Tombstone was an eyewitness. "It is being said that Doc Holliday was involved in the crime," he would begin, and that was strictly true, for he himself was saying it, at that very moment.

"A passenger heard one of the robbers cough-ing . . ." The trick was to raise the brows and look expectant, holding pencil and paper at the ready. With a serious frown, he would take down the words of people who had no infor-mation at all except for what they'd heard, or thought they'd heard, or thought John Clum might like to hear, for people take great satisfaction in seeming more "in the know" than they might really be.

By noon on March 16, Clum had ac-cumulated a useful collection of assertions about the well-read gentleman from Georgia who was holding back Wyatt Earp's political possibilities.

Holliday had engaged a horse at a Tomb-stone livery stable and told the stable boy he'd likely be gone for seven or eight days.

Holliday was seen departing the city, armed with a Henry rifle and a six-shooter.

Holliday had started south but doubled back and headed for Benson instead.

Holliday got back early and had just re-turned a rented horse to the livery stable, but the horse was all fagged out and so was Holliday. He must have been riding hard to get away from the posse that was tracking the killers!

Most of this was fiction, and most of the informants knew it. Still, John Clum had been asking questions about Doc Holliday. And where there's smoke, there's fire, right?

Ben Sippy didn't think the attack on the Kinnear stage would have anything to do with him. He was the Tombstone city marshal, and the crimes had not been committed in town. Then Mayor Clum showed up at the jail and gave him a direct order. "We can't have a man like Holliday walking the streets. Find him and do your duty!"

This was not the first time Ben Sippy had found himself wishing that Virgil Earp had beaten him in the race for city marshal. The pay was less and the job was more than Ben had figured on, and arresting Doc Holliday for murder struck him as an unhealthy way to spend an afternoon.

Ben's first move was to go down to the sheriff's office, hoping to persuade Harry Woods to come along as backup, but Harry declined the invitation.

"After all the shit John Clum has printed about Sheriff Behan? Nobody in *this* office is gonna arrest a registered Democrat on that lying bastard's word."

Anybody else Ben might have called upon was already in the posse chasing the stagecoach bandits. So Ben was on his own, but he did his duty. He checked Molly Fly's boardinghouse, where Doc ate and slept. He checked the Alhambra, where Doc worked.

He checked the library, where Doc read, and the music room at the Cosmopolitan, where he played piano. Came up dry all round.

It wasn't until the night after the stage attack that he finally found Holliday, gambling in a dark little faro joint on the eastern edge of town. That was the first odd thing, because it was the kind of place favored by two-bit whores hoping to parlay a good night's take into a few days' rest.

Not the kind of place Doc Holliday usually frequented.

"Doc?" Ben said. "I need to talk to you."

"Marshal Sippy," Holliday noted, eyes on the layout. "Wait until this game is finished, sir, and you may speak to me at your convenience."

"C'mon, Doc. It's important —"

Holliday leaned back. "So is this game, and be damned to you if you break my concentration again."

"Oh," Ben said, withering under that slate-blue stare. "Sorry."

Not wanting to rile Doc further, Ben watched quietly. As far as he could see, the deal was square. Course, Doc himself would know if somebody attempted to cheat him at his own game and considering his reputation, few men would try. Two minutes later, Doc collected his winnings, which seemed to be something under fifty dollars. That was peculiar, too. Small-stakes games didn't much interest professionals, who saw no point in risking cash without a fair probability of a substantial payoff.

Another man was waiting for a game, so Doc moved to the edge of his chair and planted his cane, but he had trouble getting up and looked like hell. Sweaty, pasty-faced, tired. Drunk, too, which was a real surprise, no matter what gossips said. Sure, Doc put away a lot of bourbon, but so did many lungers — Ben's own cousin Jack among them. They drank in small doses all day long, to control the coughing and ease the chest pain.

"Now, then," Holliday said, finally on his feet. "You have something to discuss with me?"

"Yes, sir," Ben said. "Let's go over to the office."

"I doubt that is necessary. What is this about?"

"Something you might not want to discuss in public."

Drink in one hand, cane in the other, Holliday limped to a table at the back of the room. Ben followed, and they both sat down before Holliday asked again, slowly and deliberately, "What. Is this. About?"

Ben looked away for a moment. "The Kinnear Stage holdup."

"A lamentable affair. What has it to do with me?"

"Probably nothing, but . . ."

"Probably," Doc repeated. "Implying . . . what, exactly?"

"Where was you last night, Doc?"

"Why do you ask?"

"Goddammit, Doc! I'm giving you the benefit of the doubt here! I could arrest you right now —"

"On what grounds?" Holliday cried, exasperated. He stared at Ben for a moment. "Wait! Are you suggestin' that I had something to do with a holdup?"

"Well, see, people are saying you planned the robbery —"

Startled into a laugh, Holliday pulled out a handkerchief and coughed for a time, gasping, "Now, *that* is perfect irony," before he settled into the fit. When it passed and he got his breath back, he drained his shot glass, looking half-amused. "Well, sir, people may say whatever they please. It is a free country. Any amount of absurdity and nonsense may be spoken." He paused to cough again before asking, "Out of curiosity, do you have a warrant?"

"Not really, but Mayor Clum says I have to take you in."

The slate-blue eyes turned cold. "No, sir, you do not have to do any such thing. If you do not have a warrant, then what you have is gossip, which is evidently being purveyed by a Republican politician whose newspaper profits from the sale of rumor, innuendo, and character assassination. And you may tell Mr. Clum for me that if my name is dragged into his newspaper over this affair, I shall sue him for libel."

Ben could see that he was expected to say something, but nothing came to mind because Holliday had begun to tremble, as some men do when they are very angry or very scared, and since Ben didn't imagine that anybody could be scared of him, it seemed pretty likely that he was about to get killed. Which made what Doc said next a considerable surprise.

"Marshal Sippy, I have a friendship of long standing with several lawmen and I have seen many arrests. Permit me to guide you on this matter. Take whatever suspicions you or anyone else may have and lay them before a judge. If there is the slightest shred of evidence to connect me with anything remotely illegal, then you may do your best to have a warrant issued and I will engage an attorney to defend my good name. Until that time, good evenin' to you, sir."

With that, the skinny, gimpy gambler rose and hobbled out of the saloon, leaving Ben Sippy to take a long-delayed breath while considering whether $112 a month was enough to make this damn job worth its risks.

He went back to the city jail that night and got some sleep in an empty cell. First thing the next morning, he walked over to the

Epitaph office and since he couldn't exactly remember even half of what the dentist actually said, he conveyed to Mayor Clum what he took to be the essence of John Henry Holliday's message: "Doc says he'll make a sieve out of the next sonofabitch who repeats gossip about him."

After that, "things quieted down," John Clum would recall in a memoir he wrote many years later, "and tale-bearing became a lost art."

But seeds had been sown, and John Harris Behan would harvest them.

Come After Me Full-Tilt and Run Me Down

For the members of the Behan Posse, it was a relief to get away from Tombstone on the morning of March 16. As soon as they cleared the crowds, they kicked into a cavalry trot, putting the town's hysterical, shouting civilians behind them. For the next four hours, there was no noise but hoof beats, the huffing of the horses, the creak of leather, and the wind singing past their ears.

For the lawmen at least, the facts of the crimes were settled when Bob Paul's telegram arrived, an hour after the attack. Three robbers were waiting for the stage at the crest of a draw near Drew's Station. They opened fire, killing Budd Philpot outright and wounding a passenger who'd been traveling on the stage roof. The passenger's name was Peter Roring. Possibly Roarig or Rohrig. He was from Wisconsin. Bob had returned fire. He didn't think he'd hit anyone but couldn't be sure. It was dark and he was driving the team and trying to keep the wounded man from falling off the stage. Bob had delivered the strongbox and mail pouch in Benson, but the passenger had died en route. So: two murders and two counts of attempted robbery.

There was one other detail in Bob's telegram that didn't seem significant at first. Budd had complained of stomach cramps after leaving Watervale and had become too sick to handle the team. Just before the ambush took place, Budd Philpot and Bob Paul had switched sides on the driver's bench.

Bob Paul was back at Drew's station, waiting for the posse when it arrived. "C'mon," he said, leaning into the hill like a Belgian draft horse. "I'll show you where the bastards were laying for us —"

Frank Leslie shook his head. "I work alone. Stay away from the tracks."

Dismissed, the others eased past the canvas-wrapped body lying on the front porch and went inside Bill Drew's house. Bill poured coffees all round but not entirely graciously. Didn't offer lunch, either.

"What am I supposed to do with Budd?" he asked.

"He's got a family in Calistoga," Morgan Earp said. "Wife and kids."

"Jesus," Virgil said with a sigh. "Well . . . they're gonna want the body."

"Where's Calistoga?" Bill asked.

"California, someplace," Morgan said.

"It's up near San Francisco," Johnny Behan told them.

"Take the body into Benson," Bob Paul said. "Ship it from there."

"That canvas ain't free, nor the use of my buckboard, nor my time neither," Bill said, for he'd had twelve hours to think all this through, and he was still pretty sore about how Kinnear had taken the stage-stop contract away from him a few months back and given it to some bastard in Contention City. "Then there's the undertaker in Benson and the freight charges on the train. Who's paying for all that?"

Everyone looked at the Wells Fargo agent.

"He worked for Kinnear, not us," Williams said.

"Budd Philpot died because he was sitting in my place on that stage," Bob Paul said. "They meant to shoot the guard, not the driver."

Bob was flanked by Morgan and Wyatt Earp, who had also served as strongbox guards. All they did was stare at Williams, but the combined effect of that massive wall of male silence was persuasive.

"All right," said Williams. "Mr. Drew can invoice me for the canvas and for use of his wagon. Tell the agent in Benson I said the company will pay for the embalming and for the transport back to his family. Fair enough?"

It was, so they finished the coffee and got Budd loaded onto the buckboard. There was a sharp whistle from up the hill, where Frank Leslie had been cutting sign. He was beckoning now, the buckskin fringes on his sleeve fluttering.

"I make it four men," he said, leading them to a clump of mesquite on the far side of the draw. "One stayed with the horses here. Big fella. Or fat. His prints go deepest into the sand. Three others walked up here on foot. Stood around, waiting." He kicked at a few cigarette butts. "Got cold," he noted, pointing at places where the men had stamped their feet. He moved on to the next site. "Spent cartridges," he said, pointing them out in the dirt. "I found seventeen. That makes it three pistols." He looked at Bob Paul. "Sound right?"

Bob nodded. "Sure does."

Satisfied, Frank led them around the mesquite copse.

"No blood?" Bob asked as they walked.

"Just on the road where Budd fell. I don't guess you hit anybody."

"Shit," Bob said.

Frank slowed and gestured toward a trail of hoofprints that narrowed into a single file. "Moving fast. Headed for the mountains." He took a pull on his canteen, which was probably not filled with water. "Best we catch 'em quick," he said, wiping his mouth with the back of his hand. "Nothing but rock up there."

The weather was cold but windless. The tracks were easy enough to follow, for the ground between the San Pedro River and the Whetstone Mountains was gravelly sand dotted with barrel cactus and ocotillo and yucca.

"Heavy fella's horse is starting to stumble," Frank pointed out, and sure enough, they found the animal — head down and exhausted — abandoned in the foothills near the Wheaton ranch.

"Luther King's pinto," Wyatt said.

"You certain?" Johnny asked.

"Saw him on her, couple of weeks ago. Hard to miss a pinto."

They followed the trail up another hill, then dismounted and crouched down before they crested, to see what lay beyond.

The Wheaton ranch was a simple one. A brush corral, a crude shack. No animals visible. No smoke coming from the chimney.

"Well, let's go take a look," Johnny said, remounting.

The quiet remained unbroken as they approached the ranch house. Johnny called hello but got no response. The house was as silent as the rest of the place.

They took care of the horses, helped themselves to some canned beans, and bedded down. In the morning, Buckskin Frank went back out on his own, circling wide to get beyond where the fugitives' tracks merged with those of the rancher's stock. He returned to the ranch house an hour later.

"Found sign a quarter mile out. Heavy fella's on a new animal now."

"Add horse theft to the bill of particulars," Virgil said.

Johnny Behan nodded. "If they killed Wheaton, it's another murder. We are trailing some very bad men."

On March 19, they were still in the Whetstones. Steep, waterless heaps of rubble.

"We're gonna lose a horse," Wyatt warned when Roxana stumbled.

"Just as bad for them," Frank said, but half an hour later, high on an outward-facing slope, he called for a halt and sat for a time, studying the vast valley below.

From that vantage, the San Pedro River was a green ribbon of cottonwoods winding through winter-browned grasses. Dragoon Mountains to the east. The Huachucas, far to the south.

Billy Breakenridge polished his specs and squinted. "Could be, that's their dust," he said, gesturing. "What do you think, Frank?"

Frank uncorked his canteen. "Dirt devil."

"Well, their horses are gonna be as thirsty

and tired as ours," Morg said. "My guess? They think they've lost us — which they have, right, Frank?"

Frank took a pull, wiped his mouth, and declined to comment.

"So they'll think it's safe to double back to the river to water the horses," Morg pressed. "Right?"

Virgil said, "I don't see what else they could do."

"Or us, neither," Williams said. He wasn't complaining, but it wasn't like the company had lost a strongbox. It was too bad about Budd Philpot and that passenger, but they were Kinnear's problem. At this point in the festivities, he sincerely regretted having volunteered for this goose chase.

"Johnny?" Virg said. "Your posse. Your call."

"All right," Behan said. "We'll go back down and follow the riverbed. Maybe Frank can pick them up again."

By Sunday, the horses were done in and the provisions almost gone. The weather was cold and so was the trail, but anyone passing this way was likely to get a meal and a place to sleep at the Redfield ranch.

Like all the small ranchers in the county, Len and Hank Redfield did a little pasturing for the Cow Boys, but simple hospitality would be provided to anyone — outlaw or lawman — who asked for it. So that's where the posse headed, and that's where they caught the break they needed.

"Well, now. Lookee there," Virgil said, pulling up as the Redfield corral came into view. "Anything about that strike you boys as strange?"

It was a heavyset man milking a cow. With two pistols strapped to his waist. And a rifle, propped against a bucket, close to hand.

"Lotta artillery for a fella milking a cow," Morg noted.

"That's Luther King," Wyatt said.

"I believe I'd like to ask Mr. King a few questions," Johnny murmured.

Luther saw them coming. Taking off on foot was not a good plan, but it was the best he could come up with on short notice. Though he made the mesquite barrens beyond the ranch, he was not quick, and it didn't take long to surround and disarm him.

"Luther King," Johnny Behan said, "you are under arrest for the murder of Peter Roring and Budd Philpot."

"And for attempted robbery of a Wells Fargo strongbox," Williams added.

"And for an attack on a stagecoach carrying the U.S. mail," Virgil told him, adding, "You are in a heap of trouble, son."

"Horse theft, too," Billy Breakenridge reminded them.

King was still staring, open-mouthed, at Johnny Behan. "Budd? Budd *Philpot*? But we

421

didn't mean for —" King shut up then, but he'd already said too much, and he knew it.

"Who's *we*?" Wyatt asked.

Virgil caught Morgan's eye, and Morg started to chuckle.

"There he goes," Virg said.

"Ole Wyatt . . ." Morgan agreed, for their brother was staring at Luther King with a look so hard it felt like a shove, and a man with a guilty conscience always took that as a bad sign.

Which it was. Because while the rest of the posse had filled the hours with stories and jokes and idle chatter, Wyatt Earp had been riding a little ways off on his own, thinking for days about what Bob Paul had said back at Drew's Station: "They meant to shoot the guard, not the driver." And not just any guard — that's what Wyatt had finally figured out. They wanted the guard who was going to be the Pima County sheriff soon. A sheriff who would enforce the law. A sheriff who could not be bribed and would not be intimidated.

"It wasn't ever a robbery," Wyatt said. "The Cow Boys wanted Bob Paul dead, and you killed Budd Philpot by mistake."

"Now, Wyatt, let's not rush to judgment here," Johnny Behan began.

Wyatt started to argue, but Virgil had seen Johnny Behan do this kind of thing before and admired the way the sheriff handled interrogations. So he shook his head, and

422

Wyatt held his tongue.

"Luther, there are two men dead," Johnny reminded King gently, "and somebody is going to swing for that, but it might not be you."

"I swear, Johnny! I didn't kill nobody! I always liked Budd!"

"And Curly Bill always liked Fred White," Wyatt muttered.

"Wyatt, just hang on," Virgil soothed, and Johnny continued, "Luther, if you can explain to us what really happened, maybe we can work this out."

"I just held the horses!" Luther cried, looking at Buckskin Frank Leslie. "You know that, Frank! You musta seen that in the tracks!" Nobody said anything, and Luther rushed to fill the silence. "I swear, I just held the horses! Henry Head and Bill Leonard and Jim Crane went off to wait for the stage."

Morgan murmured, "All Cow Boys."

"And they *was* looking for somebody on it, I know that, 'cause we stopped a different stage before that one, and Henry said, 'No, that ain't him.' "

"But they were figuring to rob the stage, too, weren't they?" Johnny suggested. "May as well be hanged for a sheep as a lamb, right, Luther?"

"I guess."

"Luther, how much did they figure to take?" Johnny asked, like he was just curious. "Did they say anything about how much was on the stage?"

"No, sir. They didn't say nothing about that."

"That's surprising." Johnny frowned thoughtfully. He turned toward Williams, winking at him with the eye King couldn't see. "Agent Williams, what was the cargo manifest on that stage? Fifty grand in cash and bullion, was it?"

"Something like that," Williams said, playing along.

"Fifty *grand*!" Luther squawked. "Those sonsabitches! Those dirty goddam bastards!"

"Luther, were they trying to cheat you out of a cut because you only held the horses?" Johnny asked, like he was shocked at how unfair that was.

"They — Those bastards! Look, I lost a card game and I owed some fellas twenty bucks. Billy B., you know that's true. I lost twenty bucks to the Slopers. Johnny Tyler and Billy Allen, remember?"

"Yes, I remember that," Billy Breakenridge confirmed.

"And Billy Allen, he said he'd shoot me if I didn't pay up, so Henry Head said they'd give me twenty dollars if I came along with them and helped them do a job. Jesus! Twenty dollars, with them sitting on fifty grand. Those bastards didn't say nothing about no fifty grand!"

"Well, *maybe,*" Johnny suggested thoughtfully, "maybe they *didn't* figure on robbing the stage at all. Maybe they wanted to kill Bob Paul before he could take office and make things hot for them."

Luther King was looking at Wyatt now. "Mr. Earp, I swear! I don't have nothing against Bob Paul, and it wasn't me shot at that stage. It was Henry Head and Bill Leonard and Jim Crane."

"Where're they headed?" Wyatt asked.

"They said they was gonna make for New Mexico. Cloverdale, down near the border. I didn't figure on all this hard riding! And anyways, I just held the horses! I didn't do nothing wrong, so I told them I was done running. I wouldn't have stopped running if I'd killed somebody, right?" He looked from one face to the next. "Right?"

It was Wyatt who broke the silence, quoting Proverbs: " 'The wicked flee.' "

"But the righteous don't," Luther said, nodding vigorously, for his mother was religious and he remembered the gist of the text.

Satisfied, Johnny Behan pulled in a deep breath and let it out. "Well, Luther, we need to take you before a judge and get a deposition and so on."

King went pale beneath his sunburned skin. "Johnny, you can't — Jesus! They'll kill me if they know I said all that!"

It was not an unrealistic concern. And if the Cow Boys didn't get him for being a snitch, the townspeople might lynch him for killing Budd.

"Don't worry," Johnny told him. "We'll take care of you, Luther."

Which certainly sounded like a promise.

The plan was for Johnny Behan and Billy Breakenridge to take the prisoner to Tombstone, where Luther would be charged as an accessory to murder and horse theft. Agent Williams — a desk man who hadn't figured on all that hard riding, either — would also go back to Tombstone. Reprovisioned by the Redfield brothers, the Earps would stay on the trail with Frank Leslie, trying to catch the other three fugitives before they disappeared into the mountains or crossed into Mexico.

From the start, the posse had traveled light. Bedrolls on the ground. Whatever they could carry in their saddlebags. Nine days out, they were thirsty, hungry, filthy, sore, and bone-tired when Frank Leslie's little bay gelding crumpled up beneath him.

He stepped off as the horse went down. Everyone else just sat there staring at the animal for a while.

"Damn," Frank said, his voice like a metal rasp. "I liked that horse."

"Frank," Virgil croaked, "is there a chance in hell we're gonna find these bastards?"

"No," the tracker admitted. "Lost 'em for good."

"Well, boys, we're done," Virgil said. "At least we got one of 'em."

Luther King, he meant. But he was already wrong about that.

Frank got up behind Virgil, and they turned back toward home. Two dry camps later, they came across an isolated ranch and stopped there, hoping to get fresh mounts. The owner gave them a meal and let them rest up and water their remaining horses, but he claimed he had no animals to lend them.

"Old Man Clanton just bought a spread near here," he told them. "I don't want no trouble."

They got about five miles from the ranch before Virgil's horse died, exhausted by the double burden. That left Morgan on Dick Naylor and Wyatt on Roxana. Neither animal was in good enough shape to carry two men, not even Roxana, an Arab mare bred for stamina. So they took turns. Two on foot, two riding.

Buckskin Frank was wearing moccasins. The Earp brothers were in high, slant-heeled boots. Everybody was bloody-footed before long, but there wasn't a damn thing to do except . . . keep going.

■ ■ ■ ■

Thus the Gods Have Spun the Threads

■ ■ ■ ■

WOULDST THOU ROB ME OF MY PRIZE?

Seven miles out of Tombstone, they came to a rutted road and sat down to wait for one of the wagons that hauled water or lumber out of the Huachucas. Such wagons didn't have a lot of room for passengers, so they hitched rides into town, one by one.

Morgan let the older men go first. By the time he got picked up, it was all he could do to tie Dick behind the wagon and fit himself in between some water barrels.

"Where do you live?" the driver asked.

"First and Fremont," Morg mumbled.

It was afternoon when the driver nudged him awake. "You're home, young fella." Morgan snorted at that "young fella," for he felt like Grampa Earp used to look: crippled up, bent over, and creaky. Groaning, he climbed out of the wagon and stood there, swaying while the water hauler untied Dick Naylor's lead.

Morgan had always taken care of his horse before himself and the fact that he'd been riding Wyatt's favorite animal made that responsibility even more pressing, but he was so beat now, he almost cried when Lou called, "Morgan!" and ran outside to meet him.

"I'll take Dick to Dexter's," she told him while he drained the glass of water she handed him. "You go on inside. There's a bath ready and food on the table."

Eighteen hours later, he woke to a dawn of red and orange and gold. He looked to his left. Lou was sound asleep. Easing himself out of bed, he went outside for a piss, then came back in for the stack of clean clothes she'd laid out for him.

He got dressed in the front room so as not to wake her. Nothing fit. He'd lost a lot of weight in the past three weeks. Leaving his scabby, blistered, peeling feet bare, he made himself some coffee and hobbled outside to sit on the porch and watch the April sky lighten.

Lou had kept herself busy while he was gone. Must have been a couple of dozen new plants in the front yard. When she came outside an hour later, he asked, "Where'd you get all the greenery?"

She hesitated — just a moment — but he saw the shade pulled down.

"A neighbor brought them."

It sounded innocent, but she seemed troubled. "What's wrong?" he asked.

"Morgan, come inside."

He knew she had bad news. Was she leaving him? Had his mother died? "What's wrong?" he asked again.

"Luther King got away."

"What?"

She made him sit at the table before she handed him a week-old copy of the *Nugget*.

Luther King, implicated in the Philpot-Roarig murders, escaped yesterday from the sheriff's office. Undersheriff Harry Woods went outside the jail for a short time. Suspect King quietly stepped out the back door of the jail. He had been absent but for a few seconds when he was missed.

A confederate on the outside had a saddled horse in readiness for him. It was a well-planned job to get him away.

King gave the names of his partners in crime at the time he was arrested. Their names were Bill Leonard, Jim Crane, and Henry Head. King was also an important witness against John "Doc" Holliday.

"What's Doc got to do with it?" Morgan cried. "What in hell is going on? Luther King never said a word about Doc Holliday!"

"They're saying Doc planned the stage robbery."

Morgan fell back against his chair. "Well, that is the stupidest thing I ever heard! Is he under arrest?"

"Not anymore. The judge said there wasn't any evidence, but Harry Woods is saying Doc was the one who had a horse ready for Luther King to ride away on!"

There was more, but Morgan had heard enough.

Somebody was banging on the door. "Hell," Wyatt muttered. "Now what?"

Whatever it was, he devoutly hoped it could wait until sometime next year. Bearded, befuddled, he felt like he'd been beaten with a club, but when he heard Morgan calling his name, he put both hands over his face, winced at the sunburn, rubbed the crust out of his eyes, and sat up on the side of the bed.

"C'mon in!" he called, staring at the raw wreckage of his feet. Morgan yelled back that the door was locked, so Wyatt got up to open it.

"Get dressed," Morg snapped, angrier than Wyatt had ever seen him. "We're meeting over at James's place. Virgil's on his way. I've got to go find Doc." He waited. "Wyatt! You awake?"

"Yeah," Wyatt said, looking around for some trousers. "What's going on?"

"I'll explain later. Just go on over to James's."

Virgil was already sitting at one of the tables when Wyatt got to the tavern, and he was furious. "Harry Woods let Luther King get away."

"*What?*"

Virg held up a copy of the *Nugget*. "Says here, Harry left the jail and Luther just up and walked out the back door."

"Which wasn't locked," James called from behind the bar. "Woods is blaming Doc Holliday for it."

Wyatt stared. "But . . . That don't make any sense at all! Doc don't even know Luther King!"

"Well, he knows Bill Leonard," Virg said, "and everybody knows we were chasing after Bill and Henry Head and Jim Crane."

"Doc's a friend of ours. Why would he work against us like that?"

Virgil tapped the newspaper. "According to this, Doc helped Luther King escape because he didn't want Luther to testify against him."

"Testify against him for *what*?"

"Planning that damn stagecoach attack." James came over with coffee for Wyatt and pulled up a chair next to Virgil. "There's been rumors for weeks. Word is, one of the robbers was a lunger, and now people are saying it was Doc Holliday, not Bill Leonard."

Wyatt shook his head, dumbfounded. "Luther never said a word about Doc. He said it was Leonard and Head and Crane. The whole posse'll testify to that!"

"Don't be so sure," James warned. "Behan's

backing Harry Woods' story."

Wyatt's jaw dropped, but the door had opened. Doc and Morgan were headed for the table. It was hard to tell who was hobbling worse: Doc on his bad hip or Morgan on his battered feet.

"They are not just callin' me a murderer and a thief," Doc said as he and Morgan sat down. "They are callin' me incompetent as well! If I wanted to steal a Wells Fargo shipment, I'd have done a better job of it. God a'mighty! Just shoot a horse! You could take whatever you wanted from the stage."

"It gets worse," James told Wyatt. "People are saying Doc poisoned Budd Philpot, and that's why he got sick the night of the holdup."

"Pilin' absurdity on top of slander and libel," Doc cried. "I was nowhere near Watervale when Budd was there, and why would I do such a thing in the first place?"

James shrugged. "I guess the idea is that you wanted Budd sick so that Bob Paul would have to drive. That way he wouldn't have the shotgun in hand."

"This just don't add up," Wyatt said, rubbing his face with both hands. "Go back, Doc. Why would anybody think you had something to do with this?"

"I was out of town the night the stage was attacked. Evidently that single fact is sufficient to justify draggin' my name through

436

the mud."

"Where were you?" Virgil asked.

It was a simple question, but Doc didn't answer right away. "I was on my way to Charleston," he said finally. "For a poker game."

"Well, that's easy then!" Morgan cried, flooded with relief. "Who did you play? They can vouch for you."

"I didn't make it that far, Morgan."

The others shifted uneasily in the silence that fell, for it seemed like Doc was deciding how much to say. Or how to say it. Or making something up. He seemed relieved when a couple of Chinese came in for beer.

James turned to yell, "We're closed!" but they didn't understand, so he got up and shooed them out, locking the door.

"Doc," Morgan said, "just tell us what happened."

"You know where the Charleston road bends around those three big hills?"

They nodded.

"I was robbed on the highway. There were two of them."

"Hell," Wyatt said.

"You get a look at any of them?" Virgil asked.

Doc shook his head. "Flour-sack masks."

"Horses?" Wyatt asked.

"Bays. Nothing special — nothing I noticed, anyway. I was not at my best," he admitted.

"The game had a ten-dollar ante. I was bringin' just about everything I had to the table. Somebody must have seen me takin' cash out at the bank. I don't believe the robbers knew who I was, but I was afraid they'd come after me for braggin' rights! 'I killed the ferocious *Doc Holliday*!' " He paused. "This will not sound good, but . . . I was close to Bill Leonard's place, so that's where I went."

Virgil groaned. "You're right. That don't sound good."

"Who's Bill Leonard?" James asked.

"He's a goldsmith," Virgil told him. "Melts down stolen coins and jewelry to make big gold rings for the Cow Boys."

"Doc, how do you know Bill Leonard, anyways?" Morgan asked.

"I met him in the Las Vegas sanatorium. He used to work with dentists. I was bored. We talked now and then, that's all. Anyway, he wasn't home when I got to his place. Nobody was there. I rested a few hours and rode back to the city in the morning."

"Did you report the robbery to Harry Woods or Ben Sippy?" Virgil asked.

"I didn't dare! Virgil, if something like this gets around, I may as well carry a sign that says, 'Rob me at your convenience.' "

"Did you tell *anyone*?" Morg pressed. "Mrs. Fly maybe?"

Doc went still, then straightened suddenly.

The movement set off a coughing fit, and James got him a drink. "I pawned a gold watch for forty dollars," Doc said when he could speak again. "The pawnbroker might remember that. And Ben Sippy saw me playin' faro that night. I would never do that if I weren't damn near to broke."

"Pawning a watch and playing faro are not exactly proof you weren't in on a *failed* robbery," Virgil pointed out.

Doc's face fell. "You're right . . . The funny thing is, I almost told Marshal Sippy. He said I was accused of bein' in on the holdup, and I said, 'That's ironic,' but I didn't tell him why and —"

"Cui bono?" Wyatt said.

At a loss, Morgan asked, "Coo-ey what?"

"It's Latin," Doc told him, astonished. " 'Who gains?' "

"It's what Eddie Foy told me about politics, back in Dodge," Wyatt said. "Remember, James? The trick is, you have to ask, *Cui bono?* That's how the Romans said it. You have to ask, Who gets the good of it?" He looked around. "Why would anybody drag Doc into it? There's no reason Doc would want Bob Paul dead. So if Doc's accused, who gains?"

"Gimme that newspaper," Virgil said. Silently he read the article again, looking up when he got to the part about Luther King quietly stepping out the back door of the jail. "Well, who left the damn cell unlocked?" Virgil asked, throwing the paper down in disgust. "That's gotta be Harry Woods's doing. Which makes him negligent or complicit."

Doc said, "I was at work when *that* happened! There are two dozen witnesses who can tell you I was dealin' at the Alhambra when Luther King escaped."

"But why blame Doc?" Morgan asked. "Must be a thousand men in this county more likely to rob a stage."

"To hurt me," Wyatt snapped. "To ruin my chances in the sheriff's election next year. To make me look bad because Doc is my friend."

Virgil looked skeptical. "I don't know, boys. Behan was right there with us, chasing Luther King and the others down. Maybe Harry Woods did this on his own."

"Wyatt," Doc said softly, "if you want me to go, now is as good a time as any. I will pack up, buy a ticket, and leave tonight."

"No," Wyatt snapped. " 'The wicked flee when no man pursueth, but the righteous are bold as a lion.' " He stood, wincing when his weight settled onto his feet. "I can fix this, Doc." And he sounded confident, like it was a harness that needed mending, or a sprung plank in a boardwalk.

"What's the plan, Wyatt?" Doc asked warily.

"Find the real killers and shovel this shit right back onto Behan."

Doc and his brothers watched him leave.

"Gentlemen," Doc said when the door had

440

slammed, "correct me if I am wrong, but didn't y'all just spend two weeks tryin' to do exactly that?"

"Never confuse stupidity with malice. It's nearly always a mistake, and it'll get you into useless feuds." That's what Johnny Behan would have said, had Wyatt Earp bothered to ask him why Luther King had been allowed to escape from the county jail.

In point of fact, it was Undersheriff Harry Woods who decided that it would be in Johnny Behan's best interests if Luther were unavailable to be prosecuted for a variety of felonies in connection with the attack on the Kinnear stagecoach. When Johnny Behan came to the office after a badly needed night's rest and found out that his chief deputy had simply let Luther go . . .

Well, no one can curse like the Irish.

For the next hour, the undersheriff was informed at length and in detail that his presumption in this matter was in error. It would have been a political triumph to send Luther King to prison, if not to the rope. Holding at least one man accountable for the crimes would have gone a long way toward dispelling the *Epitaph*'s ugly insinuations that the sheriff himself was in league with the county's outlaws. Furthermore, that desirable outcome would have been accomplished without stirring up trouble with Old Man

Clanton, Curly Bill Brocius, Johnny Ringo, or anyone else, because Luther King really was just a hanger-on and none of the Cow Boys would have given a good goddam if he'd been convicted as an accessory to murder, attempted robbery, and horse theft. Now it was going to look like Johnny gave an order to let Luther escape in order to appease the Cow Boys and to prevent unsavory allegations of collusion from coming out at Luther's trial.

Only when his boss's initial fury had been spent did Harry try to say anything, and all he got out was "Hell, Johnny. I'm sorry. I didn't think —"

"No! You didn't, God damn you! And that's the trouble! Nobody thinks! Nobody ever *thinks*!"

That observation became an additional tirade on the general theme of being surrounded by fools and bunglers until worldly realism and saddle-sore exhaustion set in. Sitting at his desk, his wind-chapped, sun-scalded face in his hands, Johnny eventually muttered, "Well, goddammit, what's done is done," and began to assess his situation with as much dispassionate composure as he could muster.

He had not intended to make enemies of the Earps but when they found out Luther King had escaped, there would be hell to pay. Which was a pity. Johnny and the brothers had worked well together on this posse, and that was how he liked things to be: cordial, professional. Sure, he and the Earps would be on opposite sides as the '82 election came closer, but there'd have been be no reason for hard feelings, if not for Harry's imbecilic initiative.

Sighing, he stared out the office window, his mind blank, until his eye was caught by a thin, bent figure wrapped in a blanketlike cloak, moving slower than the foot traffic around him.

"Harry," he said quietly, "when Billy and I brought Luther in, you said folks were talking about Doc Holliday being the lunger who was involved with the holdup, right?"

"Yeah, but Luther said that was Bill Leonard, not —"

"Shut up," Johnny snapped. Face still, he took a piece of paper out of his desk drawer and began writing. "This," he said, handing it to his undersheriff, "is what you are going to publish in the next edition of the *Nugget.*"

Harry frowned when he got to the last sentence and read, " 'King was an important witness against Holliday'?"

"Yes. Against Holliday."

"Johnny," Harry said cautiously, not wanting to set off another tongue-lashing, "Luther didn't say anything about Doc Holliday."

"No, you idiot! I'm saying it. We're saying it. The *Nugget* is saying that Luther said it. Jesus *Christ,* Harry!"

443

Getting a grip again, Johnny stood and went to the office window.

"I warned Wyatt that Holliday was trouble," he said softly. "He should have followed my advice. And maybe I'll be doing him one last favor now . . . If Wyatt Earp has any brains at all, which is questionable, he'll tell Holliday to get out of Tombstone on the next stage. But he won't. Wyatt will stick with that obnoxious, dangerous, venomous drunk because they're *friends.*"

He turned then to his undersheriff. "I'm not going to fire you, Harry, but from this day forward — now and forever, amen — you and your newspaper are going to make Wyatt Earp carry Doc Holliday on his back, exactly the way John Clum and the *Epitaph* have saddled me with the Cow Boys."

It was nothing personal, even then. Using John Henry Holliday against Wyatt Earp was a simple act of political pragmatism. That's how it would have remained, if not for Josie Marcus.

She'd selected her clothes carefully, seeking just the right balance between charming and desirable. Her dress was dove gray and peach pink, very becoming against her skin. Barely visible at the top of the neckline: black lace, a subtle hint about what lay beneath.

Inspecting her tinted cheeks — color subtly

applied — she rehearsed her lines as she set off for the Cosmopolitan. She would take her cue from Wyatt. If he was still exhausted, she would look concerned and say, "I've been so worried about you. I hope you won't think me too forward, but I just had to see how you were." On the other hand, if she saw what she hoped for when he opened the door — surprise, pleasure, yearning — she would give that shy, silent man a knowing smile and lead him to the bed herself.

"Miss Josephine!" Mr. Bilicke said when she entered the lobby that morning. "What can I do for you today?"

"I was hoping to see Mr. Earp," she said casually. "Is he in?"

"I'm afraid you just missed him. He left about half an hour ago."

"Kwand meem," she said, miming mild disappointment with an insouciant wave of her small, gloved hand. "It was nothing important. I was passing and thought I'd pay a call."

"Would you care to leave a card? Or shall I tell Mr. Earp that you're looking for him?"

If she said yes and Wyatt didn't return the call, it would be a silent message she didn't want to receive. "No, thank you," she said. "I'm sure I'll run into him later."

She stepped to the door and paused for a moment on the boardwalk to pop open her parasol. That was when she noticed Johnny Behan.

Their paths had crossed before. Tombstone was big, but not that big. In the past two months, Johnny had seen her with other men — important men, rich men — at the Maison Doree, at the Schieffelin Theatre, at the Can Can Café. She would glance at him with a defiant little smile. He would pretend she was invisible. *I'm glad to be rid of you,* they told each other wordlessly. *I wouldn't take you back if you begged.*

"Mr. Bilicke? On second thought . . ." she began quietly. Then she raised her voice. "Tell Wyatt I'll be back this afternoon."

Why did she do it?

Because she was young and in full bloom, witlessly willing to exercise the brief destructive power of beauty. Because there was still no sign from Wyatt that he knew she was free, and she wanted to give him a little push. Because Johnny's indifference annoyed her. Because she wanted to wound him and believed — rightly — that this would do the job. Because of what he'd done to her on the kitchen table.

She had seen the word "slut" on Johnny's lips before and read it there now. She lifted her head and narrowed her eyes and flounced her curls. Believe what you like, she thought as she brushed past him.

And he did. Oh, he did.

All along, he was thinking. That hypocritical, two-faced, self-righteous bastard! He was screwing you behind my back, all along.

"What's this?" Johnny asked Virgil Earp, a couple of days later.

"Expenses," Virgil said, pushing a piece of paper across Johnny's desk. "The federal marshal's office is covering part of my salary, but the rest is county."

Brows knitted, Johnny read the neatly itemized list.

Salaries: V. Earp, $32; W. Earp, $72.
   M. Earp, $72; F. Leslie: $72.
Provisions: $26.
Losses: Frank Leslie, one horse; Virgil Earp, one horse.

Johnny looked up, all innocence. "This doesn't come out of my budget, Virg."

"It was your posse," Virgil pointed out.

"Well, Billy Breakenridge is on my payroll," Johnny said, "and I'll pick up Frank Leslie's salary, as far as the Cochise County line. I can't pay him for the time in New Mexico, but I might be able to get the county to cover his horse if it died in Cochise. Morgan and Wyatt were your deputies, so their salaries are a federal expense. And your horse would be, too."

There was a long silence.

"I guess you might be right about that," Virgil said. You miserable little chiseler, he meant.

"You could try billing Wells Fargo if the feds don't cover everything," Johnny suggested helpfully. Go to hell, he meant, and take your brother Wyatt with you.

Virgil left the sheriff's office and walked a few steps away from the window so Behan couldn't see him stop and stare at the boardwalk with his jaw set and his breath coming deep and hard. "That sonofabitch," he said softly. "That son of a *bitch.*"

Still fuming, he looked up just in time to see Wyatt leaving the alley behind the Oriental. Which was strange. Because the *other* news they'd gotten after chasing Bill Leonard, Henry Head, and Jim Crane around the desert was this: Milt Joyce had refused to renew the contract for Wyatt's quarter interest in the saloon's gambling concession.

The Oriental had been a reliable source of income and one that would be hard for Wyatt to replace. Worse yet, that income would now go to Johnny Behan, to whom Milt had leased the gambling concession a few days later at a nice discount — one Democrat to another, you understand. City councilman to sheriff.

Bastards, the two of them.

So what in hell was Wyatt doing out behind the Oriental?

Virgil was about to call out to his brother when he saw Ike Clanton, of all people, leave the same alley and hurry off in the opposite direction.

"Wyatt!" Virg yelled, dogtrotting across the street to meet his brother down at the corner. "What's going on? What were you doing with Ike?"

"Nothing," Wyatt lied.

Because that's what politicians have to do.

This One Is a Fool, and Will Pay for It One Day

"It's a lot to think about," Ike said, the day they made the deal.

"You want me to go over it again?" Wyatt asked.

"Go over it again."

"Wells Fargo is offering a reward of twelve hundred dollars apiece for the men who attacked that stagecoach. That's thirty-six hundred dollars for the three of them."

Ike nodded. "I just gotta tell you where to find 'em."

"And I'll do the rest."

"You'll do the rest," Ike said. "And I get the reward."

"You get the reward."

Ike frowned. "Why don't you want the reward?"

"I'll get the credit for bringing them in, and that'll be better than money."

Ike frowned harder, suspicious again. "Better than money?"

"Yes, because I'm running against Johnny

450

Behan for sheriff next year. If I arrest Bill Leonard and Henry Head and Jim Crane, it'll look real good to the voters. And Doc Holliday will be in the clear."

"Doc Holliday," Ike said. "I don't like him."

"I know, Ike, but I do. He's a real good dentist. He'll fix you up if you get a toothache."

"He talks too fast. No. He talks slow, but he says . . ."

"Too many words," Wyatt supplied, for he, too, found Doc wordy and confusing.

Ike looked over his shoulder, getting nervous about one of the Cow Boys seeing him with an Earp. "Thirty-six hunnert. For the three of them."

"It's a lot of money," Wyatt said. "You could use it to get away from your old man. Go back to California. Maybe open another café."

"I'm a good cook," Ike said, confident about this. "I can open another café."

"And you can take your sisters with you, so your old man can't hurt them anymore. You could make a new life, Ike. Start fresh. I had sisters, too," Wyatt reminded him. "It's important to take care of them when your old man is a mean sonofabitch."

Ike's face darkened. "He is. He is a mean sonofabitch. I had to protect the kids."

"Me, too, Ike. That's just how it was for me."

Ike circled around again. "What about Billy?"

Ike had taken care of Billy, his younger brother, the way Wyatt took care of Morgan. "He can go with you to California if you want," Wyatt said, "but I think he gets along with your old man."

"Yeah. Yeah, Billy gets along with the old man," Ike agreed. "So I just gotta find out where Henry and Jim is."

"And Bill Leonard, too."

"Bill Leonard, too. I tell you. I get the reward. You get the votes. And I can take care of my sisters."

"And Doc Holliday gets clear. You got it now," Wyatt told him. "Don't tell anybody else, Ike. This has to be our secret."

"Our secret," Ike said. "Don't tell anybody else."

"I won't either," Wyatt promised.

And he kept his word, but it wouldn't matter in October. Not to Ike. Not to anybody.

THE SEASON OF
SPRING CAME ON

When Tommy McLaury went into Tombstone for supplies at the end of April, he didn't go straight to the grocery store. Instead, he rolled past Calisher's and pulled up just beyond First to see how Mrs. Earp's garden was doing and to give her one of his hound pups.

He was hoping Morgan Earp would be out of town and that Lou would be out front tending the garden so he could talk to her a while. But he had it planned out in his mind, in case Mr. Earp was there that afternoon. Maybe sitting out on the front porch reading a book. Or having a cup of coffee and a smoke.

"Morning," Tom would say. "I don't know if you remember me, sir. I'm Tom McLaury."

Morgan might not have said anything then. He was the friendly Earp, the good-natured one, but he'd remember about the mules, so Tom planned to explain how Billy Clanton came by and why the McLaurys couldn't return the animals to Lieutenant Hurst though they meant to. Then to get off the mules, Tom would say, "I am happy to see those flowers are doing well." If Mr. Earp was surprised to learn that Tommy was the neighbor who'd brought them, Tom would say, "Yes, sir, I'm the one," because his conscience was clear. He might have sinned in his heart — coveting another man's wife — but he hadn't done anything to get himself shot by a jealous husband, either. He'd say, "Mrs. Earp was trying to get lilacs to grow here, and I guessed they wouldn't do well. So I brought her plants that like to bloom in this kind of country."

There might have been an uneasy silence then, but ice would surely break when the puppy began to whimper. Tommy would hop down and go around to drop the gate. "My hound bitch had a litter," he'd say. "I was thinking — since you're gone so much — maybe Mrs. Earp would like one. I thought she might get lonely or scared sometimes, being on her own like that. A dog can be a good companion." Tommy would open the box in the wagon bed and hand over a fat, squirming pup. "There's seven others, back at the farm," he'd tell Mr. Earp. "My hounds are good dogs, but I can't keep 'em all. I'd take it kindly if you and Mrs. Earp would take this one, sir." Then they might talk about the puppy a bit, but in the end Tommy expected

454

Mr. Earp would look him in the eye and say something like "This is neighborly of you, and the flowers were, too. But no more." And Tom would take that with good grace.

From the start, he had been troubled that Lou was not free to accept his love or the life he wanted to offer her. When he brought the flowers last month and helped her plant them, Lou herself told him not to bring her any more gifts. That was a sorrow to him, but he accepted it. Thing was, he really did have eight pups to dispose of, so he told himself that if Lou took one of them, she'd be doing *him* a favor and that would make them even for the flowers. And from then on, Tommy could touch his hat to her and Lou could smile at him in a nice neighborly way, just like her husband would have wanted.

Except Morgan wasn't home that morning. He was playing pool over at Bob Hatch's Billiard Parlor when Tom McLaury brought that puppy into town.

For a long time, Morgan Earp couldn't understand the point of playing games. If he had time to pass, he preferred to read. He'd never paid any attention to billiards until he lived in Dodge and started watching Jacob Schaeffer play at Dog Kelly's saloon. These days, Jake was the world champion of straight-rail billiards, but even three years ago, when Jake was just a skinny young bartender with plenty of time to practice, Morg knew he was something special. Watching Jake nurse balls was like watching Wyatt work a horse or listening to Doc Holliday play piano. You couldn't hardly believe how good he was. That's why Morg didn't even think about learning the game in Dodge. Jake set a fence that was too high for a regular person to clear.

When Bob Hatch opened a billiard parlor in Tombstone, Morgan still wasn't interested. Then Doc Holliday told him about how Bob kept a bunch of live frogs in a jar on the bar and claimed he could tell the weather from them.

"How in hell does he do that?" Morg wanted to know.

"Well, I don't imagine Arizona weather is all that difficult to predict," Doc said. "Most of the year, your best bet is 'more of the same.' If it is August and you say, 'It will be stinkin' hot tomorrow,' I calculate you'll be correct a minimum of thirty times out of thirty-one."

But Morgan stayed curious about the frogs, so he stopped in at the pool hall to ask Bob Hatch about them. Bob came from Maine, and he was kind of hard to understand until you got used that choppy, sing-songy way he talked and how he skipped his *r*'s. When Morg asked about the frogs, Bob said, "These heah ah *toads,*" and "Down east, they sing louda when a stoam's a-comin'." So Bob and Morgan got to talking about the difference between toads and frogs, and the differences between toads from Maine and toads from Arizona. During that discussion, Morg bought a beer. Bob offered to let him try his hand at billiards without charging him a table fee, and Morgan Earp's fate was sealed.

"There's no such thing as a free sample," Hattie Marcus would have told him, and she'd have been right, for once he got started, Morgan Earp could not get enough of playing billiards.

He liked the crack of the ivory balls on a well-hit break, and their hushed roll across the felt. He liked the feel of the cue in his hand, the smell of tobacco and chalk. He liked the sound of the beer mugs clinking and Bob's toads chirping. Soon, playing billiards for Morgan was like practicing piano for Doc. "It will yield to persistence," Doc always muttered when he was having trouble with a new piece, and that was the way Morgan felt about all the little puzzles in billiards. You had to see the lay of the balls after the break and find a series of moves in them. You had to vary the cue speed and shape your shots so you'd be in position for the next hit or make your opponent scratch. It was a hard game to play well, and he understood now why Doc got so cranky if you talked while he was practicing. Morgan, too, liked the way everything around him sort of faded while he was at the table.

Which is why he wasn't aware that somebody on Allen Street was hollering for him until Bob Hatch called, "Moe-gan! Lady outside. Wants you!"

Morg went to see what the trouble was, and there was Allie, fists on her hips, glaring at him from under that big slat-brim bonnet of hers.

"I knew it was going to come to this," she informed him, like he had any idea what she was talking about. "I told Virg, and he was supposed to say something, but nobody does *anything* around here except me! So now I'm telling you to get home and look after your affairs, Morgan Earp."

With that, she stalked off, her little feet going about twice the speed of Morg's and her mouth going faster than that.

"Look at you! What kind of grown man spends all his time playing with sticks and balls? When are you going to stop drifting and do something with your life? That's what she's asking herself, Morgan! Either marry her or let her go!"

It went on like that, down Allen Street and up First Street, with Morgan amused, then bemused, then confused, and sort of insulted. When they turned onto Fremont, Allie came to a sudden halt and waited for Morgan to see what she saw: Lou, standing in the front yard, surrounded by the flowers that "a neighbor" brought her.

Holding something in her arms like it was a baby.

Smiling at Tom McLaury.

"Prettiest man I ever saw," Allie declared, "and one to give you Earp boys a run for your money. He's gonna be somebody someday. He's already got two hundred acres under alfalfa! Well? Don't just stand there gawping. Do something!"

It was all body, what he felt. A punch in his chest like his heart made a fist. A great cold wave of emotion that was probably fear but which he named anger.

"McLaury!" he bellowed. "Get the hell away from her!"

Alarmed, Tommy touched his hat to Lou, climbed onto his buckboard, and slapped the reins on his team's back. He was out of reach by the time Morgan came stomping up to the house, but if Morg expected Lou to be embarrassed or ashamed, he had another thing coming.

"You had no call to shout at him like that," she started, a fat spotted puppy squirming in her arms. "He was just being nice. I *told* you I wanted a dog, Morgan. You never did anything about it and Mr. McLaury did, and I am *grateful*!"

"And you don't think he wants something in return?"

"And you think I'd *give* him something in return? Is that what you're saying, Morgan Earp? You're gone six days out of seven, doing I-don't-know-what up in Benson and Tucson, and you have the nerve to ask me if I'd cheat on you? I'm here all by myself, and just last week, a drunk tried to get into the house —"

"Did you call for Virgil?" he asked, shocked.

"Yes, but Virg was gone, too! Allie came over with a shotgun, but what if she hadn't heard me? This neighborhood is getting worse and worse, and it's just not right to leave me alone so much! Why can't you find a job in town? You're thirty years old, Morgan! What have you got to show for it? When are you going to make something of yourself?"

"I'm making three-fifty a day with Wells Fargo. And Wyatt's got a lot of irons in the fire —"

"Oh, *Morgan*!" Exasperated, Lou put the wriggling puppy down. "Wyatt's a dreamer! First it was going to be a stagecoach line. Then it was going to be a race track. Then it was going to be water rights. Now it's the sheriff's office. His big plans never *amount* to anything. You just drift along, waiting for his nothing to turn into something, and it never does!"

Suddenly she was in tears, and it wasn't Tom McLaury, or Wyatt's big plans, or Morgan's job anymore. It turned into "What *am* I to you, Morgan?" and "Are we *ever* going to get married?" And "I want a baby, Morgan! Why don't *any* of us have any *children*?" She was sobbing by then, and Morgan was so stunned, he just stood there, gawping, until he finally said, "Damn, Lou. I didn't know you was so unhappy!"

"Well, how *would* you know?" she cried, stamping her foot. "You're never home! You just expect me to wait until you get back from Benson or billiards or the Cosmopolitan, and I *hate* it! I hate Tombstone, and I hate Arizona, and I *miss* you! Even when you're in town, I miss you, Morgan."

It went on like that for a while. Her telling him how they'd been together almost four years and she was still waiting for something to happen — and she didn't even know what she was hoping for! Just *something* that would lead to something else. Progress. Movement! Not just drifting from day to day. Him saying he was sorry and promising things would get better and swearing off billiards. He'd quit Wells Fargo and look for work in town. He told her they could go find a preacher right now, right this minute, if that's what she wanted, but she only cried harder and said that would make Allie feel bad because Virgil couldn't marry her.

By that time, the puppy was yapping for attention and making fierce little growly sounds and flinging himself about. It was comical, and when she was calmer, Lou wiped her eyes and picked him up again. "I'm keeping him," she warned.

"He got a name?" Morg asked cautiously.

"Higgs," she decided.

Why Higgs? Morg wanted to ask, but he didn't want to risk getting her started again. "Higgs," he said. "Higgs is good. Higgs it is."

"Doc," he asked a few days later, "you ever think about kids?"

"My cousins Robert and George send me photographs of their children now and then."

"No, I mean having kids. Of your own."

Arched brows rose high over slate-blue eyes. "Well, now. Is Miss Louisa . . . ?"

"No. She'd like that. We're not doing anything to prevent it, but . . ."

They were taking a break, sitting amid the beer kegs and crates behind the Alhambra. Now that Morgan had quit Wells Fargo, Doc was training him on the faro table. Wyatt was going to bank Morg when he got good enough to deal on his own, but that seemed a long way off. Doc said faro was a stupid game, but it was fast. Morg found the bets hard to follow and hated being indoors so much.

"It's kinda strange," Morg said. "Six of us brothers, and Newton's the only one with kids."

Doc took out one of those thin, black cigars

he favored now because they were easier on his lungs than cigarettes. "Newton's children were born before the war, were they? Before he enlisted?"

"Now that you mention it. Why?"

" 'A night with Eros, a lifetime with Mercury . . .' "

Doc stopped, choking on the first draw, as usual. What happened next was so much a part of him that you hardly noticed. The cough. The handkerchief. The flask uncapped. A sip or two of bourbon to dull the pain in his chest. Everything back into his pockets. Then he'd pick up with whatever he was saying as if nothing had interrupted the thought.

"Folks had bigger families before the war, in my observation. If men were lucky enough to survive the fightin', they were usually unlucky enough to bring a souvenir home to their wives and sweethearts. Venereal disease has run rampant ever since. The damage is internal, but it can interfere with what Mr. Darwin calls reproductive success. Children may not be in the cards for any of us whose lives have not been pure."

"Oh," Morgan said. "Damn."

"Yes, indeed," Doc said softly. He looked at Morgan sideways. "Thinkin' about ghost lives, are we?"

"Yeah," Morgan said. "Maybe."

Not his own so much but Lou's, for she

was not the wife of a clean-living, hardworking, sweet-faced farmer with a big spread and
a good future ahead of him. No, Lou was
shacked up with a man who meant well. A
man who was good-natured, if not ambitious.
A man who had just realized that Higgs might
be the closest thing to a baby they'd ever
have.

Doc was leaning back in his chair, eyes narrowed in speculation. "You know what you
need, son?"

"What?"

"A decent suit of clothes. Marine-blue
gabardine, I should think. With a chalk stripe
perhaps. That, and a justice of the peace."

"Doc, what in hell are you talking about?"

"You. Marryin' Lou."

"Lou doesn't want to get married," Morg
said, a little too quickly. "She said a wedding
might make Allie feel bad because Virg can't
marry her."

"Very thoughtful. Very considerate. I would
expect nothin' less of Miss Louisa, but two
witnesses are all you need. Nobody else has
to know." He looked away. "Make her your
wife, even if you can't give her children."

Morgan chewed on that awhile before he
asked, "What about you, Doc? You ever think
about being married?"

"All the time," Doc said, "but she's in a
convent now."

Morgan just about fell off his barrel. "Kate's

in a convent?"

Doc's wheezy laugh lurched into a serious coughing fit, but his eyes were merry over the handkerchief. "God a'mighty, Morgan! If you could see your face! No, not Kate. There was a girl back in Georgia I might have married if I hadn't come out here for my health. Martha Anne will always be dear to me, but she is a bride of Christ now. At my best, I could not have rivaled Lord Jesus, and I am a long way from my best."

Doc ground the stub of his little black cigar into the dust. Morgan stood and offered the dentist an arm for leverage.

"As for Miss Kate," Doc concluded wryly, "she is a foul-mouthed, pigheaded Hungarian harridan who has made it amply clear that she would not have me on a silver platter." He looked northward, toward Globe, Arizona. "Even so . . . I miss her."

BITCH THAT I AM — A CAUSE OF EVIL AND A CURSE!

There are women who do not wish to be pursued. During a dozen years of active frontier prostitution, Mária Katarina Harony had often declared, "I pick and I choose!" That was no idle boast. In the grim world of two-dollar house girls, Kate Harony had always named her price, getting what she demanded and doubling the fee if a john dared to argue.

"I know what I'm worth," she'd declare. "If that's more than a cheap bastard like you can afford, be damned to you."

Men had lined up, year after year, hoping to be accepted. How many of them? Four thousand? Five? Maybe more. Too many, that's for sure. She was thoroughly tired of men and their lust. Tired of the whole damn business.

It's a rare whore who anticipates that the market for her wares will turn. Rarer still: a whore who saves her cash and makes plans for what comes next. Kate Harony was a realist who'd always kept an eye out for the next opportunity and in the beginning, that's all Doc Holliday was. A way out. A way up.

Of all the men who'd had her, Doc alone asked the right questions and showed an interest in the answers. He alone knew her for what she was: the pampered, well-educated daughter of a Budapest physician. Fluent in four modern languages, familiar with the Greek and Latin classics. Exiled by war, impoverished, orphaned, fostered out. Ruined by the guardian who should have protected her, she'd run away, and it was in a string of frontier brothels that she learned her seventh language: a vulgar and ungrammatical English. Doc, too, had lived with luxury in childhood, with poverty in adolescence, and with hardship in adulthood. He admired the nerve and self-possession she brought to the only work a girl could get paid for on the frontier. His respect meant a great deal to her. So did his cash. So, eventually, did he.

She never meant to love him.

He didn't make it easy, for if Doc deplored the way Kate made her money, she was infuriated by how he spent his. They had traveled together off and on since 1878, a pair of souls chained together in the fourth ring of the Inferno — the miser pushing a boulder up a hill while the spendthrift shoved it down. Doc could win in an hour what Kate earned in six months, but he'd spend it just as quickly. He insisted that they live in a town's best hotel, that they eat in the finest restaurants. It was French frocks for her, English suits for him, lavish parties for his friends. And then there was the stupid way he'd slip a few bucks to anyone he felt sorry for! She understood that he was trying to recapture childhood's careless abundance, but they weren't aristocratic children anymore, and the way he squandered money drove her crazy. The very fact that he had walked away from their saloon in Las Vegas — just *gave* her his interest in it — proved what an idiot he was about finances. And how could he possibly believe it was wrong to kill a dangerous, crazy, drunk bastard like Mike Gordon? Doc did the world a favor when he shot that mad dog down, but she couldn't make him see that.

She had no reason to stay near the sanatorium after he left, so she sold out and cleared enough to buy a six-bedroom boardinghouse in a silver camp in northern Arizona. She'd gone from silk to calico before, but this time she wasn't drudging for an Iowa bastard who called himself a foster father but worked her all day and rode her all night. This time, by God, she was on her own and liked it that way.

She divided the six rentals into two twelve-hour shifts. "You don't need no bed when

468

you're working," she told each miner. "I'll give you a discount to share." That was a lie but one they fell for, each of them hoping that she was part of the deal. She hired a cook, learned to make plain, cheap meals in quantity, fired the woman, and did the work herself to reduce expenses. "The goddess of parsimony," Doc called her once, and he hadn't meant it as a compliment.

Then, he started sending all these telegrams, each one more provoking than the last. Why did he waste money on Western Union when a penny stamp would have sent a whole letter? Was he afraid she would see from his handwriting that he was sick again? Was he trying to trick her into coming to Tombstone so she would nurse him like she did in Dodge? "George Sand was an imbecile," she'd mutter at night, rereading the stack of messages before she turned down the lamp and went to sleep.

The telegrams finally stopped coming at the end of April. In what appeared to be a final contact, Doc had sent a pair of earrings. Indian turquoise set in Mexican silver. "I thought of your eyes when I saw these," he wrote, his beautiful copperplate handwriting firm and controlled. "Perhaps you will think of me when you wear them. In the meantime, *dum spiro, spero.*" That seemed to be the end of it. Which was a relief at first. But as the weeks passed, she began to wonder if he really was sick. *Dum spiro, spero:* While I breathe, I hope. Was that some veiled reference to his disease?

She was too damn busy to sit and read a newspaper these days. They were just advertisements and bullshit anyway. Still, when a month had passed with nothing further from him, she asked Florence at the grocery store if there'd been anything in the news lately about Doc Holliday.

Learning that Doc was a suspect in a stage robbery back in March confirmed her opinion of journalism. Doc hated dealing faro because it made him feel like a thief to take money from men who didn't stand a chance of winning a game they didn't understand. Kate was about to tell Florence, "I know Doc — he'd starve before he'd steal!" But before she could, the man behind her in line piped up.

"Yeah, ole Doc, he'll shoot you just to see if his gun works. He's wanted in Las Vegas, too. Killed his wife. Took her up into the mountains and — *bang!* Shot her right in the head."

Kate choked a little on this "news" but played along. "That poor woman!" she cried, making her eyes round and serious. "Except . . . I heard Doc Holliday, he always uses a knife when he kills women. How do you know he shot her?"

"I helped bury her," the man said, proud of this swift invention.

Kate lowered her voice. "I wouldn't noise that around, mister. They'll call you accessory to murder and string you up!"

Doc would have thought that was a wonderful story.

In May, she began to think that it would be nice to get away from Globe for a while. She'd certainly earned a rest. Twelve men meant twelve breakfasts, twelve lunch pails packed, and then twelve dinners. Fifteen thousand meals, with all the shopping, cooking, serving, and cleaning that entailed. And then there was the laundry, and all the beds, and making sure the miners settled up with her before they gambled and whored and drank their pay away.

A little trip to Tombstone might be nice. Everybody said it was a real city, not a shit hole like Globe. She could stay with Bessie and James Earp — she'd known them for years professionally and counted them as friends. Florence was tired of working for the son of a bitch who owned the grocery store, and she'd been asking about Kate and her going partners on the boardinghouse. This would be a good time to see how that might work out; Flo could look after the business while Kate was gone.

A few days later, when she'd made all the arrangements, Kate went to Western Union and used one of Doc's paid-reply forms to send a telegram to Bessie Earp.

ARRIVING BY EVENING STAGE MAY 25
STOP DONT TELL DOC STOP

She knew Bessie would ignore the second part of the message. She knew Doc would be waiting for her at the depot and that he'd treat her like a princess — he always did. She would be haughty, perhaps a little scornful at first. Then she'd relent, and they'd have a few drinks, and the fun would begin. She'd take some cash down with her, too, and let Doc parlay it into something more. Maybe even set up a few poker games for him. It'll be just like old times, she thought.

And to everyone's misfortune, she was right.

There was a long list of people who'd died abruptly in and around Tombstone during its first three years of existence. When Mária Katarina Harony awoke on May 27, 1881, she did so with an absolute certainty that she would soon be counted among them. This conviction did not come to her from the abstract philosophical assurance of the famous syllogism arising from the premise "All men are mortal." It arose instead from two objective facts: Someone angry was banging on a door, and the noise was going to kill her.

472

The need to rid herself of that last shot of whiskey battled with dread of the spasmodic violence that would precede relief, but the mere thought of vomiting was now enough to trigger the act. Rolling onto the side of the bed, she threw up over the edge.

This would be the high point of her day.

I will never drink again, she thought. It was a vow she had made before. This time she meant it.

"Kate! Damn you, open the door!"

She recognized the voice. It was Wyatt Earp's. And he had just cursed her. Wyatt never cursed.

She tried briefly to open her eyes, but daylight felt like a knife in her skull, and she sank onto the pillow. *Ó, Krisztus!* she thought. What have I done this time?

"Doc?" she called in a tiny voice. "For pity's sake, get the door."

There was no answer.

Out in the hallway two men were exchanging tense, quiet words. A key was fitted into the lock. An instant later, the door was flung open with such force that it slammed against the wall, and there stood Wyatt like an avenging angel, his face twisting when he smelled the puke.

Next thing she knew, he was jerking her upright, not caring when she cried out in pain and fear. "You are trouble," he said, his voice low and mean. "You've always been trouble,

473

but you have really done it this time. Get up and get dressed."

She was still drunk. Her fingers were clumsy on the buttons, her mind three steps behind what was going on. Glimpses of the past thirty-six hours flickered by.

Champagne, she remembered. She and Doc had started with champagne.

No. Not champagne. They had started with dismay.

She'd given no thought to appearances while running the boardinghouse, working in comfortable cotton dresses, leaving her corsets and silks stored away until the day she packed for Tombstone. Doc had always had an eye for fit and registered the straining fabric around her middle, but if she had waxed, he had waned. They were the same age — not quite thirty — but he was gray and thinner than ever. She had forgotten how bent he had become, his bones weakened by his disease. My God, she'd thought, he's an old man! And he knew what she was thinking. And yet, within moments, all that was forgotten. There was the quick, murmured banter in French and Latin and Greek: shared amusement at absurdities they saw all around them in that striving, busy, bumptious town. A swirl of hotel staff. The door closing behind them, the bed before them . . . His merry cry, "Not dead yet!" in the laughing, breathless aftermath, and the drowsy ease that followed. Room service, and the first bottle of champagne. And then what? What went wrong this time? Something about her being a walkin' abacus. "I can see you addin' it up in your head! It's my money, darlin'. I'll spend it as I please."

Later, he had to go to work, and she went with him to the Alhambra. And then . . . Oh, Jesus. That girl! Kate thought, as Wyatt gripped her arm and propelled her down the hotel stairs. It was about that girl!

Small, dark. Wild curling hair. Flashing eyes, and a great show of "Aren't I adorable?" The little tramp showed up at Doc's table, saying something about "I'm always lucky when I play you, Doc," and Doc said, "Luck has nothin' to do with it, sugar." That must have been when the fight began.

"Please," Kate begged Wyatt when they passed by the hotel bar on their way to the lobby. "Let me have one drink. Just one!"

"Shut up," Wyatt snapped, pausing at the desk only long enough to tell the clerk, "Collect from Behan. He checked her in. It's his bill."

Behan? she thought. Who's Behan?

The sunlight was catastrophic. Wyatt steered her off the boardwalk and across the crowded street. "You're hurting my arm!" she cried. "Where are we going?"

"To court. You're going to take it all back."

"Take *what* back? What's going on?"

The courtroom was already filled when Wyatt marched her up the aisle and sat her down in the front row. A bailiff called, "All rise for Judge Spicer." Thoroughly frightened now, she looked around, trying to make sense of all this, but her eyes went wide when Doc was brought in. Unshaven. In shirtsleeves. Shackled.

"Goddammit, Behan," Virgil Earp cried. "Take those things off him! You should have had Luther King in irons, not Doc Holliday!"

"Once bitten, twice shy," the sheriff said reasonably. "I don't want another murder suspect escaping."

Murder suspect? Kate thought. Wait! *That's* Behan?

Suddenly the argument over that girl came back to her. Kate knew faro mechanics when she saw them — the sleight of hand, the nudge of bets from one card on the layout to another. Most dealers cheated punters that way, but Doc was feeding money *to* this little bitch, and Kate demanded to know why. The girl was just a friend, Doc claimed. He helped her out now and then. And if Miss Josephine *were* more than that, he muttered, Kate had a hell of a nerve expectin' monogamy from others. And then . . . what happened then? A lot of yelling.

She left the Alhambra, went looking for a way to get back at Doc. There was a saloon just down the street. The bartender there hated Doc's guts, too, and showed her his crippled hand. Suddenly there was a handsome, half-Irish charmer at her side. Johnny, he said his name was. And he was so sympathetic, keeping her glass filled, asking why she was angry at Doc. When she told him about that little tramp, his eyes went small. "Infidelity is a terrible thing," he said. Commiseration. More whiskey. They were two jilted lovers, taking comfort in each other's company, but at some point Johnny started talking about that stagecoach robbery, suggesting things about Doc. None of it made any sense, but she didn't care. She just kept drinking, agreeing with Johnny about what a louse Doc was, the way Johnny had agreed with her about what a slut Josie was.

"Mary Katherine Harony, approach the bench."

She was sworn in, shown a piece of paper, asked if that was her signature scrawled on the bottom.

"Yes," she said, "but I don't remember signing nothing."

She was told to be quiet. Her statement was read to the court. Dr. John H. Holliday had planned the Kinnear stagecoach attack. He was a deadly shot. She'd seen him kill dozens of men. He told her he'd killed Budd Philpot and the passenger, both. The Earps had inside information about Wells Fargo shipments and they knew when the strongbox would be full. They were in on the robbery, too, and wore disguises; that's why Bob Paul didn't recognize them. She'd seen the disguises in a steamer trunk in Doc's room. The disguises were made of black rope tied to look like long beards.

That was when people started to laugh.

"I never said none of that!" she cried as the judge banged his gavel. "I don't know nothing about that robbery! Doc would never steal!" She twisted in her chair. "Judge, please! We had a fight. I was mad at him, that's all! If I signed that paper, I didn't know what it said. I was drunk!"

"*That,* Your Honor," said Doc's lawyer, "is the first thing out of this woman's mouth that my client will not dispute."

"Doc, please! I didn't say none of that!" Kate cried, but Doc wouldn't look at her, his thin, lined face ashen in the harsh morning light. "I'm sorry! Please, Doc! I'm sorry!"

"Oh, for heaven's sake," Judge Spicer muttered. "Sheriff Behan, I can't hold this man on a statement given by an angry, drunken woman. There's no *evidence* here."

Weeping, she barely understood the legal maneuvering that followed.

The sheriff, making a case for setting bail at $5,000: "He's a suspect in a capital crime, Your Honor."

Doc's lawyer, protesting: "Your Honor, my client doesn't have anything like that kind of money!" Something about "a continuance, if it please the court."

Virgil Earp shouting something at Johnny Behan. Doc being taken out of the room, irons clinking. Morgan calling: "We'll raise the money, Doc!" Wyatt and another man, talking to the bailiff.

Spectators, laughing about "black-rope beards" as the room emptied.

The sound of her own sobs, filling the silence that was left.

She waited for Doc in front of the jail on the day he was bailed out, trying again to apologize, to explain. Doc wouldn't even look at her. Wyatt Earp spoke for him. "Go back to Globe, Kate. And don't come back." She tried again at the Alhambra. Morgan Earp stopped her before she could get to Doc's table. At the back of the room, Doc went on dealing, his eyes on the layout, his face expressionless. She sat outside his boarding-house next, until his landlady threatened to have her arrested for loitering.

In the end, she went to see James and Bessie Earp, hoping they would intercede, but Bessie was a southerner like Doc, and she saw no way back.

"They laid hands on him, Kate. They put him in irons, and they set his price like he was a field hand. You sold him down the river for a bottle of whiskey."

"If those charges stick, he'll hang," James said.

"In the meantime, he has to live here," Bessie continued, "among men who are draggin' his name through shit. He has to swallow their insults and tolerate their jokes —"

"Because if he talks back," James said, "Behan will throw him in jail again. And if he jumps bail, it'll bankrupt Wyatt and me, both."

"Against all that," Bessie said, "sorry don't count for much."

Kate opened her mouth, but there was nothing more to say.

"Go back to Globe, honey," James advised. "That'll be best for everyone."

The next morning, sitting side by side on a bench outside the Oriental, Cochise County sheriff John Harris Behan and Tombstone city councilman Milton Edward Joyce watched Doc Holliday's woman climb aboard the morning stagecoach and settle herself for the long journey north.

Even at a distance, they could see the marks of prolonged weeping. The swollen eyelids, the puffy face.

"Doc Holliday is a cruel, cold man," Johnny murmured. "I believe he has broken that poor child's heart."

"The dear girl was a gift from Jesus to us both," Milt said solemnly, "and I'm that sorry to see her go."

"We had a wonderful evening together," Johnny confided, straight-faced. "Not that she'd remember it. Christ, but she was drunk!"

Milt smothered a laugh — not very successfully — and for a few moments the two gave themselves up to quiet, elbow-nudging glee as the coach pulled away.

"And now she's left the wicked Doc Holliday here in Tombstone," Johnny observed, "hung like a millstone around Wyatt Earp's neck."

"God bless her! What's next, then?" Milt asked cheerily.

Johnny stood and stretched luxuriously before surveying the busy street before him. Mule-drawn ore wagons, delivery vans, saddle horses. Pedestrians hurrying to accomplish as much as they could before the heat of the day set in. "Word is, Wyatt Earp just mortgaged everything he owns to post bail for Doc Holliday."

Milt stood, too, and came to Johnny's side. "So we know exactly what his property is worth at current market prices."

"County taxes ought to be adjusted accordingly," Johnny said.

"I imagine," Milt murmured, "it would do no harm if I were to mention that to the city assessor."

"At your earliest convenience, if you please,

Councilman."

"Shall we go after John Meagher, too?"

Meagher owned the Alhambra, and he'd helped Doc post bail.

"Leave him alone for now," Johnny said, "but . . . Perhaps the city ought to reconsider the valuation of James Earp's tavern."

■ ■ ■ ■

THE PEOPLE OF
TROY CRIED OUT
IN FEAR

■ ■ ■ ■

A Seething Flood of Flame Rolled Closer

There is no shade in the high chaparral. Cat-claw and white thorn and palo verde are rarely taller than a half-grown child. A sizable man can reach the top of many mesquite trees, though he'd pay for that foolishness with an armpit full of thorns. There is barrel cactus and prickly pear, cholla and a lot of ocotillo, but only snakes and rodents can rest in their shadow.

Even in a mild year, the summer heat is ferocious, but 1881 was the hottest anyone could remember. In mid-May, the temperature was well into the nineties by five in the morning. Rats panted in their lairs and lizards were breathless. Dogs dug holes under board-walks and hid. Draft horses died in their traces. Paint blistered and flaked off wood.

Encased in corsets, wrapped in layer upon layer of flounced fabric, Tombstone's ladies gazed longingly at the white cotton simplicity of a Mexican shift. In woolen suits or heavy denim, lawyers and engineers, accountants and carpenters, blacksmiths and bankers, merchants and mechanics — anyone who worked above ground — envied those who labored in the constant cool darkness of the mines. Those with old and aching wounds — Doc Holliday, James Earp, Milt Joyce among them — experienced some relief from their pains, though not enough to compensate for the malevolence of the weather. Two ice factories ran around the clock but could not keep up with demand. Driven by a furnace wind, the acrid summer dust was inescapable; laundrymen and housewives despaired. Grit peppered food and tainted drink. It settled in the hair, in the ears. Noses clogged with it, and eyes felt scoured. Consumptives weren't the only ones who suffered from chronic coughs.

Sunset brought little relief. Rainless thunderstorms cracked and boomed and tore sleepless nights to pieces. Dogs were kicked. Women were beaten. Children were whipped. Drinking became a blood sport. Anything could set off a fight. A misheard word, a shoulder brushed. Anything.

On the last day of May, Editor Clum warned, "A high tide of crime threatens to inundate our city's streets." The stagecoach killers were still at large. Geronimo was stirring up trouble again. Cow Boy raids on cattle herds — foreign and domestic — were bolder by the week. Curly Bill Brocius stayed out of town, but the younger, wilder rustlers frequented Tombstone's bars and brothels after collecting their cut of the summer cattle sales. Drunk and singing, they'd link arms and parade down the center of Allen Street, blocking traffic in both directions: daring someone to complain, hoping Ben Sippy would try to arrest them. Shimmering with belligerence, elated by the prospect of a fight, they broke windows, shattered saloon mirrors, and started brawls with miners. Business suffered. Schoolchildren were at risk. Townspeople were scared to go out at night. An accountant's wife had been accosted in broad daylight.

In early June, Mayor Clum proposed an amendment to the town charter. "Tombstone is a city, not a mining camp," he argued. "Cities appoint police chiefs who work at the pleasure of the administration and are not subject to the whims of the electorate." After some discussion, Council agreed and the duties of the police chief were carefully defined. Ben Sippy could continue in the role, but from now on he was to prevent breaches of the peace. He was to suppress riotous behavior and disorderly assemblages. He was to arrest and jail every person found violating any law or ordinance, as well as any person found committing acts injurious to the quiet and good order of the city, including public intoxication, brawling, quarreling, vagrancy, and the public use of profane or indecent language.

To the mayor's surprise, a majority of City Council went on to pass the ordinance that Virgil Earp had recommended right after Fred White was shot. Carrying guns was now forbidden within city limits. And Tombstone went beyond Dodge City's response to violence. Banned weapons included knives as well as every type of firearm, although permits to carry pistols would be issued, if applied for.

The reaction was immediate.

The *Nugget* condemned the ordinance with a furious editorial that began, "Our forefathers gave us the right to carry arms" and ended with a list of ways its readers could circumvent the law. Sales figures at Spangenberg's gun shop tripled, and a shooting range was added to the back of the store where customers and "sporting folks" could test their purchases.

Scrawled death threats began arriving at the mayor's home. "Clum you are a ded man" was typical, but one neatly written letter showed evidence of education. "You have stepped beyond your legal bounds, Mayor Clum, and you shall pay the price. *Sic semper tyrannus!*" Upon opening that one, the mayor's first thought was of Doc Holliday but as Tombstone's postmaster, John Clum had access to samples of his handwriting on

488

envelopes the gambler regularly posted to Savannah and Atlanta. Holliday used an elegant Spencerian script, not the plainer McGuffey style of the death threat.

"Dr. Holliday, what do you make of this?" Postmaster Clum asked the next time the Georgian came in to mail a letter.

"*Tyrannis* is spelled wrong. I would judge this the work of a literate man who has come across Latin now and then, but who has not studied the language in a formal way."

"Any idea who might have sent it?"

"A southerner might be more inclined than most to quote Mr. Booth in this context, and while I hope never to stoop to slander . . . I have seen Mr. Ringo at the library. You might check his handwritin' on the records there against this note."

It was a match.

A few meditative hours later, Mayor Clum decided that it might be a good time to take that trip up to St. Louis he'd been considering.

There is no such thing as whiskey too bad to drink. That was the prevailing attitude on the American frontier, but on the afternoon of June 22, 1881, the owner of the Arcade Saloon reluctantly concluded that common wisdom was sometimes in error.

Cursing his supplier for a villain and a thief, he told one of his boys to roll the offending

489

cask of god-awful rye into the alley behind the bar and dump it.

The workman took that opportunity to have a quiet smoke. When he was done — not wanting to take a chance on setting anything ablaze in a town constructed from tinder-dry pine — he carefully dropped the smoldering stub of his cigarette into the enormous puddle of spoiled whiskey. It was an innocent mistake. Never having seen a chef flambé food, he believed that any liquid would put out the ember. Fifty gallons of alcohol burst into flame.

Pushed by a dry, hot desert wind, the blaze spread with stunning speed. Buildings bordering the alley were engulfed even as the workman's screams raised the alarm. Miners boiled out of the pits. Offices and stores emptied. Every able-bodied man ran toward the center of town. Hundreds set to work, dipping buckets into horse troughs, flinging water against forty-foot walls of fire. They might as well have puckered up and spit, for all the good it did.

Frantic, they battled smoke and heat to bring out people trapped inside stores and offices and hotels. They beat burning boardwalks with wet blankets, tore burning canvas awnings down with bare hands, climbed on one another's shoulders to ax away burning balconies. When all that that failed to slow the fire, they hitched mule teams to chains and pulled down whole buildings, still hoping to contain the blaze, but the conflagration only got fiercer as liquor casks in saloon after saloon added fuel to the flames.

Dark against the afternoon bright sky, a column of black smoke drew the eyes and curiosity of rootless young men who called their saddles home. As the sun went down on what was left of Tombstone, those who'd fought the fire salved blistered skin, coughed soot and ash from seared lungs, and fell exhausted onto whatever makeshift beds were available on the unburned edges of the town. While they slept, Cow Boys from miles around converged on the city, whooped with delight at the entertaining scope of the destruction, and searched through the smoking wreckage for intact bottles of brandy, bourbon, Bordeaux, and beer.

That was the scene greeting Mayor John Clum as he stepped down out of the night coach from Benson, just past midnight on the morning of June 23. Young drunks, celebrating devastation. Laughing. Singing. Dancing in the embers.

Behind him, weary travelers who'd anticipated comfortable rooms in the fine hotels of "the Paris of Arizona" climbed stiffly into the starlight and stared wordlessly at a thin, bent man trudging toward them through the ruins.

Soot-smeared and filthy, he was recognizable only from his exhausted limp and his terrible cough. Out on bail, even Doc Holliday had fought the blaze.

"There are beds in Schieffelin Hall," he told the passengers, lifting his chin toward a large building that had escaped the fire intact.

The visitors collected their bags and set off for whatever shelter might await them, but John Clum and John Henry Holliday remained side by side, watching the horseplay of reveling Cow Boys.

"Hell is empty. All the devils are here," Holliday noted hoarsely. "And where have *you* been, Mayor Clum?"

"St. Louis," John said. Before he could register his own tears, his unconscious weeping turned to laughter that was just this side of hysteria. "I went there to buy a fire engine and two hose carriages for the city."

The dentist put a comforting hand on the mayor's shoulder. "Irony rules the day."

Morning brought no joy.

Close to seventy businesses had been wiped out. Some $300,000 worth of property had been destroyed in an afternoon. The Cosmopolitan and Grand Hotels. The town's nicest saloons — the Oriental, the Crystal Palace, the Magnolia — were gone, along with the Arcade, of course, where the fire started. Two breweries. A dozen brothels and gambling halls. The Key West Cigar Shop. The ice cream parlor. The bowling alley. The Western

Union office. The Tombstone Municipal Court. The Safford and Hudson Bank. The offices of mining executives, lawyers, architects, and engineers with all their records. Restaurants, stores. Gone. All gone.

After the first night's scavenging, there was nothing left to steal except the ground itself. Without landmarks and streets, property lines were once again in dispute and the infamous Tombstone Townsite Company launched a second attempt to seize downtown real estate. Jim Clark and Mike Gray distributed tents to hungover Cow Boys, paying them to sit on newly vacated lots in the cheerful hope that some of the legitimate owners had been killed during the fire. Having been elected largely on his promise to fight the Townsite Company's fraudulent claims, Mayor Clum ordered Chief of Police Benjamin Sippy to clear the lot-jumpers out.

Chief Sippy gave it a try, but the Cow Boys were on him like starlings mobbing a crow. After ten days, he decided that somebody in his family had just gotten terribly, terribly ill and that he himself required "a leave of absence" so he could rush to his unfortunate relative's bedside.

Starting immediately.

City Council met in emergency session as armed property owners confronted armed squatters amid the ruins. The first order of business was to organize a volunteer fire department. (Its grim motto: "Better late than never.") Second on the agenda: naming a replacement for Ben Sippy, who was unlikely to be seen again.

The motion to appoint Virgil Earp as Tombstone's new chief of police carried without a dissenting vote.

Mayor Clum had just administered the oath to Virgil when a Western Union rider burst into the meeting with news that he'd been unable to convey via telegram because the Tombstone wires were down.

"The president's been shot!" he cried. "Some crazy sonofabitch walked right up to him and put a bullet in his back!"

Anarchy had arrived.

HERE WE WILL
STAND OUR GROUND!

Mayor Clum was the first to speak. "Deputize as many men as you need," he told Virgil Earp. "Get squatters off the land and guns off the streets. We'll back whatever you do."

Virgil left the meeting and went to find his brothers. They rounded up twenty-five other men, many of them Union veterans Virg knew he could rely on. Deploying his deputies on the edge of what had been Tombstone's business district, he strode alone to the center of the ruins and announced in a booming, resonant voice, "I am Police Chief Virgil Earp. I intend to enforce all city ordinances and to maintain order. Town lots remain the property of those who held title to them before the fire. All disputes regarding titles will be adjudicated in the courts. Lot jumpers squatting on the property of others are ordered to vacate *now.*"

There was laughter and mockery in response, and a taunt from one self-confident drunk: "Well, come on 'n' git us then, why doncha?"

This was an error in judgment.

On Virgil's word, twenty-seven armed and sober men on horseback swept through the tent camp, jerking canvas shelters up and away, throwing lassos, dragging squatters to the city limits, and driving them out of town.

Done, in half an hour.

In the following weeks, Chief Earp's men patrolled Tombstone day and night, in fourteen teams of two. Walking slowly and deliberately through town, each officer cradled a shotgun or Winchester in his arms. With the police highly visible and quickly responsive to any threat, order was restored. Businesses reopened in temporary quarters while crews of Chinese laborers swiftly cleared the wreckage.

Western Union reestablished a wire; it was taken as a good omen that the first telegram received in Tombstone after the fire was an announcement that President Garfield would likely recover from his gunshot wound. Tombstone would recover, too, everyone vowed. It was going to rise from its ashes, bigger and better than ever, just like Chicago had. City Council entered into negotiations with a new telephone company to provide service throughout the town. Another water company announced plans to lay pipe from the mountains. ("This time for sure!" everyone said sarcastically.) Even news that the lower levels of several silver mines were flooding was greeted with cheer. The water was not potable, but it could be pumped out and sprayed on the dirt streets to keep the summer dust down or made available to firefighters in emergencies.

With construction sites under the watchful eyes of Virgil Earp's police force, pilfering was minimal. The summer heat continued unabated and tempers could still flare, but brawls, knife fights, and shootings were stopped before they started, the potential combatants knocked cold before they had a chance to come to blows. No one was above the law. Mayor Clum himself was arrested and fined for riding his horse through town at too great a speed.

New buildings went up with astonishing dispatch, but it was not merely a town that was built that summer — it was a genuine community. Twenty thousand individuals had traveled to Tombstone for reasons of their own; after the fire, a sense of common purpose united miners and merchants, wheelwrights and prostitutes, bartenders and ministers.

Tombstone felt itself joined to the rest of the country as well, for President Garfield's condition became a national obsession as the summer of 1881 passed. Each morning began with a breathless wait for the daily bulletin telegraphed to the nation by the president's doctors. If the news was encouraging, the mood was buoyant. Any setback — another bout of fever, another agonizing failure to dig the bullet out of his back — was met by murmurs of anxiety and concern.

If Tombstone's Republicans felt as though a beloved brother or father or son was fighting for his life after a shocking and unprovoked attack by a madman, others in Cochise County snickered at the long faces of those whose darling president had been shot and wished aloud that ole Charlie Guiteau had done a more thorough job of shooting that Yankee sonofabitch. They muttered complaints as well about the Earps, who were using their badges as an excuse to beat up anybody they didn't like. And though signs of hostility were confined to sullen looks and muttered backtalk when the Cow Boys visited town, there was lurid speculation about what might happen to those Yankee law-dogs should they dare to ride out of Tombstone.

Mayor Clum and the Tombstone City Council did not mind at all that rowdy visitors found Virgil Earp's enforcement of every ordinance oppressive and excessive. If those visitors came into town for supplies and a good time but left the next day with crushing headaches and ringing ears and fogged minds . . . well, that was just too bad.

"We're all in this together," Tombstone's

citizens told one another that long, hot summer. "Cow Boys be damned! It's us against them," everyone said.

The shining silver city on the hill against barbarians at the gate.

Which was precisely *not* how Johnny Behan had wanted things to go.

He was out of town the week of the fire, down in Bisbee again, meeting copper-mine executives and financiers. They were Republicans to a man, but he had stressed his effectiveness at working across party lines when he was sheriff of Yavapai County, and he made a strong case for himself as a man who understood the concerns of those in the mining industry as well as the issues confronting cattlemen and farmers in southeastern Arizona.

"If Republicans and Democrats work together, Cochise County can be the engine of prosperity for the whole nation," he told them. "The war's been over for years, gentlemen. Let's stop fighting each other and pull together!"

News of the fire did not arrive until three days after the blaze, when the Tombstone telegraph wires were restrung. Johnny rode for home as soon as he heard. All along the way, he was met by outraged constituents who claimed the Earps had taken over the city. Walking around like they owned the place. Stopping men on the public streets, demanding that they hand over weapons. Coldcocking anyone who argued. Arresting people for shit like cursing, for crissakes! Prissy goddam sonsabitches . . .

When he got back to town, Johnny went straight to Virgil and conveyed Democrat sentiment to Tombstone's new chief of police, one lawman to another.

"I answer to the mayor and City Council, not to the voters," Virgil told him. "The charter calls for me to *prevent* disorder, not to deal with brawls and shootings after they happen —"

"Virg, I understand that, but Democrats are citizens, too, and —"

"Hell, Johnny! I'm not checking voter registration cards! If Democrats don't want trouble with me, tell 'em not to break the goddam law."

"But there are all these new ordinances," Johnny started to point out.

"Yes, and they're posted all over town."

"Virg, half the men in Cochise County can't read. You of all people oughta know —"

Virgil's mood shifted from annoyed to hostile. "Oughta know what?"

"I'm just saying that even someone like Wyatt would have trouble reading those signs, and —"

"You leave my brother out of this," Virg snapped. "Anyways, this is a city matter,

Sheriff, not county." So it's none of your god-dam business, he meant.

And that, Johnny discovered, was the consensus throughout the city. Nobody would give him the time of day. For months, he'd been urging the formation of a volunteer fire-fighting brigade, presenting it as a bipartisan organization that could get men from both sides of the political divide working together for the good of the community. The June 22 fire was a dramatic demonstration of the wisdom of his plan, but when he brought up the matter with City Council — just as a citizen of Tombstone, mind you, not as a politician running for anything — there were indulgent chuckles around the room. "You're right, Johnny, but you're a little late," he was told. "We took care of that when you were down in Bisbee."

Worse yet, Wyatt Earp had actually run into a burning building — *twice* — to rescue a woman who was trapped inside, and in recognition of his bravery, he had been elected recording secretary of the Tombstone Volunteer Fire Brigade. "I'm real pleased to hear it," Johnny said, but he was thinking, *Secretary!* Christ, that's a laugh! Wyatt had a good memory, but Johnny would've laid dollars to dimes that Wyatt was telling his younger brother what happened at the meetings so Morgan could write up the minutes for him.

The final slap in the face came when Cochise County's district attorney reported to the federal district court that the felony case against John Henry Holliday was without "the slightest evidence to show the guilt of the defendant." Judge Wells Spicer promptly dismissed the charges. It took three hookers and a quart of whiskey to get through *that* night, but when the hangover receded, John Harris Behan was prepared to face the facts.

Doc Holliday was a free man, his bail money released. As far as anybody knew, he'd left town already — thus depriving Johnny of the brush he'd hoped to tar his rival with. Wyatt Earp was a town hero: a brave firefighter, a fearless lawman, with clear title to his property and a real shot at taking the sheriff's office in the county's first election. That crazy little weasel Charles Guiteau and a local fire had dragged Cochise County straight right back to 1865. Sixteen years after Appomattox, it was "The Battle Hymn of the Republic" against "Dixie" all over again.

A bipartisan coalition was no longer realistic.

So. Wyatt Earp would have Republicans, Tombstone, and Millville. Johnny Behan could count on Democrats, Sulphur Springs Valley, and towns like Charleston and Galeyville. Thanks to Holliday's drunken girlfriend, rumors were still going around that the Earps had been in on the stagecoach robbery back in March, which might give Watervale and Benson to Johnny as well.

And thinking of girlfriends . . .

While there was no doubt in Johnny Behan's mind that Wyatt was screwing Josie Marcus, it came to him that it might be useful if Mattie Blaylock got caught turning a trick. That would be easy enough to arrange, and then Harry Woods could suggest in the *Nugget* that Wyatt was a pimp. Better yet, they could catch Mattie during a raid on Ah-Sing's opium den one night! That would put a dent in Wyatt Earp's shining armor. His brother had a tavern that catered to Chinks, too. Maybe Harry could convince people that the Earps were pro-Chinese . . .

I can do it, Johnny thought. I can still pull it off.

In the meantime, the Earp brothers themselves couldn't have been more helpful, for each time one of them took a man's gun away, or knocked some poor sonofabitch cold for disorderly conduct, or imposed a fine for vulgar language, they made an enemy of that man and all his friends. And every enemy of the Earps was another angry voter who'd support John Harris Behan for sheriff, come November 1882.

"Can you believe this?" Virg asked, holding up the *Epitaph* at breakfast a few weeks later.

"Behan just hired Frank Stilwell as a deputy!"

"He hired Curly Bill Brocius to work with Billy Breakenridge, too," Morg said. "Tax collection!"

"Pushing up county revenue," Wyatt said, "and Behan's take."

"Yeah, I guess a man could say no pretty easy to a short fella with specs on," Morg said, "but with Curly Bill smiling behind Billy B.? You'd pay pretty quick."

Higgs's tail thumped against a table leg. Morg tore off a little piece of toast and slipped it to him.

"Morgan," Lou said, "you're teaching him to beg! More coffee, anyone?"

Wyatt held up his cup, and she refilled it. The others shook their heads.

"Stilwell's a killer," Virg said flatly. "Who's Behan gonna hire next? Johnny Ringo? Old Man Clanton? That mouthy little bastard Willie Claiborne?"

Tired of shop talk, Lou asked, "Has anyone seen Doc lately?"

There were blank looks around the table.

"Been a while," Morg admitted. "We've been kinda busy, honey."

They'd made well over a hundred arrests in the month after the fire, but things had settled down now that everybody understood Tombstone tolerated no nonsense. Virgil was going to tell City Council it was safe to lay off most of the men he'd deputized in June.

In the event of trouble, the chief would call upon his brothers Wyatt and Morgan, with the Vigilance Committee available as reinforcement. He was keeping just two officers on the payroll: James Flynn and A. G. Bronk, both tough, reliable men who took no sass.

Which meant it was time for Morgan to go see John Meagher about getting his job back. "I'm going over to the Alhambra today anyway," he told Lou. "I expect I'll see Doc there."

"Well, tell him I miss him," Lou said, "and invite him for supper."

"Doc gave notice just after the fire," John Meagher told Morgan. "We got the bail money back after Spicer dismissed the charges, and Doc said something about taking a rest cure. Haven't seen him since. He didn't look good, Morg. I figured he went back to that sanatorium."

Morgan frowned. "Seems like Doc woulda told me before he left town."

"Yeah. Well, anyways," Meagher said, "with him gone, we're short a dealer, so if your brother's still willing to bank your game, I'll give you a table."

Still thinking about Doc, Morg hesitated for a moment before he snapped to. "Thanks, John. I'll start tonight."

He meant to go home and tell Lou that, but decided to stop by Molly Fly's first, to

505

see if she knew where Doc went.

"Thank the Lord!" Molly Fly cried. "Oh, Mr. Earp, I've been so worried about him!" Leading the way up the stairs, she filled Morgan in on the past month, her voice dropping as they got closer to Doc's room. "He won't let Dr. Goodfellow come and see him anymore. There's bleeding deep in one of his lungs, but he says there's nothing to do about it but rest. At first, he'd take a little soup or something, but now he doesn't touch the trays I bring up. He just sleeps. And he's so thin! Why, you can hardly see him under the sheet!"

Quietly, she opened the door and stood aside as Morgan went in.

"Jesus," he said. "Oh, Doc . . ."

Eyes sunk in his skull. Ribs barreled from the constant labor of hauling in air. The whole body — just bony hills and fleshless valleys.

"Mrs. Fly, why didn't you tell us he was this bad?"

"I wanted to, but he made me promise I wouldn't!"

Morgan picked up a bottle of laudanum. "Do you know how much of this he takes at a time?" The landlady shook her head, but judging by the number of empties in a wastebasket, the answer was obvious: too much. Not a rest cure, Morgan thought. Eternal rest.

"Get Louisa," he told the landlady. "Tell her to find my brothers. We'll take him home to my house."

When Mrs. Fly had hurried off, Morgan sat on the side of the bed and gripped Doc's shoulders. "Doc, wake up! C'mon, you gotta get on your feet. Sit up! C'mon, Doc. You gotta get up and walk."

"Please," Doc whispered. "Please. Just . . . let me go."

George Goodfellow was a decently trained physician, but he'd had little experience treating tuberculosis. "John, I know you don't want to hear this," he'd said, "but you really ought to consider permanent retirement to a sanatorium."

"Why? So I can die of boredom instead?"

"Be serious," George snapped. "Your life is at stake, dammit."

What young Dr. Goodfellow could not have known was that John Henry Holliday was all but broke. Lawyer's fees had nearly cleaned him out in May. There would be no more help from home. When Kate's allegations were reprinted in Atlanta's papers, his family had given up on him. The only one who still answered his letters was Sister Mary Melanie, and nuns had very little in the way of ready cash.

He hadn't worked since the fire, when — in the literal heat of the moment — he had risked his life amid soot and ash and smoke, hoping to save the piano in the Cosmopolitan Hotel. That, at least, should have been obvious to George, and there was an edge in Doc's voice when he pointed out that "sanatoria — like physicians — want payment for their services, however useless they might be."

His friends' kindness and generosity had been almost limitless, but there comes a time when a proud man would rather die than ask for more. So he'd used the last of his savings for the last of his expenses. He laid in a supply of bourbon and laudanum, paid Mrs. Fly for a month in advance, hoping that would be long enough to finish the job, and took to his bed.

There was a time when he hated laudanum. The taste was bitter and nauseating, but this hemorrhage was deep in his chest. The pressure and pain had never been worse, and bourbon couldn't touch it.

Once, Mattie Blaylock came to see him. "I told you laudanum was good," she said. That might have been a dream.

There were a lot of dreams. One of them was beautiful. It was a dream of his own death. Not of dying itself, for he'd watched this disease kill his mother and knew how terrible his end would be. The dream was of . . . afterward, and in the dream, he could breathe again. Easily. Fully. Thoughtlessly.

"This is heaven," his mother told him. "We

are in heaven now, sugar."

No one who does not live with constant pain can imagine the toll it takes. The way it grinds you down. The sheer damnable tedium of it.

His mother was waiting for him, but his friends would not let him go.

Eat this, they said. Drink this. Keep fighting, Doc.

We love you. Don't give up.

WOULD THAT THIS FRAILTY HAD AFFLICTED SOMEONE ELSE!

Late summer rainstorms are normal in Arizona, but not even Chiricahua elders had seen anything like the drenching August downpours of 1881. Thunder that year did not boom or rumble and roll; it exploded like a bomb. Lightning bolts flashed blindingly, terrifyingly close. It was one storm after another, every afternoon, each more astonishing than the last. Day after day after day.

In Tombstone, packing crates floated down the flooded streets. Gales ripped off new awnings and sent freshly painted signs flying. Water poured into mine shafts, clogging the pitheads with rubble. Ore wagons bogged to the axle before rolling three yards and stamping mills had to be shut down. Roads washed out and repairs were impossible. Even when laborers could get to the damage, the next storm would undo all their work. Stagecoach service and mail delivery ceased. The city was cut off from resupply.

Vagrants stood around under leaky wooden

galleries, watching busier men splash across streets holding squares of tent fabric over their heads. Merchants passed the time making lists of stock on hand and of stock to be ordered, if the damnable rain ever ended. In livery barns, harnesses were mended and leather was cleaned, to pass the time. In homes, wobbly chairs were fixed and stockings were darned. New shirts were sewn and old ones were cut up for quilts by those imaginative enough to believe they might be cold again someday, for the rain did nothing to abate the heat.

Sweating and wretched in Lou and Morgan's front room, propped up with pillows on their chaise, John Henry Holliday tried and failed to be grateful for his rescue.

There were frightening, snarling outbursts that took everyone by surprise, even Doc himself. He would weep afterward, ashamed of his bad temper, powerless to control it. Then he'd curse Morgan's meddling in a voice halfway between a whisper and a whine. "Damn you, Morgan! Damn you! If you'd just . . . let me go, this would . . . be over by now."

"It's the pain," Morg would say. "He don't mean it." But Lou suspected that Doc meant every word and sometimes she, too, thought it might have been kinder to let Doc go.

I love Morg, she would remind herself when Doc was at his worst. I love him. I do.

How could you not admire a good-hearted man who, seeing that a friend was sick, would, without a moment's hesitation, bring him home to be cared for and looked after? Even if Morgan *had* thought to ask her first, it wasn't as if Lou would have refused. She was as fond of Doc as Morgan was. But everything was so much harder this time!

Back in Dodge when he was ill, Doc had a lot of friends to care for him. Now Kate Harony was gone. Mattie Blaylock was worse than useless. Allie was busy helping Bessie, whose tumors were getting worse. The brothers did what they could, but they all had jobs. There was no one to share the burden with Lou here in Tombstone, and no way to escape it, either. In Dodge, Doc and Kate had a place of their own. Lou could stay a few hours and then return to a home that was neat and clean and didn't smell of fever sweat. Here, the sick man was an inescapable presence, no matter how quiet he tried to be.

Doc himself was different now. Peevish, contrary, abrupt. Beaten down by his illness. More hopeless, less stoic. As awful as it had been then — watching the poor man fight for air, hour after hour, trying not to drown in his own blood — it was worse now, with the bleeding trapped inside his chest.

They didn't want him to end up a hophead like Mattie Blaylock, so Lou had to refuse when he begged for more laudanum. It broke her heart, but she was hot and irritable herself, and weary of his misery.

"I don't . . . want to die," he whispered once, "but I don't . . . want to live like this." And Lou knew exactly how he felt.

Then one glorious morning, Josephine Marcus showed up at the door with a basket of groceries.

"Doc has always been so nice to me," Josie said. "When I heard he was sick, I just had to visit. And I thought of some things he might like to eat. I hope you don't mind."

"Mind?" Lou cried. "Oh, Josie, I could throw myself at your feet and kiss your hem!"

Across the street, Mattie Blaylock was standing on the porch, her hair snarled, her wrapper untied. "Jew slut! I know what you're doing! First Wyatt, now Morgan!"

"She's visiting Doc," Lou called.

"You want 'em all, don't you!" Mattie yelled. "Greedy goddam Jew."

"Has she always been crazy?" Josie asked, but before Lou could respond, Josie was inside and in motion, unloading her basket, laying out ingredients. "You are doing me *such* a big favor! The only thing I miss about living with Johnny Behan is having an oven. Well, I miss seeing Albert every day, too," she amended wistfully, but shook that off swiftly. "I'm going to make a cheesecake for Doc. Very easy to digest. It'll put some weight on him, too."

She came again the next morning, and the next, and soon they had a routine. Lou and Morgan were up at sunrise, for Morgan was working the day shift at the Alhambra, which was busier than ever because the miners had nothing to do except gamble and drink the beer that was still being brewed locally. Morg left for work at seven. Josie arrived at eight and while she looked after Doc, Lou did laundry, washing sweat-sodden sheets and shirts, hanging them on the line. Happy to get out of the sickroom for a while, Lou would just sit in the porch rocker afterward, waiting for the sheets to dry, which only took an hour or two. Then she'd bring them in and get them ironed before the next cloudburst.

At noon, she and Josie had a meal on the table. Wyatt often came for lunch and to visit the dentist. Afterward, Lou cleared and washed the dishes. Josie read aloud until Doc fell asleep. Wyatt liked to listen, too, but he worked nights — as Josie did, though no one ever talked about that — and he sometimes fell asleep in the heat, like Doc. Tired herself, Josie would gaze at the two men for a time and then whisper to Lou, "I'll just sneak out now — before the rain starts. Time for the cuckoo to sing."

That had become their nickname for Mattie Blaylock. The cuckoo. When Mattie was awake, she spent her time peering through her curtains, keeping tabs on everyone's comings and goings. Rarely dressed, often drunk, always angry, she still had enough sense left not to yell at Wyatt, but when she saw Josie, she'd pop out onto her porch, like the little bird in a German clock, yelling, "Bitch! Jew slut! I see what you're doing. You've got to have them all, don't you! First Wyatt, now Morgan."

Which was absurd. Josie hardly ever saw Morgan, and she rarely spoke to Wyatt. In fact, her entire attention seemed quite focused on Doc, and Lou began to wonder if he wasn't the one Josie had her heart set on.

Josie was really good with him. "Sick people are like that," she'd say when Doc was fretful or despondent. "Besides, in this weather — who *isn't* a little crabby?" She was full of energy and chatter and good cheer, but somehow she didn't set Doc's teeth on edge. Maybe it was because she complained about things, too, and that gave Doc permission to feel as bad as he really did, instead of trying to pretend that he was fine.

"I'd have thought all this rain would cool things down," Josie said one morning. "Dry heat is bad, but *this*!" She waved at her face with both hands and laughed at her own discomfort. "This is horrible! And poor you, with a fever! I don't know how you stand it, Doc."

"I might as well've . . . stayed home, in Atlanta," he muttered, "instead of comin' all . . . the way to Arizona to die."

"Don't talk like that," Lou said automatically, but while Josie didn't exactly change the subject, she always found ways to distract Doc.

"The weather is awful in Washington, too," she told him. "They're hoping to make Mr. Garfield more comfortable with a new machine. It's an air blower that pushes an artificial breeze over a big chest of ice. A navy engineer invented it, just for the president. They say it brings the temperature in his room down by twenty degrees! I wonder if we could set up something like that here?"

Nothing came of the notion, but she got Doc interested in how such a device might work, and that gave them all something fresh to talk about.

She always stopped at Western Union on the way to Lou's. The morning bulletin from Garfield's doctors was good for half an hour of discussion every morning. Once, however, she reported that the latest attempt to remove the bullet from the president's body had led to an infection, and the dentist flew into a sickly, startling rage.

"His surgeons . . . are killin' him! Idiots . . . still think a filthy . . . gore-spattered frock coat is . . . evidence of their . . . vast professional experience. They won't even . . . wash their hands, let alone rinse . . . their instruments in carbolic!"

"Doc, please!" Lou cried. "Don't upset yourself —"

But Josie asked, "What's carbolic?" Which made for nearly fifteen minutes of more reasonable conversation before Josie got up and took something out of the oven.

"Here," she said, bringing Doc a dish of something bland and custardy-looking. "Try this."

"Not hungry" was always his first reaction, but when Josie pouted, he always gave in. "All right. I surrender. What have you . . . made for us today?"

"Noodle kugel. Try one bite and I promise I won't nag anymore!"

"You are . . . a shameless liar."

Which was true, of course. Josie never gave up until he finished everything on the plate.

"It's a match made in heaven," Josie told Lou once. "Doc needs to eat. I love to cook. Every bite he takes feels like a curtain call."

Lou smiled at that, but she couldn't help thinking, Maybe she'll marry him and he'll be off my hands forever.

The idea made her very happy, for reasons both kindly and selfish.

"Mr. Garfield is being moved to the Jersey shore," Josie reported one morning. "They're hoping ocean air will help."

517

It didn't, and a week later, a national day of prayer and fasting was declared. "Tombstone's ahead of the times," Josie noted. "We're already fasting!"

The roads remained impassable and food supplies were dwindling. There was no starvation, for beef was available in monotonous quantity, but it took real thought to make the most of a narrowing selection of ingredients if you wanted more than meat. Josie's "night work" sometimes gave her access to hoarded delicacies, which she shared with an exuberance that made Lou forget how the girl had earned them. One day she arrived with a miraculous can of peaches and declared, "God knows what we'll do tomorrow, but today? I think we've got just enough flour for cobbler! We'll use the juice to sweeten the batter and save the last of the sugar to sprinkle on top."

Later, when she stooped to take the cobbler out of the oven, Josie said, "You know you're in Arizona when the oven is cooler than the kitchen!" But she and Lou had fun.

It was still hellishly hot in late August, but the thunderstorms gradually became less frequent and the cloudbursts shorter. Road crews were able to make repairs and on September 1, supplies began to reach Tombstone again. Everyone's mood lifted, though drinking remained the town's most popular pastime.

At the Alhambra, a drunk named Howell Creevey entertained the entire saloon by taking bets that he could put a live tarantula in his mouth.

"Saw it myself," Morgan told Doc. "He did it three times without getting stung."

"Self-preservation," the dentist murmured. "I have seen . . . Mr. Creevey's mouth. The tarantula . . . would have died."

That was the first real sign that Doc had turned the corner. He could say only three or four words at a time, but the fever had abated. The chest pain had diminished. He was quiet-eyed and calmer now.

The president's condition, by contrast, continued to deteriorate.

"If Mr. Garfield's . . . doctors had left that poor soul alone," Doc told Josie one afternoon, "he'd be up . . . and walkin' by now."

"And so would you be, if you'd stop talking and eat more — *Oy, mein Gott!* I keep hearing my mother's words coming out of my mouth. 'Eat! Eat! You're too thin! I made this just for you!' "

"Tell me about her," Doc suggested. Stop shoving food at me, he meant.

"She's too boring to talk about." Then, struck by a thought, Josie sat still. "It just now occurred to me that she moved from Prussia to New York to California. Across Europe, and across the Atlantic, and around

519

the Horn to the Pacific . . . No wonder she wanted life to be boring! She'd enough adventure already."

"When did you . . . see her last?"

"Goodness! Almost three years. I should write more often, but . . ."

"You're not sure . . . what to tell them."

She shrugged and changed the subject. "There was another telegram from Kate this morning."

Stopping as she did to get the latest news from Washington, it was natural for her to take delivery of the telegrams and bring them to Doc. This morning's message was in Latin: SINE AMOR NIHIL EST VITA STOP.

"What does that mean?" Josie asked.

"Without love, life is empty. My own words . . . comin' back to haunt me."

Josie sat back in her chair and crossed her arms. "Doc," she said, "be honest. Do you still love Kate?"

He looked away, his face hardening in the effort to stop tears that still lay near the surface.

"I thought so," Josie said. "Listen, what Kate did was awful, but Johnny Behan put her up to it. And believe me — when that louse wants to be charming, he is impossible to resist."

They were both thoughtful for a time. Then Josie put her hand on Doc's. "Yom Kippur's coming," she told him. "On the Jewish calendar, it's a day to ask forgiveness but . . . also a day to grant it."

That was what Wyatt and Lou saw through the front window on their way in for lunch: that moment of quiet intimacy.

"A match made in heaven," Lou murmured, not realizing how deep those words would cut.

"I just remembered something I gotta do in town," Wyatt said. "I'll eat over at the hotel."

Hell, he meant. I waited too long, and now I've missed my chance.

Once the roads were dry and solid, the ore wagons began rolling again and the mines and mills returned to full capacity. Stagecoaches were back on schedule by early September. Robberies resumed.

The Bisbee coach was the thieves' first target. They got away with jewelry and cash from the passengers, along with a strongbox containing $2500. Deputy Sheriff Billy Breakenridge, Deputy Federal Marshal Virgil Earp, and special officers Morgan and Wyatt Earp, promptly tracked down robbers, who turned out to be none other than Deputy Sheriff Frank Stilwell and a friend of his named Pete Spence.

"Shall I tell Sheriff Behan you've resigned?" Billy B. asked Stilwell.

"Go to hell," Frank said.

Bail was set at seven thousand dollars. Which should have been enough.

The summer heat moderated from lethal to merely brutal. The worst seemed to be over for Doc Holliday, and he had made his intentions clear. He would begin a careful exercise regime and go back to work at the Alhambra as soon as he'd regained some stamina. The moment he had any kind of income, he'd stop imposing on Morgan and Lou and move back to Mrs. Fly's boardinghouse. Morgan had his doubts about the wisdom of this plan, and despite her eagerness to get some privacy back, Lou fretted about a relapse. But when Doc told Josie, she said, "Good! Because I've been working on a surprise for you, and you have to walk all the way to Sixth and Allen to find out what it is."

And that, he realized, was Josie's most endearing trait: She approved. Whatever you wanted to do, she believed that it was good and that you were right to do it.

By September 5, Doc Holliday was seen again on the streets of Tombstone, leaning on his cane, visibly weakened but walking a little farther every morning on those broomstick legs of his.

"Hey, Doc! I thought you left town!" the tactful would say, while the more bluntly honest might admit, "Damn, Doc! I thought you was dead."

"Not far from it," he'd tell them. And yet,

all odds against, he'd lived beyond his thirtieth birthday, and now he had two simple goals: add distance to his walk each day and find out what Miss Josephine was up to. Often she accompanied him on these walks, a tiny dynamo, chattering and cheerful.

So many new buildings had gone up since the fire in June, he hardly recognized the town, but when he finally rounded the corner of Sixth and Allen, he stood still, startled to see that a large two-story building being constructed on the very spot where Fred White had been shot.

"It's called the Bird Cage, and it's going to be a variety house!" Josie told him. "Billy Hutchinson is an impresario. He and his wife, Lottie, are going to bring all the best touring performers to Tombstone. The main floor's not done yet, but there'll be a stage on one end and a three-piece orchestra."

"Impressive," Doc said, trying not to remember Fred's screams. He concentrated on breathing for a few moments before he admitted, "I am not sure . . . I understand why you wanted . . . me to see it."

"It's a surprise!" She giggled and danced a bit, wrapping small hands around his bony arm. "Now that I'm sure you can get here, I'll tell Lottie to let us in on Sunday morning. Do you need to rest a while, or shall we go straight home?"

He could still see Fred. Bleeding in the street.

"Let's go on back," he said.

AH, IF YOU AND I COULD ESCAPE THIS FRAY!

There was nothing inappropriate about Tom McLaury's note. *Mrs. Earp,* he'd written, *you might think after all that rain, there should be Flowers again in your garden. Do not worry the plants are not Dead. They need some cold before they come back next Spring. Respectfully, T.M.*

Lou had nothing to hide, and yet . . . she never mentioned the note to Morgan. She folded it and kept it tucked into an apron pocket.

Sometimes she took it out to read again when she was alone. That might have seemed suspicious but in all honesty, she wasn't tempted by Tom McLaury. Not really. His boyish face and those beautiful, earnest, yearning blue eyes — they put her in mind of her brothers when they were little. That's all. A few minutes of conversation with Tom were all she'd needed to size him up. She knew instinctively that he was not the kind of man who could protect her and maybe that was what she found so hard to shake off: the idea of a life in which she wouldn't *need* to be protected.

So, yes, she saved that note, though she kept it to herself.

Because she loved Morgan Earp. She did. He was as decent a man as Lou had ever known. He had a talent for happiness and a sunny, even temperament that made each day with him a pleasure. She loved his curiosity and how tickled he was when he learned something new. She loved his tenderness at night. The joy was still there. The affection. The daily satisfactions. To her surprise, things had actually gotten better between them after she yelled and cried. Maybe Bessie was right. "Honey, the Earp boys mean well," she'd told Lou, "but sometimes you have to hit them with a shovel to get their attention."

Morg worked in town now. He came home every evening and when she saw him round the corner with that big grin on his face, her heart still rose. "Wait'll you hear what happened today!" he'd call. The stories he told were always funny, never mean-spirited. While Lou would not have chosen to live in Tombstone, she had a three-room house of her own here and a discreet gold ring on one finger. She understood the seasons better and despite the harshness of the landscape, she knew that Arizona would provide bright blue days and pleasant weather in the spring and fall. She hardly heard the noise from the steam engines down at the mines anymore. She had learned to pay attention to the flute and twitter of nearer birdsong.

Even so, sometimes — sitting out on the front porch, listening to the buzz and squabble of a tiny darting mob of hummingbirds and watching Higgs chase lizards with clumsy puppy zeal — she would take that note out of her pocket and allow herself to wonder what her days and her nights might be like with the shy, thoughtful, sweet-faced farmer who had brought her a wagonload of spring beauty and a puppy's exuberance to ease her loneliness and to make her smile.

Different, she decided. Not necessarily better. Just different.

"Bitch! Slut!" Mattie shouted, announcing Doc and Josie's return.

Lou slipped Tom's note back into her apron pocket and gave Doc a steadying arm as he climbed the veranda stairs.

"It's official, Lou," Josie announced. "Sunday morning, nine o'clock, at the Bird Cage. You and Morgan are invited, of course. Tell Morgan to get Wyatt to come. If Virgil and Allie would like to attend, that would be very nice, too."

Winded but pleased with himself and his progress, Doc asked, "Miss Louisa, do you know . . . what this . . . is about?"

"No, she doesn't," Josie said, "so don't

waste your breath asking her."

"She's been working on something," Lou told him, "but she won't say more than that. Are you going to dance for us, Josie?"

"It's a *surprise*!" Josie cried, exasperated. " 'Surprise' means you don't know what it is until it happens. I'll see you at nine on Sunday."

"Jew slut!" Mattie yelled, standing in her doorway across the street. "I know what you're doing. You have to have them all, don't you! Wyatt, Morgan, and now Doc."

"Good mornin', Miss Mattie," Doc called as loudly as he could. "I hope . . . you feel better . . . soon."

"Go to hell!" Mattie yelled. "And take those bitches with you!"

It was a day for surprises. That's what Wyatt would remember about September 18, 1881.

First off, Virgil and Allie showed up at the Bird Cage that morning. Wyatt hadn't expected them to come, for Allie had been slow to warm to Josie.

Then Albert Behan joined them, noticeably taller than the last time Wyatt had seen him. No surprise there — kids grew like weeds in the summer. The round freckled face was still that of a little boy, but Al shook hands like a grown man with the Earps and their ladies. When he was introduced to Doc Holliday, he said, "Josie and my father have both told me

a lot about you. I'm inclined to believe Josie."
Which made everybody laugh. "I'm supposed
to be at church," Al said, "but Josie and me
have breakfast every Sunday instead. It's not
lying. It's just not telling. Anyways, my dad
sleeps in, so he doesn't know the difference."

"Nice to know the sheriff is up on events in
town," Virgil murmured.

"No wonder he can't seem to arrest anybody," Morgan said, spitting into the street.
"Doesn't even know what's going on in his
own house."

"Doc, you all right?" Wyatt asked, for the
dentist looked kind of peaked.

"Certainly," Doc said. "Certainly . . .
Just . . . a little . . . out of breath."

"I'll be right down!" Josie called from her
hotel window across the street. When she
emerged at street level a minute later, she
had sheet music in her hands. Doc went still,
and her face lit up. "Don't expect much," she
warned him, "but I'll do my best!"

Lottie and Billy Hutchinson arrived to let
them in. "The Bird Cage will be the finest
building in Tombstone when we're done,"
Billy bragged. "Two stories aboveground and
a cellar below. This open area in the center
here will be general audience, but we're running galleries along both sides with box
seats."

"I've got velvet curtains on order," Lottie
told them, "and there'll be upholstered chairs

in the boxes."

"Theater on the main floor, gambling in the cellar," Billy said, but his eyes were on Doc Holliday, for — like a man in a trance — Doc had worked his way around piles of construction materials and now stood still, staring at what they believed was the surprise Josie had promised him.

"It's a J. P. Hale square grand," Billy said with quiet pride. "Came in that last shipment of goods before the roads closed. Not as splendid as a Chickering — what a pity to lose that beauty in the fire! Still, plenty good enough for the acts we'll have."

"Wyatt," Josie said, "bring that chair over for Doc, would you, please? And put it right there?"

Next to the piano, she meant, not in front of it.

That was the next surprise, for it was Josie herself who sat on the piano stool. Hands hovering over the keys, she murmured, "No need to rush."

In the silence of the half-finished theater, she began to play. Slowly, tenderly. As though a child were sleeping in the next room. Letting each note linger in the heart and in the ear. It was just one piece, perhaps three minutes long, but she played it well. When she finished, no one clapped or even breathed, for they were still inside that sacred place that music can sometimes create.

Finally, Josie herself broke the spell, going to Doc's side, kneeling before him, reaching up to wipe the tears from his face with her own hands.

"Well, now," he said, voice fraying. "Ain't you something."

"Oh, Doc, you wouldn't credit how I practiced! I left out the hardest parts, and it still took weeks and weeks to learn it. 'Traumerei' is the only thing in the world that I can play."

"And you are my only pupil," Doc said when he could speak again, "but I cannot imagine . . . one who might have . . . pleased me more."

They all went over to the Can Can Café for *dim sum* after that, even Albert, who sat next to Josie with a proprietary air.

They tried a couple of dozen little dishes of strange Chinese foods. The girls made a fuss about how good it was. Morgan and Virgil joshed Quong Kee about bird's nest soup and asked if he'd make cow pie dumplings next, but there wasn't a scrap left on the table by ten o'clock, when church let out.

Al told them he had to get home. That was the signal for the rest of them to leave as well. Morgan tried to pick up the check, but Wyatt told them, "I took care of it already."

Everyone stared at him, boggled, for Wyatt was the tightest man with a dollar any of

531

them knew.

"What's next?" Virgil asked. "Talking horses? Honest politicians?"

"Nah," Morgan said. "He's not paying! He just won a bet with Mr. Kee!"

"Hush up, Morgan," Doc said. "Thank you, Wyatt. You are very kind."

Virgil needed to get back to the city marshal's office. Morgan was late for work at the Alhambra. Doc said he'd escort Allie and Lou home, if they didn't mind walking at a snail's pace. That left Josie with Wyatt, who walked her back to her hotel over on Sixth but couldn't think of anything to say along the way.

When they got to the door, he just stood there like an idiot on the boardwalk, turning the brim of his hat around and around in his hand.

"Well," Josie said, "it's been a lovely morning, but . . ."

"That was real nice," Wyatt said. "What you did for Doc."

Relieved that he had finally spoken, she smiled happily. "He's been so sick . . . I just wanted to do something special for him. He has such a terrible reputation, but it's like you said — people get the wrong impression. I think he's sweet."

Wyatt looked away, then made himself say it. "He is lucky to have you. I know he'll treat you good."

She blinked. "I'm sorry?" Frowning, she squeezed her eyes shut for a moment, then looked at him again. "Wait! You mean — you thought Doc and I . . . ?" There was a startled laugh. "No! No, no, *no*! I mean, there's nothing wrong with him, but — No! Wyatt, Doc's still in love with Kate."

It was Wyatt's turn to be startled. "Kate? Oh, hell! Don't tell me he's gonna take her back!"

"Now, see, that's exactly why he didn't say anything to you! He knew you wouldn't approve."

"Darn right, I don't approve! She drinks and she's bad-tempered, and — Hell, she almost got him hanged! Why in the world would he take her back? That's just plain foolishness." He stopped. "But then . . . you and him . . . you ain't . . . ?"

Eyes bright as sunlight on water, she waited, letting him work it out.

"So then, you and me . . . I mean, if you wanted . . . we could —"

She squealed then, like an excited little kid. And leapt into his arms. And planted a kiss on his lips. Right there, in broad daylight. On a public street.

"Oh, Wyatt!" she cried, half-exasperated, half-thrilled. "My God! I thought you'd *never* ask!"

He had known one good woman, and a fair

number of bad ones, but he had never known anyone like Josie. She was not shameless, or indifferent to what he did, or merely tolerant. She was joyful. She was *glad* of him.

When he finished, he thought their first time was real fine. He would never know that she was thinking, Well, that was dreary.

She was, by then, an accomplished actress who liked men in general and found them endearingly fragile. So she waited, letting him drowse a while before she rose on one elbow and gazed down at him with a face full of challenge and fun.

"I suppose you think you're done?" she asked, brows high.

She brought his hands to places he had never touched. She made him slow down and then commanded, "Now!" and rose to meet him. When she cried out, he froze, thinking he had hurt her. Sweating, breathless, she lay back a few moments later and *laughed:* a throaty, deep, satisfied laugh.

Seeing his confusion, she smiled. "You didn't know a woman could feel that, too?"

Dumbfounded, he shook his head.

Eyes warm, she kissed him again. "Don't worry, Wyatt. I know enough for both of us."

The church bells woke them early the next morning. That was a surprise, too, for it was Monday.

The tolling was slow, not the rapid clanging

of a fire alarm or the stately announcement of worship services.

Wyatt got up and went to the window to see what was going on. Behind him, still in bed, Josie said, "Don't move! My God, I could look at you for hours."

Startled by the remark, he turned, covering himself with his hands.

She giggled. "I had no idea men could blush all the way down!"

Then it struck them both: The slow tolling of bells was funereal.

"Hell," Wyatt said. "Garfield musta died."

The gunfire began a moment later. He reached for his clothes, and Josie groaned, "No! Don't go!"

"Virg might need me," he said, bracing for the kind of argument he used to have with Mattie. *Your brothers always come first. I'm always last.* But that was another surprise, for Josie sat up, small breasts bare to the morning light, her eyes serious.

"You're right," she said. "Go. *Go!* I'll be here when you get back."

Down on the streets, there were crowds of people. "The president's dead," he heard someone say, and that's what he'd expected, but it was still a shock to hear the words and his heart sank.

Joining the throng that was headed to the Western Union office, he witnessed for himself the way the town — and the nation — was divided. Republicans were struck dumb by the news: half in grief for Garfield, half in dread of what a Chester Alan Arthur presidency would mean to the nation. Democrats adjourned to the saloons to celebrate the death of an abolitionist who'd meant to oppose the reestablishment of white rights across the old Confederacy.

Wyatt found Doc Holliday in the crowd near the Western Union office.

"I would not have voted for the man," Doc admitted, "but this —" He lifted a fine-boned hand toward the street, where small groups of Cow Boys were now tearing down Allen on horseback, shooting at the sky and racing beyond the city limits before the police could do anything about the ruckus. "*This* is indecent."

■ ■ ■ ■

DENSE THE
BATTLE-HAZE THAT
ENGULFS THE BRAVE

■ ■ ■ ■

STRIFE STRIDES
ACROSS THE EARTH

The September 21 meeting in Mexico City began with condolences, of course. His Excellency Ignacio Mariscál, head of the Secretariat of Foreign Affairs, conveyed his government's heartfelt sympathies to the bereaved citizens of the United States, which were gracefully accepted by His Excellency Philip Morgan, minister plenipotentiary of the United States legation to the Republic of Mexico. These pro forma courtesies were followed by murmurs of genuine personal regret upon the passing of James Garfield. Mental notes were made to wait a few days before any private assessment of the new president's character — or lack of it — were exchanged.

Then they came to grips.

"Despite these grievous circumstances," Sr. Mariscál said briskly, "our ships of state cannot be allowed to drift. As you well know, the conditions on the Arizona border are now and have been — for many months — outrageous. Cattle raids. Drunken predation on

539

peones. Rape, sir, of our women. Our gray-haired elders beaten. And now the Cow Boys have murdered sixteen Mexican nationals on U.S. soil. Civilians, sir. Honest merchants, robbed of over three thousand dollars and killed by criminals who are known to your officials but who are permitted to roam free."

"Your Excellency, I agree fully that the border situation is regrettable, but since President Garfield was shot in June —"

"I understand that there has been a constitutional crisis since the attack on your president, but please! Do not dare to offer excuses. Conditions on the border are more than regrettable, sir. They are dangerous — very dangerous! — but when my government protests, nothing is done. Worse than nothing, for insult is added to our injuries when members of these very outlaw gangs are deputized by the sheriff of Cochise County."

Philip Morgan, who had not been invited to sit down, shifted uneasily on his feet, one of which still ached from a wound he had sustained thirty-some years ago, not far from this office. "Sheriff Behan's decisions in this matter are lamentable, but he is within his legal rights to deputize anyone he deems suitable. My understanding is that none of the men he employs has been convicted of any crime —"

"Only because their fellow outlaws provide alibis for them in court!"

"Nevertheless, according to the rule of law —"

"The rule of law in Arizona is utterly corrupt. Do you dispute this?"

The American remained silent.

"No. I thought not. And so: I am instructed by my government to demand *again* that the United States deploy troops on our mutual border to control these murdering thieves —"

"And I, Excellency, must explain again that the *Posse Comitatus* legislation bars the U.S. military from any association with civilian law enforcement."

"Then declare *martial* law!'

"If we were to do that, there would be an insurrection in Arizona and, quite likely, in Texas and New Mexico as well."

"If you fail to do so, the consequence will be worse than insurrection."

Mariscál paused then, to settle himself, for what he was about to say carried the immense weight of armies, of destruction and disfigurement and death, of widows and of orphans.

"I must remind you, sir, that when our nations last went to war, the pretext used by President Polk for *your* invasion of *my* country was the killing of twelve of your nationals by Mexican soldiers on *disputed* territory. That, sir, is the legal precedent. Our case for war against the United States now is stronger than the one Polk made then."

It was a stunning statement, and both of

them knew it. Ceremonial formality fell away. They became, for the moment, merely two old men who had fought on opposite sides, three decades earlier.

"Ignacio, are you serious?"

"Philip, my friend, if the United States does not control these border gangs, there are those within my government who are urging an armed invasion of Cochise County to wipe the bandits out. Furthermore, I cannot promise that the *rurales* of the state of Sonora will be patient much longer. They are policemen, but each is a man like any other. How long do you expect them to maintain discipline when Americans abuse and murder their people with impunity? Without justice, there is only revenge."

Ignacio Mariscál stood then and came close enough to grip Philip Morgan's arm. "You must persuade your government to do whatever is necessary to bring the border under control, whether the means to that end are legal or not."

Over the next few hours, urgent messages flew from the office of Philip Morgan to that of Secretary of State James Blaine and from there to the executive mansion, now home to the amiable hack who'd just become the twenty-first president of the United States.

Chester Alan Arthur was no one's idea of a great man, not even his own. He'd been placed on the Republican presidential ticket only to appease the New York political machine. As James Garfield slowly died of iatrogenic infection, Vice President Arthur hid in his New York City apartment, refusing to exercise presidential authority while Garfield lived. Told that the president's long agony was over, Arthur wept with fear before taking the oath of office. In Washington, three days later, he had yet to rise to the occasion.

"I am inclined to defer to the local authorities," he said when Secretary Blaine told him of the latest communiqué from Mexico City. "This is a matter for the territorial governor, surely. Let Frémont take care of it."

"Mr. President, I'm afraid that Governor Frémont has taken a indefinite leave of absence." Secretary Blaine cleared his throat before adding with dry diplomacy, "For his health."

"Well, there must be somebody in charge out there!"

"Yes, of course, sir, there is an acting governor, but John Gosper's position is somewhat analogous to your own, sir. He is new to his office." And he's fighting out of his weight class, Blaine thought.

"Interior!" Arthur cried with sudden inspiration. "This is the Interior Department's responsibility! Get Kirkwood on it."

Save me, he meant. I don't know what to do.

■ ■ ■ ■

Another round of communiqués followed, this time between Washington and Prescott. Asked by Interior Secretary Samuel Kirkwood for his assessment of the situation in southern Arizona, Acting Governor Gospers could provide no comfort.

EFFORTS TO CONTROL BORDER BLOCKED BY DEMOCRATIC LEGISLATURE STOP FUNDS FOR 100 MAN RANGERS FORCE DENIED STOP INFLUENTIAL AMERICAN RANCHERS PROFIT FROM STOLEN MEXICAN STOCK STOP SALOON INTERESTS BENEFIT FROM COW BOY MONEY STOP COCHISE COUNTY SHERIFF BEHAN PAID TO WINK AT CRIME STOP PARTISAN NEWSPAPERS INFLAME OPINION STOP NO PROSPECT OF IMPROVEMENT STOP RECOMMEND AMENDMENT OR REPEAL OF POSSE COMITATUS STOP

There's nothing I can do, he meant. For the love of God, send troops.

Day by day, the list of Mexican dead grew longer. Outraged and fed up, Governor Luis Torres of the state of Sonora ordered a force of two hundred men to the border and gave their commandant a single order: Keep the Cow Boys out.

Apprised of this, American Major General Orlando B. Willcox took the precaution of requesting additional troops in order to deal with "the Indian problem" in the Dragoon Mountains, where the cavalry would also be in position to deal with a Mexican invasion.

In Prescott, U.S. Marshal Crawley Dake informed his superiors that he'd need five to ten thousand dollars to cover the expense of sending a posse after Cow Boy raiders who'd just killed four more men in Sonora. He was informed that no treaty covered cross-border law enforcement. Furthermore, since the crime was committed in another county, the Marshals Service could not arrest the perpetrators, if indeed they could be caught.

In Tombstone, Allie asked Virgil, "Do you think there'll be a war?"

"Well, now, Pickle," Virg said, "everybody's trying to avoid that."

Yes, he meant.

Meanwhile, the Arizona Territorial Legislature passed a bill outlawing gambling by minors.

If Ignacio Mariscál or President Arthur or Virgil Earp had asked Newman Haynes Clanton what he thought about borders, the old man would have laughed in their faces. "Some educated goddam fool takes a ruler and a pencil to a map? Why, that boy thinks he done something! But borders don't mean *nothin'* out here."

Old Man Clanton had, in fact, just peeled off sixty head of cattle from a herd that mooed with a Spanish accent, but pushing the animals across the imaginary line wasn't the important part. It wasn't until you had them in a high-sided gorge called Skeleton Canyon that you could make a fire and have a drink and bed down for the night.

Last job of the season, he thought, easing his bones onto the stony ground. This'll set us up until spring. It was a gamble, pulling off a raid this late, but the summer rains had made for perfect pasturage that fall, and the old man reckoned they could fatten one last herd of scrawny Mexican stock before the snows.

Now, lying in his bedroll, listening to cattle lowing and to men snoring, with a few quiet months stretching out before him, he had begun to think about the future.

He'd just turned sixty-five, still tough enough to ride for days when there was a profit to be made, still young enough to take a certain rowdy pleasure in a dash into Mexico for a little shopping trip. Even so, it was time to consider a different angle on the business.

Why keep supplying the big bugs? he was asking himself. Why not hold on to this herd? He had three big spreads in three broad valleys. Far from any town, each ranch was ringed by mountains like castle walls. You could see for miles in any direction, and nobody could get near you without their dust giving them away a day before they arrived. Why not buy some decent breeding stock, like Henry Hooker or John Slaughter, and become a big bug himself? Or maybe work both ends . . . send Billy down to run the raids. Keep the best stock, sell the rest on.

Course, Billy was nineteen and thought he knew it all. But I'll teach him different, the old man was thinking. I'll train him up right, and then —

"El viejo es mío," a thick-bodied, dark-skinned man of middle years said softly.

He was lying belly-down along the rim of Skeleton Canyon when he said it, and his companions didn't argue. They were used to taking orders from the one who had just claimed the old man as his own, though they wore no uniform that could identify them as policemen or soldiers. They might have been . . . silver traders, perhaps. Or tequila merchants. Tobacco smugglers, maybe, who'd crossed the border to do business.

Or relatives of a boy who'd died defending his family's cattle.

Whoever he was, the middle-aged man breathed out to steady his aim, and with that sighing exhalation, he murmured, *"Vaya al diablo, pendejo."*

The old man's head jerked and lolled. An instant later, the men on the canyon rim fired down on the sleeping figures below.

Within moments, Charley Snow, Dixie Lee Gray, Billy Lang, and Jim Crane joined Old Man Clanton in hell. Billy Byers — shot in the stomach — lurched away into the desert darkness to die.

Harry Ernshaw fled as well. His nose was permanently shortened by a passing bullet, but he lived to tell the tale.

"Good riddance." That was the reaction to the Skeleton Canyon murders among mining executives, investment bankers, and the Arizona politicians who owed their appointments to Washington. Whoever cleaned out that nest of vipers had the gratitude of the entire Republican Party, the legitimate Arizona business community, and most of the editorial writers around the territory.

"Goddam greasers never woulda had the nerve to come so far north." That was the conventional wisdom in the rougher bars of southeastern Arizona. But if not the beaners, then who *had* killed Old Man Clanton and his men?

No one speculating on this topic had anything to go on, apart from a reflexive contempt for Mexicans. Having rejected the most likely identity of the Skeleton Canyon killers, however, many men spent many hours working their way through many bottles, discussing potential suspects.

In Tombstone's Dragoon Saloon, someone pointed out that Skeleton Canyon was over in New Mexico and only a federal marshal could cross that border to make an arrest. Well, Virgil Earp was Tombstone's chief of police, somebody else said, but he was a U.S. marshal, too. Virg himself had been plenty visible since the fire, but his brothers Morgan and Wyatt hadn't been seen much recently. Neither had their friend Holliday.

It was about then that Johnny Ringo went outside to take a piss against the wall. He was buttoning up when he saw Doc Holliday gimping down Toughnut, leaning on his cane.

Alert to the possibility of getting jumped during his therapeutic walks around Tombstone's streets, Doc Holliday took note of Ringo's unblinking interest. His first thought was, He can see how sick I've been.

Ringo, he believed, was taking malicious satisfaction in a lunger's misery, for whatever reason that might be significant to the strange, hostile, vicious drunk.

Glassy-eyed with drink, Ringo simply stared from across the street at first. Then — and this was the unnerving part — malevolence was replaced by a gleeful, open-mouthed, nearly joyous smile. With the loose, unsteady gait of the very drunk, Ringo returned to the saloon, chuckling to himself and full of purpose.

It was, Doc thought, as though Eden's serpent had just thought of something wondrously amusing to lie about.

DRUNKARD!
DOG-FACED, QUIVERING
DEER-HEARTED COWARD!

The balance of the spinning world shifts when a beloved and benevolent father dies. The weight of a constant presence is lifted away. Unanswerable questions are asked in the middle of the night. Could I have done more? Said more? What should I have asked while there was still time? What did he mean by those last words? Beyond the questions, there are practicalities. Have his taxes been paid? What about all these bills? Is this claim on the estate legitimate? What should I do next? And next, and next, and after that? Even a devoted and competent son may falter, overwhelmed and at a loss.

But what if the father was a mean-spirited, violent, contemptuous old bastard? What if the son's education was sketchy and his brains regularly rattled in childhood? What if he often woke to the sting of a knife blade held against his throat and the smell of whiskey on the old man's breath. *I made you. You're mine. I can do anything I want to you and nobody can stop me. Nobody.* What if the son himself drank far too much whenever he escaped the old man's notice?

Daddy's dead, Ike would think. He's gone. He ain't coming back, and I'm glad.

Then he'd worry about ghosts and wonder if his father could hear his thoughts and return to harm him in some way. A dozen times a day, Ike would glance over his shoulder, cringing in anticipation of a blow, a threat, a sneer. He would see himself with his father's missing eyes and hear that absent tongue wag all day long. *You're an idiot and everybody knows it. You're soft, like your mother. You should be wearing a dress, you worthless, sniveling little girl.*

"Ike, you look like you could use a drink," Ringo would say, and he was always right. It took a lot of whiskey to make the old man's voice shut up.

People kept showing up at the ranch. They wanted Ike to make decisions, to answer questions, to pay money the old man owed or deliver goods he'd promised to provide. But the old man had always treated Ike like a half-wit hired hand and never told him one thing about the business. So Ike would just stand there, not knowing what to say.

Ike's little brother, Billy, would laugh at him for looking so confused, but Ringo was kind. Ringo stuck up for Ike.

"They got no right to look at you like you're stupid," he'd say. "Nobody has that right, Ike. You want respect, Ike? You have to take it. You have to fight for it."

"Fight for it," Ike said.

"Leave Ike alone," Curly Bill would tell Ringo. "He's funning you, Ike."

Used to be, Ike liked Curly Bill more. Now Ringo was his friend.

"I'm just helping Ike think," Ringo would say. "He likes it when I help him think, don't you, Ike? You need help thinking."

"I need help," Ike would agree. Then he'd have another drink with Ringo.

It took some time for Ike to put all the pieces together in his mind. The first thing to come clear was that he didn't have to go to California after all. I can take care of the girls here, he thought. Or they can get married. They don't have to ask permission. The old man's dead, and he ain't coming back.

I can open a new restaurant, he thought, and that's when he remembered promising to tell Wyatt Earp about where those men were. Because that was the plan, before the old man got killed. Ike was supposed to find where Bill Leonard, Henry Head, and Jim Crane were and tell Wyatt Earp. Wyatt was going to arrest them. Ike would get $3,600 from Wells Fargo, and Wyatt would get votes when he ran for sheriff next year.

Except before Ike could do that, Bill Leonard and Henry Head got killed by the Hazlett brothers out in Ánimas Valley. The Hazletts could have collected $2,400 from Wells Fargo for doing that because the reward was twelve hundred apiece, dead or alive. But then Johnny Ringo killed the Hazlett boys because they killed Bill and Henry. And then Jim Crane got killed in Skeleton Canyon with the old man.

Now nobody would get the Wells Fargo reward. Not Ike, nor the Hazletts, nor Ringo. Ike thought that was a pity. It was a lot of money and would have been nice to have, even though he didn't have to move to California now.

At first Ike didn't remember anything about Doc Holliday being in on the deal. Then one night when all the boys were sitting around drinking, Frank McLaury started in about how crooked the Earps were and how they were all pimps and their women were all whores, and how they held up that stagecoach themselves. Frank could prove it, too: The Earps blamed Bill Leonard and Henry Head and Jim Crane for the crime.

"It's just like when that goddam army lieutenant blamed Tommy and me for stealing those mules, when Hurst really stole the animals his own self!"

Billy Clanton usually got a laugh out of that

554

because he stole those mules. It always tickled him how Frank was so convinced of his story that he'd tell it to Billy's face and expect to be believed. But Billy Clanton wasn't with Ike that night. He was off in Charleston, whoring with Little Willie Claiborne, who was celebrating his release on bail after shooting Jim Hickey in the face.

Curly Bill was there, and he used to find Frank's notions funny, too, but Bill didn't laugh much anymore, and that evening, he got all broody about how Wyatt Earp had bent a pistol over his head after that accident with Fred White.

"I bet you any amount of money nobody hit Doc Holliday's head when *he* got arrested for that holdup," Curly Bill said. "Two men dead, but Holliday can get away with anything 'cause the Earps are always there to protect his bony carcass."

"Yep," Ringo agreed, "and now all four of 'em are gonna get away with killing Old Man Clanton."

Which made everybody stop talking and look at Ringo.

So he told them about how Holliday and the Earps were the ones who killed the old man in Skeleton Canyon. "I saw Holliday gimping around Tombstone myself," Ringo said. "I asked him, 'What happened to your leg, Holliday?' And that skinny goddam lunger started bragging! He said, 'Me and the Earps ran down Old Man Clanton and his boys, and we killed them sonsabitches in Skeleton Canyon.' But, Ike, your daddy pulled out that little pocket gun he carried in his boot. He shot Holliday in the leg. So your old man got a little of his own back before Holliday killed him."

"Holliday killed him," Ike said, dazed.

"Yep. And bragged about it."

"Bragged about it."

"The Earps'll protect him," Curly Bill said bitterly.

"They're all in on it," Frank said.

"They're all in on it," Ike said.

"They'll never get convicted!" Frank went on. "Earps always have an alibi. Oh, I was with Wyatt. Oh, I was with Doc. Oh, I never did nothing wrong in my whole life . . . And then the goddam liars'll turn around and pin the blame on somebody else."

"Pin the blame . . ." Ike said.

"Somebody's got to pay," Ringo said softly. "When one of ours is killed, we gotta make the bastards pay."

"Make the bastards pay," Ike said, but even then, he was still thinking, The old man's dead. He ain't never coming back. And I'm glad.

Sometimes Curly Bill would warn, "Ringo's playing with you, Ike."

"I'm just teaching a parrot to talk," Ringo

would say.

"C'mon, Juanito," Bill would say. "Leave Ike alone."

Ringo would just wait until Curly Bill wasn't around, and then he'd start in again about that goddam lunger Holliday killing Old Man Clanton.

"I can't think straight," Ike would protest.

"Well, try thinking crooked then," Ringo would tell him, with that angel smile of his. "It's in the Bible, Ike. Eye for eye. Tooth for tooth. Life for life."

"Eye for eye. Tooth for tooth," Ike said, beginning to squirm.

"If you're tired of being hit, you have to hit back, Ike."

"Hit back."

"You want respect, Ike? You have to take it. You have to fight for it."

"Fight for it."

"Pull a gun, Ike. You pull a gun, you're on top. Pull a gun and you'll get some respect — just like *that*!" Ringo would say, snapping his fingers.

Ike rubbed his face with both hands. He hadn't shaved in a long time. His beard was getting as bushy as the old man's was.

"One of ours gets killed, we have to kill a few of theirs," Ringo told him. "That's how you get respect, Ike. You gotta make 'em pay."

Don't talk back, Ike thought.

"Make 'em pay," he said.

■ ■ ■

Then there was the night when Ike and Billy were up late, drinking and talking about the old man.

"You recollect that time he told you to get up on the roof, Ike?"

"Jump!" Ike yelled in the old man's voice.

Billy giggled, just like when he was five and saw it happen. "Yeah, he kept telling you, 'Jump! I'll catch you!' "

"I'll catch you!" Ike remembered.

"So you jumped, and then *bang!* He just stepped back and watched you hit the ground."

"Don't! Trust! Nobody!" Ike roared, making his voice as fierce as the old man's was.

"You learnt yer lesson yet, boy?" Billy roared, the same way. Then he made his voice humble, like Ike's was that day, even though Ike was twenty-four when it happened and should have been a man. " 'Yes, sir!' you said. 'Yes, sir, I learnt my lesson!' "

Don't trust nobody.

The old man was dead. The dread wasn't. The dread was still there. A deep hole waiting — wanting, needing — to be filled.

Ike began to go over the deal with Wyatt in his mind. Ringo couldn't help him think about this. Ringo was being friendly now, but he could be a mean sonofabitch, too. Even Curly Bill was scared of Ringo sometimes.

You can go to California, Wyatt said. You can open another café. Just tell me where Henry Head and Jim Crane and Bill Leonard are. You get the reward, I get the votes, and Holliday gets clear.

Then one night, the hole filled up. *They're all in on it.*

Wyatt Earp must've told Doc Holliday. What if Holliday brags on that? And what if Ringo finds out I was gonna sell Henry and Jim and Bill to Wyatt Earp?

He'll kill me, Ike thought. Ringo will kill me, just like he did the Hazlett boys.

Respite in War Is
All Too Brief

"It defies logic. It insults common sense," Doc admitted when he told Josie Marcus his plans. "Kate is selfish and mercenary and impossible to live with, but when she's gone? I miss her like I miss breath. Madness, I suppose. Or plain stupidity."

"You love her," Josie said firmly. "Love isn't stupid."

Eyes narrow, he glanced sideways at the girl, marveling at the lack of cynicism. "That, sugar, is an eminently debatable assertion, but . . . Well, I calculate Kate and I are even now. This will be a fresh start."

They were going to meet halfway. In Tucson. In mid-October, when the weather was good. They would spend some time alone in a town where no well-meaning friends could question the wisdom of this reconciliation. They would see if they could work things out.

Doc wired ahead to reserve a modest but clean room on the outskirts. I'm not a spendthrift, he meant. Unaware of this, Kate got to town early and booked the best room in the best hotel. I'm not a miser, she meant. I love you, and I wanted to please you. That's what they really meant, though neither could say it aloud.

Instead of arguing, they split the difference: a nice room in a decent hotel just off the central plaza. They were careful with each other at first, but care soon turned to tenderness, and tenderness to that deep satisfaction in each other's company, which they always remembered more clearly than the anger and the fights. In that state of grace, they began to discuss what was left of Doc's future. We don't have much time, they agreed. Let's make the most of it.

They had no real ties to Arizona, and the territory grew more dangerous by the week. Five Cow Boys had been killed recently. That left at least thirty-five others to raise hell with impunity. Outlaws from Texas, New Mexico, Colorado, and California were joining them, for Cochise County was considered the last, best place in the country for men who would not be governed. The Chiricahua Apaches were making trouble again, as well. Why stay in this hellhole? That was what they asked themselves in the quiet of their Tucson bed. Arizona was ferociously hot in the summer, numbingly cold in the winter, and plug-ugly most of the year. All Doc had to show for eighteen months in its climate was another fist-sized hollow deep inside his right lung. Kate was ready for a change as well. Why not just pack up and go?

They settled on the Rockies, for there was reliable research coming out of Switzerland: Whatever caused tuberculosis, the disease seemed to need high concentrations of oxygen to do its worst. Sanatoria in the Swiss mountains were having considerable success with advanced cases of the disease; the higher the altitude, the more efficacious the treatment.

Why pay doctors, Kate asked, if simply spending time in thin air could cure you? She could open another boardinghouse — in Denver, maybe. Doc could do a little gambling, and Kate would look after him. They would live frugally and wait the disease out while the mountains did their work.

That was their plan, four days before the gunfight.

If anyone had asked, "What about Ike Clanton?" Doc would have answered with a question of his own: "You mean the idiot who told that revoltin' joke about oysters? What about him?"

Ike was panicking, is what.

"Ringo knows," he insisted, pleading with Wyatt to understand how scared he was. "He looks at me funny! He knows all about it."

"Keep your voice down!" Wyatt said, his own voice low, for if there was so much as a rumor of him being involved with Ike Clanton, any edge he had over Johnny Behan in the sheriff's election next year would blow away. "Ike," he said, trying to stay patient, "did you tell Ringo?"

Ike shook his head, eyes wide.

"Well, then, he *can't* know. You and me are the only ones who know. But if you keep talking about it like this, the whole town'll know!"

"The whole town'll know," Ike repeated, close to tears. "The whole town'll know! And Ringo will kill me!"

Exasperated, Wyatt gripped the man by the arm and steered him deeper into the alley. "Ike, nobody knows. It's over. All three of the men who attacked that stage are dead now. The deal is off! You didn't tell anyone, did you?"

"No!"

"And neither did I," Wyatt told him. "So nobody else knows!"

"But you told Holliday he was in the clear!"

"No! I didn't, Ike! Holliday don't know."

"Holliday will tell Ringo and Ringo will kill me!"

It went on like that — round and round and round — until Wyatt was ready to kill Ike himself. "Holliday don't know, and I'll prove it to you," he said finally. "Go home. Stay out of Tombstone and stay quiet. I can fix this, Ike. Don't worry."

"Don't worry" was what Ike said, but what he thought was this: *Don't trust nobody.*

"You know where Doc is?" Wyatt asked Morgan that night, over at the Alhambra. "John Meagher says he took a couple of weeks off."

"Yeah, I was afraid he was sick again, but Molly Fly said he looked fine and he was going to Tucson to visit a friend for a while."

"Well, go on up there and find him, will you?"

"In Tucson?"

"Quick as you can," Wyatt said. "I need him here, Morg. It's important."

"No." Kate moaned. "No. No. No. No. No."

She didn't sound alarmed, only annoyed, so Doc kept his eyes on the table until the cards played out half a minute later. "What is it, darlin'?" he asked then, but when he looked up, he knew what had upset her. Morgan Earp was standing in the doorway of the gambling hall, searching faces.

Doc raised a hand. Morgan came straight over.

"Wyatt needs you," he said.

"Did that other molar finally crack in half? Morgan, I warned him —"

"No, it's something else. He wouldn't tell me what's going on, but he needs you back in Tombstone right away."

"No!" Kate cried. "No, no, no, no, *no*!"

"Doc, *why?*" she demanded, back in their room. "Wyatt Earp crooks his finger, you don't even know what he wants, and you go running! Why?"

"Because Morgan asked me to."

"And I'm asking you not to!"

Doc opened the wardrobe and pulled out his valise. "I don't believe this will take long, darlin'. While I'm in Tombstone, I'll close out my affairs. When I get back to Tucson, we'll go on up to Globe and do the same for you. Then, I promise, we shall stamp the dust of Arizona from our feet."

"I'm coming with you."

Deliberately misunderstanding, Doc turned, a shirt in hand. "Of course, you will! Colorado's as much your decision as mine —"

"No. I'm going with you to Tombstone."

"Morgan and I will be takin' a freight train to Benson, darlin'."

"If you can take a freight, I can take a freight."

"And it's a bad road from Benson to Tombstone —"

"If you can do it, I can do it."

He'd learned this much: When Kate made up her mind, he might as well quit arguing. "Suit yourself," he said.

No Time for Speeches Now.
'Tis Time to Fight!

They were all tired. That was part of it.

The McLaury brothers got up long before dawn on the day of the gunfight. Their youngest sister was getting married, and Tommy needed to clear up some business in Tombstone before he and Frank left for Fort Worth. That's where their brother Will lived with his three little kids. The six of them were going to take the train north to Iowa so they could all be there for Sarah Caroline's wedding.

Virgil Earp was still recovering from a punishing but fruitless effort to track down three men who'd broken out of jail a few days earlier. His posse had covered nearly 100 miles when a sudden torrential rainstorm left them with no trail to follow. On October 25, they returned to Tombstone, frustrated and beat.

Before leaving on that goose chase, Virg had deputized Wyatt as a town policeman so that Officers Flynn and Bronk had backup during the chief's absence. A few hours after he went to bed, Wyatt was called out when a brawl erupted between the day-shift miners of the Goodenough and the Tough Nut. Near as anybody could make out, a disputed call in the eighth inning of a baseball game played the previous Sunday had inspired a lingering sense of injustice that flared up in the middle of the night.

Morgan and Doc were weary as well, having just completed the rushed trip from Tucson at Wyatt's request. Doc got Kate settled in at Molly Fly's a little after midnight on October 26, but he and Morg decided they'd best find out what Wyatt was so nerved up about. Morgan went looking for Wyatt, and Doc went over to the Alhambra to wait for them.

Always randy, Little Willie Claiborne and his best friend Billy Clanton had ridden into Tombstone for some fun. They spent the final hours of Billy's life drinking, gambling, and whoring. Which he might not have regretted, even if he'd known what was going to happen.

And Ike? Ike was hitting the bars and drinking to drown the dread. He was scared again, and muttering to himself, and went looking for Wyatt, hoping for reassurance. Instead, he found Doc Holliday.

Who was, by then, sitting in the Alhambra's restaurant, letting his split pea soup cool while he waited for Wyatt to show up and explain the abrupt summons to Tombstone. Doc had, in fact, just begun to eat when a shadow fell over his table and a man who looked vaguely familiar said, "If you told him, I'll kill you before he gets me."

Blinking, Doc put his spoon down to free his hand. "Pardon?"

"If you told him, I'll kill you!"

Still trying to place the man, Doc frowned for a moment and then sighed. Elephant boogers, he thought, recognizing Ike Clanton, who stank of horse and sweat and liquor and fear.

Feeling very tired, Doc asked, "Told what to whom?"

"You know who, and you know what!"

"I assure you, sir, that I do not."

"Don't you 'sir' me! Don't you try to get around me! I know what you told him, and I'll by-God kill you for it! You hear me, Holliday?"

"People in El Paso can hear you," Doc said, beginning to lose patience, "but I suspect they don't know what you're talkin' about, any more'n I do. Why not shout it at *them,* so we'll all know?"

It was about then that John Meagher sent a busboy to find an Earp or two, for while Doc Holliday was skinny and sickly, he did not take much crap. Ike could get on anyone's nerves, and now he was yelling about how

Doc had killed somebody. Though the rest of the diners seemed entertained by the farce, Meagher knew it was only a matter of time before dishes or a window got broken, so he went over to Doc's table to see if he could settle things down on his own.

"Anything wrong?" he asked Holliday.

Halfway between bewilderment and annoyance, Doc began, "Mr. Clanton here seems to have some notion about me —"

"I got a notion!" Ike echoed. "Damn right I got a notion!"

"— but I cannot seem to make this impenetrable block of drunken Arizona imbecility understand that I have no idea what he is shoutin' about."

"Ike," Meagher said, "if you're not going to play cards or get something to eat, move on."

But Ike wasn't having that. "I know my rights!" he declared, with Frank McLaury in his head. "It's a free country! I'll go where I please!" And then it was Ringo inside him, making him yell, "Gimping around, bragging about it. Eye for eye! Tooth for tooth!" And then the old man took over and Ike sneered, "Our secret. Hah! Our secret. You can't fool me. I don't trust *nobody*! I never woulda turned on them boys if Wyatt hadn't made me that deal. And *you*!" Ike cried in summation, pointing at Doc. "You are a killer and a goddam liar!"

"Oh, Jesus," John Meagher sighed, for while

Doc would not have disputed the first assertion, he took violent exception to the second and would have caned Ike to the floor if John hadn't got between the two men, pushing Ike backward, meaning to dump him outside on the boardwalk.

"Take your hands off me!" Ike was hollering. "I know my rights! Take your goddam hands off me! I'll get you, Holliday!" he yelled over Meagher's shoulder. "I'll get you before he gets me!"

Which is where things stood when Virgil Earp arrived and coldcocked Ike without so much as a howdy-do.

A sudden silence fell. Fascinated diners around the room sat back to take in whatever happened next.

"Goddammit, Doc," Virg cried, "what in hell was that about?"

Wide-eyed, Doc looked up from Ike's inert body. "Virgil, it beats me hollow. I have only been in town for half an hour —"

"And you're in trouble already?"

"I swear, Virgil! I was just eatin' my supper when that tragic example of nature's cruelty started accusin' me of tellin' somebody something, and I have not the slightest idea what he meant by any of it! I only came back to Tombstone because Wyatt said he needed me, and Morgan — Wait! There they are! Wyatt, what in hell is goin' on?"

Before either Wyatt or Morgan could say

anything, Virg held up his hands for silence and then pressed his fingers against tired eyes. "Morg, take this idiot to the jail," he said, nodding at Ike, who was beginning to come around. "No charges. Just let him sleep it off there. Wyatt, do you know what this is about?"

"Yeah," Wyatt said. "Go to bed, Virg. I'll take care of this."

Nobody in the restaurant was near enough to hear what was being said at the table in the far back corner. What they could see was Wyatt Earp leaning over his elbows, making his case with sober earnestness as Doc Holliday's face registered first confusion, then disbelief, and finally what appeared to be a retreat into prayer, for it was then that John Henry Holliday put his head in his hands.

" 'Laughter of children. Discretion of slaves. Austerity of virgins,' he chanted softly. 'It begins in loutishness and ends among angels of flame and ice . . .' " He fell silent, rubbing his forehead rhythmically with fingers that were still so powerful with a pianist's musculature he could have closed them around Wyatt Earp's throat and crushed the man's windpipe flat. "I have despaired of many things," he told Wyatt. "Health. Home. Honor. Myself. There remains just one thing I rely on, *one thing* I can put my faith in. Human folly never disappoints."

"Doc, I know you're mad, but try to understand! I thought if I could bring in Leonard and Head and Crane, I could clear you. I was trying to protect you —"

"From *what*? There was nothin' but Kate's drunken petulance linkin' me to that stagecoach attack. The charges were dismissed for an utter lack of evidence. I am no more a suspect than Molly Fly!"

"But, see, when I made the deal, you were still —"

"A grown man, damn you! *Compos mentis,* and someone who should have been consulted, at least, before bein' dragged into the middle of whatever ill-conceived scheme you've cooked up with an ignorant, drunken, cracker cattle thief who is — and I will try to be perfectly fair to Mr. Clanton — a contemptible traitor to his own kind. Now that wretch is mortally afraid that I will expose his eagerness to sell his friends out, and that they will kill him for it. As well they might! Which places me directly between Ike Clanton and whatever peace his dim, blinkered, unlettered mind can yearn for! And you —" He stopped, trying and failing to control the cough. Pale when the fit was over, he continued: "And you expect *thanks*?"

"Well, not thanks, but something, I guess," Wyatt admitted. "I didn't think —"

"That is just the trouble," Doc cried,

unknowingly echoing Johnny Behan. "No-body ever *thinks*!" He closed his eyes for a moment and lowered his voice again. "You meant well. I understand that, but . . . Wyatt, you aren't afraid of any man on two legs. Call it confidence. Call it competence. Call it an abject failure of imagination! You don't understand how very much a fearful man wants to destroy what he fears . . ." Hands fisted, elbows on the table, he paused to get his breath back. He rarely spoke so much anymore, and it was hard to keep talking now. "Wyatt, you have made Ike Clanton fear *me*. The only way he can ever feel safe is if I am dead. And now I can't even leave town! If I do, people will say Ike Clanton ran me out of Tombstone and I will be fair game for every moron with a gun between Mexico and Canada."

"Doc, I — I didn't mean for it to go like that. I was just trying . . ." To be shrewd, he thought. To beat Johnny Behan at his own game. "I'm sorry," he said.

"I am imperfectly consoled," Doc snapped. "And I am damned if I see a good way out of this."

Somebody was banging on Virgil Earp's front door. Again.

Ike Clanton had been released around four in the morning. Instead of going home or getting a room someplace, he'd been reeling from one saloon to the next ever since. Already two bartenders had come to tell Virgil that Ike was threatening to shoot the Earps and Doc Holliday on sight. "He's all mouth," Virgil told them. "Ignore him." This latest visitor was probably delivering the same news.

"Allie?" he called.

"I got it!"

Exhausted but past the point when there was a chance in hell of getting back to sleep, Virg sat up on the side of the bed and stared bleary-eyed out the window. Took a moment before he understood why it was so bright in the room. Huh, he thought, rubbing his face. Snow in October! Crazy damn weather . . .

Still only half-awake, he marveled at Ike's capacity for drink. Why isn't that idiot passed out in an alley by now? he was wondering when Allie came in, but he snapped to when he saw her face.

"That was Bob Hatch from the billiard parlor," she said. "Wyatt's alone and he's up against four Cow Boys out in front of Spangenberg's gun shop. Bob says they're liable to kill him before you get there."

"Christ." Virg grabbed his pants. "Jesus. Go tell Morg!"

"Bob went to Morgan's first, but Lou says Morg left home with Doc about twenty minutes ago. Ike has been over at Fly's, yelling about how he's going to shoot all of you."

"Christ," Virg said again, pushing his feet into his boots. "Jesus."

"Wyatt Earp hauled off and hit Tommy for nothing at all!" Frank McLaury was telling Willie Claiborne and Billy Clanton. "Just *hit* him, like he hit Curly Bill! Sonofabitch pulled Tom's own gun right out of his belt and hit him with it! We were on our way out of town! We've got every right to be carrying guns on the way out of town! He had no call doing that!"

Tom was on his feet, trying to understand what was going on. Everything seemed very loud, and his brother's voice made his ears ring. "I'm gonna throw up," he warned, but nobody was listening.

"Wearing a badge don't give him the right to go around hitting people," Frank was saying. "Assault and battery's what it is! I want that bastard arrested and prosecuted!"

"Frank, I don't feel good," Tom mumbled. "Let's go home."

"And then he says, 'I oughta kill Ike,' " Frank was telling Billy Clanton. "That's just what he said: 'I oughta kill that idiot myself!' "

"Pull a gun," Ike was muttering. "You want respect? Pull a gun."

He was already carrying a Winchester and bought a pistol when Spangenberg's opened. He was still outside Fly's Photography Studio, but in his mind he was already back at Spangenberg's. "I want another gun," he was going to say. "Treat me like a dog! Hah. I'll fight'm all. Eye for eye!"

"Go home, Ike. You're drunk." That's what he expected Spangenberg would tell him, because that's what everybody was saying. They were all against him. "Come back when you're sober," Spangenberg would say.

"You're all in on it! You and the Earps. And Holliday," Ike muttered. "You're all in on it."

"Mr. Clanton," Molly Fly was saying. "Dr. Holliday isn't here."

There was another woman with her. Small and blond, with a funny accent. "He's gone. He don't live here no more," that one said. "Go away. Leave us alone."

"You're all in on it," he told them. "I'll get him. You'll see."

Scattering threats as dark as any the old man had hurled, Ike left Fly's and was out on Fremont when his brother Billy saw him and waved.

"Ike! We're over here!" Billy called. "Jesus, what happened to your head? Did Wyatt Earp hit you, too?"

"They're all in on it," Ike told him. "All them Earps. And Holliday, too."

By three in the afternoon, there was a crowd in front of the police chief's office. Everyone had been expecting a brawl, but word was getting around that the Cow Boys were carrying guns in defiance of town ordinances and that the Earps were going to have it out with them.

"Ike has come by twice to threaten me," Doc was saying. "He's frightenin' the women. I won't have it, Virgil. This has got to stop."

"It's not just Ike," Morgan reported. "His brother Billy's here, and both of the McLaurys. Willie Claiborne's with them, too. They've got a dozen guns among them."

"And they've been buying more," Wyatt said.

Virgil took a breath. The appearance of Willie Claiborne was a bad turn. The Clantons were rustlers. The McLaurys were fences. Claiborne was out on bail after shooting a blacksmith in the face, and that little shit was trouble.

Members of the Vigilance Committee were showing up now, each newcomer offering help. Which was the last thing Virgil Earp wanted: a bunch of jumpy civilians, ready to shoot. There'd be bodies all over the street.

"Chief Earp!" Mayor Clum called, pushing through the crowd. "There are five armed men in the O.K. Corral!"

And *that* was the best news Virgil had heard all day. "They got horses?"

"Yes, but —"

"Well, then, they're probably on their way out of town," Virgil said, flooded with relief.

"As long as they leave, I won't move against them."

"Those men are defying the law, Chief. It's your duty to disarm them," Clum insisted, and he began to work the crowd. "Just six weeks ago, this nation lost a great man to assassination. But Tombstone has learned from the murder of President Garfield. We have beaten back anarchy. We have reestablished the rule of law in this city. The Cow Boys are threatening to kill public servants, but we shall have no Guiteaus in Tombstone! Chief Earp and his deputies will enforce every ordinance, without exception!"

Morgan was watching Johnny Behan cross the street. "What does he want?"

"Votes," Wyatt said, but Behan was careful to address the officer in charge.

"What's the trouble, Chief?" he asked.

"Some of your constituents from Sulphur Springs are in town," Virgil told him, "and they're looking for a fight."

"They can have all the fight they want," Morgan muttered.

"Shut up, Morgan," Virgil snapped. "I don't need anybody mouthing off."

Doc was wound up tight and Morgan was standing shoulder to shoulder with him, ready to fight. But Ike Clanton was just a drunk, talking big. Billy Clanton and Willie Claiborne could be trouble, and Frank McLaury would strut like a bantam rooster, but

Wyatt had clocked Tom McLaury, and Tommy was about as inoffensive as they came. Something else was going on here, and Virgil was damned if he could put a finger on it. Which meant that Johnny Behan might just be of use.

"Ike Clanton's been making drunken threats all night," Virg told him, trying to sound bored. "Says he's gonna shoot us and Doc Holliday on sight. He's down at the O.K. Corral with his brother Billy now, and they've got the McLaurys and Willie Claiborne with them. Wyatt had a run-in with the McLaurys this morning outside of Spangenberg's gun shop."

Behan frowned. "So they're heeled?"

"Goddam right they're heeled," Morgan said. "Pistols, shotguns, rifles."

Behan glanced at Doc Holliday. "And why is this man armed?"

"Mr. Clanton says he intends to kill me," Doc told him. "I have a right to defend myself."

"It's legal," Morgan said. "He's got a permit."

"And I've deputized him," Virg added. "Just in case."

"All right," Behan said, like it was his place to be satisfied or not with that explanation. "Let me try to iron this out, Virg. If you go, there's sure to be a fight. Those boys won't give up their guns to a Yankee."

Watching the sheriff walk away, Editor Clum told Virgil quietly, "That will make Behan the hero of the story. You should've sent Wyatt."

"This ain't a story," Virgil snapped. "And it ain't an election, Mayor."

I am the only veteran in this mess, Virg thought, his heart pounding against his ribs.

Wyatt and Morgan had stood up to plenty of drunks with guns and Doc was game, but he was just a dentist who played cards. None of them had ever been in combat. Virgil had. He'd seen plans go to pieces when the shooting began. He'd seen men freeze under fire, or break and run, or panic and empty their guns long before they were within range. He'd seen his brother James, shattered and bleeding. His dreams were filled with terror and chaos, and . . . And this *felt* like the war, all over again. It was politicians saying, "Let's you and him fight!" It was rebels with guns, hollering about their rights, waiting for you to come and get them, and —

Blinking hard, he got his bearings and raised his voice to cut through the noise of the crowd. "Everybody! Just *calm down*!"

"Chief, this is a city matter," Clum insisted. "It's not in the sheriff's jurisdiction."

Well, if Johnny Behan could damp the fuse on this, he could take all the credit he wanted. "Those boys are his friends," Virg told the mayor. "Let's not make a war out of this."

"No, sir!" Frank McLaury was telling the sheriff. "I'm not going anywhere! Wyatt Earp assaulted my brother and nobody's got the right to tell me to go home and forget about that."

"And he hit my brother, too," Billy Clanton said. "Look at Ike's head!"

"I'm not telling you to forget it, Frank," Johnny Behan soothed. "I think Tommy might well have a civil suit against Wyatt. And Ike, as well, but for now? Let's let things simmer down."

"You're in on it," Ike complained. "You're all in on it!"

"Frank, Billy," Behan said, "take your brothers home, all right?"

"We have a wedding," Tommy said to no one in particular. "Let's go. Please, Frank. I've got a headache. Let's just go."

"I'm not going anywhere!"

Down at the corner of Fourth Street, Willie Claiborne was keeping watch.

"They're coming!" he yelled. "The Earps are coming!"

ON THEY STRODE, LIKE A CONSUMING FIRE

"Behan has failed," Johannes Fronk told Virgil. "The Cow Boys are refusing to leave town. They are out on Fremont now, heavily armed."

Fronk's low, calm, lightly accented voice carried the weight of experience. He sold case goods in a store near Fly's Photography Studio, but he'd had a distinguished career before settling in Tombstone. A Prussian army officer. A Secret Service agent during the Civil War. Chief of detectives in the Los Angeles Police Department. "Already you are outnumbered. Others may come. I advise you: Do not wait longer."

Virgil took a breath. "Wyatt?"

"Nothing to do but go and make the fight," Wyatt said finally.

"About time," Morgan muttered. "Doc's freezing. Let's go."

Eyes bleak, Wyatt looked at Doc directly for the first time that day. The dentist was shivering violently. It might have been the cold. The wind was raw, and it was snowing again.

"This ain't your fight, Doc," Wyatt said. "No call for you to mix in."

Wrapped tight in that gray woolen cloak of his, Doc stared, hard-eyed. "That is a hell of a thing for you to say to me." You made it my fight, he meant. I am damned if I will back down now.

"If you wish my help," Johannes Fronk was telling Virgil, "I can furnish to you ten good men."

Virg shook his head. "This is just a misdemeanor arrest," he reminded everyone. "Doc, gimme that cane of yours." Handing his own shotgun to the dentist in exchange, he said, "Keep this outta sight. I don't want any more excitement than we got already."

Tom McLaury was bent over, hands on his knees, staring wet-eyed at the puddle of puke between his boots. Usually throwing up made you feel better. Not this time. And his head hurt worse, too.

Willie Claiborne was yelling something, down at the corner. Eyes bleary, Tommy glanced up and saw four men come around Fourth, and it looked like they meant business.

"Frank?" Tom called. "I want to go home."

Willie Claiborne was sprinting back to join Billy Clanton and Ike. Sheriff Behan passed him, going the other way, and hurried down to speak to Virgil Earp, who listened for a moment. The police chief was carrying an ebony cane with a silver top that gleamed dully in the wintry gray light. Looking angry, he pointed it toward Frank and Willie, whose pistols were in plain sight.

Leaving the sheriff behind, the Earps were striding up Fremont now. Three abreast. Trailed by someone with a limp, who could not quite keep up with them. That dentist, Tommy thought vaguely, remembering Louisa's introduction. A friend of the family, she'd called him.

The nausea hit again. He was still gasping when Frank grabbed his arm and jerked him upright, pulling him back toward a narrow vacant lot between Fly's Photography Studio and the O.K. Corral. "Stand there," Frank ordered, pushing Tommy behind Billy Clanton's horse. "Don't move!" So that's where Tom was when a booming bass voice shouted, "I am here to disarm you. Throw up your hands! I want your guns."

"You got no right to take our weapons!" Frank yelled.

He and Billy Clanton put their hands on their pistols, half-drawing them in warning. From beyond Billy's horse, Tom heard two quiet clicks out on the street.

Virgil Earp shouted, "*Hold!* I don't want that!"

Firecrackers, Tommy thought, because that's what the gunfire sounded like: those strings of Chinese firecrackers that go off one after another, twenty or thirty of them in a row.

Stupefied, he saw it all, everything happening at once, but slowly, too.

Billy Clanton — down, his belly blooming red. Still alive, still firing.

Ike — on his knees in front of Wyatt Earp. Pleading with him, flung aside, scrambling away.

Willie Claiborne — right behind Ike. Both of them running away.

Then Frank went down and he was still alive, but the Earps were still shooting. They mean to kill us, Tommy thought. They mean to kill us all.

The dentist was still out on Fremont. Tommy saw the shotgun in his hands, but Holliday seemed as stunned as Tom himself. Suddenly Tom's mind cleared and he reached over Billy Clanton's saddle for the Winchester in the scabbard.

The horse pivoted away from the pressure on her flank, carrying the rifle out of reach. Arm high, Tommy saw the dentist snapping out of the same kind of horrified immobility.

There was a bright flash then. It felt like Billy's horse had stepped on him somehow, like his chest had been crushed, and the next thing he knew, Tom was sitting on the ground, his back against a wall or a fence or something, and he was watching everything through gun smoke and snowflakes, all the sounds muffled, like he was underwater.

"Tommy!" Frank screamed. Still alive, still firing.

"Ike!" Billy Clanton wailed. Still alive, still firing.

Virgil Earp — down. Still alive, still firing.

Morgan — down. Still alive, still firing.

Wyatt — still standing, taking careful aim, like a man shooting at beer bottles or tin cans. Each shot separate. Bang. Bang. Bang.

Billy Clanton — hit twice more. Dead.

Frank — gut-shot, still alive, dragging himself toward the street, toward the dentist who'd just emptied both barrels of a shotgun into Tommy's chest.

"I've got you now, you sonofabitch," Frank said.

He fired one last time and had the satisfaction of seeing Holliday go down before someone put a bullet through Frank's own head.

Silence fell.

It's cold, Tommy thought, watching the snow and slipping sideways.

A face appeared in the sky above him. An angel, he thought, gazing at her.

He smiled, and darkness closed over his eyes.

■ ■ ■ ■

Firecrackers. That's what the shooting sounded like to Louisa Earp, too: firecrackers going off, right down the street. Misdemeanor, she thought, for fireworks had been outlawed since the fire in June.

A moment later, she realized that it was gunfire and she began to pray. Not Morgan. Please, God, not Morgan.

She would not remember pulling on her coat. Or going out on the porch. Or seeing Morgan on the ground. Or running toward him. She would never forget her blank mind being shocked into awareness when she stumbled, almost, over Tom McLaury.

She stood over him, staring down at the farmer in disbelief. Watching the light fade from his eyes.

She saw the blood next, hot red pools of it melting the snow-frosted dirt. Blood everywhere. Dead men. Blood splashed all around them on the ground.

"Virg!" Allie was yelling, running barefoot down the street, for she hated shoes and never wore them inside and hadn't taken time to put them on. "Virg! Virg! Virg!" Higgs was there, too, whining, and Lou went down on her knees at Morgan's side, and Morg was saying over and over, "I'm all right, I'm fine, honey," but he wasn't. He *wasn't*! He was bleeding from both shoulders, his coat and shirt and pants all red and wet. "Clean through," Virgil was telling Allie as Wyatt pulled him off the ground. "It went clean through the calf, Pickle. I'll be all right." A few yards away Ike Clanton was kneeling beside his brother's corpse and he was crying, "Billy! Billy! Billy!" Kate was there now, too. A curtain of blood was sheeting down the side of Doc's trousers. "The same hip!" he was saying. "Goddammit! The same one!" But instead of moving toward Molly Fly's house as Kate wanted him to, Doc pointed at Ike and shouted at Wyatt, "Why in hell didn't you kill *him*?" Dazed, Wyatt said, "His hands were empty," as though that explained everything but he looked stunned and couldn't answer when James got there and asked, "What in hell happened?"

Which is what everyone in town was asking, except for the schoolkids who'd been on their way home when the gunfight broke out, and who were staring at the dead men or pointing at Mattie Blaylock because she was wearing nothing but her nightgown and her hair was all wild and she was laughing, like it was the funniest thing she'd seen in years.

"He's all yours now," Mattie sneered when Josie came running up First Street. "I hope they hang that coldhearted bastard!"

But Wyatt wasn't hit, and Josie bent at the waist, trying not to faint with relief. "You threw us, Johnny!" Wyatt was shouting. "You told us you disarmed them! You threw us!" When Josie looked up, Virgil was on his feet, and Allie had slipped under his armpit, supporting him as he hopped on one leg, the other one red with blood. Kate was cursing like a cavalry trooper as she helped Doc limp away. Three bodies were being loaded onto a wagon. Morgan was lying on the ground, pale and still, with Lou next to him, weeping.

Oh, my God, Josie thought, Oh, God, no! Morgan's been killed! But Wyatt was calling for a doctor and a stretcher, and he barely glanced at Josie when he told her, "See to Lou," who was crumpled on the ground, hysterical now, crying over and over, "He's dead! Why did they kill him?"

"Lou, it's all right," Josie soothed. "He's still breathing! He'll be all right."

"He's dead! I *saw* him die! Why did they kill him? Why is *Tom* dead?"

"Tom?" Josie asked, bewildered. "Tom who?"

And none of it made sense. None of it. None of it. None of it . . .

■ ■ ■ ■

PAYMENT FOR MY
BROTHER'S BLOOD

■ ■ ■ ■

HEADLONG DESTRUCTION
SWINGS OUR WAY

An inquest was convened. Wyatt Earp did not attend. He considered it a legal formality. The fight happened in broad daylight with hundreds of witnesses. How could there be any dispute about what happened?

Wyatt had a tin ear for the *vox populi* at his best, and he was not at his best in the days that followed the shootout. And while a drinking man might have taken time to belt a few back under the circumstances, Wyatt was teetotal, so he was unaware of the arguments taking place in Tombstone's smoky saloons.

Doc Holliday started it. No, it was Morgan Earp!

Well, I was there and *all* of the Earps had drawn their guns before they even turned onto Fremont.

Of course they did! All night long, Ike was going around saying he'd shoot them on sight.

Johnny Behan had already disarmed those boys, I tell you! The Earps shot them down like dogs.

If Johnny Behan already took their guns, who in hell shot Virgil and Morgan and Doc Holliday? Answer me that!

All right, I will! Wyatt shot them himself. They got in the way when he was shooting at Billy and the McLaurys. I saw it with my own two eyes!

Even if he'd known what people were saying, Wyatt would not have cared. He had women and wounded men to protect.

The bullet that passed through the meat of Virgil's calf hadn't hit the bone, Virg just needed bandaging and rest, but Morgan was in trouble. A bullet had gone in one shoulder and out the other: a long, terrible tunnel of a wound, sideways across his back. The slug had dragged pieces of Morg's shirt along with it and Dr. Goodfellow had to open up the track of the wound and dig the fabric out. Nobody said it out loud, but everybody knew if infection set in, there was no way to amputate a man's shoulders. Doc Holliday's hip was creased but he was following Goodfellow from bed to bed, making sure the bandages were boiled clean and the instruments were rinsed in carbolic.

"Wyatt, there's nothing more you can do," Josie told him some time long past midnight. "Mr. Fronk has guards around everyone. You need rest."

So did she. He could see it in her face, her

dark eyes shadowed with fatigue. That was when his own exhaustion hit him.

"All right," he said. "All right."

Josie fell asleep the moment she put her head on the pillow, but tired as he was, Wyatt lay awake hour after hour, going over and over it in his mind.

Nothing like the gunfight had ever happened before, and yet . . . It felt familiar somehow. He tried and tried to place that feeling of being there and doing it before and finally realized that he couldn't remember a time when he *didn't* have that trick of folding up into himself.

Going deaf and mute and watchful. Seeing nothing but the hands.

He must have been five or six the first time. Morgan was real little. Who set the old man off? Virgil, probably. Or James. Didn't matter. Nicholas Earp would beat the daylights out of anybody he could get a grip on. Mother. The girls. Anybody. You had to step back into silence while the old man roared. Let the words go by, empty as a breeze. Watch the hands. Pay attention to what the hands might do next.

In that state of mind, everything slowed down and it felt like he had all the time in the world to make a decision. Step in to protect Morgan and the girls, or let his older brothers — Virgil and James and Newton — deal with the threat to themselves or Mother.

In the dark before dawn on October 27, it came to him that he'd been practicing his whole life for what happened yesterday. The ability to make haste slowly had allowed him to aim and fire without panic, to place each shot carefully — each bullet meant to protect someone he cared for. He had saved Virgil and Morgan. He'd saved Doc.

He'd taken lives to do it.

He was a Methodist. He went to church twice a week. He knew that killing is as bad as sin gets, but he was not sorry. He could not find a way to be sorry.

He was three when Morgan was born. It was thirty years ago, but he could clearly recall standing at his mother's bedside. "This is your baby brother, Wyatt," she said. "You have to love Morgan and protect him."

Later, when Warren was born, Wyatt found out that newborn babies will hold onto whatever touches their palms, but the way Morgan had held Wyatt's own small finger still seemed special to him. It was like shaking hands. Like making a deal. *I'm your baby brother. You'll take care of me.* And Wyatt did. Morgan, so chatty in manhood, had hardly bothered to talk at all when he was little. Wyatt always knew what he wanted. *He's hungry. He needs a change. Pick him up, Ma, he wants to see.*

Funny how things turned out, Wyatt growing more silent as Morgan got older. Course, Morg wanted to speak for himself — that was part of it, but only part. Every year, Wyatt had more to keep silent about, more to keep a grip on, more to control so the old man wouldn't beat the tar out of somebody.

"When a man beats his boy, he wants a son who won't buck him." That's what Wyatt told Doc Holliday once, back in Dodge. "He's trying to make a coward. Ninety-nine times out of a hundred, it works."

"And the hundredth boy?" Doc asked.

"We can go either way. Kill the old man, or try to become a better one."

He didn't tell Doc how hard it was, trying to be a better man. He didn't say what it was like, pouring your soul into just . . . not being murderous. He never told anyone what it felt like when his grip on anger loosened.

It felt like honesty.

The shame came later.

The sun was rising by then, its first rays hitting Josie's face. She stirred and rolled toward him — away from the light — and realized he was awake. "Did you sleep at all?" she asked.

"First thing I can remember," he told her, "is Morgan holding my finger, the day he was born."

"He'll be all right," Josie said. "Virgil, too. And Doc."

"What happened . . . It was my fault. I want

you to know that."

She sat up and looked at him in dawn's pale light, her belief in him and in his decency as fierce as it was uninformed and unquestioning.

"You always do what you think is right," she said. "That's the best anyone can do."

Confusion Joins the Fight

Who said it first? John Clum wondered. Shakespeare? Cicero? Caesar? *A year in politics is an eternity.*

A year, he thought with his hairless head in his ink-stained hands. Hah! One day was enough to change everything in this godforsaken town.

In the first minutes after the gunfight, public opinion was all on the side of the law. An early rumor spread that Deputy Morgan Earp had died in the performance of his duty and there was great sympathy for the Earps on their loss, for Morgan was well liked. Then Ike Clanton was seen leaving the Western Union office and somebody said he had summoned more Cow Boys. Soon it was all over town: They were coming to Tombstone to lynch the Earps and Holliday.

A reasonable person might have expected citizens to rally behind their police force, but Tombstone was about to be invaded by a gang of vengeful outlaws. Suddenly Johnny

Behan's policy of "Live and let live" appeared to be the better part of valor, and folks began to grumble that the Earps had stirred up a hornets' nest.

Then the doctors reported that Morgan was hurt bad but likely to live. Virgil Earp and Doc Holliday's wounds were far less serious. An inch of difference in the bullets' trajectories could have severed Morgan's spinal cord, or cost Virgil his leg, or left Doc Holliday gut-shot and screaming. Even so, it began to seem as though the police had gotten off easy.

Talk shifted to the argument Holliday and Ike Clanton had the night before the fight. Nobody knew what it was about, but somebody who'd been eating in the Alhambra's restaurant insisted that Ike Clanton had started it. Then somebody reminded everyone about when Milt Joyce coldcocked Holliday last year and how Wyatt said anyone who laid a hand on Doc would answer to him. When Ike Clanton turned himself in to Sheriff Behan because he was afraid Wyatt Earp would find him and finish the job, the notion did not strike anyone as impossible, or even unlikely.

Virgil was steady, folks said. Morgan was affable. But Wyatt? Hell, he beat a man to death up in Dodge City! Who knew what he was capable of when his friend and two of his brothers had been shot?

Word began to filter out of the inquest: Tom

McLaury might have been unarmed. A counterrumor claimed that somebody had picked Tom's pistol up after the fight and was keeping it as a souvenir. Nobody seemed to know who "somebody" was and no one came forward to show the gun.

Even Earp partisans admitted that Tom wasn't near as bad as his brother Frank, so why had Wyatt hit Tom a couple of hours before the gunfight? Nobody had a good explanation for that.

Everyone had expected Willie Claiborne and Ike Clanton to blame the Earps, but Johnny Behan's testimony at the coroner's inquest was a surprise, and he wasn't shy about repeating it in public later on. "Frank McLaury and Billy Clanton were the only ones carrying weapons, and they had agreed to disarm," he testified. "When I saw the Earps come around the corner, I went to them and told them not to fight because those parties had agreed to give me their weapons. The Earps ignored me and began firing without preamble. I heard Billy Clanton say, 'Don't shoot me! I don't want to fight!' Tom McLaury threw open his coat and said, 'I have got nothing!' But Holliday cut him down. That gunfight was little more than murder."

Hour after hour, the coroner had listened to witness after witness, letting conflicting and ambiguous testimony stand without asking for clarification. By midnight, facts that had seemed clear-cut were in doubt. Those who'd initially supported the Earps lapsed into uneasy silence, leaving only the voices of those who condemned the officers and who now turned on John Clum himself during an emergency meeting of the City Council.

"I lay what happened at the mayor's feet," Councilman Milt Joyce declared in what was the opening move of a run for the city's top office. "He knew what everyone in this town knows: Doc Holliday will shoot without provocation!" Milt held up his own scarred and deformed hand. "And wasn't it Mayor Clum who told the Earps to disarm those boys? Why not let well enough alone? I'll tell you why," Milt offered. "Sheriff Behan was already on his way to the O.K. Corral. Johnny Behan could have settled matters in his own quiet, professional way, but Mayor Clum wanted Wyatt Earp to look good to the voters for next year's election!"

Which was uncomfortably close to the truth and put the mayor on the defensive. "I said to disarm those men," he cried, "not to slaughter them!" And while he regretted the phrasing the moment the words were out of his mouth, there was no taking them back.

So there it was. On the afternoon of October 26, 1881, the Earps were incorruptible, intrepid lawmen bravely marching off to protect the city from gun-toting outlaws. The next morning, they were cold-blooded killers who'd murdered three men on a public street because of some kind of personal feud between Doc Holliday and Ike Clanton. And Johnny Behan had become the odds-on favorite to win the sheriff's office in the '82 election.

As editor of the *Epitaph,* John Clum was free to interpret the events as persuasively as possible; his newspaper was on the A.P. wire, so his version of the story would be read by Eastern investors and Washington politicians. As mayor of Tombstone, he had to be seen as impartial. So he put Virgil Earp on medical leave and appointed Deputy James Flynn as acting police chief. Flynn could serve until the Earps were cleared of wrong-doing. As head of the Citizens Safety Committee, however, John Clum was within his rights to authorize a doubling of the guard around the Earps and Holliday, hoping to shield them from retaliation by the cattle thieves, drifters, and thugs who were converging on Tombstone by the hundreds: drinking heavily and talking big about lynch parties and settling scores.

The next morning's funeral cortege was far larger than the one that accompanied Fred White to his grave. Two thousand people stood in respectful silence along the route to the cemetery, which passed right by the Earp brothers' homes.

The procession was led by Curly Bill Brocius and Johnny Ringo, who held aloft a large banner made from a bedsheet and bearing a hand-lettered declaration: MURDERED IN THE STREETS OF TOMBSTONE. Behind them were wagons that bore the dead, their pale cheeks brightened by mortician's rouge. Chief mourner Isaac Clanton came next, eyes reddened, face ravaged. Ike was followed by more than a hundred men, on foot and on horseback, their pace set by a brass band playing a drinking song called "Where Was Moses When the Lights Went Out?"

"Odd choice for a dirge," Doc Holliday remarked, looking out Morgan Earp's bedroom window. "Wash your hands, George."

"John, they are perfectly clean."

"You can argue with him for half an hour," Kate Harony told Dr. George Goodfellow, "or you can save us all time and do like he says."

"C'mon," Morgan muttered. "Let's get this over with."

The physician sighed and washed up. Again. Like it or not, a D.D.S. had trumped an M.D. ever since the president died. For the past six weeks, the American Dental Association had been frightening everyone out of their wits, claiming that Garfield had needlessly succumbed to infection introduced to his body by the unclean hands of his own

604

doctors. Now all around the country, the ignorant and superstitious were convinced that tiny invisible animals caused infection.

At the Earp family's insistence, any physician tending to Virgil and Morgan's wounds was shadowed by Dr. J. H. Holliday. All George Goodfellow wanted to do this morning was inspect the incision and change the dressings, but the dentist still insisted on this senseless rigmarole about "antisepsis procedure."

Mrs. Earp and the Harony woman sat behind the patient to support his back while he swung his legs over the edge of the mattress, face rigid against the pain.

"There are too many people in here," Goodfellow said, trying to reestablish professional authority. "I need space to work."

The women left the bedroom. Holliday merely moved into a corner, vigilant as Goodfellow unwound the bandages.

"The itch is driving me crazy," Morgan complained.

"Itching means the wound is healing," Goodfellow murmured. "Apart from that, how do you feel?"

"Tired."

"You lost a great deal of blood. Fatigue is normal."

"I can't find a good way to sleep! I like to sleep on my back or my side, but everything hurts."

Holliday went to the door. "Kate? Miss Louisa? Go over to Mrs. Fly's and ask for pillows. Three — no, four at least. Tell her I'll pay for replacements, but we need them right away."

Ignoring the dentist, Goodfellow continued his examination.

"Entry and exit are mostly scabbed over . . . Swelling is somewhat reduced across the whole of your back . . ."

Holliday came forward to inspect the incision and met the physician's eyes. A portion of the tunnel looked angry. In a rare moment of agreement, both doctors made a silent decision not to say anything to Morgan about another surgery until they were certain it was necessary.

"And your own wound, John?" the physician asked.

"Granulation is well along. Kind of you to ask, George."

The next ten minutes passed in silence while Morgan's dressings were replaced with fresh bandages — boiled, sun-dried, minutely examined and accepted by Holliday as sufficiently clean. Bidding his patient good day, Dr. Goodfellow left the room, promising he'd return that evening.

Morgan had another bad ten minutes as Kate and Lou got him settled again, but when they were done, he was half-sitting in bed: his arms, lower back, head, and neck supported by pillows with a narrow gap across his shoulders so pressure on the wound was relieved.

"Better?" Doc asked.

"Hell, yeah," Morg said. "Damn. *Yes.*"

"I am very sorry, Morgan," Doc murmured. "I should have thought of that sooner."

"Will you be able to sleep now?" Lou asked anxiously.

Morgan's eyes were already closed. "Mmm."

"Miss Louisa, Kate and I will sit with him now. Please, honey, go on over to our room at Mrs. Fly's and get some rest yourself, y'hear?"

"Doc . . . are you sure?" Lou asked.

He contrived to sound hurt. "Why, Miss Louisa! After all you and Morgan have done for me! How *can* you ask such a thing?"

"Turnabout is fair play," Kate added, for she and Lou had spent long hours together back in Dodge when Doc was so sick. "I'll go with you and get a few things from the room."

The women left again and for a little while, there was no sound in the room but Morgan's soft snoring. Easing himself into the corner chair, John Henry Holliday took stock of everyone's condition three days after the shootings. His own wound was painful but could have been much worse. Virgil might be left with a limp, but he already felt well enough to be impatient with keeping his leg up. Morgan likely had more surgery ahead of him and a long recuperation, but he was young and in good health otherwise.

The crisis was nearly over. All they had to do was wait for the inquest jury to find that the McLaurys and Billy Clanton had been killed without malice aforethought by four police officers doing their duty. Then he and Kate would leave Tombstone for good.

She returned from Mrs. Fly's and handed him the new Zola novel he'd been reading before he left for Tucson. He opened the book and stared at the print for a time but couldn't concentrate and set it aside.

Kate was staring at him, her own eyes shadowed by fatigue. "You don't fool me none," she said.

For as long as Kate had known him, John Henry Holliday had been haunted by nightmares of his mother's death. Now there was a new dream that made his sleep fearsome and broke her own. Tom McLaury, reaching for that rifle. Tom McLaury, blood pouring from the crater in his chest.

"Dammit, Doc, we coulda been in Denver by now!" she whispered. "We never shoulda come back here."

"I know, darlin'. I know," he said softly. Too late now, he meant.

Five days after the gunfight, the Cochise

County coroner's jury returned a thunder-
ously unenlightening verdict: William Clanton and Frank and Thomas McLaury had
come to their deaths as a result of gunshots
inflicted by Virgil Earp, Wyatt Earp, Morgan
Earp, and John Holliday. Having failed to
characterize the shootings as either justified
or criminal, the jury left the whole question
open for legal wrangling that could easily
drag on for a year or more. Which suited
Johnny Behan and Milt Joyce just fine.

That afternoon, there was a soft knock on
Doc Holliday's door. Kate got up to answer
it. When she saw who it was, she stepped into
the hallway, shut the door behind herself, and
scowled up at Wyatt Earp.

"Doc's sleeping," she told him. "Come
back later."

"It's important."

"So is his rest! Something like this, it can
knock him back. You know that."

Down at the bottom of the stairs, a man
wearing a badge stood next to Molly Fly.
"I'm sorry, ma'am. I hate to do this, but I
hafta."

"Do what?" Kate asked, wary now. "Who
the hell are you?"

"Jim Flynn, ma'am. Acting chief of police.
I'm sorry, but I have warrants. Morgan and
Virgil are allowed to remain under house ar-
rest, but I have to bring Wyatt and Doc in."

"On what charge?" Kate demanded, voice rising.

"Murder," Flynn told her.

"Murder!" Molly Fly cried.

"You ain't serious!" Kate scoffed as the door opened behind her and Doc stepped out.

"Wyatt," he said evenly, "what's goin' on?"

"I'm sorry, Doc, but you're under arrest," Flynn said. "Ike Clanton's filed murder charges against you."

"Behan helped Ike Clanton get a lawyer," Wyatt told him.

"Against *me*?" Doc said, astonished. "But . . . I was deputized!"

"It's not just you, Doc," Wyatt said. "It's all four of us."

Kate reacted first. "What's the bail?"

"Behan asked Judge Spicer to deny bail," Flynn said, "but when I got the warrants, I went to Spicer, too. He agreed to ten grand apiece."

White, Doc slumped against the door jamb. "I can't — I . . . I don't have anything close to that kind of money! Wyatt, can't Virgil do something?"

"City Council suspended him without pay until this is settled," Jimmy Flynn said bitterly. "The whole goddam town wanted that fight, and now the bastards are cutting you loose."

610

■ ■ ■ ■

Which wasn't entirely true.

The relevant meeting had convened late at night and was not open to the public. Ore magnate Richard Gird and his armed escort had ridden in from Millville. When he arrived, Mayor John Clum had summoned two other men. Eliphalet Butler Gage, who'd presided over the development of the Grand Central Mine, came quickly. They waited twenty minutes more for the Wells Fargo agent, Marsh Williams, to show up, then decided to go ahead without him.

"He's dealing with another stage robbery, I expect," Mayor Clum said.

"Cochise County is a magnet for criminals these days," Gird said. "That scoundrel Behan has all but issued formal invitations."

"Two of my investors back east just pulled out of a deal we were ready to sign," Gage said. "I told them that the time to invest is when there's blood in the streets, but they've got other places they can put their money."

"How is the bail campaign going?" Gird asked.

"Seven backers, thirty-eight thousand dollars so far," Clum told him.

"Does that include Holliday's as well?" Gird asked, frowning.

"No. Just an oversubscription for the Earps.

Wyatt and his brother James have put up eight thousand dollars of their own for Holliday. Several others have pledged the balance — gambler friends of his."

"If it's true that Tom McLaury was unarmed," Gage said, "the publicity is going to be catastrophic."

"We've got to control this, John," Gird warned.

"I am doing my best," Clum said, "but I can't do anything about the results of the inquest. And I'm afraid I have more bad news. Both of Virgil Earp's regular deputies say they'll resign if sworn officers go on trial for doing their jobs —"

"It won't come to that," Agent Williams said, sounding confident as he came through the door. "Gentlemen, I'm sorry to keep you waiting, but I believe you'll all be pleased to know that Mr. Thomas Fitch would like to join us."

Everyone sat back. Then they all stood up.

The silver-tongued orator of the Pacific. That's what the nation's newspapers called Tom Fitch. A gifted advocate whose eloquence and force of argument had kept California in the Union. A journalist credited by Mark Twain for improving the novelist's prose style. Forty-three years old, at the peak of his powers, Tom Fitch was widely acknowledged to be the best damn lawyer west of the by-God Mississippi.

And he knew it.

Aware that he could overawe men, Fitch was all smiles and jocularity at first, but when the greetings were over, he sat at the table, opened a briefcase, put on his glasses, and laid out a stack of papers with efficient dispatch.

"I have already gone over the inquest testimony. All the witnesses called by the coroner were at some distance from the events that took place on October twenty-sixth. Nobody was in a position to see the entire incident. Gun smoke undoubtedly obscured what they *could* see. In my opinion, the jurymen were not wrong to come to a less than definitive determination." He looked up. "I understand that Sheriff Behan has been aiding Mr. Clanton in the effort to engage prosecuting attorneys for the murder charges?"

He paused to allow the others to vent their outrage.

"Obviously," Fitch said mildly, "Behan's agenda is to eliminate all three Earps as potential rivals for the sheriff's office in next year's election. No matter. He will rue the day he allied himself with Isaac Clanton. From what I hear, Ike can't count to twenty-one unless he's buck naked."

When the startled laughter died down, E. B. Gage took the opportunity to ask, "How soon will this go to trial?"

"When hell freezes over, if I do my job right," Fitch said blandly. "There'll be a preliminary hearing first, to determine if there's enough evidence against the defendants to send the case before a grand jury, which would then have to indict. Wells Spicer will be presiding over the hearing. An honorable man. Excellent lawyer. Not one to be swayed by outside pressure. Wells and I have both defended Mormons in capital cases — no easy task, believe me! He stood up to the worst kind of intimidation during the John Lee trial. I promise you: Angry Cow Boys will not frighten him. I myself will represent the Earp brothers. Dr. Holliday has engaged T. J. Drum as his attorney. Good man, Drum. He and I will present a unified defense." There was a bright smile when he asked, "Would any of you like a cigar?"

None of them were ready to celebrate just yet, but Fitch lit his own.

"Gentlemen," he said, puffing, "we are going to bury the prosecution under testimony. We will ensure that every single witness with an opinion testifies during that hearing. The more they disagree and contradict one another, the better. Every statement will be undermined until none of what they say can be believed. The prosecution's case will then hang on the version of events provided by Ike Clanton and William Claiborne." Tapping ash off the Cuban, Fitch peered over his glasses to add dryly, "Both of whom were running away while the shooting took place. It should be easy to prove that neither man has eyes in the back of his head."

Brows up, Fitch held out his cigar case again. This time, Gage and Gird accepted the offering.

John Clum hesitated. "If I may ask, sir, who will be paying your fee?"

"Am I speaking to the mayor of Tombstone or the editor of the *Epitaph*?"

"The mayor," Clum said. "My officers took an oath to enforce city ordinances. They were told to prevent trouble, not simply to react after it happens. The Earps — and even Holliday — did their duty at the risk of their own lives. If they face trial for that, Tombstone will never be able to hire another policeman and anarchy will prevail. I understand that drawing out the preliminary hearing as long as possible will help to prevent a trial. Many hours mean big fees, and I imagine that your rate is commensurate with your experience and reputation. Wyatt Earp has money. His brothers are not rich men. I have a divided City Council, and I cannot pretend that Tombstone will undertake to foot the bill. So, I ask again: Who is paying you?"

There was a moment of silence. Tom Fitch made his face completely impassive, but when he glanced at Agent Williams, they all understood. Every stagecoach robbery ate away at Wells Fargo's balance sheets. Anything that curbed the outlaw element of Cochise County was to be supported, and no price was too high. Not even Tom Fitch's.

"I am working *pro bono,*" Fitch lied, smooth as you please. Then he grew quite sober. "Gentlemen, the police officers in this case will be exonerated — I promise you that. However, I must also warn you that this will not end in the courtroom. My fee is nothing. Before this is over, there will be hell to pay."

WHAT ATONEMENT FOR BLOOD SPILT UPON THE EARTH?

William McLaury was not alarmed when the Western Union boy appeared at the door on October 27. He'd been expecting a wire telling him that his younger brothers were about to leave Tombstone and were on their way to Texas so they could all travel to Iowa together for Sarah Caroline's wedding.

Bereft and benumbed since his wife's death in August, Will was grateful for the distraction of travel. For weeks, he had concentrated on wrapping up legal affairs for his clients so he could leave his law practice with a clear conscience. He'd made a good start on packing his bags and the children's. He was taking woolens, mostly. Iowa was chilly in November. He'd send summer things for the children later. His older sister, Margaret, had agreed to take them in. Will couldn't make a living and care for three little kids as well.

Neighbors had looked after the children since Malona's death, but all three were home now, excited about seeing their uncles

Frank and Tom, looking forward to the wedding up in Iowa.

The messenger wouldn't meet his eyes when he handed Will the flimsy folded paper. That was the first sign. Messengers weren't supposed to read what they delivered, but sometimes . . . Well, they knew.

The boy waited for a tip, but Will just closed the door and sat down in the nearest chair, too stunned to notice when the telegram fell from his hand.

REGRET TO INFORM YOU THOMAS AND FRANK MCLAURY KILLED OCTOBER 26 STOP DIED INTESTATE STOP GEORGE PRIDHAM APPOINTED ESTATE ADMINISTRATOR BY PROBATE JUDGE LUCAS STOP

His son, John, picked up the telegram.

"Are they gonna be late?" John asked, eyes full of concern. There was supposed to be a party for his eighth birthday. It wouldn't make up for his mother being gone, but having Uncle Frank and Uncle Tom there would be special. "Pa?" he asked again, "are they gonna be late?"

His father started laughing but in a scary way, for he was crying at the same time.

"They *are* late," William McLaury said, just before he broke down entirely. "They are the late Tom and Frank McLaury."

Once more, he attended to the busyness of death. Making arrangements for the children to go back to the neighbors. Wiring word to his parents. Following the telegram with a letter.

I have no details, he wrote. *I believe their deaths must have been an accident of some kind. A fire perhaps. I am leaving for Tombstone on the 28th to take responsibility for their estate. Embrace Sarah Caroline for me and tell her I am sorry to spoil her celebration. Yours in grief, William.*

The journey to Tombstone was a complicated and wearisome combination of trains and stagecoaches. Four nights in bad hotels. Five long days lost in misery as he stared out at the desolate cactus-marred countryside, trying to come to grips with it all. Malona had been consumptive for years. Her terrible death was no surprise, but to lose Tom and Frank as well seemed a great injustice, even before Will knew how they had died.

Somewhere along the line, he bought a paper and managed to read for a few minutes. The big news seemed to be a street fight in Tombstone.

Trouble is likely to arise from a recent

shooting of some Cow Boy criminals in Tombstone, A.T. An investigation of the shooting will begin soon. A large amount of money has been raised to assist the prosecution of the Police by friends of the Cow Boys. Arizona Governor Gosper has requested that a company of cavalry from Fort Huachuca be sent to protect Tombstone from Cow Boy reprisals, should the Police be exonerated.

General William T. Sherman has requested authority from the U.S. and Mexican governments to cross the border to pursue, capture and arrest Cow Boys and bring an end to this scourge, but the *Posse Comitatus* law renders our government powerless to prevent these marauders from using the mountains and desert of southeastern Arizona as their asylum. No one in Washington seems to understand the need for action.

He read no more. The words seemed to pass beneath his eyes without sinking into his mind. And anyway, the Cow Boys were of no interest. His brothers were alfalfa farmers, not cattlemen.

On the second of November, suffering from a head cold that mercifully explained his red eyes and swollen nose, Will McLaury climbed down stiffly from the stagecoach, collected his bags, and trudged into the Grand Hotel. Tired and sick as he was, he knew he would not rest until he'd seen his brothers' graves.

"Can you tell me where Tom and Frank McLaury are buried?" he asked the desk clerk, whose eyebrows had risen when he'd seen the new guest's signature.

"You passed it on the way in, Mr. McLaury. I'm sorry for your loss. The cemetery is about a quarter of a mile back on the Benson road."

It felt farther. Uphill, with a frigid wind pouring down out of the highlands that surrounded the town. The grave was easy to pick out. Freshly mounded, with a single plank marker that served for both boys.

FRANK AND TOM McLOWRY
Murdered in The Streets of Tombstone.
OCTOBER 26, 1881

The name was spelled wrong. That was what he noticed first. It took a moment before another word registered. *Murdered.*

"D'you know them?" someone asked.

Startled, he took a step back and nearly fell. When he caught his balance, he saw two men sitting on the ground. Empty whiskey bottles nearby. Another bottle, half full, passing between them.

"My brothers," he said. "My little brothers."

"Drink? You look like you could use one."

The man who offered the bottle would have been handsome, if not for his eyes. They were the eyes of a drunk, half-hidden under lazy lids, but there was something else about them that gave Will pause. Still, he took a pull, coughed, and handed the bottle back. "Who killed them?"

The dry, unblinking eyes flickered with amusement. "Tell him, Ike."

The second man — Ike — showed enough emotion for the pair of them. "Doc Holliday and the Earps," he said, breaking down. "They killed my little brother, Billy," he said, pointing at another fresh grave. "And Holliday killed my daddy, too."

John Ringo and Ike Clanton walked with him back to the Grand Hotel, telling the whole story along the way. Will McLaury was a sick and exhausted man, barely able to think, but he could not sleep after what he heard and spent the whole of his first night in Tombstone pouring his outrage into letters to his parents, his sisters, his law partner.

"The cause of Frank and Tom's death was murder," *he wrote over and over.*

Some time ago <u>Holliday,</u> one of the murderers, attempted to rob the strongbox of Wells Fargo & Co. and in doing so shot and killed the driver and a passenger. The other parties engaged in the murder of Thomas and Frank, the <u>Earp brothers,</u> were also part of the attack on the coach. Young Bill Clanton, a boy 18 years, knew the facts about the attempted robbery. He told his brother J. I. Clanton, and Tom and Frank as well. They had the facts for a prosecution of Holliday and the Earp Bros., and Holliday had information of that. He and the Earps killed Tommy and Frank and young Clanton to keep this matter of the robbery quiet.

There will be an indictment against Holliday and I think two of the Earps for the stagecoach murders and attempted robbery, and they will be hanged one day for murdering Tom and Frank and young Clanton. Even after he was mortally wounded and <u>lying on the ground,</u> Frank raised on his elbow and fired several shots wounding three of the murderers. Two of the scoundrels are hurt badly, but Wyatt Earp and Holliday walk the streets heavily armed. They have cowed those who might testify against them. The town's people are in Sympathy with us but only <u>ranch-men</u> dare come forward to give any information in court.

I will see to it that Holliday and Earp are jailed lest important witnesses Isaac Clanton and William Claiborne be killed before they can tell the truth of this in court. The men who killed Tom and

Frank will be <u>punished</u>. I regard it my <u>Duty</u> to see that these brutes do not go unwhipped by Justice. I will join the prosecution and I think I can hang them. I could put an end to this myself, with a knife or a gun. I cannot afford to do it nor can I conspire at it, but this thing has aroused all the Devil that is in me.

W. R. McLaury

Out on bail during the preliminary hearing, Wyatt Earp felt like a caged bear in a carnival: half-feared, half-pitied. There were stares and catcalls whenever he left the hotel room he shared with Josie. Most days he spoke only with Tom Fitch. Sometimes he went to visit Virg and Morgan. He wasn't exactly welcome when he did. Like Kate Harony, Lou and Allie suspected that Wyatt was to blame for what happened and they weren't wrong, though they couldn't have said exactly how — not yet.

Now it was all going to be made public, and he needed Morgan's help.

"I'm sorry, Lou," he said, standing on their veranda. "I gotta talk to him."

"Wyatt, can it wait? He's not feeling well —"

"I'm awake," Morg called. "C'mon in, Wyatt."

Lou left them alone. Wyatt stood in the

bedroom door for a moment, a sheaf of paper in his hand, trying not to let his surprise show. It had only been a few days since he'd looked in, but the change in Morgan was startling.

"I know," Morg said. "I look like hell." Thin-faced, unshaven, feverish. "At least I'm not as skinny as Doc yet."

It was an attempt at humor. Wyatt tried to smile.

"They're gonna have to cut again," Morg told him wearily. "Some of that goddam shirt is still inside somewheres. Sit down. How's the hearing going?"

"Good, I guess. Fitch is tying them up in knots, objecting all the time, just to throw everybody. He's letting the prosecution witnesses talk, but then he compares that to what they said at the inquest. The stories keep changing, so he keeps asking questions until they say, 'I don't know' or 'I guess I was wrong about that part.' " Wyatt held up the papers in his hand. "Morg, when the prosecution's finished, Fitch is gonna call on me. I'm supposed to read all this in court."

"Jesus," Morgan said. "That's a lot."

"That's what I told him. Fitch says it'll help if we have one story. Not dozens, like the other side. He wrote it up, but I have to read it."

"Lemme see."

Morg had to keep his elbow down on the

bed so he wouldn't move his shoulder, and he had to hold the papers up in his hand, trying not to move his head much because that pulled on his shoulders, too. Every now and then, as he read, he'd stop to ask a question, like "Why'd you hit Tommy McLaury that morning?"

"Doesn't matter anymore."

"He say anything about Lou? Goddammit, I told him — !"

"No! No. It was just . . . The McLaurys had been listening to Ike. One of them repeated something behind my back, and I was tired of the guff. I hit the nearest. Might've been Frank who said it, but I guess I hit Tom. Hard to tell 'em apart."

"Yeah," Morg said. "Same as us, I guess."

He went back to reading, but about halfway through he started to frown, and when he was done, he looked troubled. "Wyatt, this ain't how I remember it. I told Fitch it was Doc who — He was standing behind me, see? When he cocked the shotgun, I thought he saw somebody make a move, so I —"

"Shut up!"

Morg blinked.

"Morgan," Wyatt said carefully, "the way you remember it could get you hanged."

There was a long silence.

"I don't know, Wyatt," Morg said finally. He let the papers drop to his lap and laid his head back against the pillows. "I don't know.

I gotta think about this."

But Wyatt didn't have time for Morgan to think. He had to learn the whole piece by heart. He had to sound convincing. The story had to be specific, logical, and complete, Fitch said. Otherwise, this thing could go to trial, and if it did, Morgan would pay the price for Wyatt's mistakes.

Reading printed stuff was hard, but this was in Fitch's handwriting, with curlicues and flourishes and what all. Knowing that the task was beyond him, he left Morg's house and went back to his room at the Cosmopolitan, ignoring the jeers and hard looks. Who else could help, if not Morgan? Doc was hardly speaking to him. Virgil and James had always made fun of him for not being able to read very well, but if they understood how important this was —

He opened the door to his hotel room. Josie was in bed.

With a book.

He hated to admit any kind of weakness, especially to her, but when he stammered it out, she didn't sneer or mock him or act shocked or anything.

"Lots of people have trouble reading. Maybe you just need spectacles. Oh, Wyatt, you'd look so distinguished in spectacles!" she cried.

He thought his heart would burst, though

he didn't quite know why. "I'm pretty sure my eyes are fine."

"Well, we'll take you to an optometrist when this is all over, just to make sure. In the meantime? This'll be just like learning a piece for the theater."

She rewrote the pages so they were printed plainly, underlining important words or writing them big, so he could keep track of where he was in the story. "You have such a good memory!" she'd say when he got a stretch of words down pat. She believed he could do this. She believed every word in the statement. She believed in *him.*

Once, he tried to tell her the truth, but she waved his scruples off.

"Oh, Wyatt, it's not lying. It's just making the story a little simpler. You have to make it easy for people to understand."

It was almost more than he could bear, but he kept on. Morgan's life was at stake.

CUT DOWN THROUGH THEIR OWN RECKLESS FOLLY

Judge Wells Spicer spent the whole of November 1881 discovering things to admire about William McLaury and Tom Fitch.

Both attorneys were formidable in their own ways. Given the great Tom Fitch's decades of experience and national reputation, Spicer had expected the older man to triumph easily, but William McLaury brought energy and surprising legal agility to the proceedings. It was like watching a Texas longhorn in a contest with a good stock horse. The outcome was not inevitable. Sometimes the longhorn won.

The hearing went on far longer than anticipated. Twenty-one days in session. Thirty witnesses. Documents. Depositions. Objections, motions, rulings. McLaury held his own at first, but his was a Sisyphean task. Ike Clanton was the boulder he had to push up the hill, and that rock just kept rolling back down on him. Under Tom Fitch's gentle, curious, persistent questioning, Ike changed his story repeatedly, each new version less convincing than the one before.

Even if Ike hadn't been such a sad spectacle in the witness stand, his testimony was all but irrelevant. To constitute the crime of murder, there must not only be a killing but felonious intent. That was the sole legal issue in this hearing.

Was there bad blood between Wyatt Earp and Ike Clanton? Yes. Was there an argument between Doc Holliday and Ike Clanton the evening before the gunfight? Yes. Had there been an altercation between Wyatt Earp and Thomas McLaury on the morning of the gunfight? Yes. None of it mattered. When the attorneys for both sides had said and done all they could, felonious intent — and nothing else — was what Wells Spicer had to rule on.

Of course, the community would expect the judge to address the events preceding the gunfight and he did so at the very beginning of his finding. "Given the events of the preceding night," he wrote,

I am of the opinion that Chief of Police Virgil Earp committed an injudicious and censurable act when he called upon Wyatt Earp and John H. Holliday to assist him in arresting and disarming William Claiborne, the Clantons, and the McLaurys. Yet I can attach no criminality to his unwise decision. When we consider the lawlessness and disregard for human life on the frontier; the existence of a law-defying element in our midst; the fear and feeling of insecurity in our city; the violent men who have been a terror to Cochise County, keeping capital and enterprise away from our city; and when we consider the many deadly threats publicly made against the Earps and Holliday, we can understand that in this emergency Chief Earp needed the assistance and support of staunch men whose courage, coolness, and fidelity he could depend on.

So. Granted: Virgil chose his deputies unwisely, but there was nothing felonious in that.

It is clear in my mind as well that Chief Earp honestly believed that when the Clantons and McLaurys and Claiborne passed through the O.K. Corral to Fremont Street, their purpose was not peaceful. The prosecution holds that their intent was to leave town; nevertheless, it has been established during this hearing that it was reasonable for Chief Earp to believe that they intended to resist any attempt to arrest or disarm them, and that they intended to attack the police. Many citizens had reported threats to him. They publicly insisted that Chief Earp perform his duty to arrest and disarm the Cow Boys, as they termed Claiborne, the Clantons, and McLaurys.

And that was of the essence.

Should Virgil Earp have abandoned his clear duty as an officer because its performance was likely to be fraught with danger? Or, was it not his sworn duty to the law-abiding citizens of this city, who looked to him to preserve order and security, to arrest and disarm those men? There can be but one answer, and that answer divests the defendants — both regular and specially appointed officers — of a presumption of malice or illegality.

When those officers marched down Fremont Street to the scene of the subsequent homicide, they were going where it was their duty to go; they were doing what it was their duty to do; they were armed, as it was their right to be armed, when approaching men they had reasonable cause to believe were both armed and contemplating resistance.

So much for felonious intent, but what of the facts regarding the Cow Boys?

It is beyond doubt that William Clanton and Frank McLaury were armed and made such quick and effective use of their guns as to seriously wound Morgan and Virgil

Earp and lightly wound John Holliday.

There remains a dispute as to whether Thomas McLaury was armed at all, except for the Winchester rifle that was on the horse beside him. I will not consider this question, as it is not of controlling importance. It is beyond doubt that the Clantons and McLaurys had among them at least two six-shooters in hand, other pistols holstered, and two Winchester rifles on their horses. Thomas McLaury was with a party making felonious resistance to arrest. In the melee that followed, he was killed. The fact of his being unarmed initially cannot itself incriminate the defendants.

He could have run away, Wells Spicer thought. Ike Clanton and Willie Claiborne did, and they lived.

The prosecution claims that the deceased were shot while holding up their hands in obedience to the command of the chief of police, but the inquest found that William Clanton was wounded along the length of his right wrist. Witnesses testify that he fired his pistol thereafter with his left. The trajectory of his initial wound is compatible with a man aiming a pistol, not holding his hand in the air. Similarly, the wound to Thomas McLaury's right chest, below his right arm, could not have been received with his hands on his coat lapels demonstrating that he was unarmed, as claimed by the prosecution. His wound is consistent with testimony that he was reaching over a horse for a rifle when he was fatally wounded.

Who started it? That's what everyone would want him to decide, but that had no bearing on whether these three homicides were murder.

I cannot say which party fired first. Some witnesses testify that each of the deceased yielded to a demand to surrender. Other witnesses of equal credibility testify that William Clanton and Frank McLaury met the demand for surrender by partially drawing their pistols. All witnesses agree that the initial discharge of the firearms from both sides was almost simultaneous. As the defendants were police officers charged with the duty of arresting and disarming men who had previously declared their intention not to be arrested or disarmed, they had the right and duty to meet force with force, under the statutes of the Territory of Arizona.

Which left only Ike Clanton to deal with.

The testimony of Isaac Clanton that this tragedy resulted from a scheme by the Earps and Holliday to assassinate him in order to silence him about their robbery of the Kinnear stagecoach . . .

Spicer paused, searching for the proper phrasing.

. . . falls short of credibility. If the purpose of the confrontation was to kill him, he would have been the first to fall. Mr. Clanton was not injured at all. His claim to be unarmed was believed by Wyatt Earp in the heat of the gunfight; he was allowed to run away unharmed by Wyatt Earp, the very man Mr. Clanton says conspired to kill him.

Beneath a mountain of words, there was but one conclusion, and Wells Spicer now reached it with little hesitation.

There being no sufficient cause to believe the defendants guilty of felonious intent to murder, I order them to be released.

He reread the decision and then signed his name with a flourish.

Wells Spicer, Magistrate, Arizona Territory. November 30, 1881.

For generations, the McLaury family would remember that the Earps and Holliday were exonerated on Sarah Caroline's wedding day.

They had all hoped for a different outcome, of course, but Ike Clanton's pathetic performance on the stand undermined those of more reliable witnesses, whose own testimony was partial and contradictory, leaving Will with no effective rebuttal to what Tom Fitch established under questioning.

That much Will himself could accept. What galled him was the dismissive, insulting phrase: "not of controlling importance."

Tommy wasn't armed, but that cut no ice with Judge Spicer! No, the police were just doing their jobs. Tommy was in the wrong place at the wrong time. Too bad for him! Too bad for his family. Being unarmed and killed by the police is not of controlling importance.

It ate at Will, that awful phrase.

It ate at Johnny Ringo, too. "Your brothers' blood cries out to me from the ground," Ringo would whisper, his voice silken, his eyes glazed by drink as they sat in the back of a shadowy saloon. "You have to make them pay."

"Eye for eye," Ike would say over and over. "Tooth for tooth."

But William McLaury was a lawyer, loath to give up on the justice system. There remained a slender hope that he could get a grand jury to review the testimony and come to a different conclusion. He also had his brothers' affairs to settle, a task that became more distressing as it progressed, for everyone in Tombstone was now chiseling away at the McLaurys' estates. The undertakers wanted $280 for the funeral they'd given Frank and Tom, which seemed a lavish fee for stacking the boys, one above the other, in a single grave with one wooden marker for the pair of them. The valuation of the boys' land, farm equipment, and livestock came in far lower than anticipated, and Will suspected the assessor had friends who wanted to buy it up cheap. A lumber mill in the Huachucas presented an unpaid bill and while working through Tommy's books to confirm the purchase, Will found out that the boys weren't in business together at the time of their deaths. That opened up some troubling questions about Frank's livelihood, especially when several Cow Boys claimed that Frank had owed them money for "cattle transactions." And despite their seeming friendship to Will during the hearing, neither Ike Clanton nor Johnny Ringo would forgive debts they said Frank owed them. They had no paper to back their claims but after a month in Ringo's dead-eyed company, Will wasn't eager to engage in a dispute with either of them, in or out of court.

His expenses in Tombstone mounted. Bills were piling up back in Fort Worth. He had no income from his languishing practice, but he soldiered on in the cold and blustery weather of early December, growing more downhearted as the dark days passed. He came to dread the mail, for there was often a sweet and wrenching message from little John, begging his daddy to come home, but in the end, deliverance came in a letter from his older sister Margaret, whose son had recently graduated from law school.

Let your nephew Charlie take over the estate work, Margaret wrote. *Go home to your children, Will. We have lost our dear brothers and you have lost your dear Wife but your babies have lost their* sweet Mother *and I know they yearn now for their Father to comfort them. Go to the children, William. Do not leave them longer in the care of Strangers. Let Providence work its will in the rest of these affairs.*

It had been a year to test anyone's trust in Providence, but when Charlie arrived, shortly before Christmas, Will packed his bags.

Three drunk and sullen men saw him off the day he left Tombstone. Ike Clanton, Johnny Ringo, and a friend of theirs who'd just gotten out of jail. Frank Stilwell, his name was.

"Your brothers' blood cries out to me from the ground," Ringo murmured.

"Eye for eye!" Ike said. Several times.

"Goddam Yankees won't get away with this," Frank Stilwell vowed.

A Yankee himself, Will just nodded, and he shook hands with all three of them before he boarded a stagecoach bound for the Benson railway depot.

The road passed by the Tombstone cemetery. Will couldn't see his brothers' grave, for it was just over the hill and out of sight. Although he had by then accepted that there was nothing more he could do, he prayed with all his might to the God in whom his sister still had faith.

"Damn them," he whispered. "Damn the Earps. Damn Holliday. Damn all of them to hell."

■ ■ ■ ■

THE GODS WILL
DEAL DEATH TO
THOSE WHO KILL

■ ■ ■ ■

THOSE LEFT ALIVE AFTER HATEFUL CARNAGE

Tombstone was glad to see the end of 1881. Hell of a year, everyone said, shaking their heads. Fire, flood, famine, blood in the street.

Nobody felt much like celebrating, but the city did its best. There were church socials, recitals, a masked ball, and a charity auction. The Bird Cage Theatre threw a grand opening party with skits, magic acts, comedians, and a large staff of "dancers" happy to entertain any gentleman's desire to . . . dance. More genteel entertainment, "suitable for ladies," was available at Schieffelin Hall. On Christmas Day, Al Schieffelin himself dressed up as Father Christmas to distribute gifts to more than 250 children.

Many of those kids had been behaving strangely lately. Sucking their thumbs, wetting their beds. Waking up with nightmares. Begging to skip school. No amount of punishment seemed to correct these new transgressions, but a few of the more perceptive parents noted that the trouble had started back in October when the kids had watched three men die in the street. "Honey, that's all over now," such parents lied. "Everything is going to be fine."

Those who could afford it — Johnny Behan included — decided it was time to send their children to boarding schools back east. Whole families were packing up, and for the first time since Ed and Al Schieffelin stared down at the glorious numbers Richard Gird had calculated for their initial silver assay, the population of Tombstone began to drop.

The Earp women were among those who hoped to leave that wretched town. *Ever since our troubles began, we have had guards around us,* Lou wrote to her sister. *It has been disagreeable to be so unsettled, but most of the Cow Boys have now drifted out of town. They will go back to stealing stock, no doubt. Virgil is walking though he must use a cane. We believe Morgan is out of danger. His shoulders still give him pain and he is very weak I am afraid. We had to give Higgs up. I could not break him of jumping on Morg.*

And truth be told, neither Lou nor Morgan wanted a constant reminder of Tom McLaury. The dog was Josie's now.

"We girls are sewing again and it is a pleasure to be busy," she continued, though the truth was simpler: The Earps needed money. Virgil didn't exactly get fired after

Judge Spicer cleared him, but City Council had quietly allowed John Flynn's appointment as chief to remain in force. Allie was pretty bitter about that. Virg was still a federal deputy marshal, but he got paid only if he could transport prisoners. Too lame to mount a horse, he was almost broke. Morgan could hardly move his arms, so he'd lost his job dealing faro at the Alhambra. The doctors couldn't predict what he'd be able to do when he healed up. Tend bar for James, maybe? Two crippled Earps, selling beer to Chinese laborers.

Wyatt had been keeping everyone afloat with income from the two gambling concessions he still had. Then Tombstone announced the new tax assessments. All the Earp property had been revalued, even James's tavern. Suddenly the family owed $6,200 more than the year before. Wyatt had mortgaged the house Mattie lived in and was selling property off to pay the debts, but he was losing ground.

"There is still good money in making tents for prospectors," Lou closed, "and we all look forward to better days."

She signed the letter and dropped it off at the post office before joining the other girls over at Allie's. Mattie was long past helping with the sewing, but Kate was there, and she and Bessie were keeping things lively.

"Allie, d'you ever hear the one we used to

tell about Wyatt?" Bessie asked. "Seems he gets to town fresh off the farm and before he's been there ten minutes, a streetwalker comes over and says, 'C'mon, big boy. Let's have a little fun.' "

Kate picked the story up. "So that big dumb hick, he thinks, 'I guess the rumors was true! City girls can't keep their hands off a handsome man like me.' So this girl, she takes him to her crib, but instead of hiking up her skirt, she says, 'Now before we get started, there's the little matter of the fee.' "

Bessie finished, "So Wyatt says, all bashful and humble-like, 'Ma'am, that's real nice, but I wouldn't think of acceptin' money from you!' "

When the giggling died down, Lou grew serious. "Bessie, why is Wyatt so different? James is sweet, and Virg is like a big friendly bear, and Morgan — well, you know what I think about Morg! But Wyatt is so . . ."

"Cold?" Bessie suggested.

"Stupid," Kate said flatly.

"Ignorant," Allie said. "That's what Virg says. 'Wyatt's ignorant, and he's afraid if he opens his mouth, people will find out.' "

"If he opens his mouth," Kate said, "they'll see what a good dentist Doc is."

"Will Doc start a new practice when you get to Colorado?" Lou asked. "His cough seems better. Maybe he could do fillings and make dentures again."

Kate slumped in her chair. "He ain't coughing so bad right now, but . . . he's got no *joie de vivre*. Hell, what's the English? No *snap*. He don't even play poker no more! He just deals faro and gets along from day to day." She sat up straight, as though to signify that she had enough energy for both of them. "We was doing good in Las Vegas with that saloon. We're gonna buy a new place in Denver, or maybe go up higher in the mountains."

"When y'all leavin'?" Bessie asked.

"Me? Day after tomorrow. My lawyer found a buyer for the boardinghouse. There's things to do and papers to sign up in Globe. Doc's gonna finish out December at the Alhambra. John Meagher's shorthanded, and Doc owes him a favor for posting bail during the hearing. First of the year, though, we gonna meet up in Prescott. Then we're gone for good! Arizona's been nothing but trouble for him."

"Arizona's been nothing but trouble for all of us," Allie said, pedaling away at her sewing machine. "Virg keeps getting letters from his parents out in California. They want the brothers to settle in Colton with them."

Bessie rolled her eyes. "I like Mother Earp. The old man?" She shuddered. "He's a piece of work, that one is."

"Well, Morgan won't be able to travel for a while yet," Lou said, "but when that time comes, we can't leave Tombstone fast enough to suit me."

■ ■ ■ ■

Which were John Clum's sentiments exactly. He had started receiving anonymous death threats when the gun laws went into effect in June, but the level of menace reached new heights within hours of Judge Spicer's decision. "The sooner you depart for a healthier clime, the better for yourself," one read. "If you stay here, you are liable to get a hole in your coat at any moment."

The Earps, Doc Holliday, and Tom Fitch were also getting things like that, but Wells Spicer was the main target. Last week the judge insisted that the *Epitaph* print the entire text of the latest note he'd received, along with Spicer's own written response: a far-ranging litany of insult and contempt, followed by an open invitation to the yellow sons-abitches to come ahead and try him.

"Judge, do you think that's wise?" John had asked warily.

"If the bastards want me," the portly, balding, fifty-year-old Spicer replied, "they know right where to find me."

"Exactly," John said, but the judge was adamant, so the *Epitaph* ran the story. John had even written an editorial about the campaign of intimidation that was being waged, trying to match Spicer's brave words with his own. But it was time to face facts.

The *Epitaph* had lost circulation and advertising since the October gunfight. Once again, Editor Clum was as close to broke as makes no difference. And if Mayor Clum had any illusions about his constituents rallying behind him in his hour of need, those fantasies evaporated during the December meeting of City Council, when boos, catcalls, and rancor made it clear to him that there was no point in running for reelection.

Reassessing his plans for the future in the quiet solitude of his bedroom on New Year's Eve, he came to the conclusion that he would prefer not to live in a town where the gravediggers were more prosperous than the newspaper owners. On January 1, 1882, he announced that he would be leaving for a few weeks, ostensibly to visit family back east.

Two days later, having "temporarily," handed the *Epitaph* over to his assistant, he climbed aboard the evening stage to Benson. As the gaslights of Tombstone receded into the darkness, he felt the tension in his shoulders ease.

One hour out of Tombstone, masked gunmen opened fire on the stage.

The horses panicked and ran until the wounded left-lead animal staggered to a halt and died in harness, a couple of miles on. When the stage jolted to a stop, John Clum clambered out and walked into the night without a word to the other passengers. For hours he struggled alone across treacherous, broken ground. Toward dawn, battered and cactus-torn, he heard the distant rumble of the Grand Central Quartz Mill. At the superintendent's home, he borrowed a horse, rode to the Benson depot, and caught an eastbound train.

Certain that he had just survived an assassination attempt, he did not stop traveling until he arrived in the nation's capital. There he begged for reappointment as Indian agent on a nice, peaceful reservation, for two years among the civilized white men of Cochise County had rendered John Philip Clum profoundly nostalgic for the humor, dignity, and steadfast friendship of savages.

There were those who called his flight to safety an act of cowardice. John Clum himself was inclined to consider it realism. Either way, he never looked back. And he lived to tell the tale.

Dispatches from Arizona to Washington had increased in frequency and urgency as the end of 1881 approached. There were few responses. President Chester Alan Arthur had been kept informed of the situation along the Mexican border, but most of President Garfield's cabinet had resigned rather than work for his successor. Many departments were still in transition and, naturally, offices were closed during the holidays, so no one was around to read the letter Federal Marshal Crawley Dake sent to the Justice Department in December, demanding to know why funds had not been appropriated to fight the outlaws in Arizona. Dake was enraged as well by the way Virgil Earp had been treated for doing his duty, and infuriated by Sheriff John Behan's collusion with the criminal elements of Cochise County.

I have some of the bravest and best men in the Territory in my employ, he wrote in December. *I will no longer tolerate efforts by the Sheriff's office to deter my deputies from hunting down stage robbers, mail robbers, train robbers, cattle thieves, and all that class of murdering border banditti.*

By the time his letter was delivered, however, the attorney general had resigned and was headed home to Pennsylvania.

Secretary of State James Blaine had left Washington as well. He wasn't coming back and the Senate was on Christmas recess, so his replacement hadn't been confirmed, which is why there was no one around to be alarmed by Arizona Governor Gosper's frantic letter predicting war with Mexico if the Cow Boys were not reined in.

Furthermore, Gosper wrote, *in the absence of swift and decisive federal action, the law-abiding citizens of Cochise County are likely to form vigilance committees to protect their*

651

persons and property.

Gosper's letter was filed by a clerk, who then forgot all about it, but the message proved prophetic as the people of one Arizona community after another gave up on their government and took the law into their own ungentle hands.

Galeyville declared itself off-limits to any stranger who came into town bearing arms. When a Cow Boy named Prairie Jack yelled that it was a free country and dared anybody to come and take his gun, he was promptly beaten to death by the assembled citizenry. A perfunctory inquest ruled this death justifiable homicide.

Less than a week later, the town of Shakespeare hanged five men without benefit of due process. All of the deceased were said to have ridden with Curly Bill, although one of them might just have *looked* like somebody someone once saw with Curly Bill. "They served our community a good purpose," crowed an editorial in the local paper, "for they have started our cemetery."

Shortly thereafter, out in the chaparral nearby, a man named Joe was discovered riding what was said to be a stolen horse. He was lynched; the horse wound up in his accuser's possession.

And if the Mexican border stopped lawmen from pursuing bandits, Arizona's vigilantes were not so particular. The bullet-ridden body of a kid named Wercher was discovered by the *rurales* on the Sonora side. He, too, was said to have stolen a horse, but there were rumors that he might simply have stolen the heart of the wrong man's girlfriend.

In Tombstone, anonymous death threats were now arriving at the homes of Sheriff John Behan, *Nugget* editor Harry Woods, and Councilman Milt Joyce. "We know which side you're on," the notes usually said.

With one such letter in hand, an armed and drunken Milt Joyce went after Virgil Earp in public, shouting abuse, making accusations. Virg dropped his cane and slapped Milt across the face. Sheriff John Behan dragged Milt away before anything worse could happen and brought him before a judge for disturbing the peace. This act of political neutrality earned him no thanks from Milt Joyce or the Earps.

"Please, Virg," Allie begged that night. "Please. Let's just go."

But Morgan was still too hurt to travel, and his brothers wouldn't leave Tombstone without him.

THE BRAVEST IS HIT.
THE BEST WILL DIE.

Frank Stilwell never figured on being in jail so long on a goddam robbery charge. Hell, he got off scot-free after killing a Mexican waiter up in Prescott.

Even so, he'd been sitting in jail — off and on — since back in September when him and Pete Spence got arrested robbing the Copper Queen Mine payroll off the Bisbee stage. Bail was set at seven grand. Curly Bill collected it and sent a couple of boys to get Frank and Pete released, but the judge had some horseshit rule about how people on bail couldn't post bail for other people.

So Frank and Pete sat there stewing until somebody explained a few things to the judge, who came to see the unwisdom of his previous attitude. Yes, the judge noted, the Earp brothers and Billy Breakenridge *had* found a broken-heel bootprint where one of the robbers mounted a horse and rode away. And yes, the posse *had* tracked that horse to a town where a big-mouth cobbler told them he'd fixed a boot heel for Frank Stilwell, but that cobbler might've been lying. And anyways, he was no longer available to provide testimony. Besides which, Frank Stilwell wasn't the only man in the world with a broken heel on his boot. Could've been anyone.

So Frank and Pete finally got out of jail. Pete took off, but Frank Stilwell had a saloon in Charleston to run, which is where Virgil Earp showed up a week later with a federal warrant for attempted robbery of the U.S. Mail. And that was horseshit because Frank didn't even know the Bisbee stage was carrying a goddam mailbag! He just wanted the strongbox and whatever pretties him and Pete could take off the passengers.

So Frank went back to jail, and without Pete for company this time. He still wasn't worried, understand. A mail-robbery charge didn't scare Frank Stilwell, by God. He just hated all that sitting.

Before long he took to pacing the cell, and with so much time on his hands, he began to meditate on injustice and oppression. He saw patterns that had been obscure to him before and looked for explanations as to why some people had it so easy while others were sitting in jail for no good reason. Which is why Virgil Earp came to occupy Frank Stilwell's thoughts to a larger extent than all the other sonsabitches who always came along to spoil things. Because that goddam mail robbery charge was purest malice. Harassment and persecution, that's what it was, same as when Virgil's brother Wyatt kept riding by the saloon back in Charleston — all biggety and full of himself, like he was daring the Cow Boys to come out and try something.

Frank didn't have anything against Morgan Earp yet, but he was probably a biggety sonofabitch, too. Goddam Yankee sons-abitches, Frank thought as he paced his cell. Coming down here, where they weren't never wanted. Throwing their weight around. Somebody oughta take those bastards down a peg.

Then one day in late October, the jailer brought him a copy of the *Daily Nugget* and said, "Hey, Frank, looks like some friends of yours made the paper." And there it was, in black and white, as if Lord Jesus his own self had descended on a cloud to confirm all Frank Stilwell's darkest suspicions about the Earps.

Billy Clanton, dead. Little Billy! He was just a kid. And the McLaurys, both of them dead, too! Frank McLaury . . . all right, there'd been times when Frank Stilwell had wanted to shoot that mouthy little gamecock himself. But Tommy? What in hell had Tom McLaury ever done, except be pretty to look at? And who'd done it? Why, none other than the Earps! and that skinny lunger sonofabitch friend of theirs, Doc Holliday. First he kills Old Man Clanton, and now that bastard went and killed poor Tommy McLaury!

Those sonsabitches, Frank thought over and over. Those lousy goddam Yankee bastards. They've been gunning for us from the start! Well, they won't get away with this. I swear to God — they won't get away with this! Soon as I get out of here, the Earps are dead men. Them and that sonofabitch Holliday, too.

That's what Frank Stilwell was thinking when he finally got out of jail in late December. And that's what he kept thinking, all the way to Tombstone.

When Deputy Sheriff William Milton Breakenridge saw Frank Stilwell lurking in an alley near the corner of Allen and Sixth, he took a few moments to think things through, for this was as unwelcome an encounter as he'd experienced since going to work for Johnny Behan. And that covered a lot of ground.

Billy B. took a lot of guff for being small and clean-shaven, for wearing specs and having a care for his clothing. The past twelve months had provided ample opportunity for the dapper little deputy to wonder if Sheriff Behan's orders weren't sometimes meant to humiliate him. It was, for example, probably some kind of joke when Johnny hired Curly Bill Brocius as an assistant tax collector last spring and then sent Deputy Breakenridge out to work with him. But Billy B. had made the strange partnership work. Together, he and Curly Bill had squeezed a great deal of tax revenue out of the ranchers of southeastern Arizona, and Billy's own cut of the collections was gratifying. So he got the last laugh that time.

There was, by contrast, nothing amusing when Johnny hired Frank Stilwell as a deputy. When Billy B. questioned the wisdom of pinning a badge on a sullen, quick-tempered thief who'd put a bullet into a waiter's face for bringing him tea instead of coffee, Johnny Behan mumbled something about fighting fire with fire. Whose fire are we fighting? Billy wondered at the time, but he was a conscientious man who did his job as best he could. He worked with Frank Stilwell when he had to, same as he worked with the Earps when necessary. A lot of frontier lawmen had played both ends against the middle. You couldn't afford to be a stickler about such things. And anyway, the arrangement with Stilwell didn't last. Billy Breakenridge had been in charge of the posse that tracked the Bisbee stage robbers down, back in September. When Frank Stilwell turned out to be one of them, Sheriff Behan decided to consider Frank's arrest to be a letter of resignation.

Now Stilwell was out of jail again, and he

was the kind to hold a grudge. Billy B. had expected the man to head for Charleston, where he had a saloon and a livery stable and friends, but here he was in Tombstone. Hanging around in an alley at dusk on the day after Christmas. Drunk, and carrying a shotgun.

Technically, this was a matter for the city police, but Deputy Sheriff Breakenridge had taken an oath to uphold the law, and that's what he did.

"Evening, Frank," he said mildly. "On your way out of town with that gun?"

"I got no quarrel with you, Billy," Frank declared. "I want the Earps and I want Holliday. Holliday first, by God! I saw that sonofabitch go into the Bird Cage, and when he comes back out, he's a dead man."

"Frank, haven't you been in enough trouble lately?"

"He killed Tommy! I want the bastard dead."

Billy Breakenridge understood, for he himself was one of the many men and women who'd been half in love with Tom McLaury. It had broken his heart to see Holliday exonerated after blowing that beautiful boy's chest to pieces, but that was the decision of the judge. Doc was free to walk the streets, just as Frank Stilwell was after killing an unarmed waiter up in Prescott. Cuts both ways, Billy thought.

"I want him dead," Frank was muttering,

tears glittering in the gaslight from the saloon across the street. "He killed Tommy, and I want him dead."

Billy put a hand on Frank's arm. "I know how you feel —"

Stilwell jerked away. "Get away from me! You don't know a goddam thing about me, nancy boy!"

Oh, Frank, Billy thought. I know more about you than you do. But when he spoke, a moment later, his voice was neutral. "I know you're breaking the law right now," he said. "And if the city police catch you with that shotgun, you'll be back in jail. So check that weapon or leave town. I'll give you five minutes to choose."

Before Frank could reply, Johnny Ringo came out of the shadows. "I'll take care of him," Ringo said, his voice friendly in the darkness. "C'mon, Frank," Ringo said, pulling the weeping man away from the street. "Now ain't the time, and this ain't the place."

About ten minutes later, Billy Breakenridge saw Doc Holliday leave the Bird Cage. Silently, the little deputy watched the gambler walk unmolested down Allen Street and go into the Alhambra, where he worked the night shift.

I just saved your life, Billy B. thought. How's that for irony?

It sounded like thunder when Alvira Sullivan

heard the noise three nights later. Hope Virg don't get caught in the rain, she thought, for it would be a pity if he came down with a cold now, just when he was so close to going back to work for Marshal Dake.

Allie didn't like him going out by himself, but Virg wouldn't be babied. He took a walk around town every evening before bed to keep his bad leg limber and ward off night cramps in the damaged calf. He'd stop in wherever Wyatt had a faro table going and smoke a cigar, or drop by James's tavern for a beer. Usually he'd be back by now.

She went to the window, pulled the curtain aside, and frowned at a cloudless sky brilliant with stars. Maybe the storm's coming in from the south, she thought, but already an uneasiness was setting in.

Pulling a shawl around her shoulders, she went out on the porch, expecting to see Virg on his way home. Instead, she saw the police chief, Jimmy Flynn, running toward her on Fremont.

No, she thought. No, no, no, no.

"Allie!" Flynn called, "I'm sorry! It's Virg—"

"No!" she wailed. "No, no, *no*!"

"C'mon. He's still alive," Flynn told her, "but we have to hurry."

Folks dressed for dinner were standing around on the boardwalk in front of the

Cosmopolitan's restaurant, talking excitedly to hotel guests wrapped in robes and blankets.

I thought it was dynamite down in one of the mines —

I was sitting on the bed, taking my stockings off —

First they attack Clum's stage, and now this! Right here in the city!

Some of the buckshot went right through my window.

They were over there by the brewery. I saw two men running —

Three! I saw three!

He was still *standing.* He was still on his feet when I got to him.

Jimmy Flynn pushed through the crowd ahead of Allie, opening a path. "Outta the way," he kept saying. "I've got his wife."

Inside, the gaslights were turned up high. Virg was lying on one of the tables. He grinned when he saw her and said, "There's my tough little mick! Don't worry, Pickle. I've still got one good arm to hug you with." But his voice was so weak! She'd never heard his voice like that. Dr. Goodfellow was cutting Virgil's shirt off, and she could see it now: his back and side, peppered with buckshot. His left arm with a huge bloody hole in the middle of it.

"Virg, did you get a look at him?" Wyatt was asking.

"That sonofabitch Stilwell. I saw him just before . . ."

Her vision went white. The room seemed far away, and she closed her eyes hard, refusing to faint. She could still hear Virg, and he was weeping now. "Don't let them take my arm! Don't let them do it."

"Virg, if it'll save your life," Wyatt began, but Virgil kept saying, "Don't let them do it! If I have to be buried, I want both arms on me!"

Doc Holliday was there now, too, getting ether ready like he did for Morg. "Watch my eyes, Virg," he was saying. "Try to be calm. Breathe in —"

"Promise me, Doc!" Virg cried. "Don't let them take it while I'm under."

"You have my word," Doc said. "Breathe in."

There were dozens of big lead pellets to dig out, and so much bone! Chunks of it. Long sharp shards, like pieces of a broken bud vase. The whole elbow was shattered, and at some point Allie's knees hit the ground.

When she came to, Bessie was beside her, on the carpet. "Don't you give up on him, honey," Bess said fiercely, and Allie knew why, for Bessie had told her about how James's shoulder had been shot to kindling during the war, and how it took months and months for him to get better but he made it.

Then James himself knelt next to Allie and

lifted her up — still strong on one side — and got her into a chair. "I won't tell you not to worry," he said, "but I will tell you this, Allie: It is very damn hard to kill an Earp."

Afterward, they carried Virg upstairs to a hotel guest room and laid him on one of those new box mattresses that were eight inches thick. People came and went. Doc, Josie, Wyatt, Lou. They told her to rest, but she would not leave Virgil's side. All night long, she sat in the chair, watching each breath, willing him to take the next one.

Sometime during the night, she heard a strange soft sound. *Pat . . . pat . . . pat . . .* That's how it sounded. *Pat . . . pat . . . pat . . .*

It wasn't until morning that she knew what it was. The mattress was soaked through with Virgil's blood. Drop by drop, it was falling onto the carpet beneath the bed. *Pat. Pat. Pat.*

At dawn that day, Federal Marshal Crawley Dake was awakened by a messenger from Western Union. He began cursing after reading the first four words of the telegram and continued to curse for a long time after finishing it.

VIRGIL EARP WAS SHOT BY CONCEALED ASSASSINS LAST NIGHT STOP HIS WOUNDS ARE FATAL STOP TELEGRAPH ME APPOINTMENT WITH POWER TO AP-

POINT DEPUTIES STOP LOCAL AU-
THORITIES ARE DOING NOTHING STOP
THE LIVES OF OTHER CITIZENS ARE
THREATENED STOP WYATT EARP

"Is there a reply, sir?" the messenger asked
when the marshal paused for breath.

"You're goddam right there's a reply," Dake
said. "God damn them! God damn them all
to hell!"

Protect the family. Make sure nobody else
gets hurt. That was the first step.

Even while the doctors were pulling bone
and lead out of Virgil, Wyatt went upstairs
and told Josie to stay in their room and not
to come out for any reason. Then he insisted
that everyone else move into the Cosmopolitan. James and Bessie. Morgan and Lou. Doc
Holliday. Even Mattie Blaylock. Al Bilicke
gave them the whole of the second floor.
Johannes Fronk, head of the Citizens Safety
Committee since John Clum left town, posted
guards at every door, inside and out.

Crawley Dake's telegram arrived a little
past seven. Wyatt Earp took the oath as a
deputy U.S. marshal and promptly deputized
Doc Holliday, Charlie Smith, Daniel Tipton,
Sherman McMasters, Turkey Creek Jack
Johnson, and Texas Jack Vermillion. Morgan
was still laid up, but with Virgil bled white
and all but dead, Wyatt swore Morgan in, too,

and made sure he had a gun close to hand, in case somebody got past Fronk's guards.

Warrants next.

Billy Breakenridge came forward to say that Frank Stilwell had made threats against Doc Holliday and the Earps a few nights earlier and that Johnny Ringo might be involved as well. Ike Clanton's hat had been found behind the brewery used as cover by the men who shot Virg. The idiot had actually written his name inside the hatband. When Wyatt appeared before the court that afternoon, he requested warrants for those three and for Peter Spence and William Brocius as well, all on suspicion of assault with intent to murder. He meant to find and arrest everyone and anyone with a grudge *now.* A judge could sort the evidence out later.

Behan's house next.

Rousting the sheriff out of bed, he told Johnny what had happened to Virgil and cut off Behan's murmurs of shock and sympathy. "I'm sending Josie home," Wyatt said. "She'll be on the Benson stage in the morning. I want a safe conduct for her."

"Wyatt, what makes you think I can guarantee — ?"

"Just get the word out, Behan. Do what you have to. If she gets hurt, you'll wish you'd never been born."

Returning to the hotel, he checked again on Virgil, who was still alive but only barely.

Ignoring Allie's red-eyed glare, he went down the hall to his own room.

"Pack," he told Josie. "You're going back to San Francisco."

"I'm not scared," she lied, wet-eyed. "I won't leave you, Wyatt."

"Take Higgs and go home," he said, pulling her valise out of the wardrobe. "I can't think about you now."

My brother is dying, he meant. *I need you to be safe.*

Of course, she didn't hear it that way. It was all on her face — what she thought, what she felt. There was never any guessing with Josie, no trying to figure her out. Shocked, hurt, angry, she stood up and began to stuff clothing into her bag.

Just as well, he thought, for she was willing to leave him now.

In the hours following the attack on Virgil Earp, Marshal Crawley Dake sent one telegram after another to Washington. He might as well have been howling at the moon for all the good it did. Despairing of support from his superiors, Dake took out a $300 personal loan from Wells Fargo and telegraphed word to the bank in Tombstone: Let Deputy Marshal Wyatt Earp draw on the funds to field a posse and seek those responsible for shooting Virgil.

Ordering Doc Holliday and Texas Jack Vermillion to remain in Tombstone to look after his brothers, Wyatt Earp and the rest of his deputies saddled up and left for Charleston, warrants in hand.

Johnny Behan watched them thunder out of town. An assault on a federal marshal, inside city limits, was out of his jurisdiction. Even if the posse brought their men in, he knew it would be impossible to hold anyone for the shooting. Billy B.'s testimony would be dismissed as hearsay. Ike's hat wasn't proof of anything but carelessness. Nevertheless, Sheriff Behan sent identical telegrams to Frank Stilwell, Curly Bill Brocius, and Ike Clanton, whom he knew were in Charleston.

```
V EARP NEAR DEATH STOP US MARSHAL
W EARP REQUESTS SAFE CONDUCT FOR
J MARCUS TRAVELING DECEMBER 30 ON
BENSON STAGE STOP GET WORD TO
SPENCE AND RINGO STOP
```

This would, of course, warn all the suspects that Wyatt was now a federal officer on his way to arrest them, but hell . . . Johnny Behan was only doing what the marshal had requested.

Almost three hundred miles north, waiting for Doc to meet her in Prescott, Kate Harony awoke after a long night spent drinking with old friends. She was only moderately hungover and found no reason to moan until she went downstairs for coffee and saw Virgil Earp's name in the headline of a newspaper somebody had left in the hotel café.

The vendetta has opened in dead earnest in Tombstone with the attempted assassination of Virgil Earp, who was dangerously wounded on December 29th. Until now some believed the threats of the Cow Boys to be idle boasts, but the shooting of Marshal Earp shows that the Cow Boys will have their revenge. Who will be next? Attorney Tom Fitch has been repeatedly threatened, as have Marshal Earp's brothers and associates. The turmoil in Tombstone is giving the entire Arizona Territory an unsavory reputation abroad, deterring the immigration of capital and respectable labor.

A brief note from Doc arrived the next day.

You will know by now what has happened in Tombstone. If I leave the city alone, I will be attacked on the road as John Clum was. Wyatt's posse has gone after those responsible. When they are under arrest, I will try to get to you. In the meantime, I am doing my best to be useful. Morgan is stronger, but Virgil's wounds are terrible. I do not see how he can survive. You were right. I never should have come back to Tombstone, but there is nothing for it now. Best you go on to Denver. I will come to you as soon as I can. JHH

"Your brother's blood cries out to me from the ground." That's what Johnny Ringo had whispered over and over while they waited to ambush Virgil Earp.

"Eye for eye," Ike said. "Brother for brother."

"They won't get away with it," Frank Stilwell muttered when Virgil Earp turned onto Allen Street. "Biggety goddam Yankees."

It was Ringo who'd made sure the double-barreled shotguns were loaded for buck, and he kept everyone liquored up while they waited for the marshal to stroll around that corner. When Virgil pulled even, they by-God let him have it and took off running afterward, which was when Ike lost his hat.

The horses were waiting in front of a saloon down on Toughnut Street. They hit those saddles and raced out of town, laughing like schoolboys. It felt good, like a dash for the border after a cattle raid, your heart beating and your horse's breath like a train engine: *chuff, chuff, chuff.*

A mile out of Tombstone, they slowed some, for there was no sign of pursuit, but they kept up a good pace until they got to Frank Stilwell's saloon down in Charleston.

670

There they bragged, and drank deep, and celebrated until dawn. Then they staggered off to Stilwell's back room and slept the sleep of the drunken righteous, and did not stir until Curly Bill Brocius kicked them awake.

"What in hell have you fools done now?" he asked, waving Johnny Behan's telegram at them. When they told him, he cursed them for boneheaded, cracker jackasses. "Virgil Earp was a federal marshal!" he cried. "This's going to bring the whole goddam government down on us!"

Slow on his best day, still half-drunk from the night before, Ike looked stupider than usual. "What should we do?" he asked Curly Bill. "What are we gonna do now?"

"Why, turn ourselves in," Ringo said with that strange-eyed, dreamy smile of his. The others howled but Ringo's serenity never wavered, for he had thought this matter through. "We're going to ask Johnny Behan for protective custody."

"But they'll put us on trial," Stilwell protested.

"Of course they will." Ringo looked at Curly Bill. "And we'll have plenty of witnesses to testify that we were here in Charleston the night Virgil Earp got shot. Won't we, Bill."

Frank and Ike waited, anxious eyes on Curly Bill, who was silent for a while but nodded in the end. Even Curly Bill was scared of Ringo.

On February 2, 1882, five suspects came before the Cochise County Court in connection with the shooting of Deputy U.S. Marshal Virgil Earp. The charge against them remained attempted murder; thirty-four days after being hit with four charges of buckshot, the marshal was still fighting for his life. Eight men and three whores swore that each of the defendants were in Charleston on the night of the attack on Marshal Virgil Earp. The case was dismissed for lack of evidence. The accused were released.

For five weeks, the Associated Press had provided the world with lurid coverage of the attack on Virgil Earp, which was labeled Cow Boy revenge for what was being called "the Gunfight at the O.K. Corral" because it took too long to set the type for "Gunfight in the Vacant Lot behind Camillus Fly's Photography Studio Near Fremont Street."

The A.P. carried news of the attackers' exoneration as well, and two weeks after the trial, the *Nugget*'s editor, Harry Woods, received a bizarre letter from England.

Dear sir, can you obtain for me a good specimen of the genus Homo known as the cow-boy? Send him to me by registered mail. I understand that cow-boys are just

672

too, too awfully utter. Yours sincerely, Oscar
Wilde

O, My Brother! I Have Been the Death of You!

There comes a time when the smart money gets out. That's what people were whispering in March of 1882. The Tough Nut's been seeping for a year, they said. That new shaft at the Grand Central just hit water. The Contention's bringing in a Cornish engine that can pump out half a million gallons a day, but who else can afford equipment like that?

Silver's done. Copper's the next big thing. Bisbee is booming, and you're less likely to get hit by a stray bullet down there.

Did you see what happened last week? Johnny Ringo and Doc Holliday almost had it out with pistols on Allen Street!

Ringo was drunk. He probably started it.

Well, I heard Holliday say, "All I want of *you* is ten paces in the street!"

The city police stepped in to stop them, but it's only a matter of time before somebody else gets killed, and I don't want it to be me.

It's time to sell out. It's time to take what you can get and go.

"Talk to Wyatt, Morg. He'll listen to you." That's what Lou was saying, and Allie, and James, and Bessie. Even Virgil said, "There's no future for us here."

The family was hemorrhaging money. The doctors' bills alone were staggering. They were still paying on Morgan's three surgeries, and Virgil needed constant care. Bessie was sick, and Mattie Blaylock required a steady supply of laudanum to keep her quiet. Al Bilicke was giving them a break on the entire second floor of the Cosmopolitan, but he couldn't carry the Earps forever. And they didn't dare go home because the death threats kept coming and it was too difficult to guard three houses.

One by one, Johannes Fronk's volunteers had drifted away. Which meant paying the replacements. Turkey Creek Jack Johnson and Texas Jack Vermillion and the others were friends, but they still needed room and board. And now Johnny Behan had persuaded Ike Clanton to refile murder charges against the Earps and Doc Holliday. There wasn't any new evidence that could overturn the earlier decisions, but this would mean more of lawyers' fees on top of everything else.

Meanwhile, their income had all but dried up. Allie had her sewing machine brought from home and the girls were doing what they could to help, but it was a pittance laid against all the bills. Wyatt still got $125 a month as a deputy marshal. James had re-opened his tavern in January, but business was way down. Even Chinese laborers knew it was dangerous to associate with an Earp.

Doc, at least, was making some money, for John Meagher had allowed him to go back to work at the Alhambra. The Cow Boys might well make trouble, but Meagher understood that Doc was trying to cover Morgan and Lou's expenses as well as his own.

The dentist was risking a bullet every time he left the hotel, but Morgan envied him. At least Doc got outside for a few minutes a day.

Wyatt was gone a lot, too. All winter, he rode out with one posse after another. Live-stock theft along the border always picked up in the spring. Bisbee payrolls were attracting thieves from all over the country and stage-coaches were getting robbed regularly. Ar-rests were made, but nothing would stick. Everybody always had an alibi. Each time a Cow Boy left the courtroom unscathed, the insolence and provocation got worse. Without his brothers to back him up, Wyatt was tak-ing the brunt of it all, and when he got back to the hotel, he was beat down to his boots.

Morgan had begun pacing the hotel hall-ways — not strong enough to ride with Wyatt, too restless to read, too bored to sit. He hated to complain, but life inside the Cosmopolitan was close to intolerable. The girls could hardly stand the sight of one another. There was a lot of squabbling, and Lou was fed up. "If I wanted sister wives," she told Morg, "I would have stayed in Utah." James and Bessie were ready to sell out and leave on their own. Even Virgil said, "This is no way to live."

"Talk to Wyatt, Morgan," they all said. "Wyatt will listen to you."

"Wyatt, do you even remember why we came to Tombstone?" Morgan asked over supper when they were alone and the time seemed right. "We came here to get rich, right? Well, the money is gone. The silver's underwater. Half the miners have been laid off. Hell, even the Chinamen are leaving town! James says his place is empty most of the time. He's in a hole, and it's getting deeper. We all are."

"The election's eight months away," Wyatt said. "With the Bisbee taxes coming in, it'll be forty grand a year for the sheriff, and I'll pay everything off."

Lips compressed with the effort to hold back what he was thinking, Morgan looked away. There wasn't a chance in hell that Wyatt would ever be sheriff of Cochise County. Even here in Tombstone, City Council and the town police force had distanced themselves from anyone who'd been involved with the gunfight. An entirely fresh slate of town officials had been elected in January.

"Wyatt," he said carefully, "people don't want to be reminded of what happened last October. Everybody wants to put it behind them. Voters. Virgil and Allie. Lou *hates* it here — she always has! James and Bessie want to leave. Doc wants to try Colorado. Let's just go. Just sell everything off, pack up, and get the hell out of here."

"I don't know, Morg . . ."

"Wyatt, what kind of life is this? We may as well be in prison! We can't hide in here forever."

"And we can't just walk away," Wyatt snapped. "It'll look like the Cow Boys drove us out. If we run now, we'll be running the rest of our lives."

They finished eating in silence. Morgan went to bed. Wyatt remained at the table. Finishing his coffee. Thinking things through.

Morgan was right about the money at least. Two years in Tombstone and they were worse off than when they arrived. The gambling concessions, the mines, the houses, the water rights — everything was mortgaged or gone. Morg was finally healing up and Virgil would survive, but neither of them would have full use of both arms again. James was talking about opening a new bar called the Three Cripples Saloon. It was a joke, but nobody laughed.

And maybe . . . maybe Morg was right

about the election, too.

Wyatt was on his way up to bed when Al Bilicke called him over to the front desk and handed him a piece of paper. The note was printed in block letters: EARPS LEAVE OR WE BURN YOU DOWN.

"Wyatt, this business is all I have," Bilicke said. "I have to think about my wife and kids."

All that night as Wyatt lay in bed, the questions circled in his mind. How long before somebody else took another shot at an Earp? How long before somebody got killed? Frank Stilwell was back in Tombstone, free as a bird, and he had a couple of friends with him. A half-Mexican named Florentino Cruz, and a breed named Hank Swilling — Apache Hank, they called that one. They were staying with Pete Spence and his wife, right across the street from Virgil's place. Torching the Earps' houses would be easy as pie.

We can't stay here, Wyatt thought. We can't go home. We can't leave town. What in hell can we do?

He was wishing Josie was there to help him figure this out when the solution came to him.

In the morning, he found Doc and asked, "How soon do you figure Virgil could travel?"

"In another month, perhaps. I still believe amputation would have been better for him, but he'll go to his grave with two arms. Why do you ask?" Wyatt didn't answer right away, and Doc must have realized that Morgan had talked to him. "We're gettin' out?" he asked.

When Wyatt nodded, Doc looked relieved. "My guess is, it'll be safe to move Virg in the middle of April, give or take a few days."

Wyatt went to Morgan's room next and asked Lou to step outside. "We can't just walk away," he told Morgan, "but we could say Virg needs another operation on his arm. We could say we have to take him to a doctor in San Francisco."

Morgan stared at him for a moment, and Wyatt got ready to defend himself. It was all right to say something nice, even if it wasn't quite true. He used to do that all the time with Mattie. You look nice. This tastes real good. So it couldn't be sinful if you saved a life by lying. It was honorable, almost.

Before he could say that, Morgan grinned that big boyish grin of his. "Hot damn," he said softly. "Hot damn. Thank you, Wyatt. You're doing the right thing."

There was muted jubilation on the second floor of the Cosmopolitan Hotel that afternoon. They would have to keep quiet about their plans, so as not to alert the Cow Boys and invite a last-minute attack, but when Virg was well enough, they'd buy up all the seats on the night coach out of Tombstone. Wyatt's deputies would act as an armed guard until they got to Benson. Then they'd take the local to Tucson and transfer to the Southern Pacific. Virg could continue his convalescence in California. Maybe all the brothers would stay with their parents for a time. Doc Holliday would come with them as far as Tucson, then continue north to Denver, where Kate was waiting for him.

Even Wyatt looked happy, but when Allie showed him a flyer about the St. Patrick's Day Ball at Schieffelin Hall, he shook his head. "I don't know, Allie," he began.

"Well, I *do*," Allie said. "We've been cooped up long enough! Virg can sit and watch, but the rest of us are going to dance tonight — even Bessie, if she feels good."

He thought it over. It was only a few blocks to Schieffelin Hall. There were a dozen men in town who could be trusted to keep an eye out for trouble. "All right," he said. "All right."

On the day of the dance, the ladies spent hours in Lou's room, primping and dressing up, giggling like girls behind the closed door. A barber came across the street, and the gentlemen got shaves and haircuts and put on their best suits. Meanwhile, Texas Jack Vermillion rounded up a substantial bodyguard.

The weather on the evening of March 17, 1882, was raw and blustery with an icy, spitting rain that made the warmth and light of Schieffelin Hall all the more splendid. Miles of Kelly green bunting festooned the windows. Gold paper shamrocks and silver punch bowls gleamed in the gaslight. Satins and silks shimmered. Crystal glittered. It was like stepping into Aladdin's cave. Town politics remained bitter and both sides were in attendance, but for a few hours, hard feelings and rivalries and suspicions were set aside.

Well-rested after a quiet winter, Doc asked each of the Earp ladies for a waltz. Wyatt danced a polka with Lou. Then the band played something slow, and everyone cheered when Virgil — gaunt and frail — took Allie for a single turn around the dance floor, holding her close with his good arm, but what everyone would remember later was how happy Lou and Morg were that night, and what a handsome couple they made: Lou in a sweet pink frock that set off the pretty flush of her cheeks as she danced and Morgan in a blue worsted suit he'd worn just once before, last summer.

"Why, it looks like their wedding party," someone remarked at the punch bowl as Lou and Morgan swept past.

"It does indeed," Doc Holliday murmured. "It does indeed."

It was seductive, that little taste of ordinary

life. Remember when we lived in houses and had kitchens and beds of our own? Remember when we could walk around town without armed guards? That's how life is supposed to be!

The next evening they all went out again, this time to see the Tombstone premiere of a comedy called *Stolen Kisses* — hours of silly entertainment and heedless laughter. It was just what they all needed.

Afterward, everybody returned to the hotel except for Morgan.

Bob Hatch's Billiard Parlor was right across the street from the Cosmopolitan. All winter long, Morgan had played games in his mind, imagining angles, thinking through the shots. After months in bed and then more months of what felt like captivity, he was dying to play for real.

Later, Wyatt would try to work out what made him go back to the billiard parlor. He was already up in his hotel room. He had his coat off and was starting to unbutton his shirt when an uneasiness rose in him. He just couldn't shake that feeling, though he knew Morgan had five good men guarding him at Hatch's.

"Hell," he sighed. Morg would rag him about being a mother hen, but he put his coat back on. It was almost his birthday. He was turning thirty-four at midnight and told himself it'd be nice to celebrate with Morgan.

Allen Street was all but empty, for it was raining again and still windy, with the cutting nighttime cold of March in the desert. The lights were blazing through the fancy painted windows of the billiard parlor. Wyatt hurried inside only to be greeted by Bob Hatch's irritable cry, "Shut that gawddam doe-ah!"

"What's the matter, Wyatt?" Morgan asked. "Couldn't sleep?"

"Just thought I'd come back and watch you play."

Which was sort of the truth, for Bob Hatch was an expert and Morgan was very good, and it was a marvel to see them compete. There were tall chairs along the wall, so you could sit and watch the games. Shaking the rain off his coat and hat, Wyatt hung them up and went over to sit by a fella named George Berry, who nodded hello and murmured, "Five bucks says your brother loses two out of three."

"What in hell happened to that wrist of yo-ah's?" Bob Hatch asked Morgan.

"Oh, this was years ago," Morg said. "Remember, Wyatt?"

"He musta been about five," Wyatt said, though he suspected Bob was only asking about this to distract Morgan from the game. He leaned toward George and said, "I'll take that bet."

"Ma always called me Angel," Morg began, "and the Bible says angels can fly, right? So one day I climbed up this big old cottonwood, and you know how brittle they are —"

Morg paused to move around the table for his next shot.

"He fell about twenty feet," Wyatt said. "Broke the wrist."

"And then Pa beat the hell out of me for being so stupid!" Morgan said cheerfully, like it was a good joke on him and it made perfect sense to wallop a child who was already hurt. Wyatt was going to say something about that, except he noticed that Morg was standing between the gaslight and a window. That could make you a target. "Morg," he was going to say, "move away from the window."

He would see what happened next for the rest of his life.

The glass exploding. The sledgehammer impact. The bloom of blood.

The first slug caught Morgan square in the back, smashing his spine and ripping out through his gut with enough residual power to slam into George Berry's thigh, four feet beyond. Before Morgan had time to hit the floor, a second bullet passed inches from Wyatt's own head, splintering the wooden wall behind him.

The rest was a blur. Men taking off into the night, guns drawn, looking for the shooters. Lifting Morgan with Bob Hatch, getting him onto a chaise longue in the card room next door. Gamblers running for the police and the family and the doctor, who hurried — again — to the side of a shattered and bleeding Earp. George Goodfellow's bleak eyes meeting Wyatt's as he shook his head with silent regret. Lou, screaming. Doc, holding her.

"Lay me straight, Wyatt," Morgan asked quietly.

"You are straight," Wyatt told him. Weeping. Soaked to the skin in his brother's blood. "You're just as straight as you can be."

"Well, then, I guess my back is broken."

In the minutes Morgan Earp had left, he joked lamely, "I have played my last game of pool" and tried to comfort those around him. "Won't be long," he promised. Mostly though, he gripped his brother's hand. "They're picking us off," he whispered. "Don't let them get you, Wyatt."

It wasn't a scene in a sentimental story. It wasn't a dime novel. There were no howled oaths, no fist-shaking vows of revenge. In the end, there were no words at all. There was just the feel of Morgan's grip loosening around his hand.

And . . . a pain drilling through his own chest. It was so deep, so physical that he unbuttoned his shirt later, looking for a bullet hole. Nothing, he thought, mystified by his own unmarred flesh. How can nothing hurt so much?

I shoulda known, he thought over and over. Frank Stilwell and Pete Spence. Apache Hank and Florentino Cruz. They're picking us off, just like Morgan said.

"Wyatt?" James said. "What's the plan?"

He turned and stared at James for a moment. I'm always wrong, he thought. Why do they ask me what to do?

"You take Virg and Morgan home to Mother," he said finally. "I'll go, as far as Benson. Then I'll track the killers down."

WRETCHED MORTALS! THEY LIVE IN GRIEF.

There was no chance now of making a quiet retreat. Stilwell, Spence, Swilling, and Cruz were seen leaving Tombstone, but the Cow Boys had eyes all over town. There was every reason to believe there'd be another attack on the road to Benson.

As word of Morgan's death spread, men who'd served Wyatt and Virgil as deputies showed up, armed and red-eyed, to escort the Earps to safety. It fell to James to prepare what was left of the family for the journey.

"What about Mattie?" he asked Wyatt.

"Yeah, her, too. I don't want her in the house if they burn it down."

"We'll need money for the trip. You got any?"

"Some. Sell the horses, I guess. Except for Dick."

While the women packed, James stopped by the lawyer's office and arranged to have the last of the Earp properties disposed of. "If there's anything left after you settle the debts, send it to Mr. and Mrs. Nicholas Earp in Colton, California," he told Bill Herring.

He went to Dexter's livery next. They bought Morgan's horse and Virgil's. Most of that money went to renting wagons and teams to transport the family to Benson. Johnny Behan came by to murmur condolences and offer $400 for Wyatt's Arab mare, Roxana, and her colt Reuben. It was a tenth of what the animals were worth, but it was cash in hand and James was grateful.

He walked to the Western Union office after that, which was when James finally broke down, writing the telegram that Virginia Earp would receive.

MOTHER MAY GOD COMFORT YOU STOP MORGAN IS DEAD STOP WE ARE BRINGING HIM HOME STOP

"Half a dollar," the clerk said quietly. "I'm sorry about your brother, sir. I'm sure he's in a better place."

"No," James said, his voice ragged and fierce. "No! Wherever my brother is, that place is better because he's in it."

Doc Holliday never left Lou's side in the hours after Morgan's death. All that night, they waited in the mortician's office while Morgan's body was embalmed.

"I can't leave him," Lou said over and over,

as though apologizing for keeping Doc from going to bed. "I just can't leave him."

"We'll stay here," Doc always replied. "We won't leave him alone."

When the body was prepared, they went in together, arm in arm, to view the remains. "So cold!" Lou whispered when she touched Morgan's hands. He was dressed in the suit Doc had bought him. Weeping, she ran a hand down Morgan's arm, along the sleeve. "It matched his eyes," she said.

Doc nodded to the mortician, who cut a curl of Morgan's hair and then took a snippet of marine-blue gabardine from a place where it wouldn't show. These mementos were wrapped in tissue paper, tucked into a little envelope, and pressed into Lou's hand.

"I can't leave him!" she said again. "Doc, I can't —"

"We'll stay right here," he told her. "We won't leave Morg alone."

At dawn, the coffin was loaded onto a flatbed wagon, wedged in tight with the family's valises and bedding so it wouldn't shift as they traveled over the rutted, gully-riven road between Tombstone and Benson. Lou and Doc would sit in the back with Morgan. Allie made beds up for Virgil and Bessie in a second wagon; Mattie would ride with them. The wagon drivers and a mounted escort were armed with rifles, pistols, double-barreled shotguns, and enough ammunition to fight off a concerted attack by the Cow Boys.

Already in the wagon bed, Virgil sat up, his boneless, aching arm strapped tight to his chest for the journey. "Where's Wyatt?" he called, and you could hear the panic in his voice. "Has anybody seen him?"

"He's over at the church," Jack Vermillion said. "Chased everybody else out."

"He's all right, Virg," James soothed. "Don't worry. I'll go get him now."

The door was open. James looked inside. It was Sunday but there was no minister, no congregation. It was just Wyatt by himself, wet-faced and pacing in front of the plain white wooden altar. James recognized the rhythm of what he was saying, for it was Wyatt's favorite psalm. *Create in me a clean heart, O God, and renew the right spirit within me.* Then the rhythm broke and the words became angrier.

"Why him?" Wyatt cried. "Answer me! Why him?"

James backed away from the door and crept down the stairs, waiting until he was a good distance out in the street before he called, "Wyatt? We're ready to go!"

A few minutes later, Wyatt came outside. His eyes looked raw, but he pulled his hat down low, and now there was no other sign of distress. "You get Mattie?"

691

"Yeah, but she's drunk. Brought a bottle with her."

"Shoulda been you, not Morgan," Mattie sneered when she saw Wyatt. "You brought us all down here to die. You ruined my life! You ruined everyone's life —"

It was Bessie who slapped her. "He never shoulda taken you in. I'da sent you right back to the street where you belonged. So you just shut your mouth, get in that wagon, and be glad we don't leave you here alone."

The wildflowers would be glorious in the spring of '82. Seeds that had lain dormant for years had soaked up the unprecedented moisture of the previous summer. Soon buds would swell, blossoms would explode, and the stony Arizona sand would offer up a lavish display of color and scent.

In a few weeks, Louisa Earp's garden would be an oasis of verbenas and primroses, lupines and gold poppies and larkspur, but on the twentieth of March, there was nothing more promising than a few green shoots along the side of the house.

With one hand on her husband's coffin, Lou watched their home disappear as the wagon made the wide turn out of town, rolling past the cemetery and a farmer's grave.

Exhausted by grief, she closed her eyes and saw Tom McLaury's face. Beautiful in death.

Cold and white as marble in the snow.

You were right about my sister's lilacs, she thought. They died, too.

Maybe the Cow Boys were down in Charleston, celebrating Morg's death. Or maybe they were around but didn't care to take on the Earps' armed escort. Whatever the reason, there was no trouble on the road, and Wyatt believed the worst was over when they reached the railway depot.

All he had to do was get Virgil, James, and the women onto the train to Tucson with Morgan's body. When that was done, he'd go back to Tombstone with Sherm McMasters and Texas Jack Vermillion and Turkey Creek Jack Johnson, collect the warrants, and begin the pursuit.

"I'm goin' with you," Doc told him after Lou was on the train.

"No," Wyatt said. "You're not."

"I am not askin' for permission, Wyatt."

"Good, 'cause I'm not giving it." I don't need a sick man who might collapse or cough at the wrong time, he meant. I can't stand to see my grief in your face.

Doc looked like he'd been slapped. Wyatt softened. "Doc, my brothers can't take care of themselves, let alone the girls. I need somebody I trust to look after them."

So it was decided: Doc would travel on to Tucson with the family. When the Earps were on the train that would take them to California, he'd continue north to Denver, as he'd meant to do before all this happened.

He and Wyatt shook hands, and Doc climbed aboard the train. He had just gotten settled into a seat by the window when a breathless messenger ran up to Wyatt Earp and handed him a telegram.

That's when everything changed.

■ ■ ■ ■

Now There Will Be Killing Until the Score Is Paid

■ ■ ■ ■

A Heart-Devouring Anger

Why *that* moment? Why not when Morgan died? Perhaps because the shock was too great, the loss too sudden and profound. But there was this as well: a lifetime of denying his own nature.

Wyatt Earp had been born, and born again, and now there would be a third life, for the iron fist that had seized his soul in childhood had lost its grip at last. The long struggle for control was over, and in its place, he found a wordless acceptance of a truth he'd always known. He was bred to this anger. It had been in him since the cradle. He'd never bullied neighbors or beaten a horse. He'd never punched the front teeth out of a six-year-old's mouth or hit a woman until she begged. But he was no better than his father, and never had been. He was far, far worse.

Gazing out the window of the train that was about to pull away, John Henry Holliday saw the moment when a pure, cold rage transfigured a man he thought he knew: a

697

man who nodded to the messenger, who dismounted, who pulled his shotgun from its scabbard, who tossed Dick Naylor's reins to Sherm McMasters and hopped aboard the train, yelling, "Wait here!" to the rest of the posse as the locomotive jerked forward and the train began to pick up speed.

"Bob Paul sent word," that man told him, swaying slightly in the aisle. "Ike Clanton is in Tucson with Frank Stilwell and Hank Swilling. They're laying for Virgil at the depot. They think they're gonna kill a cripple."

The words were factual. The tone was unemotional and cool, but what John Henry Holliday thought was *Rubicon.*

Wyatt moved up the aisle to warn Virgil and James, and to make plans with them for what came next.

He passed Mattie Blaylock on his way. "It's all your fault," she muttered again. Then she, too, saw what Doc Holliday had seen, for Wyatt rounded on her and clamped one big hand around her throat, and it was all there, in those cold, unblinking eyes. How many times he could have snapped her neck like a twig. How many times he had left the house instead and let her live. How that was over now because there was no mercy left in him. None.

"Yes," he said. "It's all my fault. And I'll have more to answer for, when this is done."

■ ■ ■

"Shit," Frank Stilwell whispered. "See that great big sonofabitch? That's gotta be Bob Paul. This place is lousy with law."

Hank said, "I count eight . . . No, ten. Two more, over by the restaurant."

Stilwell swore under his breath. "Somebody musta talked."

Hours ago, he and Ike Clanton and Apache Hank Swilling had climbed on top of a sidelined boxcar. Lying on their bellies, staying out of sight, they'd kept watch on the Southern Pacific. It was leaving for California at dusk. The Earps would show themselves sooner or later.

"Somebody musta talked," Ike said.

Florentino Cruz, Frank was thinking. That half-Mexican bastard probably figured he'd get off easy if he sold the rest of us out.

"There's the coffin," Apache Hank murmured.

A little gaggle of women appeared, along with a pair of tall blond men who had just two good arms between them. Wyatt was behind them, carrying a scattergun.

"Somebody talked," Ike was saying. "Somebody musta talked."

"Shut up, Ike!" Stilwell whispered.

He tried to line up a shot, but Wyatt was hustling everybody along, and the Earps were quickly lost to sight. Porters loaded the casket into the mail car. For a few moments, you could see that lunger Holliday helping a woman dressed in black climb in beside it. She turned back and reached out a hand to him. Holliday kissed it, and Stilwell was about to say, "Now ain't that sweet!" when the depot gaslights came on, up and down the platform.

Hank scrambled backward, out of the glare. It must've been the movement that caught Holliday's eye, for he looked up, and pointed, and yelled. That's all it took to send Ike running. Apache Hank was right behind him.

Which left Frank Stilwell all by his lonesome. Staring into Wyatt Earp's eyes.

Long afterward, men would ask, "Why didn't Stilwell kill Wyatt then and there? He had the high ground, up on that boxcar." But those men had never looked into eyes that told you, plain as speech, *There is no place you can go that I will not follow. I will find you, and I will pull your heart from your chest, and I will eat it raw.*

That's what Frank Stilwell saw, and that's why he clambered down off the far side of that boxcar, and then he by-God ran, and wished that he'd run sooner. Mexico, he was thinking at first, but soon there was nothing in his mind at all, except for *Run. Run. Run.*

He was maybe two hundred yards down the

tracks when the buckshot hit his thighs. He tumbled over and rolled down the shallow embankment and came to rest on his back in the weeds. There were stars at first, and then there was Wyatt Earp, looking down at him.

"Please," Frank said. "Please, don't kill me. Please."

Wyatt blew out a little snort of air, white in the mountain cold, and let the second charge go.

By the time Doc got there, Stilwell was long past dead, but Wyatt wrenched Virgil's shotgun from Doc's hands, put its barrels close to Stilwell's chest, blew it to pieces, and handed the shotgun back.

Breathless and coughing from the run, Doc watched wide-eyed as Wyatt pulled a pistol out next and began to empty that into Stilwell's body as well.

"Stop now, Wyatt. He's dead," Doc said. "It's over."

"No," Wyatt said, turning grief and rage into shreds of flesh and shards of bone. "No. It's not."

All men are capable of savagery. Bob Paul knew that, but he never would have expected it from Wyatt Earp, who had always seemed so steady.

Waving his men back, the sheriff of Pima County pointedly gazed toward the distant mountains, turning a blind eye to what remained of Frank Stilwell.

"I can give you until tomorrow afternoon," he told Wyatt. "Best you leave now, son."

They caught a freight back to Benson. With their backs against the wooden slats of an empty cattle car, Wyatt Earp and Doc Holliday sat alone together, in grief and in guilt.

Should've been me, they were both thinking, though for different reasons. Should've been me, not Morg.

After a time, Wyatt tried to reload the weapons. By then the shuddering reaction had set in and his hands were shaking, so Doc did it for him.

An hour passed before Wyatt spoke. "Stilwell got twenty-two hours."

It took a while to work it out, but then Doc understood. Frank Stilwell had lived just twenty-two hours longer than Morgan Earp.

A Brutal,
Indecent Slaughter

Dogs and a railyard worker found Stilwell on the morning of March 20. Dead men weren't unusual in Arizona, but nobody had seen one shot up as thoroughly as Frank.

News of the murder was swiftly telegraphed around the country. In Tombstone, the headline in that morning's *Epitaph* was unsubtle: THIS TIME THE THUNDERBOLT OF DEATH STRIKES THE OTHER SIDE.

The laconic headline of the *Nugget* would prove useful in the days to come. MORE BLOODSHED was all it said.

Inquests were convened that day in both Cochise and Pima Counties.

In Tombstone, Marietta Spence took the stand to testify in the matter of Morgan Earp's slaying. "I am the wife of Peter Spence," she told the coroner's jury. "On March eighteenth, Pete came home from Charleston, and he had two breeds with him. One was half Mexican, named Florentino Cruz. Sometimes they called him Indian

703

Charlie. The other one was called Apache Hank. His name is really Hank Swilling. Anyways, Morgan Earp walked by, and I heard Pete tell the breeds, 'That's one of them.' Frank Stilwell came that night, too. They was all armed with pistols and rifles. Around midnight myself and my mother heard the shots that killed Morgan Earp. A few minutes later, Pete and Frank Stilwell and their friends Apache Hank and Florentino Cruz — they come back to the house, and they was all of a tremble. Pete told me to get up and make them a breakfast, and we had a quarrel, so he struck me and my mother. He said he would shoot us both. He said he was leaving town and he'd leave our bodies behind him if we said a word of what we knew, but I don't care. I hope Wyatt Earp catches Pete and the others, and I hope he makes them pay."

Murder warrants for Peter Spence, Henry Swilling (a.k.a. Apache Hank), and Florentino Cruz (a.k.a. Indian Charlie) were issued an hour later.

In Tucson, the coroner's jury considered the condition of Frank Stilwell's body and concluded that there must have been a small army involved with his death. Five suspects were named. Wyatt Earp, John Henry Holliday, Sherman McMasters, John Blount (a.k.a. Turkey Creek Jack Johnson, a.k.a. Creek Johnson), and John Oberland Vermillion (a.k.a. Texas Jack Vermillion) were all wanted for murder.

Under the circumstances, the last person anybody expected to show his face in Tombstone was Wyatt Earp, but there he was, along with Doc Holliday, Sherm McMasters, and the two Jacks.

Marietta Spence was the first to see them as they passed her house on the way into town. She was hanging out laundry, but one eye was black, and from way she moved, you knew there were bruises hidden beneath her dress. "I'm sorry about your brother," she told Wyatt. "Pete's probably up in the Dragoons at his woodcutting camp. I hope you get him."

Wyatt nodded his thanks and the posse continued into town, where they returned the rented wagons and stabled the horses before checking into the Cosmopolitan.

"Wake us up at seven tonight," he told Al Bilicke. "We'll leave after dark," he told his men, but he himself went to William Herring's law office next.

When Wyatt appeared in the doorway, the lawyer assumed it was to give himself up and stand trial. Bill Herring had been drafting a defense ever since he'd heard about Frank Stilwell. "Wyatt," he said, "we can beat this. We've got Marietta Spence's testimony and I've lined up witnesses who'll swear to the threats Stilwell made —"

Wyatt brushed that off. "I need to change my will. If there's anything left when my debts are paid, I want half to go to my sister Adelia. This's her address," he said, handing the lawyer an old envelope. "The other half should go to Josephine Marcus. I don't know exactly where she lives, but her father's a banker up in San Francisco. Shouldn't be hard to find."

"Wyatt, I promise, the murder charge against you won't amount to anything —"

"A trial will take a month," Wyatt said. "Even if I'm not lynched while I'm in custody, the men who killed Morgan will get away."

So Herring drew up the codicil. Wyatt signed it, but before he left the office, Judge William H. Stilwell — no relation to the recently deceased individual of the same last name — arrived with warrants for Morgan's killers.

"Wyatt," the judge said, "if I were you, I'd leave my prisoners out in the mesquite, where alibis don't count."

That certainly sounded like permission, but it wouldn't have made any difference — what the judge said or didn't say. Wyatt only took the warrants out of habit. He knew, even then, he wasn't going to bring anyone in. He wasn't going to sit in court and listen to their smirking friends lie under oath. Oh, he was with me in Contention that night. We was playing cards, Your Honor, so he couldn't have shot Morgan Earp. Morgan was a nice fella, and it's too bad he got killed, sir.

To hell with that. To hell with them.

He was on his way back to the hotel when he heard someone call his name and turned to see the Western Union telegrapher hurrying across the street.

"Mr. Earp, I just got a wire from Bob Paul to Johnny Behan. There are warrants out for you, Doc Holliday, Sherm McMasters, and both of the Jacks."

"It was just me," Wyatt said. "Doc didn't fire. The other three were back in Benson."

"Well, that's as may be, but they're wanted all the same." The telegrapher looked around and dropped his voice. "Get some rest, sir. I don't believe my messenger will be able to find Johnny Behan until after eight o'clock this evening."

The Cosmopolitan was only a block from the pitheads on Toughnut Street. Until recently you'd have heard the constant noise of steam engines over in the Goodenough, but it was quiet that afternoon.

Eliphalet Butler Gage found that silence unnerving. It was the sound of businesses closing and capital fleeing.

You could explain cattle rustling to eastern investors. ("Nothing to do with our opera-

tions, although it does make beef cheaper.")
You could justify the gunfight back in October. ("Strict law enforcement! We tolerate no nonsense in Tombstone.") You could point out that the U.S. Mint was still buying millions of dollars of Tombstone silver. No matter what you said, investors were backing away.

It wasn't too late to turn things around. There was plenty of silver ore to be extracted from the Grand Central Mine. He needed bigger pumps, heavier timbers, more cash to pay competitive salaries to the engineers and skilled miners who were leaving for Bisbee's copper deposits. The capital would come back, if the crime problem could be solved.

I'm just going to ask Wyatt a question, Gage reminded himself, trying not to be nervous. He was certainly not going to offer the man a bribe. Wyatt had beaten a man to death for trying that up in Dodge. No, he would simply ask a question and wait for the answer. If it seemed wise, he'd offer . . . encouragement, one might say. If Wyatt looked askance, Gage could easily adjust his approach from financial backing to moral support.

When Wyatt walked through the hotel door, E. B. Gage wasted no time in coming to the point. "What would it take to put an end to this plague of lawlessness, Wyatt?"

To track the Cow Boys down and kill them all, he meant, and looking into Wyatt Earp's eyes, Gage knew that his meaning was clear. He could almost see the man doing the computation in his head. More men. More horses. More ammunition. Provisions for weeks in the chaparral. A good tracker. Payments to informers.

"Call it a grand," Wyatt said. "Tens and twenties."

A bargain, any way you calculated it. "I could get that," Gage said cautiously.

"How soon?"

Awash with relief, Gage almost wept. "Thursday. Friday at the latest. Richard Gird will kick in. Wells Fargo, too. How should we get it to you?"

"Send it to Henry Hooker's ranch. I'll head there when I can."

"The whole territory will be grateful. We'll back whatever you do, Wyatt. The governor wants this problem solved. So does Washington," Gage added for good measure. "There'll be pardons when the job is done."

His time with Josie seemed like a fairy tale now, like some story that started with "Once upon a time."

Eyes open, lying in the bed they'd shared, he tried to calculate how long they'd had together. The president died on September nineteenth. The gunfight was October twenty-sixth. The hearing was in November. The attack on Virg was just after Christmas. He sent

709

her back to San Francisco then.

A hundred days, maybe? Give or take.

I should sleep, he thought, but he reached for his pocket watch instead and did the count again. Sixty-six hours since Morgan died. Every minute felt like failure. Every breath Morg's killers took was a rebuke . . .

He must have dropped off at some point, for he sat up with a cry when Al Bilicke knocked on the door.

At seven-thirty, everyone was down in the lobby except Doc. Wyatt hoped briefly that the dentist was too exhausted to come along. Then he remembered: If Doc was still in Tombstone when Western Union delivered the telegram to Johnny Behan, he'd be arrested and hanged for sure.

"Did you wake up Holliday?" he asked Bilicke.

"Yes, sir. He told me to get him up at six. He's waiting for you outside."

And he'd been busy. The horses were saddled, the canteens filled, bags of food hung over the pommels. While Sherm and the Jacks tied bedrolls and lifted saddlebags onto their animals, Doc sat silently on that rented sorrel, Duchess. Eyes on Wyatt. Just waiting.

Wyatt nodded, accepting it. Doc inclined his head.

The rest of the posse was mounting up when the Jewish druggist hurried over with the two canteens that Dr. Holliday had asked him to prepare. "Coffee, very strong," he said, handing one to the dentist. Then, with a look of warning, he gave Doc the other. "Laudanum," he said. "Very dilute, but . . . use it sparingly."

Sheriff John Behan was on his way to the Can Can Café for supper when he saw Wyatt and the others getting ready to leave town. Starting across the street, he called, "Wyatt, I want to see you . . ." But his words trailed off and his steps slowed when he got close enough to look into Wyatt Earp's eyes.

It was, he'd think later, like bending down to pick up a belt you'd dropped on the floor the night before, only to realize that what you were reaching for wasn't your belt. It was a rattlesnake, waking after a long hibernation.

"Well, Johnny, you're seeing me now," Wyatt said. "May come a time when you see me once too often."

Behan took a little step back, and Wyatt smiled at that: a small, unmirthful smile, full of the snobbery of evil. *We're all rotten,* that smile said, *and I am the worst of all.* Johnny had seen that smile on someone else, though it would take a few days to remember who. Meanwhile, his own mouth worked briefly; in the end, he found nothing to say, and Wyatt gave a little snort of contempt.

"Run along now," he told Johnny. "I have

711

work to do."

Deputy Breakenridge arrived at his boss's side in time to hear that remark and saw Sheriff Behan flush crimson as he watched the Earp posse ride down Allen on their way out of town.

"Aren't we going to arrest them?" Billy asked.

"Not yet," Johnny said, moving smoothly toward legal high ground. "We don't have warrants yet."

It was only a quarter of eight.

The next morning, the foreman of Pete Spence's woodcutting operation noticed five horsemen approaching the camp. He kept an eye on them as they started up the mountain and when they got close, he recognized Wyatt Earp and realized it was a posse. Sherm Mc-Masters was with them. That was a surprise. Sherm didn't usually have much to do with lawmen.

"Where's Pete Spence?" Earp asked.

"Last I saw him, he was down in Tombstone."

"When was that?"

The foreman scratched his beard. "Last week, must be. Why? Is Pete in trouble?"

"When do you expect to see him next?"

"Hell if I know. He don't come up here much. Usually it's just me and the greasers. They take the trees down, I freight 'em back to town. Hey, Sherm."

McMasters nodded, but he was talking to the Mexican woodcutters, asking them the same kinds of questions in Spanish. They all looked blank and shrugged, except for the new man — a half-breed nobody knew well, who hung back and wiped his palms on his vest and edged toward the woods.

And suddenly took off running.

"That's Cruz," Sherm yelled.

Wyatt spurred his horse and disappeared into the trees. The rest of the posse followed, spreading out to keep Cruz from doubling back.

They caught up to him when he tripped and fell, a hundred yards into the woods. Cruz scrambled upright, but Sherm was good with a rope and hauled him down like a yearling calf.

"You know who I am?" Wyatt asked.

Cruz nodded, arms pinned by the lariat. *"Sí, señor."*

"Then you know why I'm here."

"Sí, señor, but I — I was just the lookout! I didn't know they was gonna shoot *su hermano."*

"Who? I want names."

Florentino glanced at Sherm McMasters. Hoping for sympathy, finding none. A moment later, the names poured out. Frank Stilwell. Pete Spence and Apache Hank came to mind first, of course, but Earp kept staring at him with those hard eyes, so Florentino kept going. Ike Clanton. Pony Diehl. Curly Bill Brocius. Johnny Ringo. Willie Claiborne. Johnny Barnes. Everybody. Anybody he could think of.

"Where are they now?" Earp asked.

"Stilwell and Hank and Ike, they went to Tucson. The others are up in the Whetstones, *señor.*" Cruz lifted his chin toward the mountain range across the valley. "They was headed for Iron Springs. That's what I heard them say, *quizás.* I don't know."

Earp seemed satisfied and Florentino relaxed a little, but he was already thinking that spring was nice in Sonora and how it might be a good time to visit his cousins in Mexico, as far away from Johnny Ringo as he could get.

"What'd my brother ever do to you?" Earp asked then.

He was frowning, but it looked like he was just puzzled and curious. So Florentino made his voice as *suave* as he could. "Nothing, *señor.* Your brother, he was a nice, good man — that's what I heard. But the others, they paid me twenty-five dollars to watch. Me, I needed *el dinero, señor.*"

"Twenty-five dollars," Earp repeated.

"Dead for a ducat," the skinny man at his side murmured.

"I just watched," Cruz reminded them, getting nervous again, looking from one hard

714

face to the other. "I'm sorry for your brother, *señor.* He never did nothing bad to me —"

Everybody back in the wood camp heard the fusillade, but they had work to do. At the end of the day, the foreman went out to look around. When he found the body, he had the boys wrap it in canvas and heave it on top of a load of logs, to be hauled into the city with the rest of a delivery.

"Another day, another inquest," people said in Tombstone.

"I examined the body of the Mexican named Florentino Cruz," Dr. George Good-fellow testified. "One shot entered the right temple, penetrating the brain. The second hit the right shoulder. A third hit the liver and made its exit to the right of the spine. A fourth struck the left thigh . . ."

When the enumeration was complete, the physician stated his opinion that the firing might have begun while Cruz was standing or running but had continued for some time after Cruz was on the ground.

"There was an absence of blood around some of the wounds," he said, "indicating that they were received after death."

Two for Morgan, Wyatt thought, leading the way toward Iron Springs. Eighty-one hours for Florentino Cruz.

STIR UP STRENGTH
TO BATTLE ON!

John Henry Holliday was counting as well.
Eighty-two hours. Eighty-three. Eighty-four.

He had been ill his entire adult life. He had
always worked indoors. Dental offices at first,
then saloons. Gambling was a desk job, really.
He had no more need to ride than an accountant or the clerk in a hardware store.
There had been horses in his youth, of
course, but he'd rarely had occasion to stay
in the saddle more than a morning, say, or a
long summer afternoon. He had never done
anything like this.

Nothing, ever, like this.

They were moving now through a landscape
as slovenly as a three-day beard, its unlovely
face covered with prickly stubble. The Whetstones were failed sandstone: an ancient
seabed that hadn't been under pressure long
enough to compact into something harder.
Uplifted, weathered over eons, broken now
into immense piles of rubble. It was evil ter-
rain. Difficult for the horse: like climbing over

a mountain of loose bricks. Difficult for the rider: constant adjustments, lying back against the cantle as the animal slid down the gullies, leaning over the horn as she scrambled over the next heap of stone. One slip, and there'd be cactus or a boulder to break the fall.

His legs were finished. He had no strength left to take up the shock of a trot, and the skin on the inside of his thighs was breaking down. But he was alive to feel the pain and the fatigue. With his cheesy lungs and broomstick legs, he had outlived Morgan Earp by almost four days.

He was working at the Alhambra when he heard the shots, but if you left the table every time you noticed gunfire, you'd never make a living. So he kept his eyes on the layout and continued to deal until John Meagher came over and said, "Morgan Earp's been killed." He stood and the whole world tilted. When his vision cleared, he was on his hands and knees, so close to the carpet of the gaming room that he could see individual grains of sand embedded in the filthy fibers, and he could hear someone howling.

Eighty-five. Eighty-six.

He leaned back in the saddle, trusting Duchess to pick her way down a gully and clamber up the other side. The two Jacks took turns watching out for him, which was kind, but he was careful not to fall behind and rehearsed what he'd say if Wyatt turned around and told him to quit.

Have I slowed you down?

Have I asked for help?

Have I uttered one word of complaint?

I will bear witness, he thought over and over. Morgan Earp was my friend, and I will see this through.

They made camp high in the mountains and got a few hours' rest. It wasn't enough. Grief, fever, sun, exhaustion. Despite himself, he was nearly asleep in the saddle when the shooting broke out.

Duchess shied and pivoted. He almost fell out of the saddle. Gripping the horn, he righted himself, frantically trying to work out where he was, where the others were, where the gunfire was coming from. Jack Johnson took hold of the big sorrel's reins, trying to control her.

Up ahead, Jack Vermillion's horse went down, pinning him to the ground. Dick Naylor was dancing and spinning as well, with Wyatt struggling for balance while Sherm McMasters — hat flying off, face stretched, eyes wide — raced toward them yelling, "Ambush! Take cover! Curly Bill is up ahead!"

It was a fluke, really. Not an ambush. The Whetstones were high desert. If you had stock to water, there were only a few places to do it. At the south end of the range, Cottonwood Springs was your best bet, so that's where Curly Bill Brocius had led seven men and nineteen freshly stolen head of cattle.

It was a meager return for the risk they'd run. These days the big ranchers were hiring gunmen to guard their herds. Rustling from the small operations was hardly worth the effort. Just that morning, Curly Bill had decided he was better off on Johnny Behan's payroll, collecting county taxes and getting a cut of the take. It wasn't as exciting as more conventional forms of theft, but Billy Breakenridge was congenial company and Curly Bill found it amusing to be a deputy.

"Somebody's coming," Johnny Barnes reported. "Five of 'em, maybe."

Ranch hands, hoping to get the cattle back, Bill thought, and he wasn't real concerned. In his experience, employees getting a dollar a day were rarely willing to die for a steer. "Move the stock," he told the three new boys, and they took off.

Bill himself and Johnny Barnes stayed low behind an embankment with Pink Truly and Al Arnold, watching the riders approach. "When they get close, blaze away," Bill said. "Make as much noise as you can. They'll run."

It wasn't until after the first barrage of gunfire that they realized who they were shooting at. Bill still wasn't worried. He'd heard that Wyatt Earp was on the warpath since his brother got killed. Bill's conscience was clear on that score, though he couldn't tell a lawman, "I was stealing stock the night your brother died."

The way Bill figured it, he'd just josh Wyatt some and then both sides would back off and go their separate ways.

"Well, hello, Wyatt!" he called. "Now, look at all of us! There's badges on every chest! I hear they're the latest thing in Paris this season."

"I'm not here to arrest you," Wyatt called.

"No? Well, maybe I'll arrest you! I hear there's warrants out for you boys, and I am a duly constituted deputy of the Cochise County sheriff's office. You come to surrender?"

Wyatt Earp was off his horse by then and advancing on them with a shotgun, not hurrying, just coming toward them, eyes steady.

Curly Bill heard Pink and Al splashing across the creek. He glanced back to see them scrambling up the other side of the bank and heading for their horses. Which left Bill all alone, except for Johnny Barnes. Barnes was gamer than most, but maybe he was just too scared to move.

Time slows down at moments like that, and Bill found himself remembering a tiger he'd seen when a circus came through Houston one time. The tiger was inside a barred wagon that was all painted up with jungle pictures on the outside. It was a little cage for such a big animal, but the tiger never stopped pacing. Two steps, turn. Two steps, turn. Two steps, turn. His head stayed steady as he moved, looking at you all the while, his animal thoughts plain in those yellow eyes. *These bars are all that stand between your belly and my rage.*

Except this time there were no bars.

Word filtered back to town. And soon there were half a dozen versions of what happened up in the Whetstones.

It was at Burleigh Springs. No, it was Iron Springs. Crystal Springs, I heard. Two men were killed. No, four. Curly Bill is dead. So are Johnny Barnes, Pink Truly, and Al Arnold.

No, it was four of Earp's men killed. Curly Bill shot Wyatt himself, square in the chest. No, it was Wyatt who shot Curly Bill. Damn near blew Bill in half with a shotgun blast.

Oh, hell, Curly Bill ain't even in the country. He's been living down in Mexico for months! Well, I heard ole Wyatt cut off Bill's head and brought it in to claim that thousand-dollar reward from the Cattleman's Association. Jesus! He cut off Bill's head? God's honest truth! I know a man who saw the body with his own eyes.

It would be months before the facts were

known. Curly Bill was buried on Frank Patterson's ranch later that day, his head still attached, along with Al and Pink. Johnny Barnes was seriously wounded and no one expected him to live. His name was added to Wyatt Earp's tally, but he survived to kill Butcher Bill Childs about a year later. He got caught and did a twenty-one-year stretch in the Missouri State Penitentiary for the deed.

At the time, however, Ike Clanton, Pete Spence, and Apache Hank Swilling were taking no more chances. Maybe Wyatt Earp was dead but if he wasn't, the risk of a trial seemed preferable to his revenge. They turned themselves in to the Cochise County Sheriff's Office. They were allowed to keep their guns so they could defend themselves, if Wyatt and his posse rushed the jail.

The Earp Vendetta Ride. That's what the newspapers were calling it now, one hundred and six hours after Morgan Earp was killed.

Few of those hours had been spent resting. As Wyatt and his men fell back toward a sheltered site with a high, broad view of the surroundings, no one was at his best.

Silent, Wyatt veered between embarrassment and outrage. He'd loosened his gun belt while they were working their way over that last mountain. After the first shots were fired, he dismounted but the belt slipped down around his knees and there he was, trying to pull the belt up while bullets whizzed around him and Dick Naylor squealed and plunged. Finally he got the belt up and got his shotgun from the scabbard and went after Curly Bill alone, furious that Sherm McMasters had abandoned him, that Doc was too sick to fight, and that Jack Johnson too busy taking care of the dentist to be any help.

Riding double behind Doc Holliday on Duchess now, Jack Vermillion was inconsolable about the horse that had been shot out from under him and kept vowing revenge for the animal's death. Sherm McMasters knew the others were thinking maybe he was playing both sides against the middle, that maybe he'd led them straight into a pack of Cow Boys. So he was loudly defending himself and kept talking about how he had no idea Curly Bill would be at the springs, and how his horse had panicked and run from the gunfire, and anyway it was crazy not to head for cover, and Jack Vermillion would've done the same damn thing if he hadn't been pinned under his horse.

Sherm kept it up while they were making camp, and Wyatt finally got hot, snarling abuse at Sherm for not sticking and at Creek Johnson, too, because he should've been up front, not playing nursemaid to Doc, who was coughing and didn't have the breath to holler, and pulled his pistol for the first time, and fired a shot into the ground to make them all shut up. Which they did.

"Wyatt, calm down," Doc said softly. "Where are you hit?"

It was only then that the others saw that Wyatt's duster was shredded. There were bullet holes everywhere they looked, and it seemed impossible that he was not shot to pieces. Astonished that he'd survived to berate them, they sat him down on a rock and pulled the coat off him to look for blood, and found none.

"My left leg feels strange down by the foot," he told them — quiet by then, almost dazed. So they pulled his boot off and his pants leg up and found nothing there, either. Almost two dozen bullets had come close enough to cut his clothes, but there wasn't a scratch on him.

"God a'mighty," Doc whispered. Fighting tears of relief and fatigue, he sank onto the rock next to Wyatt and showed them all what he had just noticed: The heel of Wyatt's boot had been shot off.

"Wyatt," he said, "Achilles himself would have envied your luck."

They were fugitives now, wanted for capital crimes in Pima and Cochise Counties. Their horses were stumbling. The food was gone. Everyone was wet and cold, for spring in the high desert can show you four seasons in a single day. A soft and pleasant breeze at dawn. Heat that threatens to bake you crisp before noon. A wave of cold that pours in from the north at midday, bringing hail and torrential rain in the afternoon. Snow at sunset.

Doc Holliday was close to collapse. The others weren't far from it, so they took a chance and stopped at the Percy brothers' ranch, which was big enough to attract rustlers but too small to support the kind of private army Henry Hooker paid to protect his cattle. The loss of even one steer was significant to them, and dead rustlers were unlikely to inspire much sympathy.

"I'm glad to see you alive," James Percy said. "We heard Curly Bill killed you."

"Other way around," Wyatt said. "Can you put us up for the night? I can't pay you."

"You're doing God's work," Hugh Percy said, but his brother James added, "Not everyone sees it that way. Behan has a forty-man looking for you. It's packed with Cow Boys wearing badges."

"Best if you leave before daylight," Hugh said.

"Can you lend us a horse? Jack Vermillion's animal was killed."

There was a long pause. The brothers looked at each other and then their eyes slid away.

"It's all right," Wyatt said. "I understand."

James, who was practical, took care of the

horses and fixed the men a hot meal. Hugh, who was tender-hearted, gave Doc Holliday his bed for the night. The dentist needed help undressing. When Hugh saw the state of those fleshless thighs and their huge burst blisters, he doctored them as best he could. Returning to the front room, Hugh said, "He's in real bad shape."

"I told him not to come," Wyatt snapped.

At three the next morning, he dragged Sherm and the two Jacks out of the Percy hayloft. They saddled up, but when Wyatt made no move to get Doc, Jack Vermillion went inside the Percy house to find him.

"I can't," Doc mumbled. "Leave me."

If you're caught, they'll hang you, Jack thought, but he'd gotten to know Doc since the big fire in Tombstone and understood the man's sense of honor. "If you're caught," Jack said, "the Percys will pay."

Doc held up a hand. Jack got him to his feet.

Later that day, a pair of prospectors noticed five men on four horses. The prospectors had been out in the mesquite so long, they had no idea who these visitors were, nor did they care. Posse? Outlaws? Either. Both. Didn't matter.

With the hospitality of the open range, they shared a frugal meal with the riders and took

special note of a sick man, who thanked them
for their kindness.

I WILL BE CALLED COWARD AND A MAN OF NO WORTH

The Cow Boys' first reaction to Frank Stilwell's death was not to ride out in search of retribution. There was a hell of a lot of liquor at Frank's saloon that needed to be disposed of first, so Johnny Behan knew where to find the posse he needed.

"I have warrants for the arrest of Wyatt Earp, Doc Holliday, Texas Jack Vermillion, Turkey Creek Jack Johnson, and Sherman McMasters," he announced.

The reaction to the last name was everything he expected.

McMasters is with them? That sonofabitch! I never trusted him!

I swear, there was always something about that bastard . . .

"These five men are wanted in Pima County for the murder of Frank Stilwell and in Cochise County for killing Florentino Cruz," Johnny continued. "There is now word of four more killings. Curly Bill Brocius. Johnny Barnes. Pink Truly. Al Arnold."

He waited again for the shouts and curses to slow before he said, "I am going after those responsible, and I am looking for deputies."

"Well, now," Johnny Ringo said, "you've come a long way to find them. Why didn't you get your men up in Tombstone, Sheriff?"

"The politics of the situation are complicated," Behan began.

Ringo's chuckle got tangled up with a cough. He tossed back a shot, cleared his throat, and said, "Politics, from the Latin. *Poly,* meaning 'many.' *Ticks,* meaning 'blood-sucking little bastards.' "

"Tombstone is for the Earps," Behan continued. "Wells Fargo is backing Wyatt. So are the mining interests and the Cattleman's Association. And I will get no help from Bob Paul. He holds a grudge against Precinct Twenty-seven." He paused to let the laughter die down. "But I hold warrants for the arrest of the Earp gang, and I will do my duty."

"Three cheers for Sheriff Behan," Ringo cried.

But if Ringo was drunk and amused, Behan himself was serious, and even the Cow Boys sobered at what he said next. "What happened to Virgil and Morgan Earp was criminal. What happened to Frank Stilwell and Florentino Cruz was *barbaric.* I need men who'll stick in a fight with vicious killers. The job pays five dollars a day. Who's with me?"

John Ringo was the first on his feet. Swaying slightly, smiling through the chest pain.
The worst man in a room full of villains and
happy to prove it.

"Swear me in," he cried with a kind of
heedless joy, for he knew precisely what he
was facing if he lived much longer. "Swear us
all in, Sheriff!"

Mountains, ravines, desert, scrub, stone,
cactus. Bad weather, worse food. Days in the
saddle, nights on the ground. By early April,
the Behan posse had traced the Earp party to
Summit Station. Fearing that the fugitives
had boarded a passing train and escaped,
Sheriff Behan questioned the depot agent,
who became exceedingly cooperative while
glancing repeatedly at Johnny Ringo and the
dregs of the Cow Boys who now rode with
him.

"No, sir, they didn't get on the train," the
agent said. "They passed through here, but
they were headed for Henry Hooker's spread.
One of them's sick, and their mounts are in
bad shape. You can catch 'em if you hurry."

Johnny Behan closed his eyes and tried to
think. He was nearing forty. City life had
softened him. His men were saddle-hardened
and many of them were young, but they, too,
were whipped.

"Take care of the horses," he told them.
"Get a meal at the station café. We'll rest here

overnight."

Sinking into a café chair, John Harris Behan put his elbows on the table and his face in his hands, looking up only to order coffee and beef stew. If anyone had asked what was going through his mind, Johnny would have told the plain truth. He was sitting there, wishing — truly, sincerely, fervently wishing — that the governor had appointed Wyatt Earp sheriff last year.

The irony was not lost on him. He had, after all, cajoled and maneuvered, brokered deals and worked hard to get where he was today: bone-weary and long past filthy. Frustrated, angry, and powerless. Even if he brought the Earp riders in, what good would it do? The Arizona justice system was corrupt, top to bottom, and all but impotent. Between allies and alibis, nobody was ever convicted of a serious crime.

A shadow fell over the table in front of him. He expected to see the cook delivering the stew, but it was Johnny Ringo.

"Now what?" Behan asked.

Almost shivering with delight, Ringo dropped a copy of the *Epitaph* in front of the sheriff. "Looks like a couple of the boys in Charleston have been busy."

God, but Ringo was strange. He was always drunk when he was in town, but he'd remained stone-sober during this ride, relishing the sheer preposterous absurdity of murderers chasing after murderers, and every damn one of them wearing a badge.

"Read the letter to the editor, too," Ringo urged. "You'll love that."

"Oh, Christ," Johnny whispered, seeing the headline.

Two men had walked into the office of the Tombstone Mill and Mining Company, announced that they were avenging Curly Bill, and shot Judge Bryant Peel's son through the heart. One of the assailants was killed in a shoot-out later that day. So was Deputy John Gillespie. Deputies Jack Young and Billy Breakenridge were wounded as well. The second killer, Zwing Hunt, had been taken into custody.

Stunned by the news, Johnny Behan tried to tally the dead. Ten men killed in the past ten days? And the letter to the editor was even more numbing, for it was from the murder victim's father — Judge Peel himself — and it was an open endorsement of vigilantism.

Perhaps I am not in a condition to express a clear, deliberate opinion, but I would say to the good citizens of Cochise County that there are cutthroats among you whom you will never convict in court. You must choose: Either combine to protect yourselves and wipe them out, or give the country up to them and be murdered one at a time. Expect no help from the Sheriff of this county, who has long shown himself a friend of the outlaws, and who is even now riding in their company, having legitimized their crimes with badges.

Ten men dead, and who did the judge single out for condemnation? Not his son's killers and certainly not Wyatt Earp, whose personal vendetta made a mockery of the badge he wore while leaving bullet-riddled bodies strewn across the territory. Oh, no. Not them! John Behan was to blame.

It was enough to drive a man to despair.

Rockefeller, Carnegie, Astor, Fisk, Gould, Mellon, Schwab, Vanderbilt, Hearst, Armour. Robber barons. That's what their enemies called men like Henry Hooker. Industrialists, they called themselves. Self-made men who scaled up operations, pushed down wages, undercut the competition, and amassed unprecedented fortunes by imposing order and stability on the chaotic free markets in oil, steel, banking, shipping, railroads, mining, and meatpacking.

Deeply religious, many of them. Frugal, hardworking men who saw in their success and prosperity evidence that they were among God's elect. Protestants, Johnny Behan noted, to a man.

When the Cochise County posse arrived at Henry Hooker's door, they'd already been on his land for two long days. The Sierra Bonita Ranch was nearly the size of Luxembourg: eight hundred square miles of fine grassland, straddling two vast Arizona counties. A fortified adobe castle sat in the shadow of Mount Graham, where rivers and creeks converged. Half a dozen barracks dotted the perimeter of the ranch, shelter for men paid to protect Hooker's property from anyone — red, brown, or white — who attempted to steal from their employer.

Long aware of the posse's approach, Henry Clay Hooker now waited on his veranda for their arrival. Compact, still strongly built at fifty-four, he wore a full but neatly trimmed gray beard that put you in mind of Ulysses Grant. And if you were wise, Johnny Behan reminded himself, you'd remember that General Grant, too, was a small and unimpressive man who was nonetheless a formidable opponent.

"Mr. Hooker," he began, without dismounting, "we have tracked a party of fugitives to your land. I have warrants for the arrest of Wyatt Earp, John Holliday, Sherman McMasters —"

Hooker did not descend the stairs, remaining eye level with the filthy, unshaven sheriff of Cochise County. "You're out of your jurisdiction, Behan. This is Graham County, not Cochise. Your warrants are no good here."

"Are those men on your land, sir?"

"I don't know," Hooker lied comfortably. "And if I did, I sure as hell wouldn't tell you."

"Mr. Hooker, the men I'm chasing are outlaws —"

"I know Wyatt Earp, Behan. If he's an outlaw, then damn the laws. Damn you. And damn your posse."

He was staring at Ringo when he said that. Ringo stared back, eyes glittering when he muttered, "Arrogant sonofabitch."

That was when Hooker's foreman showed himself and the Winchester rifle he had aimed at Ringo's chest. "It's bad manners to ride into a gentleman's yard and call him names," the foreman said. "More talk like that, and you won't need to find Wyatt Earp to get a fight. You can get one here, right now."

As the foreman spoke, the rest of Hooker's men were emerging from the barn, the bunkhouse, the cookhouse, the blacksmith's shop, the dairy.

"A nice bunch of fellas you ride with, Sheriff," Hooker remarked when the odds were visibly even. "Deputy Cutthroat. Deputy Horse Thief. Deputy Drunkard."

Johnny Behan took off his hat, wiped his face with his neckerchief, and stared at the mountains beyond the ranch house. He thought about saying, "I'm only doing my job." He considered asking, "Who else could I get for this posse?" If he was to have any future in Cochise County, he would have to swing public opinion again, to convince people that the Earp rampage was not a lawman's noble crusade against criminals who would never be brought to justice any other way. But on April 14, 1882, it came down to this: He was just too damn tired to argue with Henry Hooker.

"We need a meal and rest for ourselves and our horses, sir. Will you do me that courtesy?" he asked.

"Of course," Hooker said coolly. "You can even come inside. Your posse can eat in the barn with the other animals."

Later that year, Johnny Behan would make one last halfhearted attempt to arrest Wyatt Earp, but as he sat down at Henry Hooker's table, he already suspected there was no point. And he was right.

In the autumn of '82, he would be denied his party's nomination for sheriff of Cochise County. He would never win another election, but in years to come, governors and presidents would appoint him to a variety of offices. Before dying of syphilis in 1912, John Harris Behan would live a long and useful life of public service in places as far flung as Tampa, Florida, and Peking, China.

Even so, his reputation would never fully recover from his years in Tombstone. He would always be remembered as the man who

was bested — in love and war — by Wyatt
Earp.

■ ■ ■ ■

THIS IS THE POISON
OF DEEP GRIEF

■ ■ ■ ■

Come Back from the Battle and the Dread Affray

Elizabeth Hooker and her daughter-in-law Forrestine were used to saddle-weary visitors, and their hospitality was renowned throughout the territory. When the Earp party arrived at Sierra Bonita, they were all in bad shape, but one man was barely conscious. Indeed, if Jack Vermillion hadn't been there to lean on during those last few hours of riding, John Henry Holliday would have quietly slipped off Duchess and made a sincere attempt to die in the darkness.

While Forrestine oversaw meals for the men who were still on their feet, her tubby little mother-in-law took the sick man in hand, supplying a warm bath, fresh dressings for the sores on his legs, and a soft, clean bed. Twenty hours later, when Doc awoke at last, the little boy who'd been told to watch over him scrambled up and ran for his grandmother. Presently, the lady herself appeared in the bedroom door.

With reflexive courtesy, Doc tried to get up.

"Don't be silly," Mrs. Hooker said. "We don't stand on ceremony here, and you shouldn't try to stand at all."

"Where's Wyatt?" he croaked.

"They're all up on that ridge." She opened the curtains to show him Mount Graham, which was covered in wildflowers and glowing in the late afternoon light. "I expect they'll be down in time for supper. You missed the excitement! The sheriff was here looking for you," she told him, tidying the room. "My Henry was all for shooting it out with Behan and his cronies, but Wyatt didn't want us mixed up with his troubles. He took his boys up the mountain last night. Henry and our hands ran Behan off."

She stopped bustling and looked at him appraisingly. "Do you need help with the chamber pot?" He blinked. She laughed. "Like I said, son: We don't stand on ceremony here. And I've doctored a lot of boys."

"I can manage on my own," he whispered, "but you are very kind to offer."

"Well, then, I'll leave you to it. I've got a roast going for Wyatt and the others, but I think you're better off with something less challenging. How do you like your eggs?"

"Over easy. Thank you, ma'am. If it's not too much trouble."

"No trouble at all! I'll be back in a few

minutes with your meal."

He ate, and slept some more, and woke the next morning to the sound of voices he recognized. Wyatt, Sherm, and the Jacks were down off the mountain. And was that Big Dan Tipton? Yes, and Charlie Smith.

Allies from Tombstone. Morgan's friends.

Listening, he noticed a pile of clothing that had been cleaned, mended, and ironed while he slept. He briefly considered getting up, but the conversation in the next room was staccato and decisive. Far more than he felt ready for. He closed his eyes and did not open them again until the door hinges creaked.

"We're leaving in twenty minutes," Wyatt had just told the others.

"What about Doc?" Creek Johnson asked.

"He's not coming."

Before they could argue, Wyatt turned and went down the hall to the room where Mrs. Hooker had Doc. He eased the latch open, trying not to wake the dentist, and was counting off twenties when he heard Doc ask, "What in hell are you doin'?"

"We're leaving. It's five dollars a day for riding with the posse. You're out of pocket for your expenses, and —"

Doc sat up, bony chest pale in the daylight, those stick arms propping him up like tent stakes. "You're goin' to *pay* me?"

"Well, yeah. You lost income taking care of my brothers, and you need a stake to get started again in Denver, so —"

"So you were goin' to put cash on the bureau and leave me lyin' here, like some wretched woman you're done with."

Wyatt frowned and shook his head. Doc could be so strange. His mind just worked different, and you could never figure what was going to crank him up.

"You're as broke as I am, Wyatt. Where'd you get all that cash?"

"That's none of your —"

"Where did you get it?"

"Dan Tipton brought it."

"Damn you!" the dentist cried. "Where did *he* get it, then?"

"Wells Fargo. E. B. Gage. Richard Gird."

"And what — precisely — are they payin' for?"

Doc was pulling on his trousers now, easing them over the bandages. Wyatt tried not to see the muscles, thin as rope, that ran along the bones.

"Doc," he said, explaining as patiently as he could, "not one Cow Boy has ever been convicted of anything. Not even the judges believe any of them will ever go to jail. All the decent people in Cochise County want me to finish this. They want those outlaws wiped out —"

Doc was sitting still now. Slate-blue eyes in

a skull-white face. "So that's your plan. Deliver us from all evil."

"There are still killers out there, Doc!"

"There are killers right in this room."

"I've got backing from the governor on down. The president, even. Mr. Gage says there'll be pardons when it's over and —"

"And you *believed* him," Doc said, sounding like Mattie when she was amazed by how dumb Wyatt was being. "Wyatt," he warned, "if you take that money, you're bought. Take that money, and you're nothing but a hired killer. There won't be any pardon at the end. You'll do what the politicians and the businessmen want, and when you're finished, they will sell you down the river like a troublesome field hand."

He wanted to leave. He wanted to be outside, on his horse. Moving. Not talking, not hearing.

"Wyatt, I am beggin' you in Morgan's memory! Don't do this. I know what you've lost. I loved him, too. I can hardly bear to think of this miserable world without Morgan in it. What you've already done, that was vengeance. But *this* — This is *commerce*. Wyatt, they are paying for your soul!"

Too many words. Always. Too many words. And Doc was crying now.

"I don't have time for this," Wyatt muttered, tossing the cash on the bureau.

"All right then, go!" the dentist cried. "Go,

and be damned to you. Go, and take that blood money with you!"

"Mount up," Wyatt told the others. "We're leaving."

"What about Doc?" Creek Johnson asked again.

Wyatt picked up his saddlebags. "I didn't want him to come in the first place. I told him it would be too hard."

Creek frowned. "You mean, leave him here?"

"Hooker'll get him to Colorado."

"Wyatt," Jack Vermillion said, "Doc damn near killed himself for you."

"Not for me," Wyatt snapped. "For Morgan."

"Well, hell! That's why we're all here, isn't it?" Danny Tipton asked. "For Morgan, right?" It was an innocent question, but no one would meet his eyes or speak to him. Confused, Dan looked from face to face. "We're all here for Morgan, ain't we?"

It was John Henry Holliday who answered. Standing in the doorway. Half-dressed and haggard. His eyes reddened by fresh grief. "Tell them, Wyatt. Tell them why *you* think we're here."

They listened, and then they argued. Nobody believed in the promised pardons. Nobody was willing to leave Doc behind either, for you could see death in him now, not just illness. They wanted to get him to the Colorado mountains, where he'd have some kind of chance.

"Let things settle down, Wyatt," Jack Vermillion said. "You can come back for the rest of them later, if that's what you need to do. And I'll come with you. But let's get out of Arizona and lay low for now."

He would remember how it felt: like a fire went out. Like he'd burned so hot for so long, there was nothing left inside him but cold, dead ash.

Watching his face, Doc murmured something in a foreign language before saying it in English. "Enough. Done is done. No man can rage forever."

"All right," Wyatt said, not caring anymore. "All right. We'll go."

Henry Hooker provided an escort across his land and a buckboard so Doc didn't have to ride any farther. When they crossed the New Mexico line, they rested for a time in a border town, then moved on to a railroad depot where Doc could catch a train to Denver.

Creek Johnson made sure Doc's fare was paid and settled the dentist into a second-class car. Jack Vermillion arranged for a conductor to keep an eye on the sick man until he got where he was going.

Wyatt didn't even offer his hand in farewell. He wasn't sure Doc would take it.

747

My Pride and Glory Die, But the Life That's Left Me Will Be Long

For 159 days, newspapermen around the nation and around the world had blessed the name of Earp. Opinions about the events in Arizona had divided predictably along political lines. The Earps were stage robbers, thugs, and murderers; Doc Holliday was worse than any of them, a quarrelsome drunk and a killer. Or, the Earps were incorruptible lawmen; Doc Holliday was their loyal friend, a gentleman, and a scholar. There was a reliable market for either version, and editorials were easy to write. Law and order. Crime and punishment. That kind of thing. Interest lagged a bit after Judge Spicer exonerated the Earps, but it picked right up when Virgil Earp was attacked. After Morgan Earp was gunned down, the Wyatt Earp Vendetta Ride riveted readers and sold out multiple editions, until Bob Ford assassinated Jesse James.

A fickle public's taste for "frontier justice" abruptly waned. Editors everywhere scrambled for a new topic. It came as a relief when a large contingent of Apaches broke out of the San Carlos reservation. Before the U.S. Army caught up with them, the renegades had killed almost as many men as the Earps and Cow Boys combined, which made for exciting headlines about red savages and warpaths. Among their victims was Zwing Hunt, one of the Cow Boys who murdered Judge Peel's son. Zwing had taken a bullet in the chest when the deputies came to arrest him for that, but escaped the noose by fleeing the Tombstone hospital when he was partially healed up. Ironic, then, that ole Zwing had leapt from the judicial pot into an Apache fire.

Too ironic, for some. Too neat. Zwing wasn't killed by Indians, they said, but by Wyatt Earp. The vendetta was still on, they said. Wyatt was still out there in the mesquite, avenging the deaths of the righteous.

Counterrumors were swiftly offered. Earp and his posse were hiding in Colorado. Doc Holliday had died of consumption. Sherm McMasters was killed when the Cow Boys found out he was a snitch. Texas Jack Vermillion and Turkey Creek Jack Johnson were in jail up in Prescott. Wyatt had been dead since March — everybody knew that. He'd been killed back in the Whetstones by Curly Bill, who was hiding out in Mexico.

Two months after Morgan Earp died, a second great fire broke out in Tombstone.

Among the businesses destroyed were the O.K. Corral, Molly Fly's boardinghouse and her husband's photography studio. The site of the town's most notorious event was now indistinguishable in a field of embers and rubble, which prompted a brief flare of optimism. "The lawless past is behind us," people said. "We'll rebuild, better than ever!" But flooding in the mines was getting worse, and it was even harder to keep capital and labor in town.

Everyone pretty much forgot about Wyatt Earp, until Johnny Ringo's body was found.

The men he'd been traveling with simply left him in the desert. Waited until he was asleep. Took his horse, took the water, and took off. They were tired of the ugly cough. They were tired of the insults, the sneering. They were tired of *him.*

A small part of Johnny Ringo still remembered that it was wrong to degrade another person, but that had always been the thrill of it. Saying and doing whatever he pleased. For years, he had waited for someone — anyone — to have the guts to call him on it. It never occurred to him that they might just walk away.

What did he say last night . . . ? "You idiots are the kind of Irishmen who make a man wish Cromwell had done a better job." He didn't even think those two thick micks got the joke.

Evidently they had.

So they left in the dark. Cowards.

From the start, the headache was awful, and it got worse as the sun rose higher. Just a hangover, he told himself, but it was a bad one. His tongue felt like flannel, and his mouth tasted of sand. Squinting into the sun, he started up a slope, hoping higher ground would provide a glimpse of green that would signal a stream or a spring somewhere nearby. He had to use his hands to pull himself up the steeper parts. Halfway up, he stopped, open-mouthed, laboring for breath in the mid-July heat.

Lunger. Pathetic lunger.

"A gun is your *life* out here." That's what Martin Ringo had said moments before he provided his fourteen-year-old son with a memorable lesson in absurdity. They were on their way to California. Martin was sitting next to the Conestoga, cleaning his shotgun. "A gun is food. A gun is protection. Take care of your gun, Johnny, and it will take care of you."

What Martin Ringo didn't say was "Always check to see if the weapon is loaded." Especially if you've got a decaying chest and an uncontrollable cough.

One moment, he was talking to his son, and the next, that son was watching the top of his father's head fly into the air. Blood and brains and bone came down like rain and hail, all over the boy's upturned face.

Martin Ringo. Dead. Just like that. Buried at the side of the trail in the middle of nowhere. Left behind to rot alone, like he'd never existed.

So much for California. So much for the curative sunshine of the Southwest.

Why did the family keep going? Why didn't they go back to Missouri?

He could hear his mother saying, *Your brother's sick, too. You have to take care of him and me and your sisters now.* I'm not a mule, he told her in his mind. Don't hitch me up to pull your wagon. "None of my affair," he muttered, but his voice was almost gone.

He was climbing again. Struggling upward, grabbing at bigger rocks. Look for green, he told himself. Green means water.

Jesus, how long can it take to get to the top of this goddam slope?

Hours. Forever. He was losing track of time. The world was nothing more than the gravel beneath his eyeballs and the pounding headache behind them. It was branches clawing at him, ripping his clothes, his skin. It was cactus, blocking his way, making him backtrack and circle. Chollas — vicious things, their spikes jumping out to jam themselves into your hands and face.

Crown of thorns, his mother whispered.

"Go to hell!" he screamed, weeping now,

752

dry-eyed. Dry dry dry.

Just a swallow of water. He'd praise Jesus for a swallow of water.

Goddam boots. New. Meant for riding. Bad enough to be on foot without new boots rubbing blisters. He sat and pulled them off. Grunting with the effort. Hurling them away.

His mother stared at the bloody sock. *Well, now, that's ruined. After all the work I put into it.*

"Go to hell," he croaked. "Nobody asked you for the goddam sock."

His gun belt kept snagging on things. *Your gun is your life.* But it was so goddam heavy. And he couldn't breathe. It was too hot to breathe.

Lunger. Pathetic lunger. Die and be done with it, why don't you?

Sunshine won't help. Rest won't help. Nothing's gonna help you, lunger. The pain'll get worse, and worse, and worse. Until you die. Pull the trigger, you coward. Do it.

Pull the trigger, he told himself, and this'll be over.

Just like . . . *that.*

John Yost saw the buzzards the next day and went to investigate. He found the corpse near a clump of oak trees, maybe twenty yards from the ranch track. There was a pistol next to one hand. The feet were wrapped in a torn-up shirt. One of the cartridge belts was buckled on upside down. That was odd, but thirst will do strange things to a man. Crows had finished with the eyes and were tearing the scalp around the bloody hole in the top of the head, but Yost knew who it was. He buried the body where it lay and reported the death next time he went to town.

Yet another Cochise County inquest was convened to take Mr. Yost's statement in the matter of the death of John Ringo. The dead man's effects were listed. A small amount of tobacco and a pipe; a silver pocket watch, silver chain attached; a comb; matches; two dollars and sixty cents in cash; two cartridge belts, one each for pistol and rifle ammunition. A .45-caliber Colt revolver, Model 1876, containing five cartridges, one of them spent.

"Suicide, most likely," the coroner's jurors decided. "Ringo always was a crazy sonofabitch."

Nobody who really knew Ringo disputed that conclusion, but in the saloons of Arizona, common wisdom begged to differ. Wyatt Earp came back and got him, that's what people said. Ole Wyatt shot Ringo in the head. Then he put the pistol in Ringo's hand to make it look like Ringo did the deed his own self.

For years afterward, whenever a Cow Boy died, the rumors about Wyatt would start up again. Of course, rustlers lived dangerous professional lives, and their leisure hours often involved drunkenness and discord. As John Henry Holliday had once observed, such men were rarely inclined to express dismay or disagreement with a well-turned phrase. They didn't need Wyatt Earp to hurl them into eternity. They generally managed that on their own.

Even so, for the rest of his long life, the questions remained the same. What really happened down there in Tombstone? Did you get Curly Bill? What about Johnny Ringo? Why did you let Ike Clanton live? You're the one who got him down in Mexico, aren't you! What was Doc Holliday really like? I heard he called you a Jew boy. Is that why you two parted on bad terms? How many men did you shoot? Nine? Thirteen? Thirty? The truth was never good enough. He might say something like "Doc was a real good dentist," but the newspaper would print foolishness: "Doc Holliday was the most skillful gambler and the nerviest, fastest, deadliest man with a six-gun I ever saw."

Once, he got so tired of a reporter's badgering, he said, "Yeah. I killed Curly Bill and Ringo and Ike. I killed 'em all, and two dozen more." He was being sarcastic, but that was the only time a newspaperman took him at his word.

Virgil and James stayed in Colton with their parents after Morgan was buried. Wyatt knew his mother worried about him and wanted him to come home, too.

He could not bear the thought of her grief. He could not face his father's scorn. *Worthless pile of shit. Thirty-four years old, and not a damn thing to show for it. I knew you'd never amount to anything.*

So he moved, and kept on moving. Gunnison. Silver City. Albuquerque. Back to Dodge for a while. Assassination was a constant threat. Some idiot wanting to avenge Curly Bill. Some stupid kid wanting to get famous for shooting a man whose name had been in the papers.

He got so he hated to be approached by strangers, even polite ones, and that hatred never left him. When he was an old man, they'd say, "It's an honor to meet you, Mr. Earp," or something ordinary like that. Then they'd back away from the hard blue eyes that told them exactly what the elderly Mr. Earp was thinking.

You just want to shake the hand of a killer.

You want to use me to make yourself feel brave.

For a long time, the smallest thing could set him off. He'd catch sight of himself in a window, think it was Morgan, and grief would tear his chest open. He'd notice a shirt the color of Ike Clanton's or hear laughter that reminded him of Curly Bill's. The rage would explode again, all but impossible to control.

He feared what he might do. Cry, maybe. Or kill someone.

He began to drink again.

Jesus did not save him this time. It was a chance remark, just something he overheard one morning. He was hungover, standing midway between a bar and a café in some little town, trying to decide which would make him feel less bad: strong coffee or a morning shot of rye. Two ladies passed by, giving wide berth to the gaunt, unshaven saddle bum he'd become. He overheard only a few words: "My sister's living in San Francisco."

San Francisco.

So much had happened. So much time had passed. He had no reason to believe that Josie was waiting for him. She was probably married now, a beautiful girl like that.

He was mean to her after Virg was almost killed. He felt more remorse about that than about anything he'd done since. He wanted to tell her that he was sorry for being so mean, but with Morgan gone, there wasn't anyone to write letters for him. You could just say the message to a Western Union clerk, but you needed an address. All he knew was that her family was in San Francisco.

It was someplace to go. It was a direction.

She'd probably tell him to go to hell, but even that was a destination.

He sold Dick Naylor to a gangly stable boy who admired the horse and promised not to hit him. The kid was all excited about the notion of racing Dick in quarter-mile contests and had $7.15 saved up. The transaction yielded a five-dollar profit on the $2.15 Wyatt had paid for the horse back in Dodge.

Which made Dick Naylor just about the only investment that had ever paid off for Wyatt Earp.

He sold his saddle, too, and cleared enough for train fare to San Francisco with a little left over for a room above a bar near the depot. He went to a barber and got himself cleaned up. Then he started visiting banks, asking the managers, "Do you know a banker named Marcus?"

The city was bigger than he'd expected, with a lot more banks. He was all but broke and about to give up when he was told, "Well, sir, I know a Henry Marcus, but he's a baker, not a banker."

No, he thought, that must be a different man. Then, suddenly, it all made sense. How good she was in the kitchen. The cakes and crullers and cream puffs. The doughnuts and cookies.

He got directions to the Marcus bakery. It

wasn't far. He only meant to peek in the window. He figured he'd come back in the morning with a fresh shave and a clean shirt so he'd look more respectable when he went inside to ask Mr. Marcus if he had a daughter named Josephine.

Then he saw Higgs, asleep in the pale San Francisco sun, out in front of the store. He went down on one knee to pat the dog, who woke up and jumped on him and licked his face, wriggling and whining with joy, the way dogs do when they recognize someone who's been missing for an hour, or a day. Or a couple of years.

"Well, well," he heard Josie say. "Hello, stranger."

She was standing in the doorway wearing an apron, her springy hair bundled into a kerchief. Not a girl anymore. Filled out more.

Still kneeling by the dog, he didn't know what to say except "I'm sorry."

"Good," she said, and he could see she was still pretty mad at him.

Behind her, a fat little man in his fifties flipped the bakery's sign from OPEN to CLOSED. Upstairs, a stocky older woman with a German accent was hollering from a second-floor window: "Come up already! It's almost Shabbos!"

"My parents," Josie said.

Her father stepped out and her mother trundled down the stairs to stand at their daughter's side. Wyatt pulled off his hat and bore their scrutiny wordlessly.

"That him, Sadie?" her father asked.

Sadie. Her secret name. The name you called her if you loved her.

"Yes, Papa," she answered, eyes steady on Wyatt's. "That's him."

"So, Mr. Wyatt Earp," her mother said judiciously, "are you a Christian?"

"Mutti!" Josie cried.

"I'm just asking!" her mother said with a shrug.

"It's all right," Wyatt said. "I was, ma'am. Not anymore."

This information was taken in and considered.

"You're too thin," Mrs. Marcus informed him. "Come upstairs for supper."

Josie's sister, Hattie, arrived just before sunset with her husband, Emil. Their baby, Edna, was passed around and cooed over. "Look at this child!" Mr. Marcus cried. "Soft and sweet as challah!"

Wyatt was introduced. Eyebrows rose, for his name and reputation were known to them. Even so, they welcomed him and no one remarked upon the presence of a notorious vigilante at the table.

Josie's brother, Nathan, got there last, just before the wineglasses were filled. "Count on Nate to be on time for the booze," Hattie said dryly, and you could see that Nathan was a drinker, but Wyatt was in no position to feel superior about that. Or anything else.

There were candles and foreign prayers. There was bickering and joshing. There was a loaf of braided bread — soft and sweet as a baby girl. Brisket. Roasted carrots and parsnips. Potatoes in some kind of pudding. It was the first good meal he'd had in almost three years, and every time the surface of his plate began to show between the piles of food, Mrs. Marcus would reach over and add another serving.

"Eat!" she'd say. "You're too thin! Eat!"

For dessert, there were lemon tarts and sponge cake and molasses cookies.

"Mr. Earp, you sure you don't want a little something more?" Mrs. Marcus asked.

"Ma'am," he said, "I couldn't eat another bite," but he was looking at Josie — at Sadie — when he said that. And he was thinking, Yes. Yes, I do. I want more.

The baby got fussy. Emil said, "Ah! It must be time for the Exodus!"

Wyatt thought that was pretty clever, but everybody else had heard the joke before and rolled their eyes. There was a flurry of kisses and hugs, more doting over the baby, and good-byes. Wyatt had moved toward the door with the others, but he lingered a few moments longer, until he and Josie were alone.

"Suppose . . ." he began. "Suppose we went

for a walk with Higgs."

"Oh, Wyatt." She sighed. "I thought you'd never ask."

The dog ran ahead. They watched him sniff, and mark corners, and briefly chase a rat, circling back to check on them before ambling off to explore a pile of garbage. They didn't speak at first. They just strolled side by side through tatters of fog that occasionally broke apart, letting moonlight through to the street.

"You read about it, I guess," Wyatt said finally. "In the papers."

"I didn't believe any of it. Newspapers always lie."

He turned so she could see his face, for he wanted no misunderstanding between them. "I am not a good man. I wanted to be. I wanted to be better than — Better than I turned out to be. I have done things . . ." He looked away but made himself say it plainly. "I have taken lives. Some of them deserved it, but . . . maybe not all of them."

She waited. He said no more, and they began to walk again.

"I got rid of a baby," she told him.

He stopped and looked at her, startled.

She met his eyes. "It wasn't Johnny's. It was later. When I was working."

"I don't want children," he said. "It has to stop with me."

The anger. The violence.

They walked again, and she took his hand.

"I was wondering," he said after a time. "I was wondering if I could call you Sadie."

I love you, he meant. I always have.

WHO IN FUTURE WILL SPEAK WELL OF YOU?

If you want a story book ending, stop — now — and remember them in that tender moment. Be content to know that they embarked on a series of adventures throughout the West and that they stayed together through thick and thin for forty-five years.

But know this as well: If their story ended here, no one would remember them at all.

Where a tale begins and where it ends *matters.* Who tells the story, and why . . . That makes all the difference.

WALKING IN RUIN'S TRAIL

PILE UP YOUR RICHES AND YOUR LUXURY

The truth? He was damaged. She was difficult. Tombstone would dog them wherever they went, no matter what new dream they chased.

Silver, gold, real estate, oil, gas. Another boom, another bust. There was always another place to try their luck, but even when things were going well, Wyatt could get restless and irritable. Drinking more, talking less.

She'd ask, "What's wrong?"

"Nothing," he'd snap.

Maybe he'd run into somebody from the old days who wanted to talk about Arizona. Maybe a reporter from the local newspaper had come at him with a notebook and pencil, asking a bunch of questions about the gunfight. Soon — a week or month later — he'd be lying on his back, staring at the ceiling or the stars.

"Suppose . . ." he'd begin. "Suppose we try Utah next."

Or Idaho, or Colorado, or Texas.
And they'd move on.

Just once in their travels, it was Sadie who ran into an old friend. They were passing through Leadville and had stayed overnight in a modest hotel. In the morning, Wyatt walked right past an elderly gentleman sitting in the corner of the lobby, but Sadie thought there was something familiar about him and turned back to take a second look. Intent on going to the front desk to pay their bill, Wyatt didn't realize she'd left his side until he heard Sadie call, "Wyatt! Look who's here!"

"Doc?" Wyatt said, coming closer. "Is that you?"

"What's left . . . of me. Still on the sunny . . . side of the grass."

The crooked smile was the same as always. The hollow-eyed, fleshless face looked like a Mexican death's-head with a neatly trimmed mustache.

John Henry Holliday was thirty-five. He looked sixty.

Wyatt offered his hand. Doc would not take it. Before Wyatt could bristle, he explained, "Forgive me. I must keep my distance. We know now. The disease is contagious." He paused, breathless, chest laboring. "I am pleased," he continued, "to see you are both well." He looked away. A long, wordless stare. "I never meant to harm anyone," he whis-

768

pered, but his voice was stronger when he asked, "Miss Louisa?"

"She's got bad rheumatism," Wyatt told him, "but she's getting married again. Fella name of Peters. Kate?"

"Well. Last I heard. We have not spoken in some time. My fault." That crooked smile again. "I don't believe I shall mind bein' dead. Gettin' there has been a trial." He sat a while, catching his breath. "I heard that Mattie Blaylock is gone."

"Laudanum," Wyatt said.

"Poor soul," Doc murmured.

"Virgil is doing well," Sadie told him, changing the subject. She never liked to think about Mattie. "Allie is fine, too. So is James."

"Bessie's dead," Wyatt said.

"It wasn't tuberculosis," Sadie said quickly. "She had tumors."

"So I recall. Please, give James my condolences." Looking at Wyatt, Doc asked, "You ever go back to Arizona?"

Wyatt shook his head. You were right about the pardons, he meant. They cut me loose.

"I was arrested," Doc told him without rancor. "Colorado tried to extradite me. Bat Masterson pulled some strings. He was very kind. I would not have thought it of him. But he was very kind."

Wyatt glanced at the lobby clock. "I'm sorry, Doc. We got a train to catch."

"Of course," Doc said. "I am going up to

Glenwood, myself. The sulfur springs are believed helpful for my condition."

Sadie stood, leaning over to kiss him on both thin cheeks before he could protest or pull away. "Well, now. Aren't you the sweetest thing!" he said, with something of his old charm. "Take good care of each other, y'hear?"

Wyatt offered his hand again. This time Doc took it.

Even then, a few months before he died, his grip was surprisingly strong.

They moved on, and kept on moving.

Emil and Hattie backed a series of saloons and hotels in mining towns, but Wyatt's big break came when he heard that the Santa Fe Railway was about to begin service from Los Angeles to San Diego.

"Suppose . . ." he said. "Suppose we try California?"

Sadie liked the idea of living on the coast again. Wyatt had built up enough capital to look his father in the eye. So they moved to San Diego, and for once in his life, Wyatt Earp got into something big right from the start. When the rumored railway arrived, the town exploded, filling up with entrepreneurs and shipping magnates, lawyers and bankers, thugs and criminals, musicians and writers, gamblers and whores.

San Diego never slept in the heedless, restless years that would be remembered as the Gay Nineties. There was ragtime in the dance halls, vaudeville in the theaters, band concerts every night. Everywhere you looked, something exciting was happening.

Wyatt Earp *rode* that town, thriving on the action and distraction. With forty thousand people looking for rental houses, you could charge sixty dollars a month for a shabby little shack, but the real money was downtown. He plowed cash into lots along the streetcar lines and sold them a year later for ten times what he'd paid. At the city's peak, he was grossing $7,000 a week: turning real estate deals by day, running high-stakes faro games in fancy saloons by night.

He wasn't concerned when Sadie took to gambling to fill the long hours he spent managing his many businesses. She was an idiot about games — indifferent to odds, ignorant of strategy — but she was having fun and he didn't count the cost. Admittedly, she sometimes seemed a little blue. When he noticed, he'd take her dancing or they'd go to see a show. And she brightened up considerably when Wyatt won a racehorse on a bet, for Sadie liked the track as much as Wyatt did. He'd always dreamed of breeding horses and with money rolling in from his real estate holdings and the gambling halls, he could afford to invest in good bloodlines. She loved the beautiful animals he bought, the gorgeous silks, the betting and the screaming excitement of the races themselves. Together, they traveled the western race circuit — Santa Rosa, Santa Anita, and Santa Ana; Kansas City, St. Louis, Chicago, and Cincinnati — staying in glamorous hotels and eating at fine restaurants. It was fun for Sadie to rub shoulders with high society and there was always an illicit thrill when she was introduced as Mrs. Earp to some big shot. *Miss Josephine Marcus,* she'd think with a secret smile, *now starring in the role of Wyatt Earp's wife!*

The costumes her role required were splendid. Elaborate broad-brimmed hats; elegant wasp-waisted dresses with immense leg-of-mutton sleeves; bustles and high-buttoned shoes. When their horses lost, there was always tomorrow; when they won, Wyatt would buy her lavish jewelry. A ruby bracelet. A diamond brooch. An emerald ring.

But never a plain gold band.

Of course, she never asked for one. She had her pride.

For all anybody knew, she and Wyatt were married, though that didn't stop other women from throwing themselves at the famously dangerous Wyatt Earp. Tall and straight in tailor-made suits, he was broad-shouldered and square-jawed, with a silent aura of physical confidence few modern males could match. By the 1890s, the Wild West had become something you paid admission to see at Buffalo Bill's show, but Wyatt Earp was the real deal. Men were impressed, but women were enthralled. They'd watch him demurely through their lashes or stare at him with frank curiosity. Sadie knew exactly what they were thinking, for she had once thought it herself.

My, my, my . . . what would that *be like in bed?*

I taught him everything he knows, she'd think bitterly, and it maddened her to imagine other women enjoying the benefits of her tutelage.

"I love him, Doc, but he's not the same man!" That's what she said back in Leadville when she and Doc had those few minutes alone. "What happened after I left Arizona? He used to be so . . ." So shy, she thought. So awkward. Capable of blushing, for heaven's sake! "So upright," she said. "So — so —"

"So Methodist?" Doc suggested.

"Yes! But he drinks now, Doc, and he . . . well, he does things. And he doesn't seem to care about — about what others think." About what I think, she meant.

Doc fell silent for a time, trying to decide how much to say. In the end, he simply took her hand. "Try to remember him as he was, sugar. Try to remember the man Morgan

773

looked up to."

Now Doc was dead and here she was — five years later — living with someone she hardly recognized. She hated his drinking. She hated the endless wheeling and dealing. She hated being shut out of his life. Most of all, she hated the other women.

Oh, she could have taken lovers. She was still beautiful. She still had admirers in those days. Rich men, important men. But she didn't want them. She wanted Wyatt. And she wanted him to want her, only her.

He'd given her fair warning. "I am not a good man," he'd said, and he meant it, but she'd thought he was just being modest, or Methodist, or something.

He's only human, she would tell herself when he disappeared for an hour and came back smelling of someone else's perfume.

Then she'd hit the roulette table, blow two grand, and make him pay her debts.

"It wasn't just San Diegans," a journalist wrote later. "The whole world experienced a sort of money insanity in those days. Any financial scheme that merely promised a return drew international crowds of eager gamblers who liked to call themselves investors."

The first sign that the fun was over came when a few downtown properties were offered at a small discount to their initial asking price. Within a week, the real estate market shifted from "Grab it now, before the price goes up!" to "Wait a little while. It'll go down more."

Property values dropped, and kept on dropping. Being mortgaged to the hilt seemed to make sense during the boom, but now everybody owed more on their property than it was worth. Buildings recently bought for a hundred thousand dollars couldn't scare up ten grand. New construction stalled. Ambitious projects were abandoned, half-finished. Why put up another lavish home or impressive office block when so many others already sat empty?

It wasn't just the big shots who were getting killed. When credit was easy, working men with families bought their own little piece of the dream, and lost everything when they lost their jobs.

Foreclosures clogged the courts. There were burglaries in the dark and holdups in broad daylight. Before long, people were packing up, sneaking out of town at night, leaving homes and mortgages behind. Whole sections of the city were abandoned. Arson became epidemic. Small stores failed. So did big ones. Banks went over the edge and took depositors with them.

And exactly twenty years after the Crash of 1873, the whole dismal catastrophe repeated itself.

■ ■ ■ ■

If anyone had asked Wyatt Earp for financial advice in those days, he would have said, "Invest in sin." Vice is always the last to leave a dying town, for desperate men will rent female solace for an hour, slam down a shot of whiskey, and throw their last five dollars onto a craps table, hoping for a miracle.

On paper, his real estate investments were hit hard, but he had income from a whorehouse and saloons. He owned his horses outright and continued to race them. Like his father-in-law before him, he stayed solvent longer than most, and he was pretty sure he could ride the downturn out.

"Good times always end," he'd learned to say, "and bad times never last."

But the depression dragged on, year after year. One by one, he sold the properties and the horses off. Sadie's gambling debts mounted — a fair measure of his own drinking and philandering, which did not achieve the level of Johnny Behan's but were nothing to be proud of, either. They had a real battle once. He caught her stealing cash from his wallet. She laid into him for the women.

By that time, San Diego's business district was a ghost town. And there was a lawsuit over a promissory note that Wyatt was likely to lose. Then they got word that Sadie's father was sick.

"Suppose . . ." Wyatt said one night. "Suppose we move up to San Francisco. Might be nice for you. Living closer to your family."

So they moved on.

SAY THE PRAYERS.
HEAL THE WOUNDS.

"Wyatt, I'm so glad you're here," Mrs. Marcus whispered, her soft old face blotched with crying. "It's his heart, Sadie. He don't got long."

Leaving Wyatt with her mother, Sadie went into the bedroom and found her sister sitting at the bedside. "Oh, so now you come!" Hattie said bitterly. "Now, when you can be the heroine?"

"Girls!" their father whispered. "Don' bicker."

Inside the old man's chest, was a heart as swollen and hollow as a cream puff. Even so, his eyes sparkled when he asked Sadie about the racehorses and the journey from San Diego. Her answers were full of inaccurate cheer, but it wasn't long before he murmured, "Go on now, girls. Go help your *mutti.*"

Hattie left. Sadie watched at his bedside until she was sure he was asleep, then crept out and closed the door behind herself.

"How is he?" Wyatt asked. She shook her

head and broke down, weeping silently in his arms, her whole body shaking.

Then, without a word, she went to the kitchen, put on an apron, and began to cook as though lives depended on it. Sometimes she let her mother or her sister help. Mostly it was just Sadie in the kitchen by herself. Chopping, peeling, mashing, stirring, beating, scrubbing. Flour up to her elbows. Hands in dishwater.

"Nobody's hungry," Wyatt would tell her. "Sadie, take a rest!"

"We gotta eat," she'd say, sounding just like her mother. And that was that.

Henry died a few days later. For a week, streams of visitors trooped into the apartment above the bakery to be with the Marcus women. Sitting *shivah,* it was called.

Josie never left the kitchen. There was too much food. A lot of it was going to waste. Wyatt was at a loss until Hattie's husband, Emil — the other odd man out — clapped him on the shoulder one night.

"Our job is to say yes to whatever our wives want right now. Whatever it is, just agree!"

"But why does she keep cooking?" Wyatt asked.

"It's what she has to do," Emil said. "Grief takes everyone different."

It could be worse, he meant. At least she's not shooting anybody.

For all the sadness of Henry's passing, they would remember that island in time fondly. In the cramped little apartment above the bakery, in tears and in memories, in simply holding one another and being together after frantic years of hustle and distraction, Wyatt Earp and Sadie Marcus found each other again.

Then, on December 2, 1896, the newspapers found Wyatt.

It was just supposed to be a night out on the town — some fun after all the sadness. Wyatt had agreed to referee a $10,000 championship prizefight between Tom Sharkey and Bob Fitzsimmons. There was a nice fee involved. They needed the money. Sadie had no interest in boxing, but she dressed up and they went to dinner at the Grotto Café. Meanwhile, a few blocks away, fifteen thousand people had gathered to see the fight.

At ten P.M., Wyatt stepped into the ring and took off his coat. The audience gasped. Wyatt frowned. A police captain in charge of the event approached, but Wyatt still didn't understand what the fuss was about.

"Mr. Earp," the officer said, "you can't wear a pistol in here."

Wyatt promptly handed over the revolver that he routinely shoved into his waistband at the small of his back. "Forgot all about it," he told the cop, and that was true. His life had been under threat for fifteen years. Keeping a weapon at hand was habit.

Both managers came into the ring to argue about disqualifying Wyatt. Then the fight promoters joined the dispute. Wyatt stood back and let them have at it. He'd stay or go. Whatever they decided.

The delay lengthened. The crowd got drunker and angrier. Finally, the contest got under way, but in the seventh round — just as the spectators began to enjoy the mayhem they'd paid for — Wyatt called a foul on the favorite and awarded the decision to the underdog, Tom Sharkey.

There were screams of "Fix!" and "Payoff!" Ringside doctors, who'd witnessed the viciousness of Fitzsimmons' low blow, called the decision fair. Sharkey went to the hospital. Bookies got hammered on long-shot bets. The next morning, Bob Fitzsimmons' manager filed a lengthy complaint, alleging collusion between Tom Sharkey and Wyatt Earp to throw the fight and split the prize money.

Seven doctors testified in court to the seriousness of Fitzsimmons' foul. The lawsuit was dropped. Wyatt paid a hefty fine for carrying a concealed weapon without a permit. That should have been the end of it, but the controversy simply wouldn't die. There was too much money in it. A bartender could say,

"Fitzsimmons was robbed," and half his customers would yell, "I'll drink to that!" Newspapers lavished an ocean of ink on the affair. The *San Francisco Chronicle* — whose owner had lost big on Fitzsimmons — was brutal, lampooning Wyatt Earp as a gun-toting, backsliding Methodist, selling booze and girls, up to his ears in corruption and bribery. Wyatt couldn't go anywhere without being harassed.

Hattie and Emil canceled their newspaper subscriptions and put on brave faces in public. The Lehnhardts had already welcomed Hattie's widowed mother into their home. Now they invited Wyatt and Sadie to move in as well. Emil's candy and confections business was fabulously successful, and their new house was big enough to keep everyone comfortable.

Three months later, Sadie announced that she was expecting. She was thirty-six, so this was something of a surprise, though all the more reason for celebration. Names were discussed, but the choices were obvious. For a girl: Virginia, after Wyatt's mother. For a boy: Henry, after Sadie's father. Wyatt admitted he was hoping for a daughter, and Sadie understood. As much as she liked the idea of a son carrying on her father's memory, she knew what Wyatt was thinking. A girl could marry and escape the Earp name, which would always be a burden.

The child — a boy — was stillborn three months later. Rushing to the hospital, Wyatt slipped on the rain-slicked pavement after jumping off a trolley car and fell on his ass, right in front of a reporter.

Ridicule was added to public opprobrium and private sorrow.

By the summer of 1897, it began to seem that nothing would ever displace Wyatt Earp in the newspapers. In fact, it took just one screaming headline. "GOLD IN THE YUKON!"

Wyatt listened as Sadie read. When she finished the article, she looked up. "Suppose . . ." she began. "Suppose we go north."

"That would be good," Wyatt said carefully, for this was the first sign that she had recovered from their loss. "We could make a fresh start."

So they moved on.

The snow was already falling and the rivers were freezing up when they got to Alaska. They disembarked on the coast and traveled by dog sled to their first destination, a Yukon River settlement named Rampart. The town had begun as a Russian outpost. Decades later, it was sold to a group of San Francisco Jews, who'd built it into a profitable trading post. They were willing to give Emil Lehnhardt's notorious brother-in-law a job there. Wyatt was grateful. So was Sadie.

They found a one-room log cabin before the winter closed in and furnished it with simple handmade furniture. Sadie made the cabin cozy with blankets and down comforters and calico curtains, layering furs on the floor to keep the chill out. Dressed like an Inuit, Wyatt hunted for food that first season and trapped for pelts.

"Snug as a bug in a rug," he'd say when he opened the door to the perfume of fresh bread and the aroma of roasting ptarmigan or moose stew.

"Eat!" she'd say, sounding just like her mother. "You're too thin! Eat!"

He was almost fifty. She was nearing forty. Age was mellowing them both. There were no reporters in Rampart. No scandals, no drinking binges, no gambling, no silent brooding. They were content together, and they welcomed others into that contentment.

Most of the men who headed to the Klondike had been thrown out of work by the Panic of '93. A hundred thousand started the journey north; barely a third would reach the gold fields. Some turned back. Many died along the way. Overloaded ships went down in storms or were crushed by ice floes. Men were buried alive in avalanches or simply got lost and froze to death.

Fifteen hundred miles from the nearest doctor, injuries were often fatal. So were failure, liquor, and loneliness. Men killed themselves in Alaska, but not in Rampart, where the Earps saved lives in their own way. Bright lights and warm food could make all the difference to someone considering a bullet to the head. Men left Sadie's table determined to endure another day of numbing cold and darkness. On their way out the door, such men would tell Wyatt what a lucky fella he was. He agreed, and Sadie was pleased.

In the deep blue Arctic nights, beneath glowing green ribbons of light, they put their troubles behind them and made a genuine home for each other. Amid the birch and aspens and spruce that descended low mountains to flat and frozen water glistening with snow, they were granted a season of happiness.

There would be other dreams to chase, other booms, other busts. Over and over, they would move on, but no matter where they went, memories of that first winter in Alaska would sustain them.

Until memory itself began to fail.

ON THE SAD
THRESHOLD OF OLD AGE

Hollywood was their last boomtown.

That's where they met John Flood. They met actors like Tom Mix and William S. Hart there, too. Charlie Chaplin said hello to them once, and so did the famous writer Jack London. But John Flood was the important one. John would be the son they never had.

After Alaska, they spent years in the California desert, prospecting for silver and gold and oil, but settled life grew more alluring as they grew older, especially after they saw their first movie. They were in town buying supplies when *The Great Train Robbery* came out in 1903. Fascinated, they returned to the theater over and over, trying to work out what was fake and what was real.

"The office is just painted canvas and props," Sadie whispered, "but they must have put the set right next to real train tracks."

Wyatt muttered about the things the movie got wrong. "You wouldn't hit anybody if you waved a gun around like that," he'd say, but what bothered him most was the way the actors pretended they were shot. "Nobody throws their arms up in the air and staggers around like that. You just *fall.*"

"They need someone like you to tell them how it really was," Sadie decided.

Wyatt scoffed, but when Sadie got an idea in her head, you couldn't pry it loose with a crowbar. Whenever they were anyplace near a movie theater, they'd go see the newest Westerns and she'd start in on her consultant notion again. Eventually she wore him down and when Wyatt was in his sixties, the idea began to seem like it might pay off.

"Suppose . . ." he began one night. "Suppose we try Los Angeles."

She was past the change by then, plump and plain, but Sadie screamed and clapped her hands like a little girl. "Oh, Wyatt, it's going to be grand! We'll meet movie stars and live in a real house and I can bake and maybe they'll even put *you* in a movie! You're handsomer than any of those actors."

They packed up and headed for Hollywood in the summer of 1911 and rented a little house on the edge of town. Wyatt started hanging around the back lots where the weekly one-reel Westerns were being filmed, hoping that studios making movies about the "Old West" would pay him well for his firsthand knowledge.

To his dismay, nobody seemed to give a

damn about getting things right, so he fell back on faro, as he always had when they hit a new town and needed a stake. Sadie was having fun fixing the little house up — recutting quilts for curtains while the bread dough rose — when a policeman came to inform her that her husband was in jail.

She had to use the rent money to bail Wyatt out. He wouldn't tell her what happened. Wouldn't speak at all until they got home. He seemed stunned. Not befuddled, but weary. "Faro's illegal here," he said finally, and that was all she could get out of him.

With the faro bank confiscated as evidence, they had no cash for rent or an attorney. Then the press dredged up Tombstone and the Sharkey-Fitzsimmons fight again, and the next morning, it was all over the papers: NOTORIOUS MARSHAL ARRESTED IN RAID ON BUNCO GAME!

Wyatt was ready to go back to the desert, but Sadie wasn't willing to give up on Hollywood before they'd had time to make a mark there. Taking matters into her own small hands, she whipped up a chocolate-caramel layer cake and brought it to their landlady, in lieu of rent.

"It isn't fair!" she cried as the landlady forked into the cake. "There were two other men involved, but my husband got all the terrible publicity. Everything was put on him because he's Wyatt Earp! Now we need a lawyer, and we are not rich people. Please, could you just wait a week or two our payment? Hattie Lehnhardt is my sister. I know she'll send us something to tide us over. My husband would be so grateful if you could give us a little time."

Doing the notorious Wyatt Earp a favor had a certain risqué appeal. Hattie Lehnhardt was the wife of the fabulously wealthy Emil Lehnhardt, "California's Candy King." And the cake really was good.

"Well," the landlady said, finishing a second piece, "I can wait a few days for the rent. In the meantime, we have a neighbor who might be able to advise you."

"A lawyer? One who'll work for free?" Mrs. Earp asked. "Have another slice! This is one of my husband's favorite recipes."

"Mr. Flood is a mining engineer, not a lawyer, but he's so smart and very organized! He is an orphan and a bachelor, poor man. He has a roommate, but I think he's lonely. And much too thin! He'd benefit from some of your baking, Mrs. Earp. Would you like an introduction?"

The answer was yes, so the landlady invited Mr. Flood over that evening and offered him a piece of Sadie's cake.

"Mr. and Mrs. Earp haven't any children, and they are getting on in years," she told him. "I think they'd enjoy it if you visited them now. Why not say hello and see if there isn't something a nice young man like you could help them with?"

Thirty-three in 1911, John Flood wasn't all that young, nor was he as lonely as that friendly matchmaker believed, though he was indeed a very nice man.

He was only three when the famous gunfight took place, but he'd read the papers and knew the stories. Naturally, he was curious about the infamous Wyatt Earp. So when Mrs. Earp sent a note asking him to visit the following Sunday, John accepted the invitation.

There was coffee and a plate of perfectly browned macaroons set out on a crisply ironed tablecloth. Everything was neat as a pin and spotlessly clean in the ramshackle little house, though the coffee was in chipped mugs, the faded tablecloth had been repeatedly mended, and the table beneath it was a rickety old thing, tipsy on the uneven floor.

"I know what you're thinking," Mrs. Earp said, all pudgy warmth and bustling hospitality. "How dreary! What a dreadful little place!"

"Oh, no, it's lovely," John lied.

"Well, believe you me," Mrs. Earp confided, putting a flirtatious hand on his arm, "after all those years out in the desert — prospecting for gold and oil with Mr. Earp — any place with a roof and no snakes is a palace in my book. Wyatt, come and meet Mr. Flood!"

Dressed simply in khaki trousers, his white cotton shirt buttoned all the way up, Wyatt Earp was tall and trim, with a full head of silver hair and a neat white mustache. Straight as a lodgepole pine, he towered above John, who was thirty years younger and a slender five feet four. Looking up at that suntanned, handsome face, John was for a breathless instant eight years old again, the age he'd been when his father died.

He took the large, strong hand the old man offered and . . .

That was that. He fell in love.

"Should I be jealous?" Edgar asked when John came home, burbling about the visit.

"No!" John cried, startled, as he often was, by the way Edgar just seemed to *know* things. "No, but . . . it's nice, somehow. I fixed their table, and they were so grateful!"

John Flood and Edgar Beaver had been together only a short time by then, but among the things Edgar just seemed to *know* was this: There was a part of John that needed a family, that yearned to be somebody's son. John had lost both parents and his only sister in quick succession when he was very young, and while John himself never made that connection, he was aware from the beginning of the deep satisfaction he found in helping the Earps.

The couple seemed a little lost in the modern world. Neither had been educated much beyond the basics. Although they knew John wasn't a lawyer or an accountant, to them, a college man was a college man, even if he'd run out of money before he finished the engineering program at Yale. He wasn't able to offer much more than moral support after the bunco charge, but he celebrated with them when the charges were dismissed because the police had bungled the raid, arresting Mr. Earp before the faro game got under way. Soon the Earps were relying on him for advice about electricity, and the new income taxes, and where to find a good dentist, and he solidified his position as their adviser when he suggested that they lease one of their more promising oil claims to Mrs. Earp's sister.

"Mrs. Lehnhardt has the capital to develop a well," John told them, "and she could provide you a steady income from the royalties."

Hattie agreed to the deal. The well came in. The yield was moderate and Hattie's checks were small but they were regular and made all the difference to the Earps financially. John was pleased with how things turned out.

It wasn't a chore to visit them every Sunday afternoon in those early years. Mrs. Earp always had fresh coffee and pastries on the table, and all three of them loved to talk about cinema. The Earps always went to the

Saturday matinées, though they often found the newsreels disturbing, especially after 1914, when war broke out in Europe.

"What in hell are they fighting about?" Mr. Earp asked John, but nobody really understood that.

"No more war talk!" Mrs. Earp would declare. "It's much too dreary!"

Movies were more fun. Not surprisingly, the couple favored Westerns. Mrs. Earp liked Tom Mix and thought he was very funny. Mr. Earp thought the actor's big hats and fancy costumes were ridiculous, but admired his trick riding. In his opinion, William S. Hart movies got a lot of things right, though it bothered Mr. Earp more and more that every movie had a gunfight like the one in Tombstone.

"You'd think street fights like that happened all the time," he'd say. "And the movies make people believe you could tell a man's character from the color of his hat. It wasn't like that."

"They're turning my husband's life into money," Mrs. Earp would complain, "and we aren't getting a penny, Mr. Flood. It just isn't fair!"

Mr. Earp's dismay and Mrs. Earp's indignation came to a head in 1922, when the *Los Angeles Times* printed a series of sensational articles about Wyatt's exploits in the Old West, based on an exclusive interview with the notorious old marshal about the gunfight at the O.K. Corral.

"A man came by and asked a lot of questions, but my husband told him to leave," Mrs. Earp told John. "The paper just made up the answers!"

"Made me sound like an idiot," Mr. Earp grumbled. "I never woulda said Doc Holliday was a 'merry scamp.' "

"I don't see how they can print stories about my husband without his permission," Mrs. Earp said. "It's not fair, Mr. Flood. They're making money from his story, and we aren't getting a penny. Surely that's not legal! There must be something we can do."

"I have a friend . . ." John said cautiously. "Edgar is a journalist. Perhaps we can consult him on the matter."

The following Sunday, over coffee and an excellent applesauce spice cake, Edgar Beaver read the clippings Mrs. Earp had saved, and listened to Mr. Earp's concerns about the articles, and felt for himself the responsibility of being asked for advice by an earnest old man and his anxious old wife.

"What's required is a letter to the editor," he told them, accepting a "second slice of cake" pressed on him by Mrs. Earp, who may not have noticed that he'd already had two pieces. "Don't complicate it with outrage or emotion, Mrs. Earp. All you need is a calm, factual letter correcting the errors in the article."

He finished the third piece of cake, but when Mrs. Earp began to repeat for the fourth time that it couldn't possibly be legal to print things like that and complained again about people making money by slandering her husband, he stood and excused himself, saying, "I'm afraid I really must dash."

John stayed on to help the Earps compose their letter, refuting the article's objectionable content, point by point. A few days later, the *Los Angeles Times* printed a retraction.

"You did it!" Mrs. Earp cried when he arrived that afternoon, wrapping him in a jubilant, cushiony embrace. "John, dear, you did it!"

"Thank you, son," Wyatt said quietly, offering his hand.

It was the first time they'd called him anything but Mr. Flood, and John was touched to his heart. He'd never seen Mr. and Mrs. Earp happier, and yet . . .

When he got home, he was depressed and uneasy.

"Something's wrong with Mrs. Earp," he told Edgar, "but I just can't quite . . . put my finger on it, I guess."

Edgar's judgment was unclouded by affection. He'd known after that third slice of cake. "Wyatt is a magnificent old thing, but Mrs. Earp reminds me of my aunt Lillian.

Mark my words, dear boy. She's already a little batty and she's going to get worse."

■ ■ ■ ■

NOW LET ME WIN
NOBLE RENOWN!

■ ■ ■ ■

GIVE THE BARD
HIS SHARE OF HONOR

Wyatt, too, had seen the signs, but senility is slow and sly and subtle. Small strokes — pinpricks of the brain — change people little by little. Those who watch dementia creep up to claim a mind make light of early lapses. They explain away the repetition and strange behavior. They try not to see what's happening.

Sadie had always been dramatic. She'd always had a tendency to dwell on things. And when she was just getting started on some mania, it could seem quite reasonable for a while.

"What we need is an *authorized* version of the gunfight," she decided after the *Times* backed down. "You have to set the record straight, once and for all. John Flood can write it up. It'll be no trouble at all for a college man like him! He's here on Sundays anyway."

John was charmed by Mrs. Earp's confidence that he could tell her husband's story properly. Though dumpy and frumpy at sixty-two, Sadie still had a way of shining her eyes at a man and making him feel he could accomplish anything, simply because she had faith in him. Wyatt was slower to yield to her enthusiasm. He hated talking about the past in general and Tombstone in particular. When anybody brought the gunfight up, he'd plead, "Can't we talk about something more pleasant?" But Sadie insisted, over and over, that an authorized version of the story was required. Wyatt would give John Flood the facts. John would type it up, the way he'd typed the letter to the *Times.* That would settle things once and for all.

When Mr. Earp finally agreed to cooperate, John felt honored to be entrusted with the old man's memories. He himself believed that he could compose a calm, factual rendering of the events in Tombstone.

And so it began.

Sunday after Sunday, John Flood and Wyatt Earp worked their way through the mules, the stagecoach robbery, Kate's drunken accusation, the deal with Ike, the gunfight, the maiming of Virgil, the murder of Morgan, and the vendetta that followed.

"It's heartbreaking," John told Edgar. "It's hard for him to talk about what happened. Mrs. Earp is getting more and more upset. She didn't witness any of it herself, and Mr. Earp tells her not to listen, but she refuses to leave while he's talking."

At first John thought she was being brave, facing up to the truth of her husband's violent life. Sometimes, though, he got the feeling that she was monitoring what John heard. Once, when he asked, "When did you and Mrs. Earp meet? Was that before the gunfight?" she stopped the conversation cold. And if Mr. Earp started to talk about his brother James or his sister-in-law Bessie, Mrs. Earp was adamant: This was not material for a William S. Hart movie.

"Movie?" John asked, startled. "Is there going to be a movie?"

"Oh, yes!" Mrs. Earp said breezily. "My husband's story is perfect for William S. Hart. You'll write the screenplay. Mr. Hart will make a movie that tells the story of Tombstone as it ought to be told, and all our money worries will be over!"

John glanced at Mr. Earp, who rolled his eyes and shrugged.

"Mrs. Earp," John said carefully, "I am competent to write letters for you and Mr. Earp, and I'm doing my best with the Tombstone story, but that's not the same as writing a screenplay! What you're asking me to do . . . Well, it's like expecting a sandlot ballplayer to break into the big leagues."

"Oh, but just imagine your name on the credits, dear! Screenplay by John H. Flood! It'll be so exciting!"

"Bill Hart! That old ham?" Edgar said when John got home that night.

"Mrs. Earp is convinced that a movie about her husband would be a hit. She wants me to write a letter to Mr. Hart and offer him an option on the story."

"Hart's completely washed up, dear boy. He's been trying for years to get his magnum opus financed. Nobody will touch the project."

John looked miserable. "It's . . . very difficult to say no to Mrs. Earp. I know it sounds crazy, but I . . . I want to do this for her."

She was the closest thing John Flood had to a mother. He found it inexpressibly sweet when she called him "John, dear," and Edgar was fairly certain the old girl was fully aware of that.

"Well," Edgar sighed. "I suppose there's no harm in trying. Send the letter. Let Bill Hart be the one who disappoints her. Then she'll blame him, not you."

Edgar was right: William S. Hart was box office poison in 1923.

The first in a long line of Shakespearean actors to leave legitimate theater for harlot Hollywood, Bill Hart had arrived in Los Angeles at the age of fifty. He got work almost immediately in a series of one-reel cowboy movies, which were already madly popular in 1914. Nobody seemed to mind that his acting was stagey and mannered and stiff. Audiences would pay to see anything that moved in those days, and studios were satisfied with anything that made a buck. But Bill Hart had spent two years of his childhood living on the Minnesota frontier. Like Wyatt Earp, who was sitting in the dark watching those Westerns, he was annoyed by the absurd screenplays and the stupid mistakes in those early oaters. So he began to write and produce his own movies.

That's when his career really took off, for his films portrayed the Old West with a zeal for authenticity that was immensely appealing to those who were sentimental about a by-gone era, which had lived ugly but read romantic and ennobling. A William S. Hart movie brought "wilderness" and "pioneer days" inside theaters. Grown-ups could gaze at dramatic painted landscapes without heat or dust or rattlers. Children could enjoy the gun play without catching a stray bullet. And everyone — including Bill himself — was captivated by the character he played in every film. A good bad man.

A man who did wrong for the right reasons.

For almost a decade, William S. Hart was the biggest celebrity in the world, but as moviegoers grew more sophisticated, his acting began to seem laughable. Box office revenues fell. The fan mail disappeared. By 1923, Bill Hart was a has-been, and he knew it. Which made it all the more thrilling when he got a letter signed by Wyatt Earp.

During the past few years, that letter read, *many wrong impressions of the early days of Tombstone and myself have been created by writers who are not informed correctly, and this has been a concern I feel deeply. I am now seventy-five and realize I am not going to live forever. I want any wrong impression to be made right before I go away. The screen could do all this, I know, with yourself as the master mind.*

Later on, Bill Hart found out that the letters from Wyatt were written by a man named John Flood, who'd looked after the aging Earps for years. Still later, Bill learned that Flood had to rewrite everything over and over, for Mrs. Earp was never satisfied with how he put things, even if she'd dictated the letter to start with. Even later, Bill came to understand that it was Mrs. Earp who felt such deep concern about Wyatt's reputation, not the old lawman himself. But when he got that first letter, Bill Hart wrote back personally.

Yes, he agreed, Westerns were popular but — regrettably — not William S. Hart Westerns, according to the big studios, anyway. Fed up with their negativism, Bill was busy trying to produce his first independent film. At the moment, he wasn't able to take on

Mr. Earp's project, though he sympathized with what he thought was Wyatt's distress. *It makes my hair stand on end when I read things about the West that are not true. I can imagine what it must mean to one like yourself, who has been through it all, to have false stories printed about you.*

He closed by urging Mr. Earp to find a good writer to tell his story and promised to take a look when it was all down on paper. He meant exactly what he said: He'd take a look. His letter was not an option contract, let alone a promise to produce a movie.

But that's not how Sadie would see it.

When they got the letter from William S. Hart, she felt like a girl again. How long had it been since the dreary world seemed so full of promise? Ages and ages and ages!

Dear John's idea about the oil royalties had saved them from destitution, and now his screenplay would make them rich! Of course, she was a little frightened as well, for there were elements of her husband's story that concerned her. Things that would not be right for a William S. Hart movie. "What Mr. Hart wants is a nice clean story, with pep!" she'd tell John.

That became her constant refrain: John must write a nice, clean story, with pep. "Keep it clean," she'd remind him when he left each Sunday evening, and she'd give a conspiratorial wink before she added, "You know what I mean."

"I'm sorry, Mrs. Earp," he'd say. "I'm not sure I *do* know what you mean."

Sometimes she'd laugh and say merrily, "Of course you do!" But sometimes she'd wring her hands and insist again, "It has to be *clean*!"

"Clean, clean, clean! She sounds like Lady Macbeth," Edgar remarked at the end of '23. "Methinks that lady doth protest too much. I know what you and I are hiding, dear boy. I wonder what dirt Mrs. Earp has under her rug."

Draft after draft, John did his best for her, trying to guess what she wanted. Pep seemed to involve making up dialogue, but John Flood was a middle-aged engineer and not much given to imagining lively conversations among men who were about to shoot one another. Clean was easier. Clean meant that neither gambling nor saloons could be mentioned. Faro was considered a bunco game now, and Prohibition was national law. Mrs. Earp wanted nothing in the story that could cast a shadow on her husband's reputation as an incorruptible lawman. At the same time, she was buying bootleg whiskey for Wyatt and laughed the inconsistency off when John asked about that as gently as he could.

Mr. Earp almost always had a glass in his

hand, though John never saw him drunk. The old man would nurse a shot for an hour or more and then pour himself another. "Takes the edge off," he said once. "Softens things, some."

When John asked about how slowly he drank, Mr. Earp looked surprised. "Never thought about it before, but . . . That's how Doc Holliday used to drink. Little by little. Unless his chest was real bad . . ." He drifted off for a time. That was happening more as he moved into his late seventies. "Doc was a real good dentist," he said then, and his eyes came back to John's. "He was a real good man. Better'n me. He spoke the truth when I didn't want to hear it."

All the same, to please Mrs. Earp, John took any reference to liquor out of the manuscript.

"It has to be clean," she'd say every Sunday as he left. "Keep it clean, John, dear!"

Months turned into years. John knew that what he was writing was bad, and it was getting worse by the week. Every Sunday Mrs. Earp asked for changes that snarled the story and introduced logical errors. She never made these demands where Mr. Earp could hear her. She'd pull John into the kitchen or follow him out the door and put that flirtatious hand on his arm and smile up at him from beneath her lashes.

"John, dear, you can't write about *that*,"

she'd say on days when Mr. Earp had re-
counted something violent or illegal. "It's
much too dreary! Much too . . . complicated.
The story needs more pep!" More phony
dialogue, she meant.

Sometimes, though, she'd speak up and
argue with her husband.

"It drove a lot of men crazy," Wyatt told
John Flood in 1925. "The way Ike Clanton
repeated things. How slow he was to get what
you were saying."

"But you trusted him?" John asked.

"I guess. Yeah. When I made the deal, I
trusted him. That was probably stupid."

"Ike was stupid, not you," Mrs. Earp
snapped.

Mr. Earp looked at her. "We both got hit a
lot when we were kids, Sadie. Hell, you're
supposed to hit kids. Spare the rod, spoil the
child. But Ike's father, and mine? They was a
lot worse than most. People talk about knocking sense into a kid, but getting hit like that
can scramble up your thinking."

He turned back to John Flood, who was
startled by how worked up the old man was
getting.

"I saw it when Milt Joyce bashed Doc
Holliday. It was the same with Curly Bill.
Maybe Ike got hit so much, he never got over
the scrambling. And he got hit again the night
before the gunfight. And then he was drinking because he was so scared Doc Holliday

would tell the Cow Boys about Ike ratting on them. Don't you remember, Sadie? I told you the night of the gunfight! I *told* you it was my fault!"

"It wasn't your fault! None of it was your fault!"

"I made the deal with Ike and he got scared, and —"

"You can't write that, John! The gunfight was not my husband's fault!"

"I'm not going to lie, Sadie!"

"Wyatt, it's not *lying.* It's just making the story simpler, so people can understand it right!"

"My goodness! Look at the time!" John said, leaving them to battle this out on their own.

Then there was the Sunday when Ann Ellen appeared.

"John, dear, I've been thinking," Mrs. Earp said, her eyes sparkling with mischief. "There really ought to be a little romance in this story. Every William S. Hart movie needs a leading lady! Let's call her Ann Ellen. Quite a pretty girl of . . . let's say nineteen. She's in awe of Wyatt Earp. Sheriff Behan is in love with her, but she really did like Wyatt better. The sheriff was very jealous, and of course that made things difficult for Wyatt, too."

"Oh, ho!" Edgar cried when John brought this tidbit home. "So *that's* the dirt under her rug? A love triangle? How disappointing! I was hoping for something juicier."

There was something juicier, of course, and Sadie regretted bringing up romance as soon as John Flood left the house. As the week passed, she became increasingly distressed, imagining the salacious curiosity that might be aroused if "Ann Ellen" were introduced to John's screenplay. Why, some nosy reporter might travel down to Tombstone and interview old-timers about that love triangle. Those old-timers might remember not just Josie Marcus and Johnny Behan but Wyatt and Mattie Blaylock. Worse yet, they might recall a girl who went by the name of Forty-Dollar Sadie, who certainly wasn't Josie Marcus, but . . . Well, mistakes could be made. There were people still living in Tombstone who hated Wyatt. One of them might be cad enough to reveal how Josie had supported herself during the months between Johnny Behan and Wyatt Earp.

And if that was dragged out into the light . . .

No romance, she decided over and over. I must tell dear John. No romance. It's all too dreary. Dreary dreary dreary.

All week long, she went over it in her mind, afraid that she would forget in daylight what was a maddening circle of words in the darkness. No Ann Ellen. No romance. I must tell John. It's all too dreary.

■ ■ ■ ■

So. No Ann Ellen. Ann Ellen was evidently too much pep for a William S. Hart movie, but John Flood's relief did not last long. Every time he thought the manuscript was finished, Mrs. Earp would make some new demand or insist on more changes, all while pleading with him to finish the story so Mr. Hart could get that movie made and they would all be rich.

"John, dear, I've been thinking. Let's take some of the emphasis off Tombstone, shall we? That story has too much blood and thunder, don't you think? It's much too dreary!"

"John, dear, I've been thinking. You really ought to write about our adventures in Alaska as well."

"John, dear, I've been thinking. Mr. Hart loves stories about childhood on the prairie! Let's add some things about Mr. Earp's youth in Iowa."

Every few weeks, Mrs. Earp would dictate another letter reporting fictitious progress on a screenplay that John Flood couldn't possibly write and that Bill Hart would never produce. Then John would go home and take a headache powder.

"Dear boy, it's been two *years* of Sundays!" Edgar complained in 1925. "Tell her you quit. Tell her you have beriberi and you're going to New Guinea for the cure. Tell her anything, but stop this insanity!"

"Edgar," John asked one night in 1926, "do you know anything about a writer named Walter Burns?"

"Never heard of him. Why?"

"He's contacted the Earps. He wants to do a book about Tombstone."

Edgar sat up straight. "Then he's brilliant! Perfect for the job! A Shakespearean genius with great commercial instincts. Tell Mrs. Earp he'll make them rich and famous. We'll change our names and run away to Mexico. With any luck at all, she'll never track you down."

"Don't be flippant."

"I can be flippant or I can be murderous," Edgar replied grimly. "That woman has stolen three years of your life! She'll never be happy, and that makes you unhappy, and that makes me unhappy. I swear, John, this is a quadrangle worthy of Freud. I'm ready to kill your mother figure so you can sleep with your father figure and be done with it!"

"I'm serious, Edgar."

"So am I."

"Just . . . find out about Burns, will you?"

A few days later, Edgar dropped a folder of notes on the table in front of John. "Walter Noble Burns is a Chicago literary critic.

Competent reviews of important authors — H. G. Wells, Maxim Gorky, Edith Wharton. He just published a biography that makes a hero out of a vicious little killer named Billy the Kid. It's selling like crazy. Sam Goldwyn bought the movie rights for ten grand."

"Then why do you look like you just sucked on a lemon?"

Edgar sat down across the table. "Word is, Burns is a shameless plagiarist and every fact in his book is questionable." There was a long pause. "Look, the Earps are your friends, not mine, but I can't help thinking that Wyatt deserves better."

John's face went blank, then lit up. "Edgar! Why don't *you* write the biography?"

"I'd rather be buried alive." Edgar said promptly. "Besides which, I write for a living and I don't accept payment in pastry. No . . . If Mrs. Earp wants someone to throw buckets of literary whitewash on Tombstone, then Walter Burns is her man. Get him to visit the Earps and for the love of God, make sure that they say yes."

But they didn't.

The moment Burns mentioned doing research in Tombstone to supplement his interviews with Wyatt, the deal was dead for Sadie. For Wyatt, refusing Burns was a matter of loyalty to John Flood, along with sheer fatigue, for he was in his late seventies by

813

then, suffering from what he called "plumbing troubles" and mortally tired of talking about the old days.

"We already got a fella writing about me," he told Burns. "He's worked on it for three years. I'd hate to change horses now."

"So I've been scooped? Ah, that's too bad," Burns sighed with apparent good grace, though he was thinking, Then why in hell did you ask me to come all the way to Los Angeles? "Who's the publisher, if I might ask?"

There wasn't one. John Flood's manuscript had been turned down by every house in New York, and the rejections were brutal. "All but unreadable." "Stilted and florid." "Diffuse and pompous." Not even a cover letter from William S. Hart had helped. Wyatt didn't go into all that, but he admitted that John's manuscript was not up to snuff.

"Suppose . . ." he suggested. "Suppose you take what John's written and polish it up for us?"

A retort about "editing amateur work gratis" formed in Walter Burns's mind, but it was quickly suppressed by the prospect of getting access to research that could be pirated. "I'd be happy to take a look at it for you, Mr. Earp. And perhaps you and I could still work together . . . What if I were to focus my Tombstone story on Doc Holliday?"

"That'd be real good," Wyatt said warmly.

"Doc got blamed for a lot he didn't do. I'd like to square things for him before I die."

But Wyatt Earp was front and center when *Tombstone: An Iliad of the Southwest* came out, in 1927.

"Listen to this, John!" Edgar cried gleefully, reading in bed. " 'His hair was as yellow as a lion's mane, his voice as deep as a lion's. He suggested a lion in the slow, slithery ease of his movements and his gaunt, heavy-boned, loose-limbed, powerful frame.' Does that sound like a crush to you? Is Burns married?"

"I don't know, and I don't care! Edgar, the man lied to Mr. Earp's face. He said he was going to edit my manuscript and write a book about Doc Holliday."

Edgar continued to read in a radio announcer's baritone: " 'Roughly molded by the frontier, he had the frontier's simplicity and strength, the frontier's resourcefulness and its unillusioned self-sufficiency.' Is 'unillusioned' a word? 'He followed his own silent trails with rough-shod directness . . . Whatever he did, he did in deadly earnest. He was incapable of pretense: cold, balanced, and imperturbably calm.' My God! It just goes on and on! 'A natural master . . . Brains and courage . . . The dominant qualities of a leader . . .' " Edgar looked up and saw John scowling. "What?"

"Edgar, he said he was writing about Doc Holliday. Mrs. Earp is furious."

"She wanted a hero. Burns delivered. I can't see why she's upset."

"Well, she is, and you have to come with me tomorrow. I'm afraid she'll have a stroke if she doesn't calm down about this book. She wants to file a suit against Burns. Mr. Earp is worn out with it, and I can't get her to give the idea up. Maybe she'll listen to you — she still talks about how you got the *L.A. Times* to back down."

"But I didn't! I just told you to write a letter!"

"Edgar, *please*!"

It came down to this: John Flood loved the Earps. Edgar Beaver loved John Flood. "All right," Edgar said. "All right, but just this once."

The Stroke of Death Will Not Come Quickly

She was happy with the Burns book in some ways. She liked that Johnny Behan was portrayed as vain and ineffectual. She was immensely relieved that there was no mention of a southwestern Helen of Troy. Nor was Mattie Blaylock even hinted at. None of the Earps' women figured in the story. *Tombstone* was a story about men, written by a man, meant to be read by the kind of men who wore suits, and worked indoors, and chafed at the modern world's restrictions, and sometimes thought yearningly about just plain *shooting* some sonofabitch who richly deserved it.

Even so, she kept circling back to the lawsuit. Pacing, fuming, crying. "We have to sue that lying sneak! That low-down, lying phony! How could he sit at our table and tell my husband he was writing one thing when he was writing another? It's not fair! This can't be legal!"

When Edgar visited, he let her repeat these

complaints three times before he said, "Mrs. Earp, your husband is a public figure. Walter Burns has written a story that's the opposite of libelous. Mr. Earp is portrayed as a fearless lawman meting out frontier justice to bad men. It's a nice clean tale," he could not help saying, "with a great deal of peppy dialogue."

Temporarily derailed, Mrs. Earp stood still, but her face remained set in what was becoming a permanent scowl of bewilderment and pique.

"But there's not a penny in it for us!" she cried, pacing again, off on a new tangent. "And if there's a movie made, we won't get anything from that, either! We are not rich people. My husband is old and ill. We have no savings, and there's no pension from any of the towns he served. Now that this book is out, there'll be no market for an authorized biography. What is to become of me?" she demanded, wringing her hands. "What is to become of me?"

Tired of the drama, Wyatt excused himself to lie down for a nap. Mrs. Earp hardly paused in her vilification of Walter Burns. Edgar listened a while longer, then signaled to John that it was time to go home.

"She's bats, dear boy," he warned when they left. "This won't end well."

"I can't just walk away from Mr. Earp," John said stubbornly. His voice was rough when he spoke again. "He hasn't got much time left. I will see this through."

Johnny Behan's son, Albert, had kept in touch with Sadie over the years, but when he saw the Earps in Los Angeles at the end of 1927, he was startled by the changes in them. At seventy-nine, Wyatt was alarmingly thin and obviously sick. The state of Sadie's house was almost as shocking. Dusty, disordered, and just . . . not clean.

As always, there was cake on the table, only it was store-bought — not bad, though not as good as the marble cake Sadie used to make for him. When he finished his second piece, he declined the third and came to the point of his visit.

"I hate to bring this up, but Billy Breakenridge is working on a book with a ghostwriter. He told me they plan to do right by my father. Mr. Earp, they're going to say you and your brothers were all corrupt and the gunfight was an outlaw dispute that my father tried to stop. They're going to say all the men who died at the O.K. Corral were unarmed."

Wyatt stared at him, astonished. "But . . . Judge Spicer went over all that in the hearing! If they was unarmed, how did Virg and Morgan and Doc get shot?"

"They're going to say you shot them yourself, by accident."

"But . . . that's plain stupid!"

"That evil little queer," Sadie muttered.

"Albert, Billy Breakenridge sat right where you're sitting, just last summer! 'I want to talk about old times!' " she said, making her voice high and whiny. "I made him breakfast! Biscuits and strawberry jam, and eggs and bacon and coffee —"

"Al, I don't understand," Wyatt said. "Me and my brothers, we always worked fine with Billy B. Why would he say that about us?"

"Because he's an evil little queer, that's why," Sadie muttered.

"There's money in controversy," Al said. "His writer thinks everybody who bought the Burns book will buy Billy's, too. They're calling it *Helldorado.* It's a catchy title."

"Billy's probably broke, too." Wyatt sighed. "We're all old and broke, Al. The best of us died young. The rest of us have lived too long."

Sadie was still muttering. "That evil little queer! He's an evil little queer."

"Sadie! Stop it," Wyatt said sharply. "You're stuck again."

"It's our story, and everyone is making money but us," she said, breaking through one circle maze only to wander into another. "We are not rich people! My sister has money. People think we don't need anything because Hattie is rich, but my husband is old and ill, and we have no savings, John!"

Wyatt met Al's eyes before he said, "This is Albert Behan, Sadie, not John Flood."

She didn't even pause. "There's no pension from Dodge or Wichita or Tombstone. We have nothing! And now that evil little queer is going to take the bread from our mouths!"

Albert left a few minutes later, but Sadie kept on about Billy Breakenridge and how people were stealing from them, and no pension, and so on. Wyatt told her that things weren't as bad as she thought, but when she got like this, it was more useful to say, "I'm hungry," or "Take laundry off the line," or "Read me the paper." Sometimes chores distracted her, but this time she was hooked good and solid.

Come Sunday, she was still nerved up about Billy B.'s book and started in on it again the moment John Flood came in the door.

"Billy Breakenridge sat right where you're sitting, just last summer! 'I want to talk about old times!' " she said, her voice high and whiny. "I made him breakfast! Biscuits and strawberry jam, and eggs and bacon and coffee. And now that evil little queer is going to take the bread from our mouths! You sit right down at that typewriter," she ordered. "You're going to write a letter to Houghton Mifflin. Tell them we want every copy of that evil little queer's book destroyed, or we'll sue. If they publish it, we'll get a lawyer and we'll sue them and that evil little queer for damages. He won't get away with this," she

821

vowed. "We're going to stop him in his tracks. That evil little —"

"Sadie!" Wyatt roared.

Shocked into silence, she stared at him.

"I'm out of tobacco," Wyatt said, slowly and distinctly. "Go to the store — *right now* — and get me some tobacco. And when you get back, I want you to keep a civil tongue in your head."

She stood there. First blank, then confused, then defiant. She settled on belligerent capitulation. "Of course," she said with theatrical lightness. "Whatever you say. I'll let everyone steal from us and run roughshod over you, if that's what you want. I'll just go get tobacco for you! I'll be your little errand girl."

Muttering, she put on her hat and gloves, snatched up her purse, and stalked out of the house, leaving two silent men surrounded by dusty furniture and piles of newspapers and unwashed dishes — so unlike the tidy home John Flood had first visited sixteen years earlier.

"I'm sorry, John," Wyatt said, scrubbing at his face. "She was never *mean* like that, before . . . She gets these ideas and just goes around and around. She's younger than me, but . . ." He looked away, helpless. "Old age takes people strange sometimes."

Milk-white, John stood. "I — I think I have to go."

Wyatt got to his feet, which wasn't easy anymore, for his insides hurt something fierce and no amount of whiskey seemed to help.

"You've been real patient with her, son. And real kind to me. I hope you can forgive her and . . . I hope you'll come back."

John was at the door by then, reaching for his hat. When he turned, it was all on his face. Everything he'd felt. Everything he'd never said.

Coming close, Wyatt offered his hand and when John took it, Wyatt held on for a few moments.

"Give Edgar my best," he said. "He's a good man. So are you."

"Yes, sir," John said, his voice thready. "Thank you, sir. I'll see you next Sunday."

"Honestly, dear boy, I can't decide if you're a saint or an idiot," Edgar said.

"Mr. Earp is dying," John said. "I won't abandon him now."

"The question is, What happens when the old lion leaves us? What on earth are we going to do about his wife?"

We, John thought. *We.* I'm not alone in this.

On good days, she was as cheerful and perky as a parakeet. Her habits of hospitality remained intact, and visitors sometimes brought out her old sparkle. Thoughtless pleasantries bubbled out of her. She could be charming, as long as you wanted what she wanted you to want. But if you refused a fourth piece of cake or disagreed with her about something, there'd be a stunning avalanche of emotion. Uncomprehending surprise, weeping reproach, furious denunciation. She had trip wires, too. Topics that set her off. She was endlessly worried about money and convinced the neighbors were stealing from them. She told horrible kike jokes and laughed uproariously at them herself.

She was different before, you'd remind yourself. Poor Wyatt, you'd think as you left the house.

"How do you stand it?" John asked him once.

"I was no prize, John," Wyatt said. "She put up with a lot from me."

The man who would immortalize Wyatt Earp didn't know about Mrs. Earp's peculiarities, but Stuart Lake knew other things in 1928. He knew Lowell Thomas was still making a lucrative career out of selling Lawrence of Arabia. He knew the public remained hungry for stories of individual heroism — even now, a decade after losing a generation of nameless men to the Great War's senseless slaughter. He knew people were still fascinated by the Tombstone gunfight, and he knew Mr. and

Mrs. Earp thought they'd been cheated by Walter Burns.

So right off the bat, Stu Lake offered to split the proceeds of a biography down the middle. *I'm proposing a fifty-fifty, horse-high, bull-strong, hog-tight deal,* he wrote, demonstrating the lively style he intended to bring to the project. *You do the telling, I'll do the writing and the whipping into shape.* As his bona fides, he offered his experience as Teddy Roosevelt's press agent at the turn of the century: playing up TR's cowboy persona, framing his adventures so they had maximum political appeal. *I am the man for the job,* Lake wrote. *Give me a chance and I'll do you proud.*

The reply came from a Mr. John Flood, who said he acted as the Earps' secretary. Mr. Earp was not in good health; Mrs. Earp would need income after his passing. Mr. Flood himself had spent three years interviewing Mr. Earp about his life, but his own manuscript had not been acceptable for publication. He would make his notes available to Mr. Lake. *I am not interested for one moment as to financial remuneration,* Flood wrote. *The purpose is to square Mr. Earp and make provisions for his wife.*

Which was damn decent of the man. Or really naïve.

Given Mrs. Earp's many and shifting concerns, the contract negotiations were something of an ordeal but a week after signing, everything John Flood had written was on Stu Lake's desk. It took all summer to sift through the material, separating what seemed factual from a great deal of bad dialogue. In September, Lake was ready to meet Wyatt himself in Los Angeles.

Perhaps he should have gone sooner, but Stu Lake hadn't realized how sick the old man was. And traveling was difficult. Meeting new people meant acknowledging his leg. "Shrapnel," he'd say briefly. "France, 1918." His femur had been shattered; survival cost him two years in military hospitals. A long series of awful operations had left Stuart Lake with a heavy limp. His right leg was four inches shorter than his left.

"Virgil's arm was like that," Wyatt said. "He's dead now. They all are. I'm the last."

Which turned out to be the longest statement Wyatt Earp would make to his biographer. Of course, Wyatt had never been much of a talker, and in his final months, he was fighting a chronic infection and worsening pain.

"He was delightfully laconic," Lake would recall. "Exasperatingly so."

Mrs. Earp provided far too much pastry while her husband doled out bare facts, a few words at a time. Stu Lake pumped for names, dates, details. It was like pulling teeth — a process with which Wyatt Earp was familiar, and one that he enjoyed about as much as answering questions. By the end of '28, the writer considered it more productive to mail written questions, even knowing that Mrs. Earp was answering them on Wyatt's behalf.

Mr. Lake, my dear husband is not at all well, she wrote the first week of January 1929. *Do visit again soon, for I am afraid he is not long for this world.*

For once, she was not exaggerating a situation to heighten the dramatic effect.

He died as he'd lived, nearly silent at the end.

All my life, he thought, lying in bed, waiting for it to be over. On the move. On the run.

A year. Two. Three at the most, and we'd move on. Monmouth, Illinois. Pella, Iowa. San Bernardino, California. Lamar, Missouri.

Wichita. Ellsworth. Abilene. Dodge.

Tombstone.

Denver. Gunnison. El Paso. Austin. San Antonio. Aspen. Salt Lake. Ouray. Coeur d'Alene. Eagle City.

San Diego. San Francisco. Rampart. Nome. Los Angeles.

Forty-seven years more than Morgan got.

Shoulda been me, he thought.

Sadie was at his side when the old desire to leave everything behind rose up in him again.

"Suppose . . ." he began. "Suppose . . ."

Then he moved on, one last time.

. . . .

FOR GENERATIONS STILL UNBORN, HE WILL LIVE IN SONG

. . . .

ONE GENERATION DIES AWAY, ANOTHER RISES UP

The obituaries did not reveal the poverty and illness of his final years. They did not mention his widow's deepening dementia. They paid no homage to John Flood's years of devotion. They discreetly overlooked the business failures, the booze, the women, the scandals. They rehashed the gunfight and the vendetta, but they did not say, "He upheld the law until he took it into his own hands and crushed it."

They called him the Lion of Tombstone and sold a lot of newspapers. It wasn't lying. It was letting a lucrative legend replace an old man's life.

After the funeral, John Flood helped Mrs. Earp respond to the thousands of condolence letters from admirers of the Walter Burns book *Tombstone*. John was determined to send a reply to everyone who'd written, and he spent months typing the thank-you notes and getting Mrs. Earp to sign them.

He paid for the postage himself.

In the summer of 1929, Stuart Lake began to realize that he now had the undivided attention of Wyatt Earp's widow. Her letters were typed and grammatical at first, scrawled longhand and erratically punctuated later. She asked for progress reports and details about how he was handling various elements of the story. She questioned him about publishers and serial rights for magazines and movie options. She wanted to review his work. She exhorted him to tell a nice, clean story with pep.

He agreed to make drinking and saloons incidental to her husband's life. He was willing to present gambling as the nineteenth-century equivalent of playing golf. Gradually, he found himself creating a Wyatt Earp who was sober and single, fictionally articulate, virtuous and just: the courageous embodiment of frontier justice, fighting Cow Boy crime in Tombstone like Eliot Ness facing down gangsters in modern Chicago. None of it was good enough for Mrs. Earp.

She wanted not just Achilles and Adonis but meek and mild Jesus as well. Stu Lake's patience began to fray. *Mrs. Earp,* he wrote, *you do not desire a biography but a eulogy!* It was a measured response to her interference, so he was stunned when she wrote back to tell him she was withdrawing her permission for the biography, threatening to consult a lawyer if he went ahead with it. Horrified, he wasted hours explaining and reexplaining things she had misconstrued and distorted. Hoping to convey to her that her "contributions" to his work were making a difficult task harder. Reiterating his admiration and respect for her husband. Trying not to hate her.

When the stock market crashed in October of '29, she panicked, though she had no investments to lose. She begged dear Mr. Lake to publish as soon as possible, pleading poverty and starvation. Stu wrote to John Flood directly and was assured that Mrs. Earp's sister provided her with an income, but the frantic handwritten letters continued. *Please, Mr. Lake! I must have an advance on our royalties. I will soon be out on the street!* You and half the population, the writer thought, gimping past breadlines and soup kitchens, wondering how long it would be before he himself joined the destitute on the dole.

At least twice a day for the next eighteen months, he despaired of transforming John Flood's notes and Wyatt's monosyllabic mumbles into something worth reading but, week by week, he chipped away at the task. There was nothing else he could do. The alternative was beggery.

And damn if all the work didn't pay off.

When *Wyatt Earp: Frontier Marshal* was published in 1931, it became an immediate and enduring bestseller. Stuart Lake's one and only book would be the solid cornerstone of its crippled author's financial life, and as much as he had come to dislike Mrs. Earp — as much as he resented her endless importuning — he sent half the royalties to Wyatt's widow, year after year after year.

Mrs. Earp, he wrote once, *I am bewildered by your continuing criticism of my portrait of your husband. I did everything I could to ensure that his story would please you.*

His biography was indeed everything that Sadie had hoped for and nothing that she dreaded. But by 1931, she was too far gone to read it.

"She was here again," Edgar often reported when John got home from work. "Banging on the door and yelling. This has to stop, dear boy."

"I'll write to her sister," John would promise.

Hattie replied just once, making the facts clear. *Mr. Flood, I do what I can for my sister though I am myself a widow in poor health. Sadie receives regular payments from Mr. Lake and I provide additional income, but I cannot keep her from gambling her money away or spending it foolishly on frivolous lawsuits. She is her own worst enemy.*

"Papa spoiled her rotten," Hattie told her daughter, Edna. "She'd make a fuss until she got her way. She was always dramatic, and now she's playing a crazy old lady. Well, let me tell you: Your aunt Sadie is crazy like a fox."

She'd get on trains and tell the conductor that she'd already given him her ticket. If he argued, she'd accuse him of trying to extort money from a defenseless old widow. Then she'd cry, and her distress seemed very real. She'd pull the same thing on landlords, who'd write to her sister for the rent because Hattie always sent it. She would go to certain restaurants, blithely expecting to eat for free. "I am Mr. William S. Hart's guest," she'd say. And the funny thing was, if the owner sent Hart the bill, the old actor would pay.

Crazy like a fox. Except . . .

Sometimes she got lost. She'd stand on a street corner weeping, and when someone approached to help, she'd open her old leather handbag and show off yellowed newspaper clippings, telling the stranger that she was Wyatt Earp's widow. "Sure you are, toots," a Good Samaritan might say. She'd be escorted to the nearest police station, and one of the cops would make sure that she got home all right. She'd feed him stale cake and he'd sit with her a while. Listening to her talk about Wyatt Earp. Wanting to believe her.

Sometimes she'd disappear for months. Edgar would check the police blotters and obits. Then they'd find out that she was with her niece, Edna, in San Francisco or that she'd been taken in by another, more distant relative.

During one such absence, John Flood and Edgar Beaver moved away from the neighborhood they'd shared with the Earps since 1911. When they bought a place on Fourth Avenue in 1939, they listed themselves as "business partners" on the deed. For years afterward, they felt a lingering sense of guilt and relief, knowing that Mrs. Earp was no longer likely to show up at their door, screaming threats and making demands. They closed the book on her sad story.

So did the rest of the world — too busy now with Hitler, Mussolini, and Hirohito to care about a crazy old lady who claimed she was the widow of a legendary frontier lawman.

After Pearl Harbor, the young men who'd grown up watching bloodless movie gunfights at Saturday matinées joined real armies and fired real weapons that ripped through muscle and gut and brains, shattering bones, pulping limbs, tearing off heads. In the movies, the good guys always prevailed but all through 1942, the Axis powers won battle after battle.

In December of that year, the Selective Service notified men born between 1877 and 1897 that they, too, would be required to register for the draft.

"The war must be going a lot worse than FDR is willing to admit," Edgar said, "if America really needs a pair of old nellies like us."

He and John weren't called up, but like everyone on the home front, they followed the war news obsessively, studying the ebb and flow of battles around the world. There was growing optimism in '43, and by the end of 1944, the war seemed all but over. The British were pushing forward in Burma. Marines were clawing their way from one godforsaken Pacific island to the next. On the eastern and western fronts of Europe, the Allies were rolling toward Berlin.

Then, in December, Hitler threw everything he had left at the troops along the Rhine, hoping to beat them back before they could invade Germany.

With the titanic Battle of the Bulge in the headlines, the world did not notice the passing of Josephine Sarah Marcus Earp. The *Los Angeles Times* ran a brief obituary, identifying her as "the widow of the picturesque western frontier gunfighter, United States

Marshal Wyatt Earp." The cause of death was listed as a heart attack, with dementia as a secondary factor. She was eighty-two.

No one grieved. By the end of her life, she'd worn out her welcome everywhere. William S. Hart paid for a cremation but didn't attend the brief service. John Flood was informed, but he and Edgar stayed away. Her ashes were sent to her niece, Edna, in San Francisco. Like Wyatt's, Sadie's urn was interred in the Hills of Eternity Jewish cemetery near those of her parents, her brother, Nathan, and her sister, Hattie.

"We live too long," Wyatt said once. In Sadie's case, it was hard to argue. And yet, she got her way in the end.

Sadie always got her way.

Overpowered by Memories, Both Men Gave Way to Grief

Peace never lasts, but wars eventually end. In 1945, hundreds of thousands of American soldiers, sailors, airmen, and marines came home and began making up for lost time. Marrying in battalions, having children in brigades. Snapping up houses in brand-new suburbs. Buying cars and refrigerators. Smoking, drinking, and eating as much steak as they could pile on their plates. After fifteen years of Depression poverty and wartime rationing, Americans denied themselves nothing. It was a giddy era of fads and crazes, and television was the biggest craze of all. Broadcasters struggled to fill hours with shows that advertisers would sponsor. To everyone's surprise, the most lucrative market turned out to be that army of postwar babies, millions of whom were advancing on kindergarten like a conquering horde.

Every morning, while their weary, fecund mothers stayed in bed, grateful for an extra hour of sleep, those kids sloshed Borden's milk into bowls of Cheerios or Frosted Flakes or Sugar Pops and sat down in front of the TV, staring at the Indian-chief test pattern until the day's programming began. Quietly mesmerized by *Romper Room, Howdy Doody, Mighty Mouse,* and *Captain Kangaroo,* they sucked in hours of advertising, to the immense gratification of Madison Avenue.

From the start, cowboys were big with the kids. Gene Autry. Roy Rogers. *The Lone Ranger, The Adventures of Wild Bill Hickok, The Cisco Kid.* Things really took off in September '54, when Davy Crockett and Annie Oakley hit the small screen. By October, every little boy in America had to have a coonskin cap like Davy's and all the little girls needed a plastic-fringed skirt and vest for Halloween. In December, they all asked Santa for toy guns and cowboy hats. Slap a picture of Fess Parker or Gail Davis on anything at all — lunch boxes, pencil pouches, cereal boxes — and you could sell millions of them.

Once the little darlings had softened up their parents, the ad agencies went after adults directly and began to sponsor Westerns that would appeal to the whole family. Most early series were adapted from radio shows like *Death Valley Days* and *Gunsmoke,* but in 1955, ABC broke new ground by optioning Stuart Lake's book for a TV series starring

Hugh O'Brian.

A reporter from *Variety* heard that the real Wyatt Earp used to hang around the back lots when movies were just getting started, so he asked around at the studios, and the rumor turned out to be true.

"Wyatt mentioned a fella named Flood was writing the true story of the gunfight at the O.K. Corral," the old-timer remembered.

So the reporter tracked John down and showed up at the house, hoping for a quote he could use in a piece about O'Brian. "Mr. Flood, I've been told that Wyatt Earp said you were like a son to him," the reporter began. "Do you have any comment?"

John stood in the doorway, not moving, and cleared his throat before he spoke. "It's nice to know Mr. Earp felt that way."

"What did he tell you about the gunfight?" the reporter asked.

"I have nothing else to say."

Edgar had retired years earlier but retained a certain sympathy for journalists grubbing up column inches. "Come on, John! Give the kid some material."

"I have nothing else to say," John repeated. "Mr. Earp hated talking about the gunfight, and I will respect his preference." Then he closed the door.

"I think we should get a television," Edgar announced the next morning.

"I don't want one of those ugly things in the house," John said. "Television is nothing but game shows and fake wrestling. I'd rather listen to music."

"It's not all claptrap," Edgar said, scanning the new fall schedule in the newspaper. "There's that Edward R. Murrow show, *See It Now. Robert Montgomery Presents* . . . *Armstrong Circle Theatre* is doing plays by Paddy Chayefsky, Horton Foote, and Gore Vidal this season." He looked up. "We never go to the theater anymore, but we could watch some terrific plays right here in the house."

"Humph," John said, but he tried to be enthusiastic when Edgar carried home a sixteen-inch Zenith and sat it on a little table in front of the sofa.

Bringing in a good signal was a struggle. Edgar would fuss with the antenna. Adjust the horizontal- and vertical-hold knobs. Move the antenna again. Half the time, the show was over before he got a solid picture. It drove John crazy, as did Edgar's fascination with aluminum-clad frozen meals called Swanson TV Dinners.

"They're vile," Edgar admitted cheerfully, "but part of the experience."

Edgar loved all this modern nonsense, and John loved Edgar. He gave in to the new rituals with as much good grace as he could muster, but it was with a sense of foreboding that he settled onto the sofa to wait for the premiere of *The Life and Legend of Wyatt Earp.*

"Are you excited?" Edgar asked, carrying in a bowl of popcorn.

"My expectations are low," John replied. And yet . . .

Perhaps it was age. He was seventy-seven and no longer well; his feelings seemed closer to the surface these days. Perhaps time had softened his memories of the Earps' last years. Most likely, he was just getting to be a sentimental old fart.

Whatever the reason, his throat tightened when the earnest baritone voice-over began: "This is the story of Wyatt Earp, the greatest of the old-time fighting peace officers, a real western hero!"

Edgar snorted. "Fighting peace officers? How Orwellian . . ."

"Quiet! I want to hear!" John snapped, for a manly choir had begun to sing.

I'll tell you a story, a real true-life story,
A tale of the western frontier.
The West, it was lawless,
but one man was flawless,
And his is the story you'll hear.

"Flawless!" Edgar cried, stunned. "*Flawless?* John . . . She won! The old girl finally won!"

"Oh, Edgar," John whispered. "Mrs. Earp

843

would have loved this!"

That was true, for the series would be nice, and clean, and full of pep. Week after week, Wyatt Earp would be portrayed as a handsome, sexless, incorruptible marshal doing selfless battle with bad men who deserved to die.

And he would have a song for his epitaph.

The chorus swelled. John wiped his eyes. It's not lying, he thought. It's just remembering things the way they should have been.

Wyatt Earp! Wyatt Earp!
Brave, courageous, and bold!
Long live his fame and long live his glory
And long may his story be told!

ACKNOWLEDGMENTS

Almost twenty-five hundred years ago, Thucydides wrote of the Peloponnesian War, "The endeavor to ascertain these facts was a laborious task. Eyewitnesses did not give the same reports about the same things. Their testimony varied according to their championship of one side or the other."

That goes double for Tombstone.

There is hardly a sentence written or spoken about the events of 1880–82 that has not been disputed. I don't expect my version of the story to escape criticism. Careful historians will notice where I have trifled with strict fact: snugging up dates for the sake of narrative pacing or imagining elements of what is, after all, a novel. Nevertheless, I hope partisans of both sides will feel I've been fair to the men and women whose names and lives have been so often appropriated in the past.

I absorbed nineteen linear feet of background books for this novel, but to bring that research to life, I signed up for fifty-eight miles on horseback through the rugged mountains surrounding Tombstone. Led by Steve and Marcie Shaw of Great American Adventures, the five-day Earp Vendetta Ride was the hardest fun I've ever had. We ate in restaurants and slept in hotels, but it was still seven to nine hours a day in the saddle. Those hours gave me a sense of what it cost John Henry Holliday to ride with Wyatt Earp in the days after Morgan's death; I am grateful to Todd and Chris Cooper for their companionship and discreet kindness when I was struggling toward the end.

Thanks also go to the citizens of modern Tombstone for their willingness to share their knowledge of the town's history whenever I showed up. Bert Webster always made me feel welcome. Tim Fattig's encyclopedic knowledge of the gunfight was awe-inspiring. Doing shots in a biker bar with Stephen Keith in character as Doc Holliday remains a cherished memory.

Many people have been generous with their expertise: Joyce Aros (the Cochise County ranchers); Michael Bernal, Kenneth Brown, Carl Jenkins, Joel Lee Liberski, Randy Williams (billiards); Amy Cooke, Ann Hoffer, Susan McMullen, Susan Morris, Jean Lightner Norum, Dierdre Robinson, Christine Sharbrough (John Flood and Edgar Beaver research); Carey Granger (Tombstone silver mining); Dr. Judith Kaplan (concussion); Kimberly Loomis, Roberto Marino, Margaret Organ-Kean (genealogies); Dawood Ali McCallum (opiate withdrawl); Artie Nolan (Irish proverbs); Pamela Potter (the McLaury family); James Reichardt (legal issues); Vivian Singer (Yiddish); and Oscar Stregall (details of untreated tuberculosis). Special thanks go to Heike Erbarth for her kindness to Manfred Pütz in his final months.

For close and critical reading of early drafts of the manuscript, I thank Joyce Aros, Susanne Bach, Gretchen Batton, Eleanor Behr, Mary Dewing, Richard Doria Jr., Christopher Dussing, Jane Dystel, Miriam Goderich, Carey Granger, Jeff Jacobson, Pam Potter, Bob Price, Jim Reichardt, Vivian Singer, Jennifer Tucker, and David Twigg. Bonnie Thompson has copyedited my novels from the very start, and I am fortunate in being able to rely on her professionalism and attention to detail.

My superb agents, Jane Dystel and Miriam Goderich, have championed my work since 1995; this novel marked a difficult transition in my career, and their steady support kept me from throwing in the towel. *Epitaph* is my first book with Ecco, and the experience has been heartening. Special thanks go to Libby Edelson for taking a chance on the partial manuscript and for her sensitive and helpful editing of its final drafts. Thanks also to Eleanor Kriseman for her welcoming responsiveness and to the whole Ecco production team. As ever, I am grateful to the sales forces at both Random House and HarperCollins for making bookstores aware of my novels; to the booksellers in those wonderful stores for shoving my books into the hands of readers; and to the readers themselves for their encouragement and support ever since *The Sparrow.*

Don, Dan, and Jessie: It's time to head to La Fiesta for a pitcher of margaritas! You guys are the best.

ABOUT THE AUTHOR

Mary Doria Russell is the author of five previous books, *The Sparrow, Children of God, A Thread of Grace, Dreamers of the Day,* and *Doc,* all critically acclaimed commercial successes. Dr. Russell holds a Ph.D. in biological anthropology. She lives in Lyndhurst, Ohio.